The Essential
Yusuf Idris

The Essential
Yusuf Idris
Masterpieces of the Egyptian Short Story

Edited by
Denys Johnson-Davies

The American University in Cairo Press
Cairo New York

Copyright © 2009 by
The American University in Cairo Press
113 Sharia Kasr el Aini, Cairo, Egypt
420 Fifth Avenue, New York, NY 10018
www.aucpress.com

"The Cheapest Nights," "You Are Everything to Me," "The Errand," "Hard Up," "The Funeral Ceremony," "All on a Summer's Night," "The Caller in the Night," "The Dregs of the City," "Did You Have to Turn on the Light, Li-Li?," "Death from Old Age," "The Shame," from *The Cheapest Nights and other stories,* translated by Wadida Wassef (London: Peter Owen Ltd, 1978). Copyright © 1978 by Peter Owen Ltd/UNESCO. By permission of Peter Owen Ltd.

"His Mother," translated by Catherine Cobham, from *The Edinburgh Review,* no. 72, 1986. Copyright © 1986 by Catherine Cobham. By permission of Catherine Cobham.

"An Egyptian Mona Lisa," translated by Roger Allen and Christopher Tingley, from *Modern Arabic Fiction: An Anthology,* edited by Salma Khadra Jayyusi (New York: Columbia University Press, 2005). Copyright © 2005 by Columbia University Press. By permission of Salma Khadra Jayyusi.

"The Chair Carrier," from *Arabic Short Stories,* translated by Denys Johnson-Davies (London: Quartet Books, 1983). Copyright © 1983 by Denys Johnson-Davies.

"Rings of Burnished Brass," from *Rings of Burnished Brass and other stories,* translated by Catherine Cobham (Cairo: The American University in Cairo Press, 1990). Copyright © 1984 by Catherine Cobham. By permission of Catherine Cobham.

"The Shaykh Shaykha," translated by Ragia Fahmi and Saneya Shaarawi Lanfranchi, from *Flights of Fantasy,* edited by Ceza Kassem and Malak Hashem (Cairo: Elias Modern Publishing House, 1985, 1996). Copyright © 1985, 1996 by Elias Modern Publishing House. By permission of Elias Modern Publishing House.

"It's Not Fair," from *Under the Naked Sky: Short Stories from the Arab World,* translated by Denys Johnson-Davies (Cairo: The American University in Cairo Press, 2000). Copyright © 2000 by Denys Johnson-Davies.

"House of Flesh," from *Egyptian Short Stories,* translated by Denys Johnson-Davies (London: Heinemann Educational Books, 1978). Copyright © 1978 by Denys Johnson-Davies.

"Farahat's Republic," from *Modern Arabic Short Stories,* selected and translated by Denys Johnson-Davies (London: Oxford University Press, 1967). Copyright © 1967 by Oxford University Press. By permission of Oxford University Press.

"The Greatest Sin of All," translated by Mona Mikhail, from *In the Eye of the Beholder: Tales of Egyptian Life from the Writings of Yusuf Idris,* edited by Roger Allen (Minneapolis: Bibliotheca Islamica, 1978). Copyright © 1978 by Bibliotheca Islamica. By permission of Mona Mikhail.

City of Love and Ashes, translated by R. Neil Hewison (Cairo: The American University in Cairo Press, 1999). Copyright © 1999 by the American University in Cairo Press.

Dar el Kutub No. 16149/08
ISBN 978 977 416 242 8

Dar el Kutub Cataloging-in-Publication Data

Johnson-Davies, Denys
        The Essential Yusuf Idris / Edited by Denys Johnson-Davies.—Cairo: The American University in Cairo Press, 2008
            p.   cm.
            ISBN 977 416 242 0
            1. Arabic fiction   I. Johnson-Davies, Denys (ed.)
            892.708

1 2 3 4 5 6 7 8   14 13 12 11 10 09

Designed by Sally Boylan
Printed in Egypt

Contents

⸻

Introduction

Yusuf Idris was born in 1927, the eldest son of a man whose work required him to be away from home most of the time. Idris endured a lonely childhood controlled by parents and grandparents who seem to have been strict and undemonstrative to a boy who craved love and attention. His student years at university coincided with the era of British occupation, and these years were followed by the period of King Farouk's rule, a time marked by rampant corruption. Yusuf Idris, a medical student, was active in politics and this interest remained with him throughout his life. However, he found himself always to be against those who were in power. Even Gamal Abd al-Nasser whom, like most other Egyptians, Idris had supported in his revolution, fell out of Idris's favor, for it wasn't long before he became aware that few of the aims pronounced so eloquently by the new leader had in fact been accomplished. Inevitably, Idris was arrested for his political activities and, like so many other intellectuals, spent time in prison.

Creative writing occupied the mind of the young Yusuf Idris from his early student days, his first short story being published in 1951 and his first collected volume, *The Cheapest Nights*, in 1954, with an introduction from no less a scholar than Taha Hussein, the blind student from a lowly background who, having completed his studies in Paris, was to become Egypt's minister of culture and the leading personality in the field of scholarship and letters. Yet it was against such figures as Taha Hussein that Yusuf found himself rebelling. He felt that Arabic literature had become stagnant, that it required a revolution, and that it was no good simply adding to the culture of the past, much of which he described as being "crammed with nonsense." He was also acutely aware of the vast gulf that separated the educated classes from the man in the street, a gulf brought about by divisions of language, since the educated classes were versed in the classical language, of which the vast majority of Egyptians were ignorant or at best ill-informed. For this reason, Yusuf Idris quickly became a fervent supporter of colloquial Arabic.

In 1960 Idris made the decision to give up medicine to pursue a career as a writer and journalist. Despite his great talents and general recognition as one of the Arab world's leading writers, certainly as the short-story writer with the greatest authority and imagination, Idris lived his whole life under the impression that he had not been adequately rewarded or appreciated. This feeling came to a head when, having been nominated for the Nobel prize, he was passed over for the award in favor of Naguib Mahfouz. This should not have come as a surprise to him, since Mahfouz had produced an output, particularly of novels, which far exceeded his own. Mahfouz had also attracted the attention of translators who had translated many of his novels into English and French, and it was in these two languages that the Nobel prize committee could judge the work of potential nominees. Few translators had devoted any time to rendering Yusuf's large volume of work, mostly in the form of short stories, into the major languages. In fact, while much of his work in Arabic found its way into collected volumes of short stories, many of his stories remained virtually ignored in the magazines in which they had originally appeared. It was therefore understandable that he should not have received the same attention from translators as Mahfouz.

I feel that his stories speak for themselves and show how he differed in his approach to literature from most of his contemporaries. He had a special concern for the underdog, his works revealing a sympathetic knowledge of the disadvantaged that was mostly lacking in other writers. Much of what he felt about the way many of his fellow Egyptians were treated can be summed up in the title of the very first of his stories that I translated, "It's Not Fair."* It is one of his shorter stories, but it is no less effective for that, as it underlines the cruel differences that separate rich from poor in Egypt, differences that seem to remain no matter what the regime in power. Yusuf Idris, more than other Egyptian writers, was outspoken in his contempt for the rich and powerful and their heartless exploitation of the less fortunate and of the various forms of hypocrisy that this gave rise to. I also point out this story in particular because it is one that I have not come across in the many volumes of short stories compiled by various translators over the years; it shows, perhaps, that prolific as Idris was, especially in his earlier years, not a few of his stories have simply fallen by the wayside.

In the 1960s the BBC Arabic service decided to hold a short-story competition and asked me to be one of the judges. The other two judges were the Palestinian poet and critic Salma Khadra Jayyusi and the Sudanese writer Tayeb Salih. An initial shortlist of the stories submitted was put together by the Arab staff at the BBC, so that we the judges were left with twenty stories to read, from which we were required to choose three prize winners. I was intrigued by a rather short story entitled, if my memory serves me correctly, "The Dog." As usually happens on these occasions, the judges differed in their opinions of the twenty stories, and many arguments ensued between us. I, however, was adamant that "The Dog" should at the very least earn one of the prizes, if not first prize; in the event, it won second. I was astonished to learn later that, with the announcement of the results, none other than the Arab world's number one short-story writer, Yusuf Idris, had written to the BBC to point out that "The Dog" had in fact been written by him and had appeared in a magazine, for which Idris cited the name and date. It seemed that someone had entered the story in his own name, not suspecting that anyone might recognize it as having been written by Yusuf Idris and published in an obscure magazine. Literary competitions are fraught with such dangers, and I only hope that Idris was well compensated by the BBC.

---

* *Under the Naked Sky* (Cairo: The American University in Cairo Press, 2000).

Yusuf Idris and I would often meet during the 1960s, when I had an office in London. During this time, much of the conversation between us revolved around his writing and its comparative lack of success both in Arabic and in English translation. It therefore came as a real blow to him when he was passed over for the Nobel prize in favor of Mahfouz. Before this event, many habitués of Cairo's literary cafés had felt that if the prize were to be awarded to an Egyptian writer then Yusuf Idris was the obvious choice, that he of all writers could lead Arabic literature down fresh paths. It was not to be.

The fact remains that Yusuf Idris retains his position as the master of the Arabic short story, despite the obvious decline in the popularity of the genre in the Arab world—and indeed elsewhere. Readers looking through this select volume of his considerable output will find several stories that I translated myself. Yet despite my immense admiration for his work and the friendship between us, I did not produce a volume of his stories in English translation. Was it perhaps because publishers at the time also showed a preference for novels? This meant that until now anyone wishing to gain a comprehensive view of Idris's writings has had to look around in a large number of publications. My hope is that *The Essential Yusuf Idris* will fill that gap.

Denys Johnson-Davies

The Cheapest Nights

A little after evening prayers a torrent of abuse gushing out of Abd al-Kerim came pouring down on the entire village, sweeping Tantawi and all his ancestors in its wake.

No sooner had he rushed through the four prostrations than Abd al-Kerim stole out of the mosque and hurried down the narrow lane, apparently irritated, one hand clasping the other tightly behind his back. He was leaning forward, his shoulders bent, almost as if weighed down by the woolen shawl he was wearing, which he had spun with his own hands from the wool of his ewe. Presently he raised his brass-yellow face and caught the wind on the tip of his long hooked nose, blotched with many ugly black spots. He muttered, clenching his teeth, and the taut dry skin of his face wrinkled, bringing the points of his mustache level with the tips of his eyebrows, which were still speckled with drops of water from his ablutions.

His irritation grew as he trudged along down the narrow lane trying to find a path for his large flat feet with cracks in their soles so deep they could easily swallow up a nail.

The lane was teeming with youngsters scattered like breadcrumbs, tumbling about in all directions, and getting in his way. They pulled at his shawl, knocked against him, and made him cut his large protruding toe on the bits of tin they were kicking in his path. All he could do was lash out at them, vituperating furiously against their fathers and their forefathers, the rotten seed that gave them life, and the midwife who brought them to existence. Shaking with rage he cursed, and swore, and snorted, and spat on the wretched town where brats sprouted out of the ground in greater numbers than the hairs on one's head. But he comforted himself with the thought that the future was going to take care of them. Half of them were sure to die of starvation, while cholera would carry off the rest.

He sighed with relief as he emerged from the swarming lane into the open square surrounding the pond which stood in the middle of the town. Darkness spread before him where the low gray houses nestled close to one another, with heaps of manure piled before them like long-neglected graves. Only a few lamps shining across the wide circle of night indicated that there were living creatures packed beneath their roofs. Their dim red lights, winking in the distance like the fiery eyes of sprites, came across and sank in the blackness of the pool.

Abd al-Kerim peered into the gloom that stretched before him, the stink from the swamp winding its way up his nostrils. It oppressed him so he couldn't breathe. The thought of the townspeople already snoring behind their bolted doors oppressed him even more. But now his anger turned on Tantawi, the watchman, as he recalled the glass of tea the latter had offered him in the glow of sunset, and which his parched throat and his longing for it had forced him to accept at the cost of his pride.

It was very still in the square. Still as a graveyard; nothing stirred. Abd al-Kerim walked on, but halfway across he halted. Not without reason. Had he followed where his feet were taking him, in a few paces he would have been home and, having bolted the door behind him, there was nothing for him but to flop on his pallet and go to sleep, and there was not a grain of sleep in his eyes just then. His head felt clearer than pump water, lighter than pure honey, and he could have stayed awake till the next crescent moon of Ramadan appeared. All because he couldn't resist a glass of black tea, and Tantawi's fiendish smile.

And now he felt no desire to sleep and the townspeople were all huddled, snoring in their hovels, leaving the night to their obnoxious children. What was he to do with himself? Stay up. But where? Doing what? Should he join the boys playing hide-and-seek? Or hang around for the little girls to gather round him and snigger? Where could he go with his pockets picked clean? Not a wretched piaster with which to take himself to Abou al-Assaad's den, for instance. There he could order a coffee and then smoke a waterpipe and stay till all hours, or sit and watch solicitors' clerks at their game of cards, and listen to the radio blaring out things he didn't understand. He could laugh to his heart's content poking Abou Khalil in the ribs and then move on to where Mo'allem* Ammar was sitting with the cattle dealers and join their conversation about the slump in the market. But he hadn't a wretched piaster. God bring your house to ruin, Tantawi!

Nor could he go across to Shaykh Abd al-Megid's, where he was sure to find him squatting behind a brazier with a coffee-pot gently boiling on top. al-Sheehy would be there, sitting near him, telling of the nights that made his hair turn gray, and the days gone by when he had thrived on the simpleminded, kind-hearted folks of those days, and how he was made to repent of swindling and thieving and laying waste of other people's crops by the wily generation of today.

No, he couldn't even go there, because only the day before he had pushed the man into the basin below the waterwheel and made a laughing stock of him. They'd been having an argument over the cost of repairing the wheel. Not a civil word had passed between them since.

If only he could just grab his ferruled cane and go to collect Sama'an and together make off for the neighboring farm of al-Balabsa. There was fun to be had over there. Wedding feasts, and dancing girls, and high jinks, and merry-making, and what-have-you. But where was the money for all that? Besides, it was late. Very likely Sama'an would have gone to make it up with his wife at her uncle's, where she was staying. And the road was treacherous, and everything was pitch black. Merciful God! Why must he be the only clod in town tormented by lack of sleep? And Tantawi. *He* wasn't tormented. *He* was probably snoring away peacefully in some quiet nook. God in heaven, let him snore his away to hell!

---

* Master of a trade.

Suppose now that he were simply to go home like a God-fearing man. He would nudge his wife and make her get up and light the petrol lamp, heat the oven, warm him a loaf of bread and bring him the green peppers left over from lunch. With luck there might be a piece of pie left over too, which his wife's mother had sent them in the morning. And then she'd make him a nice brew of fenugreek and after that, pleased as a sultan, he'd sit and repair the handles of his three worn reed baskets.

Yes, what if he did just that? Would the station take wings and fly, or would the heavens collapse on the threshing floor? He knew no such thing was likely to occur. He also knew his wife. She would be lying like a bag of maize with her brood of six scattered round her like a litter of puppies. Nothing would make her stir. Not even the angel Israfil blowing his trumpet to raise the dead. And even if by some miracle she were to wake up, what then? He wasn't kidding himself. The petrol lamp was only half full and the woman would be needing it when she sat up to bake all night tomorrow. That is, if they all lived till tomorrow. And the children, growing hungry at sundown, would have devoured the last of the peppers with the last scrap of bread. And the pie was sure to have followed after the peppers and the bread. As for fenugreek and sugar, he needn't worry. There simply wasn't any in his house. And never again was he going to be offered a glass of tea like the one he had drained at Tantawi's.

God damn your soul to hell, Tantawi, son of Zebeida!

Anyone coming to relieve himself in the square at that hour, and seeing Abd al-Kerim planted in the middle of it like a scarecrow, would have thought him touched in the head or possessed of a devil. He was neither. Just a man whose perplexity was greater than he could deal with. A simple man, unfamiliar with the things of the night, the tea playing havoc with his head; his pockets stripped clean on a cold winter's night, and all his companions long sunk in deep sleep. What was there for him to do?

He stood thinking for a long time before he made up his mind. Having no choice he crossed to the other end of the square. He could only do what he always did on cold winter nights.

Finally he was home. He bolted the door and picked his way carefully in the dark over the bodies of his sleeping children, to the top of the mud oven. Inwardly he reproached the fates which had plagued him with six bellies so voracious they could gobble up bricks.

He knew his way in the dark from long habit on cold winter nights. And when he found his woman he didn't nudge her. He took her hand and began to crack her knuckles one by one, and to rub against her feet, caked with tons of dirt. He tickled her roughly, sending a shiver down her sleeping bulk. The woman stirred with the last curse he called on Tantawi's head. She heaved herself over and asked nonchalantly through a large yawn what the man had done to deserve being cursed in the middle of the night. Abd al-Kerim muttered, cursing whoever drove him to do this, as he fumbled with his clothes preparing for what was about to be.

Months later the woman came to him once again to announce the birth of a son. His seventh. He condoled with himself over this belated arrival. All the bricks of the earth would never fill up this one either.

And months and years later, Abd al-Kerim was still stumbling on swarms of brats littering the lanes, tumbling about in all directions and getting in his way as he came and went. And every night, with hands behind his back, catching the wind on his long hooked nose, he still wondered what pit in heaven or earth kept throwing them up.

Translated by Wadida Wassef

You Are Everything to Me

—〰—

All was quiet. The only sound came from the primus stove like the persistent wailing of a sickly child. It was interrupted at intervals by the noise of the metal tumbler dragging on the tile floor of the bathroom, then the sound of water gurgling out of it, and the crackling of the tin can where the water boiled. The sounds clashed and darted about like bats under the low ceiling of the room until at last the primus gave a last gasp and was silent.

It was a long time before the bathroom door opened and Ramadan heard his wife clatter in on her wooden clogs, her familiar breathing pervading the room. The clogs kept clattering up and down and the light from the lamp flickered as the sad low murmur of the woman rose and fell. Ramadan kept his eyes shut. He opened them only when he felt drops of water splash on his face. He stiffened a little at the sight of his wife standing disheveled with the wooden comb in her hand. She was digging it into her kinky hair, making long deep furrows as she pulled. Her plump face was puckered and there were wrinkles on the sides of her flat nose. She worked at the thick coils, the water splashing about in every direction, wetting her clean cotton dress with the huge faded flowers.

'Why don't you take care with that water, woman,' said Ramadan as he shifted on the bed and shut his eyes again. 'You'll break the lamp.'

He paid no attention to what she mumbled but turned over and settled down to sleep. As he pulled the quilt over his shoulder he opened his eyes a little to steal a look at his wife who was just turning off the lamp with a radiant smile on her clean face. The wrinkles had disappeared for the time being. A little tremor ran through Ramadan's body as he snapped his eyes shut. He had long known the meaning of that smile on Thursday nights.*

The four-poster shook as the woman climbed up and slipped under the covers. A strong female odor, mingled with that of cheap soap and the cotton nightdress, pervaded the intimate world under the quilt. Ramadan gave a laborious cough which he made long and deliberate.

'What's the matter?' asked his wife in a meek voice. 'You sure Sayyed is not awake?' she added after a while, in a conspiratorial tone. When she got no reply she gave a sigh which she seemed to draw from the inner coils of her soul while the bed posts shook again and she heaved herself over to place herself within the warm radius of his body. The man was breathing quickly and the hot gusts of his breath bore her off to bowers of bliss, crushing her to the marrow. She stretched a hand and touched his moist forehead, then slid it down to his fat neck where the veins stood out.

'Bless you, my dear. God keep and bless you, love,' she said in a voice like the mewing of a hungry cat. Ramadan forced himself to cough again, groaning through his clenched teeth, and the four-poster shook once more as he turned and showed her his back.

That wasn't the first time he had turned his back, or coughed, or groaned through his clenched teeth. He couldn't remember how many months ago his trouble had started. Whether it was before or after the small Bairam.** A thick fog veiled the beginning of it all. He had never given the matter a thought, nor did he dream that what had happened that day would lead him to this. Just like his neighbor from next door, the bus-driver, Si Ahmed, who couldn't have known that the fever which had seized his little girl would end in a procession of mourners filing into his house.

---

* Friday is the Muslim day of rest.
** The small Bairam is the three-day feast following the month of Ramadan.

He had attributed what happened to a chill he had caught. When the effects of the cold had gone and he found he was recovering his strength he decided to sleep with his wife that same night. The prospect cheered him up, and he went to take his position in the public square where he was on duty considerably elated, humming the only tune he knew. Cars stopped as usual at the signal of his powerful hand in its worn white glove. He stood erect in his close-fitting uniform, with the brass buttons pulled tightly over his paunch making it look like a huge watermelon. The paint shining on his cap failed, however, to conceal the grime and the signs of long wear. With his stubby pencil he diligently took the numbers of offending cars with the confidence of one who has no fear of the past, the present, or the future. He jotted them down neatly in his clear handwriting of which he was very proud. The world was fine, and he was on top of it. He ruled it with his whistle, exalting whom he wished and humbling whom he wished with merely a sign from his gloved hand.

As he wrote out his first summons for the day in his mind he was already romping in the pastures of bliss that were promised for the coming night, when he intended to shake off the dullness of that week of illness. But the cares of the day and the busy flow of traffic which he controlled from under the rim of his cap took his mind off the matter for a while and he remembered again only when he got home. He had thrown his tired body on the divan and was struggling to pull off his heavy uniform boots.

'Here, let me,' said his wife as she squatted on the floor to help him. Her soft hand went round the calf of his leg and the tip of his shoe dug between her breasts, which reminded him of the romp he had in mind and he began to tickle her with his foot while she leaned back and giggled and pushed him away. Then she rolled on her side, tightening her grip round his calf. He enjoyed the game and thrilled to the woman's voice as she squealed with pleasure, half of her willing, half of her holding back, and all of her tingling with desire.

Though a fog veiled the beginning, Ramadan could remember that night clearly. Every minute he had struggled, soaking in streams of sweat, shutting off his mind to the entire world until he and his wife and the bed were all that existed.

She pushed him from her again and again, and he damned her to hell over and over, and the struggle went on, halting only when the sleeping boy stirred and resuming when he was heard snoring again, as he drooled down the side of his mouth.

He gave up at dawn, and the woman went to sleep, but not he.

That night went and other nights came and every time he renewed the struggle, fighting desperately for his virility until at last he was forced to give up, saying to himself one morning in a voice he hardly recognized as his own: "'There is no might or power but in God.' You're beaten, man. Finished, washed up.'

Often before, he had avoided his wife at breakfast, but that day he wanted her out of his sight altogether. He could have knocked his head against the wall in his misery. It was a strange thing that was happening to him. The painful struggling every time, and the sweating, and the long nights, should have forced him to admit he was no longer a man. But he could not bring himself to do it. He burned with shame and humiliation just as if he were being paraded through the town sitting naked on a donkey, his head heaped with mud. 'You're finished, man; washed up,' he kept repeating to himself as though he were reciting the *ayah** of The Chair against evil spirits.

He cut himself a big chunk of bread but left it untouched. He got up and stood looking out of the window. Then he spat. A large mouthful which he aimed at the chicken coops on the facing roof-top. He came back and sat down at the eating board, staring at his food without touching it, chewing on his silence until it choked him. Then he got up again and slipped on his clothes, feeling his body dissolve and his limbs melt into nothing as he stole out of the house.

Standing in the middle of the square where cars milled around him and heaven and earth moved and only he stood dazed and fixed in his place, he suddenly realized the triviality of this kingdom that was his. The white gloves bothered him. His cap weighed on his head like a millstone. All day he did not trouble to write down one summons. And why should he? The

---

* A verse from the Qur'an.

world could go to hell for all he cared. He wasn't there to put it right. Damn the cars and their drivers and the traffic, and everything to do with the crazy shrieking merry-go-round where he stood.

For the first time in his life he hated the thought of his home and the wretched face of his wife, and he was in no hurry to return to either. He slid his cap down his forehead and loosened his belt as he trudged heavily down the street, the grooves in his face overflowing with despair, wishing some vehicle would knock him down and put an end to his misery. At last he reached the door of the only man in town who was a friend to all. He stood there and knocked, a thing he did not do frequently. Tantawi was not astonished. He let him in and made him welcome, asking many questions about his health and his friends and his relatives and his hometown and who had married and who had died and who was still alive. But when Ramadan said, 'Tantawi, boy, I want a whiff,' Tantawi was astonished.

Ramadan was not in the habit of taking much hashish, but that night he took an overdose to the point that Tantawi thought it best to see him home. Ramadan was too dazed to refuse or accept, much less take in his friend's questions about what was troubling him.

As he walked Ramadan wandered far with his mind, delving deep in time and place until he reached Sekina, his neighbor, in the old house by the stream, and the years following his puberty. From time to time he stopped in his tracks for no reason and Tantawi would tug at him and he had to walk on, while his mind still rambled. 'Suppose it works, boy. Suppose hash will do the trick,' he would cry as the sudden thought struck him, and he'd burst out laughing, stopping in his tracks again.

'By the Prophet, he's gone. Quite stoned,' murmured Tantawi with pity for his friend.

Ramadan nearly blurted it all out but caught himself in time and shoved the words back into his dry throat, as his shoes hit the road once more and Tantawi pulled him along by the hand.

Hashish didn't work that time, or any other time.

On the nights when he took it he would remain silent, speaking little, and when he managed to say something it was as if the words had been sucked out of him like a bad fluid; an acrid mixture of anger, resentment, and mortification. His wife would chatter on in the meantime, even though he hardly moved a muscle. His duty in the square became an agony he was forced to swallow slowly, like the hours he spent there, only half standing, The brisk salute he usually gave to his superiors deteriorated to a half-hearted motion he wrenched from himself like a bad tooth. And all the time he got more and more entangled in a coil of lies he was forced to tell the doctor in order to obtain a day or two of leave.

Normally he never went home without something for his wife. Now she became used to seeing him come with his hands empty and dangling at his sides as if they didn't belong to him.

One day he came home to find his wife's mother had just arrived for a visit. His cool and indifferent greeting made his wife blush, and her vexation reached a peak as the day wore on and his talk with her mother did not go beyond an occasional, 'And how are you?'

Finally, having had enough, the old lady retired to bed after barely going through her evening prayers, moaning and groaning from her rheumatic joints. An hour later he too was stretched out on the straw mat at the foot of the bed together with his wife and son.

He was awakened at dawn when the old lady stumbled on him as she rose to perform her ablutions for the dawn prayer. And while she recited the Fatihah,* incorrectly as usual, in her rasping voice, he couldn't help asking himself what in all hell she was doing there.

The answer awaited him in the evening when the Hagga** cleared her throat as she squatted on the floor and leaned her back to the wall, draping herself in her large white veil. 'Well, son, I shall not hide it from you,' she began.

In actual fact she was hiding from him that her daughter had sent her a letter behind his back and she began to put the matter forward with the cunning of old women. She took heart from his silence and went on to play mother and sister and bosom friend.

'And for every problem there is a solution, son, don't you worry,' she said.

---

* Opening chapter of the Qur'an.
** Title given to a person who has been on a pilgrimage to Mecca. It is the feminine form of 'Hagg.'

'Problem my foot!' he fumed inwardly. 'Solution my arse!' he raged. 'What business is it of yours? And what brings you here in the first place, you crumpled-up old witch?' The curses he sought to pour out but which he was forced to hold back stoked his fury all the more for until that moment his wife had nothing to do with his problem. She existed nowhere in that vast wilderness where he staggered alone. Now it was obviously no longer his concern alone, and God knows who else was in on it too.

The evening ended with a tremendous conflagration which overturned the eating board and blew out the lamp, and the neighbors heard it crash to the floor as he roared, 'By God, you will not sleep under my roof!'

The Hagga and her daughter were given shelter by the neighbors that night; and by daybreak the train was carrying the mother back to her village alone. And had there been room in her brother's house for her daughter too, she would not have left her behind.

At that same hour Ramadan was stealing out of their lane. When he met Abu Sultan, his greeting was curt and he avoided his eyes, hurrying along, the sooner to get out of sight. It was the same with Abd al-Razek, the newspaper boy, and Hagg Muhammad who sold beans, and everyone else he knew or did not know. Every movement betrayed his secret; every word was a calculated jab; in every smile he saw irony. Everybody knew; even the fellow near him clutching at the ceiling-strap in the train: when their eyes met, it was evident that he knew.

He darted to the center of the square wishing miserably that his body would shrink and disintegrate and vanish out of sight. Standing there in the middle was like being on display in a showcase open to the curious gaze of the crowds whose only wish was to expose him. When he failed to protect himself from their prying looks he vented his fury on the people, dealing out summonses with a heavy hand, muttering obscenities, and dragging more than one victim to the police station on the slightest provocation.

It was a sad man who stood there every day from now on. Glum, unsmiling, his face dark and lined behind the bushy mustache he no longer bothered to trim. His area became one of dread, and he became the scourge of drivers going through. Everyone knew the dark cop with the bushy mustache. His bad temper, his biting tongue, and his aversion to women drivers, particularly those crossing his square, were proverbial.

And then there was his wife.

He had worn himself out, fretting about her. Where was she that day he went home and didn't find her? She said she'd gone to Umm Hamida's whose brother was Mehanni—that boy who dressed in ironed silk caftans which clung to his thighs, and wore his skull-cap tilted at an angle. What was she doing at Umm Hamida's? And the day he caught her looking out of the window with her head uncovered. The bitch. With her head uncovered!

By and by he took to coming home late at night after he became a regular knocker on Tantawi's door. One night, after he had undressed and got into his white gallabiya, fixing his woolen cap firmly on his head, he stretched his weary drugged body on the bed while the voices of the day hummed in his ear and Tantawi's talk flickered on his memory. When the humming ceased and Tantawi faded out he realized his wife was still awake, sobbing bitterly. Ramadan that night had reached the end of his tether. The solid barrier he had placed between them was slowly eroding with her tears until only the quilt remained. He lay still, listening in silence, unable to do anything else. Finally he spoke.

'Just tell me, Naima, what is there I can do?' he asked, every fiber in him crying out in pain.

She only buried her head deeper in the pillow and sobbed louder. He shook her gently, with humility, and asked her again. Not that he expected her answer to help him much. He was simply trying somehow to cover up his failure, or at least to get someone to help him find a way out.

He began to look around to see how others in his predicament acted. He consulted the writings of old. He went to the wise and learned, he visited the shrine of every holy man in town, and he ate the pigeons and mangoes provided by Naima out of her own savings. He sucked the acid tops of sugar cane and he swayed to the beat of the tambourine when a *zar** was held in

---

* Ceremony for casting out devils.

his honor. Many times he was up at dawn in order to throw the charms written for him into the sea. Obediently he ate the pies his wife baked him,
kneaded with her own blood, and he drank all the potions the herbalist con-
cocted specially for him.

Nothing worked.

Then he made his way to the VD hospital, and there amongst the rows
of patients waiting their turn he met many others like himself. There was
comfort in being with them. The canvas bag which Naima had sewn was
filled and refilled with bottles of medicine which he dutifully swallowed.
His veins and muscles were pricked with hypodermics, and he was admitted for treatment and discharged. His mother-in-law paid them another
call, and the money she brought was spent and much more besides. Night
and day she kept on pouring out advice, and so did relatives and the relatives of relatives.

Ramadan went on desperately in pursuit of his lost virility, looking
everywhere, following every lead. All his thoughts, all his actions centered
on that one goal. It was his sole topic: at prayers on Friday, and at the café;
at the fish market and the railway station; with the male nurse from the hospital and even with his commanding officer; and still nothing changed.

They were talking quietly one day, Ramadan and Naima, sitting lazily in a
spot of sunshine on the roof. Conversation flowed gently; Ramadan was
relaxing on his day off, and Naima, having bought the sardines for lunch
early that morning, had given herself up to the luxury of doing nothing.
Ramadan was speaking in the gentlest tone for he had been giving a good
deal of thought to his wife, and he was blaming himself for much of what
was on his mind. He had chosen that day and that hour to unburden himself.

'Listen, Naima,' he began. He hesitated for an instant then gathered up
his courage and went on.

'I . . . I want to do what's right in the sight of God.'

She looked at him languidly. The shadow of a smile, playing on her face,
was about to break at his stumbling speech.

'I . . . I think it would be better if I divorced you, Naima,' he blurted out
at last.

At this she sat up sharply and turned to face him. She beat her breast with her hand and looked at him with eyes full of reproach.

'Ramadan! For shame! What is this you're saying! You are everything to me,' she exclaimed with indignation, 'father and brother; the crown upon my head. I am not worth the ground under your feet. I am only your servant, my love. How could you say such a thing! After my hair's turned gray, and yours too. . . It's not as if we're young any more . . . how could you . . .' A gush of tears stopped the words in her mouth and she couldn't continue. She unfastened her head-kerchief and wiped her tears with it as she got up and stumbled downstairs, leaving Ramadan behind, absently passing his fingers over the wrinkles on his face. He smoothed his balding head and passed his hands across his bloated belly. Absently he plucked at the hairs of his leg, most of them turned white, as his eyes strayed to Sayyed, his son.

He gazed at the boy as if he had just discovered him.

Sayyed was lying near him, his face covered with his arithmetic copy-book. Wide-eyed and incredulous Ramadan was devouring the boy with his eyes. God almighty! How could he forget he had a son, and think only of himself in this whole wide world?

'Sayyed . . . Sayyed, my boy, come over here,' he whispered hoarsely. 'Come, sit here by me . . . let me look at you. My, but you've grown, son. You're almost as big as I am. You'll be a man, soon . . . a man! And I'll have you married . . . that's right, I'll have you married to a beautiful girl. No . . . four! Four beautiful girls, and you'll be their man, son. Do you understand? Do you understand what it means to be their man? Never mind. You will, you will. And you'll have children. Do you hear? You'll have children, Sayyed, and I'll carry your little ones in my arms. These arms of mine . . . do you hear me, son . . . ?'

Translated by Wadida Wassef

The Errand

—~m~—

Whenever anyone mentioned Cairo in his presence al-Shabrawi got terribly upset. It made him feel cheated of his life and he would suddenly long to go back if only to spend one hour at al-Kobessi or Mo'allem Ahmed's in the quarter of al-Tourgouman. His memory took him back to the days when he was a conscript and he used to go the length and breadth of Cairo every week, and he would hanker for one of those daytime shows he used to attend at the National Cinema. He sighed bitterly every time, for it was not too much to ask God to arrange for the proper circumstances and a little money to make his wish come true. 'I'll give my life for one hour in Cairo,' he never tired of saying.

But he didn't have to go to quite that extreme for things looked up unexpectedly, all of a sudden, and his wish came to be realized in a way he least suspected. One day as he was sitting in his usual place at the police station, as he had for the past four years, a large crowd of people suddenly came barging in. After many questions and in spite of the racket, he was able to make out that they were bringing in a mad woman from Kafr Goma'a accompanied by her relatives and friends. Everyone was yelling at once as more and more people kept coming in, attracted by the noise, until the place was in an uproar.

A beam of hope made his heart flutter. Obviously the woman would have to be sent to the asylum in Cairo with a special escort, and he couldn't think of anyone better qualified for the task than himself.

He found it no problem to get the job. There was no need to send mediators to plead with the adjutant, since all his colleagues bluntly refused to have anything to do with it, and when he volunteered of his own free will there were no objections and the matter was settled right away.

Immediately he dispatched Antar, the errand boy from the station canteen, to inform his wife he was going away. She was to send him some food wrapped in his large handkerchief and the fifty-piaster note she would find hidden in the pillowcase.

In half an hour everything was ready: the Health Inspector's report written and the railway ticket-forms filled. All he had to do was board the train and he would be in the heart of Cairo.

He could hardly believe his luck. He couldn't believe he was going to see Cairo again and go on a tram ride and meet his old friends and dine on grilled meat at Mo'allem Hanafi's. His joy knew no bounds as he walked resolutely to the station at the head of more than a hundred people all recommending that he be kind and patient with Zebeida.

He was given a twenty-piaster tip by her father, and ten by her husband. He shook his head many times and kept up a broad smile and told everyone not to worry. He was going to be like a true brother to her, born of her own mother and father.

It was a strange procession running through the town, with al-Shabrawi at the head. People stopped to stare. Those who knew him asked where he was going.

'Only round the corner,' he replied with modesty.

'How far?' they persisted.

'Oh, only up to Cairo,' he said with feigned indifference.

'Lucky man!'

His belly tingled with excitement.

After a long wait the Delta train came puffing in. He got on with Zebeida who sat down quietly beside him. Presently the train started. Al-Shabrawi felt for his papers for the third time. They were safe in his inside pocket. Seeing all was well and everything in order, he removed his wide uniform belt and relaxed, sitting back a little, almost forgetting Zebeida.

After a long time the loitering and meandering and interminable stops came to an end and the train crawled into Mansourah like a long caterpillar. When they got off al-Shabrawi crossed the bridge holding Zebeida by the hand, all the time invoking the blessings of the Sayyeda Zeinab.*

He looked for the train to Cairo and found it crouching in its place, waiting for him. He got on and sat Zebeida near the window. When the lemonade man came round he bought two glasses which he gulped down one after the other. Then he bought a third one which he offered to Zebeida who rejected it irritably. He patted her soothingly on her back and gulped it down himself.

The train began to move. The passengers were sitting snugly in their seats, idly staring at nothing. Zebeida was looking out of the window like a child, a beatific smile on her face, while al-Shabrawi lost himself in visions of approaching bliss.

Just before they reached Simbellawen Zebeida suddenly turned round and beat her breast violently, looking at al-Shabrawi in a strangely accusing manner. The latter snapped out of his visions with a jolt.

'What . . . what's the matter?' he asked anxiously.

She gave no reply but, holding her hand above her mouth, let out a joyful trilling-cry which she followed by a string of others. A sudden hush fell on the carriage and the passengers all turned to stare. Al-Shabrawi's head reeled with embarrassment as he fumbled for an explanation. He tried to swallow but his throat felt dry. He turned to Zebeida and implored her to stop, gently patting her hand.

'There, there, now, don't worry. Everything will be alright. Please . . . .'

Finally she calmed down. But the passengers did not. They began to comment on what had just happened in low whispers that grew steadily louder, never taking their eyes off Zebeida or al-Shabrawi.

'Must be his wife, poor dear,' he heard a woman say.

A peal of laughter rang out at one end of the carriage. The man sitting in front of him woke up and cleared his throat. Two children stood on their seats to get a better view. Al-Shabrawi broke into a sweat that seeped

---

* Granddaughter of the Prophet.

through his khaki uniform. He felt like changing the bitter taste of his mouth so he opened his large handkerchief in order to spit in it but his throat was too dry and he folded it up again and put it back in his pocket.

'What's wrong with the lady, Officer?' asked his neighbor, who did not seem to appreciate the situation.

'Oh, n . . . nothing,' replied al-Shabrawi. He was able to recover his speech though his knees still felt rather watery. 'Just a little . . . ,' he said making a circular motion with his hand near his temple. The man shook his bulk and nodded knowingly. Al-Shabrawi was still moving his hand when Zebeida turned on him again.

'What do you mean, nothing? Who said there was nothing?' she asked in a shrill cry.

Al-Shabrawi looked at her with genuine alarm as she poked her face close to his. He leaned back until his head hit the wall, placing his knotted handkerchief, with its contents, between them. She peered unsteadily at the ceiling and screamed again at the top of her voice. 'Who said there was nothing? Down with the Omda* of our town Ibrahim Abou Sha'alan! . . . Long live His Majesty the King, President Muhammad Bey Abou Batta!' And another trilling-cry went up.

The carriage was now in utter pandemonium. Sleeping passengers woke up. The man sitting in front of al-Shabrawi pulled his basket from under his seat and hurried away. In one second Zebeida and al-Shabrawi had half the carriage to themselves, while the rest of the passengers huddled apprehensively in the far corner. Some left the carriage altogether while a few remained out of curiosity. Al-Shabrawi's uniform was now drenched in perspiration. He tried to force her back into her seat but she jerked his hand away.

'Down with our Omda!' she shouted again to the tune of more trilling-cries. 'Long live His Majesty the King, President Abou Batta!'

Everyone was laughing, even the boys selling peanuts and soft drinks. Al-Shabrawi joined in too, seeing no reason why he shouldn't, but he soon had to stop as the situation suddenly threatened to take a turn for the worse.

---

* Headman.

Zebeida was preparing to take off her dress, the only garment she had on. He made an effort to grab hold of her hands but she pushed him away, still uttering her piercing cries. Soon they were caught in a scuffle. He won in the end, forcing her back into her seat, and tying her down with a muffler which a passenger lent him—but not before she had flung his tarboosh out of the window. He was incensed, for throughout his years of service he had never once been seen without it, and now he had to suffer the indignity of remaining with his head uncovered expect for his cropped, scanty hair. With that much accomplished Zebeida was apparently still not satisfied. She continued her volley of trilling-cries, and every time it was down with the Omda and long live the President.

As the train neared Bilbeiss she was starting to calm down and some of the bolder passengers were encouraged to return to their seats. Infuriated by the loss of his tarboosh, it was all al-Shabrawi could do to refrain from throwing her overboard. There was nothing for him but to simmer in his rage until the train pulled in at Cairo.

He waited until all the passengers got off, then he caught her arm like a clamp and marched her out. As they walked down the platform he relaxed his grip a little when he saw she was following meekly, tame as a lamb.

The imposing structure of the station hall filled him with awe, but in his present state of mind he was in no mood to relish his surroundings or to allow happy memories to invade his thoughts. Immediately he boarded a tram, with Zebeida obediently in tow, and got off at Ataba. From there he took a short cut to al-Azhar Street where he bought himself a new tarboosh with the twenty piasters her father had given him, cursing Zebeida all the time, together with her father and his illicit money. The new tarboosh bothered him, it weighed a ton.

Taking thought he decided to get rid of Zebeida before he gave himself up to the joys of the capital. So he squeezed with her into another tram. As it wound its long, tortuous way through the crowded streets of Cairo al-Shabrawi sat reviewing all the mishaps he had suffered up until now and glumly contemplated those yet to come.

Somewhere in the middle he remembered Zebeida and threw a quick glance in her direction. With her jaw hanging open, a fatuous and placid expression on her face, she was leaning heavily on the man standing next to her. The latter had his eyes on the paper he was pretending to read, but seemed obviously to be enjoying himself. Al-Shabrawi pulled her away roughly. The placid expression vanished and a nasty look came in its place. Once again the trilling-cry went up, and again it was down with the Omda and long live President Abou Batta.

The conductor blew his whistle and stopped the car midway between stops. He went up to al-Shabrawi and ordered him to take Zebeida and get off, roundly abusing him for exposing the passengers to so dangerous a creature.

Finding himself in the street again al-Shabrawi decided it would be wiser to cover the rest of the way to the Governorate building on foot. Zebeida walked alongside on his right, her trilling-cries rending the air. A large crowd was collecting behind them as they walked along, al-Shabrawi hardly daring to raise his eyes from the ground in his mortification.

The guard at the door anticipated some sensational happening as he saw the crowd approach. Al-Shabrawi enquired about the Governorate doctor. The guard's practiced eye took in the situation at a glance. He was very sorry indeed but it was past six and there was nobody there. Al-Shabrawi's heart sank.

'And what do I do now?'

'Come back tomorrow,' the guard returned calmly.

'Tomorrow?'

'Morning,' he specified. He turned and shouted at the crowd which began to disperse loaded with a stock of anecdotes.

Al-Shabrawi begged to be allowed to stay the night. Having nothing more to add, the guard did not bother to reply, and knowing better than to argue al-Shabrawi grabbed Zebeida by the hand again and moved away.

Slowly, the enormity of his predicament began to dawn on him. With Zebeida tied to his neck there was nowhere he could stay the night. He was tired and worn out and he had had nothing to eat for hours.

He walked into the nearest café in Bab al-Khalq and sat down, keeping her close by his side, paying no attention to the many stares that fastened on them. He ordered tea and a water-pipe and was just starting to give himself up to the delicious euphoria that was spreading to his tired limbs when a sudden rumbling in his belly made him almost double up with pain. He realized he couldn't wait. He must find the toilet. When he enquired of the waiter, the latter pointed to a place not too far off. But he had to park Zebeida somewhere. He took a look round the place and noticed a man sitting near them who was wearing a coat on top of his gallabiya. It was not difficult to start a conversation with him. It turned out he was a police detective and al-Shabrawi found himself obliged to tell him the whole story, asking him in the end if he'd mind keeping an eye on Zebeida while he went to the loo. No sooner had the man accepted with reluctance than al-Shabrawi had shot out of sight.

When he got back he found the café had turned into a fun-fair, with Zebeida as the star attraction. Furiously he pounced on her and dragged her away with profuse apologies to the police detective. He walked out blindly with no idea where to go. It was getting dark and the glaring lights of the city dazzled him with memories of those bygone days, sadly overshadowed by all he was having to endure.

Probing his memory he recalled a distant relative, a student of agriculture. His memory threw up the address as well, somewhere in Giza, but when he got there he lost his way as he had only been to the house once before and that was during the daytime. He found it in the end, however, after a long search, and his relative gave him a warm welcome, asking where he'd been all this time and how everybody was. Al-Shabrawi was just about to open his mouth and explain the purpose of his visit when Zebeida, until now on her best behavior, sent up one of her choicest trilling-cries. If he had had a knife on him al-Shabrawi would gladly have cut her throat. He didn't even try to explain why he was there, but hurriedly took his leave and scuttled away allowing his relative only snatches of the story.

When the streets contained them once more, he dug his fingers fiercely into her arm and longed to crush her bones. The thought of murder occurred to him even though he knew it meant a life sentence. He was past caring. Meanwhile Zebeida was waddling along beside him like a goose, totally impervious to the threats he kept muttering at her between his teeth. Suddenly he had a flash of inspiration as the thought of murder and the life sentence he was prepared to face made him see visions that evoked the police station. He could think of no better place to take shelter that wretched night.

So they got on a bus and a moment later they were standing before the sergeant on duty at the Sayyeda headquarters. Being well-practiced by now, it did not take al-Shabrawi long to sum up the situation for him. The sergeant shook his head slowly.

'That's a responsibility I will not risk.'

'Take us into custody then,' suggested al-Shabrawi, his rage starting to mount.

'That's still a responsibility,' returned the sergeant indifferently.

As he left the building al-Shabrawi was bitterly cursing responsibility and everything to do with it, including himself for having volunteered like a fool to take Zebeida to Cairo. For a moment he considered an hotel but gave up the idea when he remembered he would have to account for Zebeida, plus the fact that it would fleece him of at least fifty or sixty piasters which anyway he didn't have. The Sayyeda Zeinab mosque, which was not far off, seemed to offer the only solution, so he took himself there and, grabbing Zebeida, pulled her down by his side as he sat down on the ground by the wall. He was now on the verge of tears and only his pride kept them back. He could think of no one in the world more miserable than himself at that moment.

The place was swarming with the usual crowd of saintly idiots and half-wits always to be found in profusion around a shrine, so that when Zebeida started up her piercing cries her voice was lost in the din of their mutterings and the chattering of the women and the giddy whirlpools of the rings of *dhikr*.* Al-Shabrawi was glad of that. Something like relief began to ease his moment at last, for now Zebeida was in her element. Nothing she could do was going to appear odd in those surroundings. It was he, rather, who was feeling out of place and he longed to lose his reason too and join these carefree people in their bowers of lunatic bliss.

---

* Religious exercise where men stand in a ring chanting the name of God.

Slowly, and in spite of himself, he began to relax, forgetting his troubles and his frustrations as he sat watching their antics. They were quite an entertaining lot. They did what they liked and nobody stopped them. He turned his attention to a Shaykh who was lying down near him at the foot of the wall. Leaning his head on his arm, the man was watching the people come and go with perfect detachment, a rapt expression on his face and a look of pure contentment in his eyes. Every now and then he would look down, then up at al-Shabrawi, then in a mocking drawl order him to repeat the profession of Allah's unity, fixing on him a relentless stare. Al-Shabrawi could only comply.

As the Shaykh lay there, his vacuous thoughts dwelling on nothing, a cigarette stub fell at his side. Nonchalantly he picked it up and inhaled deeply, enjoying the smoke with obvious relish. He fixed a rapturous gaze on al-Shabrawi as the smoke coiled slowly round his face.

'Say there is but one God,' he ordered again in dead earnest, which made al-Shabrawi chuckle in spite of himself. Suddenly he longed to lie down too, brainless and free of care like the Shaykh. That reminded him of Zebeida. He turned to look at her and was overjoyed to see she was beginning to yawn. Little by little her body relaxed, her eyelids drooped and slowly she sank into sleep.

Now for the first time al-Shabrawi was able to contemplate her face. She wasn't pretty, but her skin was fair and she was small. Her feet, weighed down by heavy anklets, were covered with bruises and layers of mud. The peaceful mask of her face now totally concealed her insanity. Al-Shabrawi noticed that her gown was torn and her thigh was showing through. He covered her up and looked away. Then he turned to the Shaykh and engaged in an endless rambling conversation with him until the latter fell asleep.

As the dark and the silence grew, and the saint's followers bundled up and lay snoring by the wall like tired monkeys at the end of a long day, al-Shabrawi realized his angry mood had left him. He couldn't recall the exact moment when it had happened; he settled down, resigning himself to the snoring that rose all around him, nearly raising the saint from the dead.

Although it had been a long day and he was worn out by the journey and all he had gone through, he decided to sit up through the night. He could hardly wait for daylight to come as he dozed fitfully, his eyes never leaving the big clock in the square.

On the dot of seven he was standing in the Governorate building waiting for the doctor and shooing away the crowd that had collected like flies. Zebeida meanwhile was sustaining a new barrage of trilling-cries. Finally the doctor arrived, and after many ordeals al-Shabrawi and Zebeida were conducted to his presence. He turned her papers over and scribbled something.

'Take her to the Qasr al-Aini to be put under observation.'

They withdrew, and hopping again from one tram to another, found their way to Qasr al-Aini. There, he stopped a man for information but got no answer. Another looked at Zebeida and walked on. Finally an old nurse showed them the way to the out-patient clinic.

The doctor in charge listened patiently to Zebeida calling for the Omda's downfall and long life for the President. And he laughed long and heartily as he questioned her and she ranted in reply. Al-Shabrawi looked on hopefully, beaming with pleasure, seeing they were getting on so well. But the doctor at last put on a serious expression and informed them there was no room in the observation department. He put that in writing on the papers.

'Where do I go now?' asked al-Shabrawi, his soul about to leap from his breast.

'Back to the Governorate.'

'Again?'

'Again.'

The entire globe seemed to weigh on his head as he walked out of the building. Thoughts of murder returned. He would kill the lot. Zebeida, the doctors, the lot, and then he would feign insanity and that would be all. But it was only a fleeting notion.

He trekked back to the Governorate building and arrived gasping for breath. The doctor turned the papers over and asked al-Shabrawi if they had brought a relative with them. His heart sank as he said they hadn't. The doctor explained that the hospital forms could not be filled out except in the presence of a relative. He must take her back where they came from.

Al-Shabrawi paled.

'You mean take her back to Dakahlia?'

'That's right.'

Come to think of it, al-Shabrawi told himself, perhaps it was just as well. But a sudden thought struck him.

'But that's not possible, my Bey, I have only one return ticket form, for me alone.'

'I told you, one of her relatives must be present.'

'Please, my Bey, I beg of you.'

'That's a responsibility I am not prepared to take.'

Al-Shabrawi had more than his bellyful of responsibility by now. Just as he was about to give vent to his fury and smash everything in sight, the air was rent by one of Zebeida's choice trilling-cries and in less than a second she had ripped off her threadbare gown and dashed out stark naked into the courtyard while everyone looked on, speechless and immobile.

Al-Shabrawi was the first to move and he shot after her like a dart. A crowd of policemen and detainees ran to encircle her. Al-Shabrawi succeeded in holding her down but she wriggled out of his hands, calling for the Omda's downfall. Then she turned and dug her teeth viciously into his flesh. He cried out in pain and came down harshly with a slap on her face. Blood trickled slowly through her teeth. She was carried back struggling and screaming, wildly shouting her battle cry, her shrieks piercing the sky.

It took four people to get her into the straitjacket.

She rolled on the ground as she fought to get free, foaming at the mouth, her face scarlet with the streaming blood. The doctor filled out a form in a hurry, and al-Shabrawi looked on horrified, his whole being wrung with pity at what Zebeida was doing to herself.

The sight of Zebeida in a straitjacket made him realize for the first time that she was really insane. It was a shock. He realized too that she had no understanding whatever of the things she was saying, that she was not to be blamed for what he had gone through, and that she had had nothing to eat or to drink since they had left their town.

The sight of her rolling and writhing on the ground filled him with pity.

'Alright,' the doctor was saying.

Now at last Zebeida was off his hands and he was finally rid of her. When that moment arrived he had promised himself a feast in celebration.

But now he felt strangely unmoved, as if none of it all had anything to do with him.

The ambulance arrived and Zebeida was hustled in calling long live to His Majesty the President, her shrill cries never relenting, to the delectation of the jeering crowd.

Suddenly al-Shabrawi darted forward like one stabbed in the heart and begged the driver to wait. He ran to the corner and bought her a loaf of French bread and a piece of *halva*, which he gave to the policeman escorting her.

'Will you see that she eats them,' he pleaded, 'and will you take good care of her? Please . . . for the sake of all your departed loved ones. . . .'

When the car rolled out of sight al-Shabrawi stole away straight to the station. He had had enough of Cairo, and enough of the whole world. From time to time he'd stare at the hand that had struck Zebeida and his flesh would creep with a sense of shame he had never known before in his life.

Translated by Wadida Wassef

Hard Up

———⟳———

A bdou was hard up. Not for the first time. The condition was chronic. He had spent most of his life until now trying to make ends meet.

He had started out as a cook, having learned the trade from Hagg Fayed, the Syrian, and mastered it to the extent that the master himself used to exclaim over the well-seasoned, perfectly-spiced sauces he could make. But then nothing lasts forever. From being a cook he got himself employed in the workshop next door to the restaurant where he was working. Then he was fired, and he found another job as a door-man looking after a block of flats ten stories high. When for some reason he quit that too, his enormous frame and strong muscles qualified him to be a porter loading trucks, until he developed a hernia. Besides good muscles he had a good voice, not a particularly pleasing one but powerful enough to bring the whole street to him when he found himself hawking cucumbers and melons and grapes.

At one time he worked as a middleman roaming the alleys night and day, in search of a vacant room. He generally succeeded in finding one, and the ten piasters that went with it. Eventually he worked his way up to the inner circles where he learned how to wangle the ten piasters from his clients without having to roam alleys or necessarily to find a room. As for being a waiter, there was none to compare with him. He remembered how, when he was in his prime, on the eve of a feast, he could handle an entire café single-handed without once delaying an order or breaking a glass.

He had a wife with whom he lived in one room surrounded by many neighbors. The neighbors were decent people on the whole, if one over-looked the brawls that erupted periodically between his wife and theirs. They sympathized with him and lent him money when he was out of work, and prayed for him to find a job and borrowed from him when he did. And so life went on providing their daily bread, growing daily more niggardly, it is true, but then, such was life.

So Abdou was hard up. Only this time it had lasted longer than usual, and there seemed to be no end in sight. His feet were worn out from calling on old friends and acquaintances, and every time he returned home and knocked on the door with a frown on his face and nothing in his hands. His wife would not greet him when she opened the door, nor would he greet her, instead he made straight for his straw mat and tried to go to sleep, shutting his ears to Nefissa's incessant chatter. But she would force him to listen, droning on about the events of the day, and the landlord's threats, and the scraps of bread the neighbors sent out of charity, and about the coming feast, and how much she was yearning for peaches, and their little girl who had died, and the boy she was expecting who was going to be born with a peach for a birthmark because she was yearning so for peaches. And she would go on and on, getting so carried away that her voice would grow unbearably shrill, until he could stand it no longer.

Nor could he stand to see the pity in the eyes of his neighbors who felt sorry for him, or listen to them wishing him better luck, because their wishes were no good to his empty stomach or to Nefissa's almost naked body.

One day on his return home Nefissa announced that Tolba had sent for him, which gave him a glimmer of hope, ungrounded perhaps, but still bet-ter than nothing. So he got up immediately and took himself over to Tolba's. Tolba was undoubtedly the best tenant in the building because he worked as a male nurse at the hospital. He was also the most recent tenant.

Tolba received him with much cordiality which threw Abdou a little out of countenance. No sooner had they exchanged the perfunctory words of greeting than Abdou was already telling him all about himself. He loved to dwell on the good old days and tell of the various jobs he had held at one time, and all the people he had known, particularly when he noticed the revulsion which his worn and threadbare gallabiya aroused. He felt somehow that speaking of his days of glory covered up for his shabby dress. He swelled with pride and he felt elated talking of the days when he occupied positions of importance. But when he remembered his present plight he grew dejected again. He deplored the evil in men's hearts, and bemoaned the old days of plenty, his voice tapering to a bare whisper which rose from the abyss of his degradation, asking Tolba on end if he could find him a job.

Tolba listened, although he interrupted him many times, but told him in the end that there was, in fact, a job waiting for him.

That night Abdou went home in a transport of joy. He spoke at length to Nefissa about Tolba's kind heart, and told her she must go to his wife next day after she'd finished with her washing for the students she was working for, and give her a hand and keep her company.

Next day Abdou was up at the crack of dawn, and by sunrise he and Tolba were standing before the Blood Transfusion Department of the hospital. He waited. Others came and waited too. At ten o'clock the door opened and they all went in. The silence impressed him. The air was permeated with carbolic acid which gave him a slight nausea. They were made to line up and a cross-examination began. They wanted to know his father's name, and his mother's, and they wanted to know what his uncles had died of, paternal and maternal, and they asked for his photograph and he could only produce the one stuck on his identity card which he always carried with him in case of an accident or trouble with the police.

They stuck a needle in his vein and drew out a bottleful of blood and told him to come back next week.

During the week he was still hard up, still searching for a job and nothing was left of the scraps of bread the neighbors had sent in charity. On the appointed day of the following week he was at the hospital department again. At ten o'clock the door opened. 'Not you,' they said to the man standing in front of him. The man refused to budge. 'Your blood's no good,' they said to him as they shoved him out of the way.

Abdou's heart sank, but when his turn came and they told him they would be taking blood from him his apprehension was gone. He stood obstinately in his place and cheered and laughed much like his old ways, resigned to wait although he was feeling very hungry.

Soon his turn came. They put his arm through a hole just large enough to hold it. He was a little alarmed but when he saw there were two other men on either side of him his fears subsided. Suddenly he felt as though his arm were encased in a block of ice. Something like an obelisk seemed to penetrate it. He gave a moan and then he was quiet. Presently he began to take a look at his surroundings. He raised his head a little to look through the glass partition behind which pretty girls who did not have crooked and protruding front teeth like his wife's and who did not wear dull black dresses like her, moved about quietly. Peering more closely he realized they were not all girls. Some were young men with clear shiny faces. He envied them for being inside with the pretty girls and he wished that by some freak he could make his arm stretch and stretch until it reached the mask on the girls' faces and he could pull it away and pinch one of those lovely cheeks.

Abdou kept watching the masked faces until they started to blur and fade out, and the glass screen began to send flashes of light, and the masks kept sliding on and off. Suddenly he felt very tired. His arm went cold, then hot, then cold again.

'How much are they taking?' he asked the man on his right.

'I don't know. Half a liter, they say,' said the man. The conversation ended there.

'Alright, it's over,' someone said, tapping his arm.

Abdou got up, walking unsteadily. When he asked for the money he was told to wait, so he waited. They gave him one pound and thirty piasters minus tax. They were even so generous as to give him breakfast.

Before going home he called at the butcher's and bought a pound of meat, and at the greengrocer's to buy potatoes, and when he knocked on the door of their room he was all smiles. Nefissa beamed with pleasure and cheerfully returned his greeting when she saw what he was carrying. She was quick to come forward and relieve him of his load, and only coyness kept her from telling him how much she loved him.

Soon she was busy cooking, and the frying smells filled the room and escaped outside to the whole building and reached the neighbors, which made some of them smile and others sigh with pity.

Abdou ate until he could eat no more and on a rash impulse went out and bought a watermelon. That night his wife, for once, did not start up her usual racket. She was docile and meek and they cooed like lovers.

Before the week was out Abdou had spent all the money. On the appointed day he went back to the hospital and stretched out his arm and they took their ration of blood and gave him his ration of money and a meal in addition.

Abdou was quite pleased with his new job as he did not have take orders from anybody, and no one bullied him around. All he was asked to do was turn up every week at that nice clean place where everything was white, and give half a liter of blood and cash in the price. His wife managed to make do with what he gained, and his body managed to replenish its blood supply, and then he went back at the end of the week and gave them more blood and they gave him more money.

And so it went on. Many people envied him.

As for his wife, it all depended. When he came home with food she'd smile in his face and nearly cry out for joy. But when he slept all week she wouldn't leave him alone. She'd nag about his skinny legs and haggard face, and tell him in no polished terms what the women in the neighborhood were saying about him. How they threw it in her face that her husband sold his blood for a living. Sometimes she'd fuss about him like a hen, seeing that he was warm enough at night, pulling up his cover if it happened to slip. By day she wouldn't let him move from his place and she'd hover round him answering his every call as if he were a sick child.

All this did not escape Abdou. It made him bitter, but then what did it matter? It's true he felt dizzy every time he gave blood, and he had to lie down by the hospital wall until late afternoon. It was also true that people talked, but at least the stove was going and the rent was paid. People could go to hell.

Except that one day when he went to the hospital as usual they did not put his arm through the hole. Instead they called him and said no.

'Why not?'

'Anemia.'

'What's anemia?'

'No red corpuscles.'

'So what?'

'It won't do.'

'And what am I to do?'

'Come back later, when you're stronger.'

'I'm strong now. Here. I can tear down that wall.'

'You'll collapse.'

'Don't worry.'

'You could die.'

'I'll take the risk.'

'That wouldn't be human . . . your own good . . .'

'And is what you're doing human?'

'That's how it is . . .'

'You mean nothing doing?'

'Nothing doing.'

That day they forgot to give him a meal, and Abdou was hard up again.

Translated by Wadida Wassef

The Funeral Ceremony

bou'l Metwalli stood in the doorway of the mosque while the midday sun poured down on him, blistering his white face. It made his hair, snow-white like a rabbit's, glow with the heat, and his bald eyelids, which he tightened against the sunlight, grow redder still. For a while he stood dodging the rays of the sun, unable to see inside except when he craned his neck to push his head into the shade within. He searched the mosque with his bleary eyes until he found the man he was looking for, sitting at the foot of a column fighting off sleep.

'Shaykh Muhammad,' he called in his quiet nasal voice. But his voice was lost in the hum that rose from the prostrated worshipers, ringing in hollow echoes against the lofty walls of the mosque. He raised his voice and struggled to make himself heard, his face reddening with the effort until it was the color of a cock's comb.

Finally the man heard him and turned his head as if he was expecting to be called. His eyes darted to the door, then he picked himself up and shuffled across. Abou'l Metwalli was relieved as he could now rest his eyes from the strain of searching. He drew his eyelids tightly together again, leaving only a narrow slit from which to follow what was going on.

'What took you so long, Mabrouk?' asked the Shaykh.

Abou'l Metwalli had no time for civilities; he did not trouble to reply.

Instead, he placed the bundle he was carrying on the bench that protruded in the doorway. It contained a dead infant wrapped in a faded blanket.

'Read the prayers, Shaykh Muhammad,' he ordered.

The Shaykh demurred. He craned his neck and looked to the left, then to the right. Then he smiled, an artless cunning smile, and was starting to say something when Abou'l Metwalli cut him short irritably.

'Just read the prayers,' he insisted, screwing up his eyes more tightly, as if in defiance of both Shaykh Muhammad and the sun. He gave his gallabiya a hard smack to mark his discontent, and tugged at his turban with both hands to set it straight, perhaps for the hundredth time since the morning.

He planted himself more firmly in his place until the Shaykh got started on his prayers. Then he let his attention drift to the pretty brawls that were breaking out all the time between the countless hawkers and their customers standing all round the mosque. But the sun was in his eyes so he moved them to the shade where a *dhikr* was in full sway. The ring included a motley crowd of people led by a half-witted Shaykh, who wore a red sash and a leather pouch slung over his shoulder. Only God knew what was inside. He was leading the *dhikr* by hitting his beads on an iron tube he was holding, while he kept up a monotonous chant, his voice even more repulsive than his face.

When the licorice-juice seller came round, and the clash of his cymbals rang in the air, Abou'l Metwalli suddenly became aware of his parched throat and he couldn't resist the temptation of the cool beads that glistened on the glass container. So he held out half a piaster to the man, and with one breath blew off the foamy top from the glass he gave him and in the name of Allah gulped down the liquid. Feeling his soul revive he dug into his waist pocket again and came up with another half piaster which he chucked at the man. Once again his throat went into convulsions as he gulped down the second glass.

It made him belch and his body became drenched in sweat. He stole a look at the sycamores a man was selling not far from him, but didn't like the look of them so he came back to the door to find Shaykh Muhammad nearing the end of the prayers, having made two prostrations.

'Peace and the mercy of God be with you,' he was saying in peroration as he stared toward the undertaker. His voice was loud and pointed, with a hint of reproof at Abou'l Metwalli. Then he dropped it to a whisper and went on to terminate the prayer. The undertaker eyed him with suspicion.

'Shaykh, would you swear on your Muslim faith that the boy was properly turned toward the *Kiblah*?'*

Shaykh Muhammad, ending his prayer, raised his voice. 'God bless and save . . . ,' he went on, but the undertaker wouldn't let him.

'Can you say in good faith that your ablutions were correctly performed?'

'. . . and save Sayyedna Muhammad and his Family, and his Companions.' The prayer was ended. 'What is the matter, brother, don't you trust me?' asked the Shaykh. Abou'l Metwalli mumbled something that made no sense even to himself. He picked up the bundle.

'How many does this one make?' the Shaykh was now asking, having wound up the prayer in a hurry.

The undertaker paused, saying nothing for a while as his irritation returned, making his small load feel like a ton of bricks. He had done his best to avoid this issue but now it seemed inevitable.

'This one makes seven, Shaykh Muhammad,' he said slowly. 'What do you mean, seven? I swear by the lady Miska, and Umm Hashem and all God's saints, this one makes eight.'

'Seven, I tell you Shaykh Muhammad, and I swear by the almighty God.'

'Look here, 'Amm** Metwalli, you're a man with a family; you can't afford to be dishonest. I swear, I tell you. Alright, let's count them from the beginning. There was that boy you brought from al-Hanafi this morning. That makes one. Then there was that girl, your cousin . . . .'

'You look here, Shaykh Muhammad, I tell you it's only seven, and if that's not true I'll repudiate my wife.'

'I tell you, man . . . .'

'And I'm telling you, only seven, and if that's not true I'll repudiate my wife.'

---

* Direction of Mecca toward which Muslims turn their faces in prayer.
** Uncle. A respectful form of address to an older person.

'Very well, we'll leave it to your conscience. God is your witness.'

'So how much have you had so far?'

'One ten-piaster piece.'

The undertaker paused to calculate.

'So now for all seven I still owe you four piasters.'

'But . . . I mean, look . . . .'

'But what?'

'I mean . . . Look, do I need to tell you? How much is a pound of tomatoes these days, hey? And okra beans, do you know how much they are? And business so slack. No proper celebrations, no funeral ceremonies, nothing coming in. And the wife, yesterday I had to buy her aspirins . . . .'

'Come on, man, don't give me that crap. You ought to be thankful. Summer's coming, and the epidemic won't be far behind, and you're going to be so busy you won't know whether you're coming or going. You've got to trust in God, man. Here, take this.'

Shaykh Muhammad hesitated, clutching and unclutching his hand, before he decided to stretch it out and take the five-piaster note the undertaker was pushing at him. He felt it with his fingers, and shrank his neck deeper inside his robe. He screwed up his eyes and blinked; he rubbed the paper note between his fingers and folded it up and nearly gave it back but thought better of it. He peered through the mist that veiled his eyes.

'Alright, Mabrouk, I'll have one piaster more.'

But nobody heard him because Abou'l Metwalli and his bundle had already vanished in the crowd.

Translated by Wadida Wassef

All on a Summer's Night

vening prayers were over. The hay was cold and piled high, and the night was dark and silvery. There was a grave and the clouds drifted over it fluttering in the air like the soft white handkerchiefs of lovers. Nearby lay our town crouching like a hedgehog, with its thorns, and sorrows, and trees, and we were there on the hay, talking, not like the grown-ups ruminating on their troubles, but mostly about ourselves. A dark force was just beginning to devastate our bodies, working a change in us which grew daily more evident and which we sensed with mixed feelings of joy and bewilderment.

Although we had many troubles we never talked about them. We worked as hard as the men, perhaps harder, for they were inclined to be indolent, sitting in the shade while they left us to broil toiling in the fields. Sometimes they begged us, sometimes they ordered us but in either case we were happy. To work was to be a man, and that's what we longed to be, and if we were made to work it meant we had grown up and that we were dependable and in the prime of life, with promise in our future. Soon we would marry and there would be processions and wedding feasts and celebration in our honor.

Having toiled all day we had voracious appetites. We devoured anything in sight and our mothers thrilled to see we were growing, and they'd feed us on the sly, much as they forcibly fed their ducks and their geese, keeping for us the choicest meats and eggs and cheese. We were growing fast, as though to make up for lost time, shaking off the paleness of a long childhood and the lean years. Our faces filled out taking the color of rich silt, our legs grew tougher, and our throats became thicker as our voices broke.

We used to sit together on the hay in the evenings, our bodies a prey to that force which made us listless, neither giving ourselves up to dreams nor yet able to curb its powerful drive. The night shuddered with our voices and our new virility as we sat in that distant spot giving vent to thoughts we dared not voice except there where we smothered ourselves in the comforting coolness of the hay.

Conversation came of itself. No one knew how it started but when it did it flowed on without end. The night was a refuge. We loved it like a beautiful woman who stirred our sleeping passions, soft and tender and ebony black, much as we hated the harsh and forbidding light of day.

We used to measure ourselves the moment we got together, each one trying to prove he was the tallest. We made bets and the loser pretended he had a pain and a swelling in the thigh which he showed the others who assured him there was no reason to worry; the swelling only meant he was growing. And then we'd go on to describe the dreams that we dreamt, or to compare our voices, feeling one another's throats. But invariably we ended up talking about women. The women of our town were like the majority of its dwellings, dark and flat and without curves. Some houses, though, were whitewashed, and we loved to imagine there was a beautiful woman inside every white house. It was about them, mostly, that we talked. For beautiful women must be easy to get, we decided, or else there was no point in their being beautiful.

Sometimes we ran wild with our imagination, working ourselves up to a mad pitch of excitement and we would start throwing hay at one another and roll about and shout and howl like wolves. But soon we were forced to calm down before we were discovered by some watchman who would send us home where there was nothing but to flop on our pallets on top of the oven and fight off the lonesomeness and the bafflement and the demons inside us that prevented sleep. Only there on the haystack, with one another, were the demons becalmed, and we found relief talking to one another.

Muhammad was the pivot on whom we all hinged. He was older but no less bewildered than the rest of us although he was more experienced. He had left our town at an early age to go to work in the city. He was always in the thick of things and he always had something to tell. What's more he knew about women, which was more than any of us could boast. None of us had any real experience of women. At most we ogled them from a distance, fearing and desiring them at the same time but quailing at the thought of anything more intimate. So we loved to listen to Muhammad, and we avidly lapped up the tales he used to tell us about his exploits. We were quite fond of him with his sprouting mustache and his long hair which he was allowed to grow as he pleased while we were forced by our fathers to crop ours short. He had a blond forelock which he was fond of smearing with Vaseline borrowed from the station-master, or failing that, with butter. His woolen skull-cap was always tilted back on his head to show off his shining forelock. He also had a hare-lip that made him appear truculent, which in reality he wasn't. He was jolly and good-natured and full of fun, and his skin was untanned by the scorching sun of the fields. He used to till the land at one time until he went to the city for some reason, and having had a taste of it vowed never to return to the plough. Sometimes as we sat with him we couldn't help feeling he was not one of us but some stranger. One of those fast and clear-witted boys from the city whom we dreaded so much. On the whole we were not given to wrongdoing and we feared transgression, but we were emboldened by his example. It was he who showed us how to fill our laps with rubble as we entered our homes and replace it with corn or barley or cotton, and walk out unsuspected. It was he who arranged to sell the loot, keeping a portion of the gains for himself and with what was left we would buy ourselves *halva* and tangerines and bamboo canes with which we loved to swagger on market-days.

That night we were sitting together, just a handful of boys from the town, their muddy feet full of cracks, their clothes in rags, their faces an indefinite blur of tanned hide. We sat exhaling odors of our dinner in the light summer air: onions and cheese and pickled peppers and sardines and leeks. The wheat was all around us, some of it swaying in the fields, some of it already tied in sheaves and lined up in small bundles like rows of prostrated worshipers. Nearby the threshing machine crouched like a kneeling camel, and the scent of the new crop floated in the air mingling with the smell of the earth, wet with dew, and the reek of our sweat which, like ourselves, had suffered a change, acquiring an odor which was intensely male.

It was nights such as this that gave Muhammad's talk its peculiar fascination. His voice, where a manly ring had already settled, unlike ours, was steady, and he held us spellbound by his manner of recounting a story. He told us about many places, near and far, some of which we knew, some we didn't, nor he himself for that matter. Strange, exotic places which called up visions of well-dressed people, and railways, and tall buildings. We usually kept him till the end, after we had exhausted our own stock of gossip about out town, and its women, and how we ogled them, and how they ogled us. And then we would let Muhammad take over.

That night we could tell from the way he began that he wanted to tell us about the Bedouin woman he had met at the village fair. But we stopped him when we saw he was beginning to cheat, rehashing things we had heard before. We wanted something new for we knew him by now. He had a trick of starting with a lengthy preamble then stopping abruptly in the middle so that we would coax him to go on, promising wheat and maize and eggs in return. Sometimes too he would clam up suddenly for no reason and nothing we said would make him change his mind.

'Listen boys,' he began that night. 'I'm going to tell you something that happened to me on condition you don't breathe a word of it to anyone.'

'Promise.'

'You swear on God's Holy Book?'

'Swear.'

'And anyone who squeals . . . .'

'Is a stinking creep.'

'And the son of a dog.'

'The son of a dog.'

'Well,' he began. 'I was going to Mansourah one day, on business . . . .'

'Liar, you've never been to Mansourah.'

'I have, I swear on the Holy Book.'

We believed him, panting with excitement. We couldn't help it. He was going to tell us about Mansourah which none of us had ever seen. But we had all heard about it, all sorts of fantastic things. We imagined it to be a vast Garden of Eden, full of Europeans and milk-white girls, and women draped in shiny *melayas** that shimmered when they walked. We imagined their bodies to be boneless, and their flesh soft and malleable like Turkish delight. We imagined their men to be sops; no match for their women who desired real men. Men like ourselves, coarse peasants with the strength of a bull.

'Go on,' we said to Muhammad.

After he got off the train, he said, he had seen to the business that took him there, and seeing he still had some time left before he caught the train back, he bought himself a loaf of bread to eat while he took a stroll down the road where the station was. It was full of big houses with large verandahs. It was late afternoon and most of the women were out taking the air. Bunches of them; had they been dealt out to the men in our town each man would have come out with a cluster.

Well, as he was going along, his eye was caught by one verandah where a woman was leaning over the railing wearing a red dressing gown.

'What's a dressing gown?'

'Oh, something like a robe.'

We were always skeptical of the things he said. We listened to him like magistrates oscillating between belief and disbelief. There was always a suspicion he was pulling our legs.

Muhammad went on with his story. He was just passing under that balcony, he said, when the woman smiled at him. He thought she was smiling at someone else but the street was deserted except for himself and when he looked back at her she smiled again. We grabbed Muhammad by his gallabiya.

'Careful now, don't you leave anything out,' we said, gasping.

'Don't worry. I'll tell you everything.'

It didn't matter whether his story were true or not as long as he kept on with it.

---

* Black silk covering worn by many women.

'Well,' he continued, 'she smiled again, boys, and my heart began to pound, and I said to myself, this is your lucky day, boy. I pretended I didn't notice and looked at her again and she laughed. I could do with a glass of *zibib*, I thought to myself.'

'What's *zibib*?'

'That's brandy, boys.'

'And what's brandy?'

'That's drink, liquor.'

Here, we got afraid. Muhammad taking liquor? We allowed him women, but not liquor. However, for Muhammad's sake we were willing to close an eye to that.

'Then what.'

'I found a tavern open, owned by a European. So I went in. "Hey, mister," I said. "Yes," he said. "Give me a *zibib*. I want the real stuff. And I want cucumbers for a snack."'

'Snack? What's that?'

'Cucumbers.'

We didn't dare repeat the question, as we were more anxious to hear what was coming.

'I drank it up, and what do you think? It turned me on. My blood caught fire. And to make double sure I ordered another one before I took myself back to her street.'

'And you went past her house again?'

'I did.'

'And she smiled at you?'

'A smile that gave wings to my soul, boys. One hell of a beautiful woman, and she was wearing . . . .'

'What?'

'She was wearing embroidered clogs, and I could see the curves of her body under her dressing gown, and she was smiling. So I looked at her and smiled. So she smiled back.'

'What for?'

'Well, I was in my best clothes. My camel-hair cap, and patent leather shoes, and my silk scarf was draped over my shoulder. Besides, I'm quite a smasher, don't forget, being young and all that. Well, I gave her a wink so she went inside and came back wearing a new dressing gown, of green silk. Then she signaled to me to come upstairs.'

'Upstairs?'

'That's right. I must say, though, I was a little shaky. I was a stranger, after all, entering a strange house just to see a woman. Suppose I were caught, where would I be? Or suppose she had relatives. Anyway, I went up. It was the two *zibib*s that did it.'

'And you went inside her house?'

'Can't you be patient? I rang the bell . . . .'

'What bell?'

'A bell at the door, with a push button . . . .'

'A bell with a push button?'

'You ignorant peasant clots. You'll never learn. Of course, stupid, bells have buttons. Well, she opened the door and told me to come in . . . a voice like spun sugar . . . .'

'And you went in?'

'Stop interrupting or I won't tell.'

'Alright, go on.'

'I stood at the door, a little uncertain. "Come on," she said, "don't be afraid, my husband is away." So I said to myself, "Come on, boy, get yourself in, you only die once."'

'That's right, Muhammad, damn you. Go right in.'

'So I went in, and sat in the sitting-room. Gilt chairs, boy, fit for a king, and mirrors on the walls, and colored baubles and things. After a while I found her coming in wearing a navy blue dress, something out of this world. She had a bottle and two glasses with her. She said, "What's your name, young man?" "Your servant, Muhammad," I replied. "You're my master," she said. "Bless you. Would you like to sit on the chair, or just make yourself comfortable, wherever you like . . . ."'

'The chair, of course, you fool.'

'No. I'm not used to sitting on chairs. I was afraid it might make me dizzy. Well, then I asked what her name was. "Fifi," she said, and then she asked if I would have a drink, and I said yes and we sat drinking, glass after glass until the room began to spin. "What's the matter?' she asked. "Are you getting tight?" "Oh, no," I replied. "Would you like something to sober you up?" she asked. I didn't dare say yes.'

'Silly boy. And did she get you anything?'

'You bet. I found her coming in with a huge tray loaded with food.'

'What was on it?'

'Turkey stuffed with pigeon, and roast potatoes, and mutton.'

'You lucky devil! And you ate all that?'

'I didn't know what I was doing. She just kept feeding me . . . .'

'Have you no shame, boy?'

'Shame, my foot. I was all wound up and I stretched my hand and I touched her.'

'Without washing your hands?'

'I washed them, damn you. Look, who's telling this story? I'm getting tired of you.'

We begged him to go on, although he didn't need to be begged. He was so carried away with his tale nothing could have stopped him.

'I touched her, boys, and her flesh was like honey paste.'

'Was her skin fair?'

'Fairer than beaten cotton.'

'And her hair, was it black?'

'Black as pitch, down to her knees.'

'Go on, tell, boy, what else? Mind you don't skip anything.'

'And her skin, boys! It was smooth and soft as silk. I said, "Please, I can't stand it any longer." She said, "Alright, come along." And she took me to the bed, and let down the mosquito-net. It was pink, I swear, and then she turned off the light.'

'Easy now, mind you go slowly.'

'Well, and I looked and saw the mosquito-net was shimmering. It must be doomsday, I thought to myself. And you know what? She had turned on another light inside the mosquito-net. There were small colored bulbs at the top, red, green, blue, yellow . . . and I looked and saw her before me, gorgeous, bewitching. She was all colored, like a sprite . . . .'

'Then what?'

'Then nothing. Boy, what a night! Better than anything in *The Arabian Nights.*'

'What happened? Go on, you've got to tell. What happened next?'

'Nothing. That's all.'

'Come on, what happened next? Don't be mean, boy.'

He condescended to add a thing or two which did nothing to satisfy our curiosity.

'Leave him alone, he's fibbing,' said one boy.

'Swear all this is true,' said another.

Muhammad swore and we got even more excited. We did not believe him. He swore on his mother's grave that what he told us was true, every bit of it.

'Did I ever lie to you?' he asked.

'You're lying now.'

'Alright, have it your way.'

'Suppose we go to Mansourah, will you take us to the place?'

'Sure.'

'Alright, let's go now. Right away.'

That was a great idea. We raised a roar and cheered and yelled and shouted as we pushed and shoved one another. We got hold of Muhammad by his arms and legs and swung him about then tossed him up on the haystack. Then we took a spin on the threshing machine. We had gone quite wild. Little clouds of hay blew up in the air and settled in our eyes and covered us with dust.

'Come on boys, off to Mansourah.'

'Off to Mansourah!' everybody shouted.

'It's too dark boys.'

'And all the digging to be done tomorrow . . . .'

But nothing was going to keep us from going to Mansourah, and we started off.

After having walked for a while we realized we had covered a large part of the way. Our town lay behind with its borders and its fields. Only then did we realize we were actually on our way to Mansourah. Already we could smell foreign soil beneath our feet. It felt different back home where everything was familiar and we moved freely. Every palm tree, every field, every house where we had played and romped in our childhood was familiar, and every man was our kin. Each one of us, blindfolded, could tell the soil of our town from that of another. Suddenly we knew we were far from home.

We were seized with panic as we stared into the dark and realized we did not know where the road was leading us. But none of us dared voice his fear. We moved on in a mass like an enormous giant with multiple heads and arms and legs, trying to melt our fears in the shelter of one another. We continued on our impetuous march, glum, silent, unbridled by reason, drawn by the magic call of Mansourah, driven in spite of ourselves.

There was only the dull sound of our bare feet on the road, like a caravan of camels. Those of us wearing shoes had long removed them and carried them tucked under their arms. We were gasping, our faces were shining, and dust kept blowing up in our wake. The night was huge and black and fearful, full of secret whispers. The plantations stretched like a vast shoreless sea. The crops stood still, moving only with the breeze, slowly, inanimately. Waterwheels creaked from afar like mourners bewailing a corpse. Gunshots sounded in the distance, out of nowhere into nowhere, and cocks crowed before their time. The barking of dogs came from reaches unknown, and a vast wind blew over a vast land, and the earth murmured, and obscure whispers came up from obscure places, sly and treacherous like the sound of huge whales twisting and turning in a sea of darkness.

Someone stretched a hand and jabbed another in the ribs and he jumped with a yell. Soon it caught on, and we were all in an uproar, shouting, jumping, and falling all over one another.

'What about her legs, Muhammad? Did she have legs like ours?'

'You call those tree stumps legs, man?'

'What were hers like?'

'Milk white.'

'Like Safeya's, the dancing girl?'

'Don't be an ass, Safeya's not a patch on her.'

'And did she have a fish tattooed on her belly?'

'What fish, you fool! What are you talking about?'

'Well what did she have on her belly?'

'Nothing. A belly like hers is not made for a tattoo.'

'And was her face painted?'

'I didn't notice.'

'How come, silly? Didn't you look?'

'I think it was.'

'And what's her talk like? Does she speak like city folk, or like us?'

'Like city folk, of course.'

We all broke into a riot again. The woman had taken substance and she was standing alive before our minds' eye, beautiful, palpable, just as we desired her.

We jogged on, pushing and shoving and laughing and talking. Every now and then we'd make a guess as to how long it would be before we reached Mansourah.

Suddenly we realized Muhammad had disappeared.

The shock was like a stab. We shot out wildly in all directions to catch him. Any doubt that he was telling the truth vanished. Every little detail of his story was indelibly engraved upon our minds. The lady of the red gown and the bottle became a vivid reality, not just another creation of Muhammad's brain. She was the woman each one of us already possessed. She was going to swoon with happiness when one after the other we were going to climb up to her iron-railed balcony. In her joy she was even going to give us each a one-pound note, for we were the strapping braves unmatched in all Mansourah.

And the swine goes and disappears!

We spread ourselves out in a tight network. By the graveyard, and the railway line, and the bridge. We were not going to let this whole venture come to nothing when Mansourah was already within reach. Another stretch and we would find our quest. Hundreds of European women, milk-white, and so beautiful you could eat them alive, sweeter to the taste than bees' honey and cream.

'There he is boys,' came a shout from the distance.

We flew in the direction of the voice and there we found Muhammad struggling with the boy who'd caught him. We threw ourselves on top of him. It wasn't difficult to pin him down. He fought vigorously, dealing out powerful blows like a man's. But we closed in on him like an army of ants attacking a breadcrumb, until at last he was overpowered and he ceased to struggle. One boy ripped off his gallabiya and tied him with it.

'What do you want now?' asked Muhammad defiantly.

'You're going to show us that place.'

'I won't.'

'Yes you will.'

'You can't force me.'

'You wait and see.'

'I'll show you, you effeminate lot of bastards!'

'Get up!'

He held fast to the ground and we dragged him up by force while he spluttered out angrily: 'It's a long way to Mansourah, I tell you.'

'That's none of your business.'

'I'm warning you. Don't say I didn't tell you.'

We walked on in silence, all of us tense and on edge. We thought of singing to relieve the tension. But we didn't know any songs. Only the girls were any good at singing. One boy knew the first line of an old lay and he started to sing it but his voice was so ugly we made him shut up. Tiny luminous dots were beginning to speckle the horizon like the eyes of grasshoppers when they catch the light. They were the lights of Mansourah which meant we were almost there. We broke into a run dragging Muhammad along until we were out of breath. Then we slowed to a walking pace. We walked a long time and still the lights were no closer, almost as if the nearer we approached the farther they receded, sinking in the dark.

'Let's go back boys,' said Muhammad.

'Shut up, you. Hurry up boys, it's getting late.'

We summoned the remainder of our strength and walked on. All of a sudden a great peal of laughter cut through the emptiness of the road. It was Muhammad. He was doubled up, unable to control himself, and when he saw us looking at him he forced himself into new convulsions.

'I got you!' he was saying between gasps. 'You bunch of idiots, I got you!'

'What do you mean?'

'You blinking bunch of idiots. You believed everything I said. I never went near Mansourah, and I never saw any woman.'

'Liar!'

'I swear boys, I never even saw Mansourah.'

'You son of a dog!'

'And you blinking idiots!'

A heavy silence fell upon us as we stared at the lights of Mansourah which now seemed to be within reach of our hands. To our fevered imagination the town became the embodiment of a woman with flesh like soft dough, draped in a dressing gown and leaning out from a balcony, beckoning for us to come. We looked back at Muhammad and found him still laughing in scorn.

'He's pulling your leg,' someone said.

'He won't show us the woman. He doesn't want us to see the place.'

'What do you mean, you swine?' snapped Muhammad angrily.

We swore at him saying we weren't going to let him go until he took us to the house. He swore back, and scoffed, and called us fools and idiots. We vowed we weren't going to let him get away with it, he wasn't going to keep the woman to himself. We ordered him to walk on, but he refused so we dragged him. He kicked one of the boys in the stomach and started lashing out wildly with his hands and his legs. We fell on him in a mass and forced him to the ground, punching at him, slapping his face. He resisted, hitting back savagely until he was overcome and we tied him down again. We smeared his face with mud and somebody spat on him. He tried to shout but we gagged him. For a moment it looked as if he was going to choke to death so we relaxed our grip a little to let him breathe.

'Drag him to the field and brand him with fire, boys,' someone suggested.

'Yes, let's.' And we dragged him into a field and started to look for matches but we found none. We'll make a spark, we decided, and started to look for flint and found some over the railway line. Now we needed a nail or a piece of iron. We found only a scrap of tin. One boy crouched on Muhammad's chest and ran the piece of tin across his legs.

'Are you going to show us that woman's house, or do you want to die?'
He made no reply. We dug our nails into his flesh and scratched. Then we
bit him. But he still wouldn't tell. We realized at last it was no use, that he
had been lying all along and we renewed the attack with savage fury.

'Come on, say it, say you're a sissy,' hissed the boy who held the tin.

Muhammad only kicked at him and cursed our fathers in return.

'Alright, give it to him, boys.' And we got to work on the flint trying to
produce a spark. A tiny part of ourselves couldn't help admiring his guts,
but for the most part we hated him for having fooled us all that time.

At last we obtained a spark and it caught on the piece of cotton. We
cheered and blew on it. It was a pale, wan, cold fire. We blew harder but
it only grew paler. No matter how hard we blew, the fire remained wan
and cold.

Not only the fire but everything all around was starting to wane. Then
something whistled in our ears like a cry for help, and we realized with horror that we were in the midst of something dreadful. We stared at one
another in a daze as slowly we began to wake to the stark reality. Our faces
were bruised and grubby, and our clothes were covered with dust. And flies.
Thousands of sticky flies droned and flew around us incessantly.

How did we come to this torment? What were our people going to say?
Surely we would be beaten and roundly abused when we returned. Some of
us would have to rise at dawn; there were the waterwheels to be assembled,
and the barns to be cleaned, and we'd had no sleep, and our eyes were bloodshot. Had they caught some infection? Was the sun also rising on our town,
back home? Why was there shock on our faces, and guilt, and remorse? Why
were they blotched and diseased and ravaged with pimples? Why did we
realize only now that we were wretchedly poor, and that there was nothing
in our homes but barking dogs and roaring fathers and screeching mothers
and the suffocating smoke of the stove?

Horrified, we began to feel our bodies and examine our clothes to see
how much damage was done. We saw ourselves with appalling clarity
which made us fear to look at the core inside.

Muhammad lay on the road like a slaughtered beast, his gallabiya in
shreds, his body limp and covered with flies. Gory wounds gaped from his

flesh and the blood clotted on his nose and down the side of his mouth and inside the cleft of his hare-lip. Slowly, dispassionately, we loosened his bonds. He groaned with pain and our hearts went out to him.

Once more we found ourselves roaming, back on the same road that saw us coming, driven in spite of ourselves. We were limping and groaning and leaning on one another. Our thoughts were dwelling on the coming dawn, rising suddenly, giving shape to the earth, with grief and care in its folds. And the harsh inexorable day loomed ahead like a huge monster, bigger than the sun. Stark and merciless, awaiting, threatening, his eyes spitting fire as we approached, awed and quivering, knowing full well there was no escape.

Translated by Wadida Wassef

The Caller in the Night

―――∽∽∽―――

It was Hagg Sa'ad's funeral ceremony. The time was just after the evening prayers when most people begin to arrive. A modest tent had been erected to receive the guests. It was lit by gas lamps that gave a pale, anemic light. They shone brightly just the same, through the blackness that enveloped our village, guiding the crowds of fellahin who came to bring their condolences. They were not used to lights by night so that they were momentarily blinded the moment they stepped inside and it was some time before they could recognize any of the people sitting there. The front seats, made of tarnished gilt with chipped edges and covered by worn faded velvet, were occupied as usual by the prominent personalities of the town.

I was considered the most highly educated man there because I was a student of medicine. Everyone insisted on calling me Doctor. The people adopted me, so to speak, and looked upon me as something of a local treasure of which they boasted to the other towns. When they went to market, the women would say arrogantly to those from elsewhere, 'Shut up, woman, at least we have doctors in our town.' And children at play stopped to stare when they saw me coming. 'He's a doctor, boys, a real one,' they'd say to one another. Adults followed me with their eyes and called blessings on me, and asked God to guard me from the evil eye and make me a joy to my father.

So, being elevated to the ranks of the prominent, it was my right and my duty to sit with them although like most others who were educated I would have preferred to sit with the majority who were poor fellahin. Hagg Sa'ad, God rest his soul, used to say of them that they were made of the rubble left over after God created the brainy folks from the soft clay of paradise.

We would rather have sat with them, as I said, because there we could be more relaxed, and we did not need to put a strain on our speech or behavior as anything we said was sure to go down as holy writ.

I was sitting in the corner near the entrance with some university students and a large number of date-palm clippers when a new group of people, who made it a point always to be seen with the educated, came and joined as. They were headed by Abou Ebeid, the orderly from the fever hospital who liked to have what he called 'the medical corps' sitting together in one place. He too practiced medicine, in a way. He examined patients, and made diagnoses, and give injections. He wore a clean white overall, a cotton gallabiya, and a tarboosh, and I must say he looked smarter in that outfit than any of the rest of us.

The last one to join us was Abdallah the barber who passed as a doctor too since besides shaving people and giving them haircuts he performed such things as circumcisions and bleedings and treated boils as well. When he saw us sitting anywhere he would give his shaving kit quickly to his assistant and order him to sit with it somewhere out of sight as though he wanted to shed his identity as a barber. Then he would come and join us with profuse greetings, most notably to me. 'You have honored us, Doctor,' he would say. He was careful to pronounce the word 'doctor' correctly with two short o's to prove to me and the others that he was enlightened and that for this reason he had a right to claim affinity to the medical profession.

We were sitting in silence, having resigned ourselves to the ugly voice of Shaykh Mustafa, the village Qur'an chanter, as it poured on us in flat tones that came through his nose. It didn't look as if he intended to stop soon. Every time he reached a cadence we thought that was the end, only to be flooded with fresh notes while he craned his neck, and frowned, and placed his hand over his right ear and strained until we thought he veins in his neck would burst. Then he would let out such a loud wail that it pierced right through the darkness, waking the sleepers in the next village and making ours shake. The only person allowed to move freely during a funeral ceremony was the head watchman. With his rifle slung on his shoulder he sauntered about in the tent to show people that the law was present. Then he would dash outside to pounce on the children who had collected to watch the ceremony and look at the petrol lamps and the fascinating patterns on the tent, and he would hack at them with his stick.

Finally we were delivered of Shaykh Mustafa's voice and his chanting came to an end. The people rushed up to thank him for his reading with voluble invocations for God to guard him and protect him from evil.

Soon after, the tent began to hum with the sound of voices as the various groups resumed their conversation in low whispers. We began to chat too, beginning with Shaykh Mustafa and what we thought of him; then we went on to gossip about the important people of the town and ended with recollections from Cairo. The fellahin could only look on and listen, keeping well out of the conversation. They followed our discussions, fascinated by the way we pronounced our words, while with their eyes they felt the quality of our zephyr gallabiyas, and closely examined Abou Ebeid's tarboosh and my wrist-watch as it flashed about reflecting the light. The infinite admiration they had for us and their absolute faith in everything we said was clearly reflected on their faces. As for Abou Ebeid, every time we happened to meet he never missed the chance to ask me some question, invariably related to medicine. Since he gave treatment to the fellahin himself, he was anxious to show them he was a great man of learning who argued with the Doctor as an equal. He was always careful to drop his local dialect and affect the genteel accent of the townspeople, so as not to put himself on a level with peasants. His tone was bland and unctuous; the same tone he used when he imposed his services on people, asking for a little milk in return or a plate of okra beans in addition to his fee. Clients' okra beans were always very good.

He irritated me. I was doing my preparatory year for medicine that year. Most of my work consisted of dissecting frogs and studying worms, and I knew nothing yet about drugs or disease. From his long experience working in hospitals Abou Ebeid had picked up the technical terms for a couple of diseases as well as the names of many drugs. He was discussing Hagg Sa'ad's long illness that night and how Dr. Hanna, the doctor from the central town, had failed to cure him and how he, Abou Ebeid, had prescribed 'Seteromycin' injection and 'Sulphata Yazin'* 3x3x5 (that's how he put it) as well as M. Alkaline, and ordered him to abstain from food altogether. But the poor fellow was seized with a sudden longing for salted fish, of which he ate a whole pound all by himself, whereupon he expired. This drew a lot of comment, for the subject of fate and destiny was one which the fellahin were equal to discussing and which they loved to ponder on.

'You don't live a day longer than it is written. . . .'

'God in His wisdom. . . .' And so on.

When Abou Ebeid got started on a subject nothing would make him stop, and he went on to tell us what happened after the man died. It was he, he told us, who got the burial license in spite of the obstacles the doctor was raising; he even got it after hours, he said, and if it hadn't been for his clever handling of the situation the man would have remained without burial till the following day. I don't remember how we got to leave him out of the conversation and confine it to ourselves alone. But I remember a discussion about the body and how long it could remain without burial. When the arguments died down, Abou Ebeid turned to me with a very serious expression on his face.

'Tell me, Doctor,' he began. He too was careful to pronounce 'doctor' correctly in order to distinguish himself from the fellahin who could never learn not to say 'doctoor.'

I turned to him, prepared to hear some silly question.

'How long after death does rigor mortis set in?' he asked me.

Everybody was terribly impressed by that expression, 'rigor mortis.' Even the barber was astounded at Abou Ebeid's learning. He looked at him with surprise and envy as though he begrudged him that much erudition. All eyes were on me now, waiting for the answer. I was most embarrassed for I hadn't the faintest idea what the expression could mean. I gave a faint smile.

---

* Attempts at pronouncing the names of the original drugs.

'Why do you ask?' I said, stalling.

'Well, you see,' he said with the air of someone throwing up a public issue for discussion. 'I had a little argument today with Dr. Sobhi. You know, the chief medical officer. I was of the opinion that it set in within half an hour, while he insisted it was two hours. What do you say, Doctor?'

I took on a knowing air.

'You're both wrong,' I said, 'actually it sets in after about one hour.'

I looked at the others and saw they were lapping up what I was saying, even though they had no idea what it was all about. There was a brief silence, and I looked at Abou Ebeid to see whether he was satisfied with the answer I gave. His eyes were on the ground, very politely avoiding mine.

I knew that confounded expression of his which he put on every time he found me in a corner, so as not to embarrass me, as it didn't do for a doctor to be embarrassed by a mere orderly.

'I say, Doctor, what's this . . . this "moris rigo?"' asked Saleh suddenly, screwing up his eyes.

Saleh was a fellah, but he was only a hireling. I believe he belonged to the family of Abou Shendi. He worked in return for food and clothing, and perhaps a small share of the annual crop. His skin was the color of dust and he was so fearfully huge that people called him the Sphinx. I don't remember ever seeing him smile, or with his eyes fully open. It was almost as if he looked with his eyelashes. They say his heart was dead because he never felt joy or sorrow or fear, and that he was the strongest man in town although he seldom displayed his strength, a little from modesty, and a little from fear of God. He spoke slowly as though every word were wrenched from him and he enjoyed the company of the educated even though he never joined their conversation. People knew he was a silent man on the whole and no one ever provoked him for fear of his mighty blows. He was never known to lose his temper, or grumble, or complain about anything.

Had not the occasion been a sad one we might well have laughed at this sudden question. As it was, the Sphinx was only asking what everyone else wanted to know, and they all turned to me to hear what I was going to say. All except Abou Ebeid who was telling me with his grin that he could answer that one. I scowled, warning him to shut up.

'Well, you see, Saleh,' I said, offhand, 'the human body is a strange thing,' and I rambled on about how the blood circulated in the body, and what made the heart beat and I went on to describe several other functions. I paused to see how this was going down and whether they had forgotten the question. But Saleh screwed up his eyes again.

'But what's this "moris" the Effendi is talking about?' he insisted.

Abou Ebeid was still flashing his cold smile at me. 'That'll teach you,' he seemed to be saying. When he saw I did not answer Saleh immediately he volunteered.

'With your permission, Doctor. Well, you see, folks, a human being is all filled inside with lime and iron and arsenic and mercuric chloride, and Markuro Cron . . . and as long as we are alive these things float about in our bodies, but as soon as a person dies they sort of get stuck together in a lump, as you might say, like a mud pie, so that when you come to feel a dead body with your hands you will find it feels exactly like a plank of wood.'

What he was saying was so preposterous they would not allow themselves to believe it until I approved. They turned to me and waited. I could think of nothing by which to refute Abou Ebeid's learning, so I nodded, which they took for acquiescence. Only then did their remarks come, all in the same breath.

'After all, a man's nothing but carrion.'

'By God, who'd have thought it?'

'Why don't you go and die, Saleh boy, so we can strew the barn with your remains, hey?'

'Just be thankful for your daily bread, and the air you breathe, you bastards.'

Abou Ebeid by now had certainly stolen the show. Everyone was looking at him with awe, as if he had the power to strike them all with rigor mortis. That was more than I could take, and soon I found myself declaiming on the subject of death and corpses with the air of an expert. I found myself telling them tales about what went on in the Faculty morgue and how we slashed at the bodies with our scalpels and how we gutted out bellies, although I had never been near a morgue in my life. They were all so entranced by my fabrications that they forgot all about Abou Ebeid and the funeral ceremony.

Meanwhile a huge man had seated himself on the reader's bench. He was wearing a caftan and cloak. I recognized him to be Shaykh Abd al-Hamid, the local preacher. It must be admitted the man was very devoted to his work. He had made himself very popular, never failing to attend every funeral ceremony in the village. He never failed to occupy the reader's bench either, the moment he had a chance, walking up to it with a staid and dignified air.

'In the name of God, the Merciful, the Compassionate,' he began. A deep hush fell on the people as they craned their necks to catch every word. They followed his sermon with great attention. He spoke in deep tones, every syllable loud and clear. Listening to his ringing voice and looking at his ruddy face anyone could see he was a well-fed man, and a glutton. There was no trace of care in his voice or evidence that he was burdened by wife or child. Surely a man destined for paradise in the world to come.

I was supposed to keep silent and listen to the sermon like everyone else but then I had embarked on a subject in which Abou Ebeid did not stand a chance against me, and I was keen to make an impression.

He was familiar with drugs and injections and high-sounding technical terms, but when it came to corpses only a doctor was competent. And so I went on with my discourse while the people divided themselves. The majority followed the sermon while the rest preferred to listen to me. I was speaking with an ear cocked to the sermon. The preacher was declaiming about the punishment awaiting the iniquitous in the hereafter and everyone seemed to be in a trance. I mean it was the palm-tree clippers who were more particularly impressed. The higher-ranking were starting to yawn, and to look at their watches, and were arguing about the right time. The preacher's haggard and desiccated audience sat nailed to their seats, their pale faces wilted like cotton leaves devastated by plant pests, their mouths gaping, their eyes bloodshot from trachoma. They were dodging the glare of the petrol lamps the better to concentrate on the preacher's lurid descriptions of the tortures reserved for sinners. How they were going to be delivered to four colossal demons who were going to make them strip and lash them with a scourge made of iron with prongs that dug into their flesh and crushed their bones. Then they were going to be moved to an upper story where they would be thrown into a blazing furnace. Every time the skin burned off, a new layer would form to prolong the torture, and when they thirsted they were going to be given the water of hell to drink, which was made of burning lava.

They followed raptly, hardly knowing what a scourge was, or lava, or a furnace. Nevertheless the Shaykh's powerful rhetoric and the strange and terrifying things he recounted had moved them to tears.

Meanwhile my imagination was running away with me beyond the bounds of credibility. I told my listeners how we thought nothing of taking our meals next to a gutted belly, and how we played cards on top of a dead man's chest, and that I was fond of carving inkwells and rulers and pencils out of skulls and human bones. I told them a tall story about an arm I had once bought from the morgue janitor and how it had caused a scare when I took it home with me to my room.

'And how much did you pay for it, Doctor?' asked the Sphinx, unable to contain himself any longer.

I pretended I was trying to remember.

'Something like twenty piasters, I think,' I said.

'Well! For heaven's sake! Then how much is a whole body?' he asked in amazement.

'I've never bought one,' I said, shrugging, 'but I should think something near a pound or two.'

'And where do they get these bodies?' asked the Sphinx, getting suddenly animated.

I hadn't the slightest idea, but I made out there was a contractor for them just like the one who supplied us with frogs during our preparatory year.

Meanwhile Shaykh Abd al-Hamid had reached the end of his sermon. The people had by now utterly lost patience, having listened for hours to the Shaykh's gruesome descriptions. When in peroration he exempted 'those who fear their God' from the horrors he described, a great roar went up as the people sighed with relief at this hope of acquittal.

I saw Shaykh Abd al-Hamid turn his plump face, clustered with sweat, to look at his audience. He rubbed his hands with satisfaction as he watched the effect of his eloquence on their faces.

I too looked at my audience. Everything was as I wanted it to be. I was on the verge of rubbing my hands with satisfaction too, like the Shaykh, when I happened to glance at Abou Ebeid and saw his silly grin was still on his face. I made one last bid to throw him in the shade. I went on to tell them how bored I had grown with the long holiday and how I longed to practice dissection again. And to show them how serious I was I declared I was ready to pay as much as five pounds for a body, if only I could lay my hands on one.

I walked away with my head high that night and Abou Ebeid saw me to the door saying, 'Go in safety, my Bey.'

I never gave another thought to the things I said that night. I forgot all about them and the 'rigor mortis' business and the iron scourges with the prongs. It was all small-talk one was bound to make where there was company and I thought no more about it.

One night, shortly after, I awoke to the sound of furious barking in front of our door until I thought the dogs were chasing Azrael himself. Then I heard a knock. It did not alarm me as we were used to having people knock on our door at all hours on account of someone being taken with sudden colic, or a case of retained urine. My father was the only one to be annoyed by the disturbance. It made him curse the day he sent me to medical school. He always feared that I should go out in the night to see a patient and get killed by someone lying in wait. Why anyone should want to kill me was a question my father never asked himself.

I opened the door to find a man standing before me bending under a huge load he was carrying on his back.

'Evening, Doctor.'

The voice was familiar, but I couldn't distinguish the face although it was the small hours of the morning and the light of day was beginning to come through.

'Who is it?' I asked.

'It's Saleh.'

'The Sphinx?'

'That's right, Doctor, I've been knocking nearly an hour. The dogs almost tore me to pieces. Here, make way.'

I stepped back a little to let him in. He put the load down on the ground. 'The goods,' he said.

'What goods?' I asked, peering into his face.

In the dim light I could see only that he was smiling. That was the first time I ever saw him smile and I realized there must be more in the matter than appeared at first.

He told me he was on his way back to his little hamlet, after having sat up rather late in the town, when he saw a body floating in the stream. His heart turned over with joy for that was exactly what he had been looking for. So he went and fished it out and laid it on the bank until he ran to Abou Shendi's house and begged him to lend him some sacking which he promised to return, forfeiting his wheat. He ran back to the stream and crammed the body into the sack, and carried it through the cornfields to avoid being seen, until he reached our house.

Dumbfounded, I tried to follow his account, staring at his enormous bulk and his swollen eyes, while I suffocated with the stench rising from the sack. Suddenly I found myself barking all sorts of abuse at him.

He waited until I finished before he spoke again.

'Easy now, Doctor. Any wish of yours is a command. This is the least I can do for you. It's not as if I'm keen on the five pounds. I'll take anything you give.'

I barked at him to take the damned thing back wherever he got it from.

He waited again until I finished then he blinked.

'Don't upset yourself so, Doctor, I'm not a greedy man, I'll settle for one pound.'

I flared up again.

'Are you mad, man? Have you gone completely out of your head?'

He made a sign of impatience.

'Alright, I'll come down. I'll take twenty piasters. Come on, same as if it were only an arm.'

At long last, after my voice had risen to a roar, and he could see from my face that my fury was genuine, he was able to realize I wasn't haggling and that I meant what I said about his taking the body back immediately. His face froze and he resumed his usual grim expression, shutting his eyes.

'Is that a proper way to treat me, Doctor? Do Effendis tell lies? Did you or did you not say a body was worth five pounds? Would you swear on the Qur'an that you didn't? Would you? '

There followed a long argument where I insisted I remembered nothing of the kind and where he repeated everything I had said word for word giving proof and evidence. I couldn't persuade him to return the body as my growing embarrassment was making me falter. But when I saw he was adamant I threatened to inform the Omda. His face darkened at that and he looked on the point of a tremendous explosion.

'This is no way no way to treat me,' he broke out. 'No indeed. After all, it's you who asked for it, and now you say you'll go and report me. I'm not taking it back, I tell you. I swear by my father's head, I'm not. You can do what you like.'

The shouting must have awakened my father, for now he was coming out of his room.

'What's going on?' he asked.

I hurried up to him, and tried to explain there was nothing, only a case of colic, but it was too late. He had already spotted Saleh standing in the doorway with a face that augured nothing good.

'What does this boy want here? He's a thief.' To all landowners all fellahin are thieves. 'He'll filch the kohl right off your eye, he will. He and his father before him. What brings you here at this hour, boy?'

As he said this, Father was walking toward Saleh who was still standing in the doorway. I couldn't do anything about what happened next. Father stumbled on the sack and nearly fell on his face, wondering angrily what had brought the thing there and what had brought Saleh.

'What's this?' he asked, feeling the bundle with his hands. 'Have you been stealing watermelon, you son of a bitch? And why should you bring it here, hey? Hey? What's the doctor got to do with watermelon?' Then, 'Well, for heaven's sake!' he exclaimed with a shock. 'That's not watermelon! What's that stink, boy? Well, for heaven's sake! For heaven's sake!' My father was shouting uncontrollably. I had never seen him so terrified before. Saleh and I rushed up to steady him in time before he fell over. I led him back to his bed. He was speechless with shock. But it only lasted a few minutes. He sat listening to me, utterly flabbergasted, as I told him the whole story. He kept shaking his head unable to believe it.

'The thief!' he kept repeating, 'the Goddamned thief and son of a thief!'

When I returned to the Sphinx I found him sitting on the ground with his back to the wall and his head hanging down. He was obviously very upset. He stood up when he saw me.

'I say, Doctor, anything wrong with the gentleman? It's all my fault! Oh my God, why did I do it?' he moaned.

I was just preparing the dressing down I intended to give him when he spared me the trouble.

'Believe me, Doctor. I never swear by my father's head in vain,' he said, bending to check the cord that tied the sack. 'But I will make an exception for your father's sake. I am so ashamed of myself. The devil be damned! What got into my head? I was going back home in peace, why did I not mind my own business? Moris rigo indeed! What's that got to do with me? But then I'd thought to myself, "The doctor will take you in with open arms, boy, you can count on that." Well, as I told you, I never swore by my father's head in vain, but this time never mind. . . .'

He stood the bundle up.

'Here, Doctor, give me a hand. Mind your clothes. Here goes,' and he hauled it up onto his shoulders with fantastic strength.

'Never mind, Saleh, I'll make it up to you,' I blurted, quite tongue-tied.

'That's alright,' he said as he turned, his bundle turning with him. 'It's only a bundle after all. Can't be worse than that scourge the Shaykh was talking about. Only a bundle, no worse than what I'm used to carrying.'

He went out of the door and had nearly disappeared in the dark when he suddenly stopped and turned to face me.

'Only try to remember, Doctor. By the Prophet, and your conscience and all that's holy, did you or did you not say you were looking for a body?'

Translated by Wadida Wassef

The Dregs of the City

1

It is almost impossible for a person to lose his wrist-watch, because usually if one takes it off one keeps it in a place that is safe and if one has it on, the strap, or whatever contraption keeps it in place, is so firm that even a skilled pickpocket can do nothing with it. That's why it must be a strange feeling for a man to turn his wrist in order to know the time and find his watch missing. 'Must have left it somewhere,' he says to himself and soon remembers where, because there aren't many places where one's likely to leave a wrist-watch lying about. That's what happened to the judge.

In the middle of a court session boredom drove him to want to know the time and when he turned his wrist, his watch wasn't there. And while the lawyer for the defense was pleading the cause for the defendant, Judge Abdallah was mentally reviewing all the places where he could have left his watch. Perhaps on the dresser in the bedroom, but he couldn't be sure. Better ask Farghali. Farghali was the court janitor, and asking Farghali was the first thing that occurred to him when something went wrong. If he couldn't find his pen, Farghali would look for it; if he mislaid a file, Farghali would know where to find it; and when he had a headache, Farghali was the first to know. Dismissing the court was no problem. All he had to do was stand up and give the order. So when the lawyer for the defense paused for breath, he saw his chance and immediately ordered the court dismissed. Everyone stood up, the puzzled attorneys wondering whether the lawyer's force of language had anything to do with the adjournment, or whether it was simply in order to investigate the law on work contracts more thoroughly.

Back in his room Judge Abdallah was about to ring for Farghali when he looked up and found Farghali already there, all of his fifty years in an upright column of bland obsequiousness. His stomach politely pulled in, his tarboosh leaning to the right so that the tassel came exactly over his right ear, he was leaning forward ready to catch every word.

'Yes, sir,' he said in a tone which years of servility had tempered to convey his submission and his perfect willingness to carry out orders.

The tassel of his tarboosh shook violently as Farghali denied knowing anything about the watch. Quite the answer Judge Abdallah expected since he knew Farghali couldn't possibly have seen his watch, but he had to ask him from sheer habit.

Probably on the dresser in the bedroom, he mused again, and the first thing he did when he got home was to look for it there. He was annoyed not to find it. Some inner pessimism, which has a habit of surfacing at such times, made him suspect the watch had been stolen. He had to make sure, just the same, so he began to search the drawers, and the bedside table, and inside the wardrobe, and under his writing table. He turned the house upside down to no effect. He had partly undressed meanwhile, keeping on only his shirt, socks and shoes so he could bend and stretch more easily in order to reach all the places that came to his mind, only to find cobwebs and heaps of dust.

He sat down to think, crossing one bare leg over the other. It annoyed him to have the even flow of his life—dull and monotonous as it was—disturbed by this petty incident. The disappearance of his watch from a room with four solid walls vexed him, as he could find no reasonable explanation for it. He was nagged by the usual sense of loss one can't help feeling for even the most trivial objects. This watch for instance was worth nothing in itself, and only the fact that he had lost it enhanced its value. It was neither platinum nor gold. Just a plain fifteen-stone Ancre he had bought before the war and which had stayed with him ever since. In fact it gave him a good deal of trouble as it frequently broke down and the cost of repairing it had come to exceed by far its original price. He didn't particularly care for it. Nevertheless, it annoyed him to part with it. Had he flung it out of the window himself he would probably not have felt a pang of regret. But losing it in this fashion irritated him in spite of himself. He didn't care about its material value. He was well off, and money had never been a problem to him. He was born and raised in easy circumstances. Even when he was a student at law school he had his own Topolino. His father was alive then, and he was used to spending lavishly.

For a bachelor, his flat was furnished quite luxuriously but that did not mean he was a rich man. Just average. In fact everything about him was average. If one were to pick a hundred men at random from all over the world and consider their height and weight and the color of their skin, the result would be something like Judge Abdallah. There were no extremes about him. Even with his tea. 'How many lumps?' Mrs. Shendi would ask as she poured his tea. And then she'd remember. 'Oh, I know. You like it just right. One and a half.' 'You know me, madam,' he'd say, looking up from his game of bridge, 'moderate, that's what I am.'

Speaking of bridge and Mrs. Shendi, it shouldn't be imagined he had made a habit of going there. In this too he was moderate. His calls were neither too frequent nor too scarce. Just enough to sustain a cordial relationship. In this respect, like in all others, he was a gentleman. A gentleman with a fixed smile he reserved for strangers. And he never took the lead in getting familiar. He spoke little and with reserved. And since life treats people according to what they are, it treated Judge Abdallah moderately, neither raising him suddenly nor suddenly pulling him down. He proceeded evenly from law school to the office of public prosecutor, and from there to the bar, just as he had planned it, and his father before him.

So that such an event as losing his watch was bound to cause a ripple.

He needed a cigarette to help him sort things out. He was not a smoker but he kept cigarettes in his desk for visitors. Occasionally, he didn't mind a puff. He got up now to light one, then came back to his place and crossed his legs. He realized then that he was practically naked. He got up again and slipped on his pajamas before anyone saw him. Not that anyone was likely to. Being a bachelor he lived alone. He did intend to marry, of course, but not before he turned thirty-five. He was thirty-two now which left him a margin of three years. The reason he had decided to marry at thirty-five was that this would be midway in his life-span, as he had reckoned he'd live to be seventy or so like his father who died at that age and his grandfather before him. There was nothing foolish about that. Many people make serious decisions in their lives based on groundless intuitions that do not stand close scrutiny.

He sat on the rocking chair beside the big wireless set. By now he had definitely eliminated the possibility of Ga'afari stealing the watch. Ga'afari was above suspicion. He had been in the family for generations, one of the many things bequeathed to Abdallah. He was a good man, naïve and loyal and wholly devoted to his master. One of those people who not only accept their destiny but look upon it with awe and reverence. The 'master' was to him a being apart whose needs were sacred. He had been with him in the house at al-Mounira and when he moved to his present flat in al-Gabalaya Street he moved down with him. He lived in, and that made him a bit of a nuisance sometimes.

Ga'afari was honest and neat in his work and he hardly spoke a word all day, which suited Abdallah as he particularly disliked idle talk. But he had found him in the way once, two years before, when he wanted to bring a girl to the flat and the presence of Ga'afari had made it awkward. He could not bring himself to walk into the flat with a girl, under the eye of that old servant who had been a witness of the family's past glories, and who had known his father and his mother and raised him from childhood. And yet he felt it was time he had a fling. Time was fleeting, he was past thirty and his years of freedom were slipping by with nothing to show for them.

With regard to women in his private life, his conduct was exemplary. Not because he considered 'such things' improper or from any moral scruples, but simply on account of a bad experience he couldn't forget. He had picked up a girl once when he was a student, together with a friend of his, and they had taken her in his friend's big car on the desert road to Alexandria. The next thing he knew was the appearance of certain alarming symptoms which, though they were treated promptly and with good results, made him vow not to come near a woman again except in wedlock. Ever since, as far as he was concerned, a woman was only a microbe with lipstick and nylon stockings, dangerous to contact. This could have induced him to marry but he stuck to his plan. Meanwhile he was nearing the deadline and his life was as arid of women as the barren desert. This state of affairs became intolerable and he decided suddenly it was time he put an end to it. That's when he began to urge Ga'afari to get married himself, and actively helped him find a wife. After that he informed Ga'afari he would not be needing him the whole day, he was free to go after lunch. All in order to clear the flat so he could be free to make the best of his remaining bachelor days.

Once Ga'afari was out of the way he intended to have the flat teeming with women, without really knowing how he was going to set about it. When he found that with or without Ga'afari things remained pretty much as they were, he was forced to give more thought to the matter. For many years he'd had little to do with women until this sudden obsession got hold of him to the point that he was prepared to overlook the microbe business. But where was he to find a woman?

In the meantime he had become a judge and although he was only a young man he had to be careful of his reputation and the dignity of his post. Nor could he confide in anyone. His immediate circle were all starchy officials in high posts. Hardly the sort of people he could be intimate with. As for his old friends from student days, his small car was one reason why he didn't have many, and even those had gone their own way. When by chance he happened to run into one of them they would be off to an effusive start full of hearty back-slapping and well-old-boy-where-have-you-been and it's-great-to-see-you, after which they would discover that that's about all they had to say to each other besides a passing remark on the good old days and the professor with the funny face.

So much for his male acquaintances. As for the females, he simply had no connections to speak of. There were a few relatives, some of whom he detested. Some were rather attractive and those intimidated him. They were either married or in pursuit of marriage, and they all had their eyes on him, having labeled him a prize catch. But he had a positive aversion to marrying a relative for no reason he could explain even to himself. He took care to keep out of their way, as the slightest motion on his part could be misinterpreted and he had no intention of finding himself caught in the end with a wedding ring.

Then there was Mrs. Shendi for variety, a fifty-year-old widow, passionately fond of bridge, who had a salon which attracted high officials of the state. She had a gift for conversation, and for smiling understandingly and listening to people's troubles. Her complexion was rather dark which suggested she came from the heart of Upper Egypt although she insisted she was of Turkish origin.

Many of her visitors were married women who were bold and emancipated. He enjoyed talking to them. Occasionally he would comment on a new hair-style of an elegant pair of shoes, but it never went beyond that. He was painfully aware of his shortcomings. He knew his appearance was not particularly impressive and that his conversation was uninteresting. All he ever managed to convey were dull platitudes which people suffered out of deference for the word 'judge' appended to his name. That's why it never occurred to him to embark on anything more intimate with the ladies of Mrs. Shendi's salon. He lacked the experience and besides they made him feel clumsy.

He cast about elsewhere. One girl abused him roundly. Another gladly accepted his invitation to the pictures and dinner afterward at the Auberge. But when his hand happened to brush hers, she stood up and walked out in a virtuous huff.

His sweeping obsession led him to try Mrs. Shendi herself. Her response was lukewarm. She gave in to him in an offhand manner and treated him like a naughty boy. For days afterward he couldn't live down his mortification or get over the fact that she was a woman of fifty and that his behavior was unbecoming for a man in his position.

Still, he did not give up. That was how he got to bring Nana to the flat six months after he started dating her. That had been a trying business because it had to be done on the quiet. It was the high cost of dating for a man in his position. He could only take her to places on the outskirts of Cairo, which he had to scout for himself first to make sure he was not likely to run into anyone he knew. And all the time they were together he would be on edge, relaxing only when she said, 'Bye, bye,' and squeezed his hand as he dropped her off.

It was quite a triumph for him when he got her to come to the flat, although his timidity did not allow him to go very far with her. He knew she was having him only because she wasn't a top-ranking beauty, and she knew it, too. Still, they managed to develop a relationship which ebbed and flowed until timidity wore off, and resistance weakened, and he developed a certain feeling for her that made him seriously consider marriage. She was pleasant, she came from a good family, and she shared his interest in law. Only the fact that it didn't take much to get her into the flat rather put him off. And the feeling nagged him without cease until he gave up the idea altogether. But he had learned a good deal in the meantime. Intimacy with one woman is revealing of the mechanics of all the others. Soon he mastered the kind of talk they love to hear. He developed an expert eye for fashion, and a knack for catching subtle details and half-tones of color. He acquired other skills as well. Flashes of wit, the glib rejoinder, the double-edged quip. And the open invitation couched in a smile, and the look that carried a world of meaning. Suddenly he'd made it and he found himself with more than one girl to his credit. One for going to the movies with, one to teach him dancing, and so on. They came and they went.

One night at a nightclub he was introduced to a group which to his surprise, included more than one member of the judiciary. He was also introduced to an entertainer, or more precisely it was she who had introduced herself, and he pulled out his wallet and treated her to an expensive drink, and she insisted on opening the door to his flat herself as they returned, both a little tipsy, later that night.

No, it was definitely not Ga'afari who had stolen the watch.

2

It must be Shohrat.

Judge Abdallah was thrilled to find himself involved in a situation which absorbed him so completely. It was more than he could keep to himself. All those suppositions and assumptions storming through his brain had to be shared with someone. He had to have Sharaf.

He got up and dialed the Actors' Syndicate. The number was engaged but he kept on trying, hardly able to wait. Sharaf was the only person in the world he wanted just now. This was a thing to be discussed only with Sharaf. He must be at the Actors' Syndicate. He had to find the scoundrel.

Sharaf and he had been friends since the days of al-Mounira when Abdallah lived in the big family house. Sharaf lived in al-Mounira too, but he came from a poorer background. That's why Judge Abdallah felt relaxed and at ease in his company. It was easy to speak his mind with Sharaf. He could tell him things he could never tell his rich friends and relatives; that's why he cared for Sharaf more than he cared for any of them even though Sharaf was by no means an important person. He had dropped out of school at an early age and drifted from one job to another for a while before he took up acting, for which he had always had a liking. He took a job acting on the radio. All his parts were short. His longest role consisted of only three words. In spite of that he was very proud of himself as an actor. He even had his own views on acting and the theater and life in general. His permanent residence was at the Actors' Syndicate.

Theirs was a peculiar relationship in spite of their affection for each other. Judge Abdallah was a busy man but there were days when he found himself with nothing to do and the world would stretch before him yawning into infinity. It was then that he remembered Sharaf. He would ring him at the Actors' Syndicate. That was the only call Sharaf ever got from anyone. 'Come along, Shafshaf,' he'd say. That's what he called him. Without asking who was calling Sharaf would immediately head for al-Gabalaya Street, sometimes by tram but more often on foot, and climb up to the elegant flat in one of the tall buildings overlooking the Nile. There would be iced water, and food, and conserves, and sometimes beer and an easy chair where he would recline to act his part.

His part was to listen. Listen to his friend Abdallah talk. And when Sharaf and Abdallah talked it was mostly about Abdallah. There are few people one can talk to about oneself without their interrupting to speak of themselves in turn. Sharaf was one of those. Abdallah would unload, droning on and on, sparing no detail, while Sharaf listened with infinite patience. He had made an art of listening to Abdallah, taking care never to appear bored or impatient, or to draw on his cigarette and shake his head mechanically, pretending to follow what was being said. He gave his full attention, his eyes shining as the situation developed, smiling when a smile was required, and coming in on time with a laugh. He made one feel he was truly concerned about one's welfare. It was not uncommon to find a listener like Sharaf, but then one knew it was only to oblige. Sharaf was not like that. He showed real concern. He asked questions, he argued, he wanted details. It was a comfort to talk to Sharaf for there were moments when he saw himself as a trivial being, a person of no consequence, particularly when he was surrounded by people whose talk was alive and witty, which made him feel miserably inadequate. With Sharaf he could let himself go, speaking with force and eloquence. He could be entertaining and witty and full of wisdom as Sharaf himself proved when he made him stop to repeat things he had said which particularly pleased Sharaf. Like the listeners to a Qur'an chanter who would ask for the repetition of verses by which they were particularly moved. Very often he wished he could get his wise sayings to Sharaf on tape just to show his friends there was nothing wrong with him. If anyone was wanting it was they.

Sometimes in his conversation Abdallah would express his private views on life and what he thought about people. Generally when a person is asked for his opinion on a certain matter in the presence of others he will say only what is conventional, out of deference perhaps, or fear of being different, or simply to avoid an argument where he could be the loser. Few people have strong personal convictions, and fewer still make them known or have the courage to uphold them. And rarest of all are those who combine courage and the power to convince, not only upholding their convictions but converting others to them. Still, the fact remains that each one of us is wise within limits, and that it is not given to all to preach their wisdom to others.

Like everyone else Abdallah had come to form his own convictions which he derived from his own experience. But those were revealed only to Sharaf. The strange thing was that of the two, Sharaf was the one to take them seriously, Abdallah being more inclined to follow others. It takes a good deal of guts to uphold one's beliefs.

Just then Sharaf walked in.

He was tall and gaunt with elongated features and an untidy mop of hair. He immediately gave the impression he was an 'artist.' He had a bashful smile and when he smiled he revealed a protruding set of teeth which nobody noticed. He went straight to the kitchen, as usual, and returned with a glass of iced water which he started to sip slowly. He removed his jacket and hung it on the back of his chair. Then he sat down and crossed his legs as he took the cigarette Abdallah offered him. Abdallah watched him impatiently until he settled down. Sharaf was quite aware of that and he took his time deliberately. At last he spoke, fixing Abdallah with his eyes, trying to guess what was on his mind this time. Was he feeling lonely? Or was it a new love affair, or some new theory on the development of crime in juveniles?

'Well, what is it?'

'The damnedest thing!'

'You've been promoted.'

'No. Shohrat stole my watch.'

'Shohrat who, the dancer?'

Shohrat was not a dancer, or another friend of Nana's, or anything to do with that category of women. Shohrat was Farghali's gift to Abdallah.

It all began with one of Abdallah's periodic rebellions against his thwarted attempts to improve his love-life. So far all the women he got to know, in one way or another, succeeded only in making him feel inadequate. He could never relax in the presence of Nana or any of the others. He had always to be considerate, always ready with sweet talk, always prompt with a smile that must never fade. To make up for his inadequacy he doubled his efforts to please while not one of them ever bothered to please him, until he got quite fed up with the lot of them and decided to try other channels. There was no reason why he shouldn't.

Next day he called Farghali and began to complain to him about the problem of domestic help. Men servants were dishonest. Elderly women were tiresome and too frail for work. Farghali bowed his head. He agreed with every word. Another time Abdallah appeared very annoyed and told Farghali he had just sacked the new servant. Farghali was extremely sorry and cursed all servants, this one in particular who certainly deserved all that was being heaped on his head. A third time, Abdallah spelled it right out and asked Farghali if he knew of a good honest woman who would work for him. She must not be too young, he was careful to stress. Farghali bowed again, he quite agreed. Abdallah appeared to be thinking. On second thoughts, he added, it would be better if she were not too old. Middle-aged, sort of. Farghali bowed once more. That was best, of course. But Abdallah changed his mind. It would be better if she were a young person after all, who could deal with the household chores, particularly as the back stairs were steep. The flat was on the seventh floor. Farghali bowed again, with a smile this time. He understood perfectly. He promised to fill those requirements by tomorrow, Friday.

It was three o'clock in the afternoon when the bell rang. Ga'afari had gone, having cleared up after lunch. Judge Abdallah opened the door himself. Farghali's smile filled the doorway. He had a habit of smiling with his eyes shut when he was pleased about something. Evidently he was very pleased now. He was out of uniform, wearing a plain suit, no doubt the gift of some previous official. Old and worn and several sizes too big, it had obviously never once known contact with an iron. His shirt looked more like a nightdress and his tie had eroded from wear to the thickness of string.

'The goods are here, sir,' said Farghali.

'Where?'

'Come along, Shohrat,' he called.

Shohrat came in. Abdallah did not look at her immediately. He felt embarrassed, and worried that the neighbors might have seen her going in. She stood in the corner near the door of the living-room. He called Farghali to his study and asked him to sit down. Farghali absolutely refused but obeyed when Abdallah insisted. Abdallah was slightly annoyed at that as he suspected there a degree of familiarity he should not have encouraged. His mind went back to the woman. He was curious to see her face so he got up and went back to the living-room while Farghali stood sharply at attention. He gave her a furtive look so as not to make her feel she was being inspected. But he found it hard to keep his eyes off her. She was not what he had imagined. What he saw was a plain, native woman of the people like thousands of others. The sort of woman who is made to be a wife and a mother. Hardly the type for a servant. He couldn't quite place her; nor could he make up his mind whether she was plain or attractive. Anyhow, he thought, she would do. He went back to Farghali and asked him what her wages would be. Farghali refused to go into anything so vulgar. He could give her what he pleased, he said, if he were satisfied, if not, there were plenty of others. Although Abdallah was not too pleased with this arrangement he gave him a cigarette. The next thing was to get rid of him, so he gave him a fifty-piaster tip which Farghali was quick to pocket in spite of voluble protests.

After he had gone Abdallah returned to the study and sat down. The woman was still standing in the living-room. 'Come here,' he called.

She came, still wrapped in her *melaya*. She stood leaning on the open door. Abdallah gave her another close look. He was quick to sense a seductive female under her strong features and her ruddy complexion.

'Your name is Effat?' he asked, deliberately distorting her name.

'Your servant, Shohrat,' she replied.

There was a feminine ring to her voice that caught his ear, and he noticed that the way she said 'your servant' was more by way of courtesy than humility.

'Are you married?'

'Yes.'

'Children?'

'Two girls and a boy.'

He was still looking at her, searching for that thing experience had taught him to look for in a woman, which revealed how far she was willing to go. It wasn't there. He noticed she was still holding her *melaya*.

'Have you had lunch?' he asked. It was three o'clock in the afternoon.

'Yes, God be thanked,' she said, her eyes on the floor.

Which meant she hadn't. He suspected she'd had no breakfast either. He told her to go to the kitchen where there was some food left over. She mumbled something about really having eaten. But he insisted and when he saw she did not know the way to the kitchen he got up and showed her. He returned to the study and sat thinking. She was not what he had expected. There was power in that woman. She was poor and wore a *melaya* but there was an air of dignity about her that women of her class seldom possessed. Perhaps it was the purity of her features. Would he dare, he wondered. Her kind was not easy to beat down.

When he heard her moving about in the kitchen he guessed she must have finished eating. He went and stood at the kitchen door.

'Have you worked before?' he asked, as a way of starting a conversation.

'No. This is the first time.'

Ah. He'd heard that one before. The lady of quality fallen on bad days. That was an old trick. He didn't want the conversation to end there so he ordered her to remove her *melaya*. She obeyed and stood looking for some place to put it. The kitchen was bright and sparkling and she dared not put it down there. Finally she laid it on the edge of the rug in the living-room. She was wearing a very faded silk dress underneath.

'Can you make coffee?' he asked with a cunning smile.

'Sugar?' The expression on her face was quite candid.

'Yes, and make one for yourself too,' he added on an impulse.

'Thank you,' she replied as she started on it.

Somehow he felt disturbed. For some reason he was aware that this woman Shohrat could see through him. He felt she knew what was in the back of his mind. Why he had spoken to Farghali, and why he was standing there now putting himself in her way? She was probably laughing at him. It only made him more determined. Suppose she were—suppose she did see through him, what then?

She was standing before the stove, her eyes fixed on the coffee pot, or at least so it seemed. He came and stood behind her.

'Where do you live?' he asked, placing a hand on her shoulder, not troubling to listen to what she replied, for what he really wanted to know was how much she responded to the touch of his hand. He felt her stiffen and he moved closer, defying her resistance. She quivered and drew slightly away as he held her more firmly to prevent her moving.

'Where are the cups?'

Beads of sweat clustered on his forehead and his throat went dry. Sharply he ordered her to clean the flat after she was through with the coffee, and then he went back to his study. She brought him the coffee there and stood respectfully before him, her eyes looking down.

Almost immediately she started to clean up. The rugs were rolled back and the chairs moved out of the way and the tile floors were flooded with water. Abdallah was watching her movements as she bent to scrub. From the back her legs were a pinkish white, and the mounds of living flesh that rubbed against the threadbare fabric of her dress called out to him with maddening insistence.

He went and stood near her pretending he was supervising her work, giving her orders. There's dust in that corner. Over there too. Bend over so you can reach it better. Her eyes were on the floor and her whole body was exposed to his gaze.

When she finished she asked if there was anything more to be done. There wasn't. She asked what time she should come next day. Half past two in the afternoon. That suited him best as Ga'afari left at two. For a moment he was tempted to have another go at her but decided to put it off for fear of another rebuff. She wrapped herself in her *melaya* and walked demurely out of the room.

When the door closed behind her Judge Abdallah cursed himself for a fool. To let a woman like that brush him off. A woman who had walked into his flat of her own free will and when nothing stood in his way. A full-blooded male in his position given the slip by a two-bit slut like her!

3

She came regularly now, every day at half past two. Every day he thought of trying and every day he put it off. Until one day she was rearranging his bed as he had ordered her (for Ga'afari usually made it in the morning) when he suddenly came upon her and took her in his arms. She struggled hard to break free, begging him to let her go. He paid no attention and after a long struggle she was forced to give in. He was thrilled when he felt her resistance collapse, even though he wasn't sure whether she was overcome by his physical strength or by sheer despair. He let her go and she ceased to struggle. What was the use now?

He went back to her after a while, curious to see her reaction after what had happened. He was annoyed to find her eyes were red and her cheeks flushed.

'What's the matter?' he asked gruffly, expecting her to mumble as usual something like 'nothing,' but he got no reply.

'What's the matter? What's eating you?' he asked again, but still she said nothing.

'I asked you what's the matter,' he repeated sharply, shaking her impatiently.

'I've never done it before,' she said slowly and the tears began to roll down her cheeks.

He refused to believe it. This imperious woman was staging an act she had probably played many times before. Did she take him for a fool or was she angling for a raise? But she never asked for a raise. And when she spoke to him after that she avoided his eyes, either looking down or busying herself with something.

He was quite satisfied with her. The best part of the experience was that her capitulation was his own achievement. It was neither his money, nor his position, nor his manner that did it but the sheer power he could exercise over her. His triumph had brought an end to the hidden struggle between her inflexibility and his weakness, for he had always known that of the two she had the upper hand. Had she been one of the ladies of Mrs. Shendi's salon and not a servant he would never have dared to go near her.

The next time he also met with resistance but it was the resistance of one who had despaired of resisting. They always got off to a stormy beginning which slowly resolved into the tranquility of habit. Her presence in the flat was a novel experience. The sound of her step, or her appearance in the doorway, her *melaya* wound tightly round her body, aroused him, and he'd find himself considering whether to have her right now or whether it would be better tomorrow. What impression was he making on her? How did he perform as a lover? He'd have her now, or maybe after lunch. He was troubled and restless. The familiar noises of the household, plates clattering in the kitchen, the broom brushing over the rugs, or her voice coming from another room, textured, modulated, provoking, fell on his ears with special impact. It was an exciting adventure which had all the ardors of expectation and all the thrills of surprise. But seldom does anything withstand the strain of habit. What was once the source of boundless joy would one day hardly cause a flutter.

His greatest hurdle at the beginning was to break her down, but once that stage was over all he had to do to get her to bed was to squeeze her hand, or smile out of the corner of his mouth, or simply ask her about her 'health.' Then she would try to elude him, and he would chase her round the flat, and what had started in jest would turn into a sweeping want that had to be answered right away. When she sensed his desire she'd start to shift about; a pale smile would form on her lips, a blend of reserve, indifference and a good deal of submission. But the moment he was through with her the smile became ironic with undertones of contempt.

When the novelty wore off and habit settled in he took to giving himself up to her with complete abandon. He omitted the niceties and he treated her as little more than a live mattress on which he sprawled and stretched and tossed and turned and relaxed without restraint. And when habit dulled the edge of excitement he began to look for new thrills. He began to whisper obscenities which he wanted her to repeat to him. Brutally and deliberately he would lay bare the most hidden reaches of her soul, even the things a professional whore would still want to keep private.

It took him a long time to realize she had not lied. He really was the only man to have had her besides her husband. If words did not convince him he was convinced by his daily observations, and by her spontaneous reactions, and the vague intimations by which the truth is always known.

One day he asked, in another attempt to probe into her being, 'Do you love me, Shohrat?'

The question sprang from an overriding need to know. What made this woman with children and a husband, who came to him from want, this woman whom he had seduced and whom he could have any time he wanted, what made her accept this situation? Was it only because being her master he had the upper hand, or did she want him for his own sake, for the male that he was?

The question preyed on his mind. He longed, if only once in his life, for a woman to desire him, any woman at all, even if it were only Shohrat. He was continually looking for evidence that she was that woman, but there was none. She was still pleased when he let her keep the change from the housekeeping money. Sometimes she would ask for a loan of ten or twenty piasters. He couldn't tell if she really needed them or if that was her way of getting what she could out of him. Nor could he tell if she was doing her best to please him for his own sake or as part of her duties as a domestic. Nothing pointed to anything definite, he could not see clear on that score because his awareness of Shohrat was confined only to the limits of his desire for her.

Meanwhile life went on as usual: work, law-suits, preambles long over-due, bridge, Mrs. Shendi, dates with other girls, drives in the car, and a hundred other things that made up the fabric of his life. Questions pounded in his head only at the instant when he desired Shohrat, otherwise he dismissed them.

Shohrat did not answer his question immediately. She looked down as she always did when he spoke to her.

'I asked you something,' he said, pressing her closer.

'Does anyone who loves another ever admit it?' The simplicity of her reply moved him. It was direct and candid which made it impossible to doubt its sincerity. It made him wonder how a woman so untutored could reason with such clarity. Had she been educated he would have suspected she was repeating something she had read in a book.

'Of course, he must,' he said to draw her out a little more.

'Then he would not be saying the truth.'

'What do you mean?'

'Love is in the heart. What is spoken aloud is not love.'

What did this woman know of love? What did it mean to her? He had read what scholars had written about it. He had discussions with his friends concerning it, people of his own background. Now he had a rare chance of picking the brain of a woman who had no experience of love.

'Tell me,' he asked, 'what's this thing, love?'

'How would I know?'

He pressed her to say more.

'How am I to know? It's love this, and love that; that's all you hear all the time,' she said impatiently.

'But you, what do you say?'

'I say it comes from God.'

'What do you mean, from God?'

'I mean one loves only if it is the will of God.'

'But what is the meaning of love? How does it make you feel? What do you want when you love?'

'Oh, come off it.'

And she would go no further. Not because she could not find an answer but because she could not bring herself to say what she wanted to say.

What begins as fun sometimes suddenly takes an unexpected turn and ends in earnest, like this discussion with Shohrat. It raised a new issue. He did not know her husband. He did not even remember whether his name was Saleh or Mahmoud although he had asked her once. Nor did he know what he did for a living. All he knew was that he had sired her three children and that for this reason there must be something between them. What was it? He wanted to know only because he had placed himself between them. He had to know which of them she loved better.

'Who do you love better, me or your husband?' he asked her bluntly one day as they lay in bed. He was sorry the moment the questions was out and would have changed the subject had he not been so keen to know the answer.

He was vexed when she said nothing. She just looked down and smiled. What did that mean? Surely she would have told him if it was him she loved better. Suddenly he was filled with a childish fury. The slut. What did she see in a man who could not even support her? Should he sack her and put an end to this issue? But he knew he was not up to facing the consequences. She had become a habit with him. She knew his ways and catered to his needs and he rather enjoyed the pleasant rut of his life with her. And then there was that irresistible pull she had on him. Perhaps it was a question of time. After all, she had spent years with her husband and only a few days with him. He would teach her how to love him, that destitute creature with a *melaya*, he would teach her yet. It became an obsession. How to subjugate this woman, how to dominate her.

His anger kept mounting until he thought he would burst.

He did not burst. An hour later he was sitting in his study submerged in the files of forty law-suits that were coming up before him in the morning. He had forgotten all about Shohrat and her husband and when he ordered

her to make him tea it was in the same tone as he ordered Farghali to call in
a witness.

4

When it started, the affair with Shohrat was a solemn experience. When he
called her it was in answer to a compelling urge; and when she came every
nerve in his body awakened to her presence. But it wasn't long before it all fizzled out into dull routine. Nothing in her stirred him any more. Her body was
nothing but a piece of property he could throw on the scrap heap any time. He
felt elated when he remembered how he had succeeded in breaking her resistance. He was the master and that's all that mattered. Shohrat did not count one
way or another. She could be another of those bits of bric-à-brac cluttering his
flat for all he cared. And yet he was often nudged by the doubt that he had not
scored a real victory. He was not certain of that victory. Did he fully possess
her? Did he dominate her to the extent of overshadowing her husband?

On the whole he didn't really care whether he possessed her completely
or whether she still belonged to another. But there were moments when his
vanity clamored for assurance. He decided to cut down her salary and see
what happened. If she stayed on his question was answered and if she quit
it was just as well.

Actually he had already begun to complain to Farghali whenever the
latter asked fawningly how things were going. He would scowl and start
to list her faults. She was sloppy, she was lazy, and it was time he tried
someone new.

When at the beginning of the month he handed her salary minus one
pound, she took it without a word and put it in her small faded wallet, her
face crimson. Next day when she didn't turn up he felt a pang of remorse
but he had no intention of tormenting himself on her account and he decided
to ask Farghali to find him another servant. But he never got round to doing
that as something more pressing had cropped up unexpectedly. Coming out
of the cinema one night he happened to catch a glimpse of Nana with a
young man. Investigations led him to discover she was having an affair with
him which vividly reminded him of his own interlude with her. For quite a
while he could think of nothing but to get her back.

Three or four days later when he was parking the car in the garage in the basement on his return from work he noticed Shohrat, wrapped in her *melaya*, squatting on the floor near the door. It annoyed him and he decided to ignore her, so he went up through the little back door connecting the basement with the front entrance to the building. But just as he expected, the bell rang in his flat a few minutes after he went in. It was Shohrat. He gave her a pale smile and let her come in. She didn't speak. Nor did he know what to say to her. He watched her indifferently as she went to the kitchen and removed her *melaya* in order to start work. He sat in his study and called her. Although a shy man by nature, he was not shy of Shohrat any more. She was perhaps the only person he knew of whom he was not shy.

'Well?' he asked.

'I had to come back,' she said looking at her wet fingers.

'Then why did you leave in the first place? Was it the money?'

He couldn't help the bitterness he felt as he said this for he remembered that the money had been his way of testing her attachment and that she had failed the test.

'My little girl was ill. I had to take her to hospital.'

He could see through the lie. Nevertheless he felt a little pity. Perhaps it was her paleness. Her face was drab and sallow. Humility made her features droop, and it looked as if that was her pride seeping out with the sweat that was dripping from her brow.

'Isn't three pounds enough for you?'

'I'm not saying anything, only Moneim has quit his job.'

'Who's Moneim?'

'My husband.'

'Oh. And why did he quit?'

'They say they're retrenching or something.'

'What does he do?'

'He's a tanner.'

'Where?'

'In a tannery, somewhere near the slaughterhouse.'

He muttered something but made no comment. Suddenly he was filled with a loathing not directed at anyone in particular. The more he looked at her pallid face, and those moist beads on her forehead, and her submission, and the more he thought of her children and her jobless husband, the more the hatred and revulsion grew. The idea of her husband's profession brought up revolting visions of dirty hides, and the stink of cattle and glue, and Shohrat's embraces and his bed.

'Alright, go,' he roared at her. She turned and went.

He cursed himself afterward for having started this conversation. It gave him no end of a headache. Where before Shohrat hardly opened her mouth, now she never stopped complaining. One day it would be about her husband. He had found a job in a dairy. Next day he had quit the job. Then it was her daughter. She had fever and diarrhea. Next her daughter was dead. And then the landlady. She was harassing them for the rent. There was no end to her tales and he had brought it all on himself. She had become a nuisance and he simply had to get rid of her. But he lacked the nerve. He was also human. He could not bring himself to sack her when he knew she was in such hardship. There was nothing but to put up with her—but even that had a limit, and no sooner would she start complaining than he would quickly shut her up. On the other hand he was still a man, and she was still that woman who had appealed to him once. And his flesh was weak even though at times he was put off by the thought of her husband's profession.

One day he heard her suddenly laugh out loud. A long, unrestrained peal that startled him. For in spite of what there was between them she knew her place, and he had a good deal of consideration for her which she herself inspired. She was not given to levity. That's why it alarmed him when he heard her laugh that way. It was coarse and vulgar, very unlike her.

'Shohrat!' he called.

'Yes.'

He thought he suspected a hint of coquetry there. When she came he found he did not know what he wanted to say or why he had called her, so he asked her if she'd got rid of the cockroach he had seen in the kitchen.

'I found him cuddling up to a female roach,' she said with a giggle. And she laughed again, loud and shrill. He stared at her, amazed. The expression on her face was new. It was no longer that of the plain good woman who was a wife and a mother he had known at the beginning. Her cheeks were sunk, and round her eyes there were incriminating shadows. Even her smile was no longer the candid smile it used to be, but an artful grimace, full of affectation. He was appalled.

He kept worrying. Had he done that to her? Was he the one who had made a whore out of that simple married woman? He knew in his heart that he was, but he wasn't going to be bothered by qualms of conscience. A man feels remorse only when he is afraid of punishment. Abdallah had no punishment to fear. What he feared was the new suspicion that gnawed at him night and day. Was he alone to blame for what had happened to Shohrat or was she carrying on with others? The doubt made him mad with jealousy. The jealousy of a master over his slave not that of a lover over his beloved. The mere thought that she should put him on a level with some errand boy or a mean mechanic was unbearable.

From now on he regarded her with suspicion. If she went out shopping he would question her closely when she returned. Where had she been? Whom did she see? Sometimes he would hear her laughing all the way up the stairs. As soon as she was inside the door he had to know why and with whom she was laughing. And he never let the slightest offence pass without comment.

The change was amazing. Before, she never dared raise her eyes when she spoke to him. Now she looked him in the face and muttered if he scolded. The former gentle soul became a hard, nagging, irritable creature. She argued and answered him back word for word. He cursed himself for his weakness. What made him put up with her?

The fact was that the more her hold on him grew, the weaker he became. Very often he could not keep up his side of an argument. Almost as if there was something in her that he dreaded. Did he fear for his reputation if she chose to speak? Should things come to a confrontation he knew he would not be equal to her brand of logic, sound and irrefutable where his arguments were based on assumptions and delusions derived from his obsession with her conduct.

Strangely, he met her arrogance with compliance. Sometimes he even played up to her in subtle ways like affecting concern for her family. That husband of hers puzzled him. She never stopped complaining about him, lamenting the day she had agreed to share his life, cursing his apathy and his indolence. But somehow it was all on the surface, as if she didn't mean what she said. Some days he was employed, but more often he was not, while she continued at her job. The children were her favorite topic. It was she who had to answer for everything to everybody, she told him, even to their landlord and her husband's current employer. Sometimes he worked in the slaughterhouse, sometimes he delivered cheese from door to door. Sometimes he made coffee in a coffee shop, and sometimes she herself would prepare the mixture for the bean rissoles which he fried and sold at their street corner. He never lasted more than a couple of days at any one job which made Judge Abdallah marvel at this family, forever hanging on the brink of destitution, wondering how they would have managed had Shohrat not been working for him. He was full of compassion for them, just as he would be for the victims of an earthquake in some distant corner of the earth. It was only compassion, however, and it was soon dispelled by the boredom inspired by Shohrat and the tiresome problems of her family.

One day around the middle of the month she came asking him to lend her a pound. It was no coincidence that it was the day after he had gone to bed with her.

'What for?' he asked, a little irritated.

'Oh, just a loan,' she replied wantonly, looking at him boldly which so unnerved him that he gave her the money. This was her last month with him, he decided firmly.

'When will you return it?'

'I'll pay it back by installments,' she answered and followed this remark with a ripple of laughter that made him shudder.

A few days later he was astonished to see her come for the first time without her *melaya*. She was wearing a new skirt made of a cheap checked material, and on top of that she wore an old rag which with a little indulgence could pass for a blouse. Her head was uncovered and her lips were painted a faint red, probably with a red pencil. She was repulsive to look at.

'What are you all rigged up like that for?'

'I'm ashamed of my *melaya* in this building. Isn't this better?' she added over her shoulder as she took a few steps forward and turned to display herself, looking at him boldly. He turned down his lip.

'And what does your husband say?'

She exploded an air bubble in her chewing-gum before she replied.

'Don't ask me.'

'Why? Where's he gone?'

'Over at the café. He's been sitting there for three months.'

'Why?'

'Out of work,' she said with a stream of laughter. She strolled across to the mirror and looked at herself this way and that. 'Well now, don't you think I look much better like this?' she asked.

He vowed to himself she must go at the end of the month. She stuck her hips on one side and passed her hand languidly in front of her face with a dramatic gesture.

'Don't you think I'd do well in the movies?' she asked as she stood striking poses in front of the mirror.

'They all say I should go into pictures,' she said again, when she got no answer, as though in reply to herself.

5

The following day she turned up in her *melaya*. He asked sarcastically what had happened. Nothing. Her old blouse wouldn't do any more, she had to have a new one. She had the material but needed a pound to pay the seamstress. This time he was certainly not giving her even one millieme. He couldn't figure out her new attitude. Whatever lay behind it portended nothing good.

He often wondered what she did after she left him. Probably walked the streets. *Melaya*-clad women were cheap. Perhaps with a skirt and a blouse she could raise her price. He was almost certain his guess was right but that wasn't his business. He was finished with Shohrat anyway. A few more days and he would tell her to go for good. She could do what she liked.

When she came the next day she asked for the pound again, saying the blouse was ready. But he wouldn't let her have it. She had borrowed enough as it was and he never expected to see his money again. Besides, he had quite made up his mind she was going. He wouldn't wait until the end of the month. He'd tell her tomorrow.

That's what he told himself every day. And every day he forgot. He had every intention of doing it as he left the flat every morning. He would go down to the garage and walk round his car to make sure it had been properly cleaned. He was certain every time to find reason to reprove the garage boy. Then he'd drive down to the court which would start to come to life with his arrival. Greetings from right and left, people shuttling to and fro, moving up and down. And Farghali, no sooner would he see the car coming than he'd scuttle downstairs, all in a fluster, to open the door and bow and take his briefcase, trotting behind him at a respectful distance. In the waiting-room he would take a quick look at a couple of cases that were shortly coming up before him, and which he had put off considering several times before for lack of time. Then the old clerk would come in, with his spectacles and his slow movements which were even more depressing than his spectacles. It took him five minutes to say good morning, and he'd hang around forever. Then coffee, and rushing madly through the files as the hands of the clock drew near to ten and the people got impatient outside in the court-room, and he heard their protests grow steadily louder. Then he'd rise and take his seat in the court-room as the sound of Farghali's voice calling the court to order made the ceiling rise like an arch of triumph.

For a while he would concentrate on the cases that followed one another in quick succession. Then his attention would start to wander, and he'd fix his gaze on the face of some witness who he found repellent or on a lawyer who irritated him. And then he'd start playing with the idea of resigning from the government and setting up a private practice.

And so the day would come to an end, and the car would take him back to the garage where he'd park it and go up. As soon as he'd opened the door and seen Shohrat's *melaya* lying on the floor like a black banner, he would remember he must speak to Farghali about firing her. He would speak to him in the morning.

But in the morning too, he would forget.

6

This, then, was the story he told Sharaf. It was all very clear. Shohrat stole the watch in order to sell it and pay for her blouse since he had refused to lend her the money. She had probably also guessed his intention of firing her. Sharaf was listening, stretched in his chair, limp and lethargic. Judge Abdallah was irritated: he had expected more from his friend than this cool response. He felt Sharaf had let him down, leaving him to deal with the situation on his own. The impudence of the woman; a mean low-down servant, to dare to steal his watch knowing that sooner or later he would find her out. That was not just impudence but an insult. That shameless woman was daring him, but he was going to show her, he was shouting now to Sharaf. She won't get away with it. He wasn't going to let her make a monkey out of him.

They sat thinking what to do, Sharaf sprawled in his chair, and Abdallah pacing the floor. It was Sunday, Shohrat's day off. That had been a new arrangement. It had been introduced when Abdallah had begun to tire of Shohrat, and he'd started to nibble around for variety. He reverted to the old game in order to clear the flat for other visitors.

The obvious thing to do was call the police, but on second thoughts it was better not to. For one thing the police have seldom been known to trouble about petty thefts. What's more, once it gets known that the police are on the track, stolen things have a habit of disappearing into the bowels of the earth. Besides if he informed the police, he would have to answer a lot of questions which were better left alone. He did not trust Shohrat not to reveal their real relationship which could damage his reputation. So there was no question of the police.

Farghali, then. After all, it was he who had brought her, on his responsibility. He must be told what had happened and it was his duty to recover the watch. But Sharaf pointed out that Shohrat might not be as naïve as she seemed; she might not give in so easily in the first round. And then curiosity might lead Farghali to pry too closely into his private affairs. It would be more prudent if Abdallah were to handle the matter himself, the better to keep things under control.

The problem was how to reach Shohrat at this time of day when neither of them knew where she lived. Farghali was the only one who knew her house, and neither of them knew where he lived either. If they waited till the next day there was no guarantee that the watch would still be waiting. It had to be now. She must be taken by surprise if they hoped to recover the watch. So Farghali had to be found. Abdallah remembered he had been in the same situation once before when he had left his keys with Farghali and the latter had to be summoned after hours. He remembered now, it was the garage boy who had found him.

He called the porter and ordered him to send up the boy immediately. He paced the floor until the bell rang and the garage boy came in followed by the huge black porter. He was only a young boy, peasant-like and in rags. He was fairly dark and obviously a runaway from his native village. It took Judge Abdallah a good five minutes to make the boy coherent, so frightened was he at being summoned by a judge, and overawed by the luxury where he stood and all those eyes fixed upon him. At first he denied any knowledge of Farghali. But under the pressure of a cigarette and many assurances that he would come to no harm, which Sharaf and the porter sustained, his memory returned and he volunteered to find Farghali. The porter was immediately given a pound and told to get into a taxi with the boy and not to return without Farghali.

While awaiting Farghali, Abdallah sat down to lay out the strategy. Suppose Shohrat were found and he were to face her, would he trust himself, when before, he, her master, had never been able to stare her down? He didn't allow the thought to linger; in his present mood he felt able to stare down a whole battalion of Shohrats and wrench from her not only his watch but her very guts. If she insisted on denying it he would threaten her with the police. But to get her properly rattled he needed to dangle a policeman before her eyes. He knew a young adjutant from the second precinct at Giza, a pleasant young man who might be willing to co-operate. But on the other hand if the young man refused, Abdallah would have exposed his private life unnecessarily.

Suddenly he had a great idea. Sharaf. Who else? Sharaf could be made to play the part. Sharaf was a little taken aback at first but gradually the idea began to appeal to him. He got up and went to the mirror and tried a few grimaces in rehearsal. He was going to enjoy this. He went back and announced to Abdallah that he was accepting the part. Abdallah cheered and his laughter, buoyed by his irritation, rang loud and hollow as Sharaf continued to fool about, ruffling his hair, making faces and striking attitudes, warming to his part.

The bell rang and when the door was opened Farghali stood panting in the doorway. The porter had refused to let him use the lift and had dragged him all the way up the back stairs. Farghali was wearing his usual old oversized suit and his dark tarboosh, slanting on one side, while sweat poured out of his face. No sooner was he told what had happened than he recoiled in horror. 'The damned bitch! The damned bitch!' he kept repeating, all the way downstairs, and until they got into the car.

Abdallah sat at the wheel with Sharaf at his side and Farghali on the edge of the back seat almost standing on tip-toe had the roof of the car allowed him. He muttered and swore. He would show her, he promised. He'd bring ruin on her house. He'd make orphans of her children. He'd get her hounded out of the neighborhood. She'd see. He kept talking of the 'neighborhood' as though it were a place known to all, and when Abdallah asked him where that would be he answered promptly, 'Right next to al-Roum Lane.' And when again Abdallah asked where that would be he named places neither he nor Sharaf had ever heard of. Finally, it turned out that the 'neighborhood' was a blind alley somewhere behind the mosque of al-Azhar.

7

Abdallah was elated as he started off on his quest for Shohrat. It was a novel and thrilling adventure not only because he was certain to recover his stolen watch but because it was going to prove his perspicacity. He looked forward to tracking Shohrat down, to catching her red-handed, to watching her reaction, observing her fear, her denial. New complications would surely crop up but he would know how to handle them. He could already see himself later, telling his friends how adroitly he had handled the whole affair. For the moment he refused to consider adverse possibilities even though they crowded in his mind. He was weary of thinking and debating and making new plans every time he discovered a leak, and from that moment he decided to shut off his mind to everything but the scene unfolding before him.

He felt himself melting into the landscape as he rolled along. He could not remember the exact moment when it happened or any specific incident that relegated Shohrat to the back of his mind. He could only recall the dim beginning from al-Gabalaya Street. The long, clean, shaded street; the open spaces and the tall stylish buildings. The peace and the quiet, except for the noiseless flow of elegant cars and a few pedestrians. The air was serene and the Nile flowed gently, and the car glided along as though on a carpet of silk. And Sharaf beside him smoking in silence, smiling with amusement when he remembered his part. Farghali was in the back, holding on to the front seat, the car reeking with his smell, spluttering into Abdallah's right ear every time he spoke.

At the bridgehead they are joined by streams of cars pouring from Zamalek, and Gezira, and Dokki, and Giza. Bright, colorful, shining, like flocks of birds. In the whirlpool of Qasr al-Nil Square their ranks are swelled by shabby cars and taxi-cabs before they diverge to other streets where movement never stops; narrower, with closer buildings, noisier, with more pedestrians. At Ataba it becomes one great merry-go-round. Automobiles and buses and tram-cars and pedestrians and horse-drawn carts mill around in utter chaos. It reaches a peak when they turn into al-Azhar Street. Here, it is a madhouse of pedestrians and automobiles, screeching wheels, howling claxons, the whistles of bus conductors and roaring motors. Policemen blow their whistles, and hawkers yell in the blistering heat. The roads and pavements are a moving mass of flesh. Everything is wholesale. Riding a vehicle, trading, and even accidents come wholesale. From time to time a warning to be careful rises above the din like the last cry of a drowning corpse.

Driving becomes an agony under volleys of abuse from pedestrians and the eloquent retaliations of Farghali, and Abdallah's determination to get even with Shohrat and avenge his wounded pride. He would strangle her willingly. Get his fingers round her neck and press, tighter and tighter. He is pressing the claxon which lets out a hoot that falls noiselessly on the enormous crowds. Traffic goes at a crawling pace, exasperating, maddening. The mosque of al-Azhar rises indomitable on the skyline, behind a haze of dust. It has stood for generations, watching the deadly struggle while it has remained constant, insusceptible to change. Then they turn to the right.

Acting on Farghali's advice they park the car and do the last leg on foot. A few paces and Abdallah begins to feel hollow as though he had been left alone in an ancient deserted place. The noise dies down, the quiet is almost tangible. He is Egyptian through and through. His father came from al-Mounira and his mother from Abbassieh. He has poor relations in Upper Egypt. He has traveled a good deal, gone to many places, and seen the extremes of poverty. Yet here was Cairo, and this place where he finds himself is part of it. The incredible scenes unfolding before his eyes amaze him beyond belief as he delves further in as though he were sinking in a bottomless pit.

The streets are long and broad at first, carrying illustrious names. They are macadamed and they have a pavement. There are crowded dwellings on both sides but they have numbers and terraces and decorated gates and the windows have panes and shutters. The shops have owners and tools and assistants and elegantly written signs. The people are clean-shaven and healthy looking. Their clothes are neat and colorful and well cut. Language is polite. The smell of burning fuel and fabrics and perfume fills the air.

The deeper inside, the narrower the streets. The houses shrink and shed their numbers. Windows have no shutters. Shops give way to stalls where the proprietor is himself the assistant and his bare hands his tools. Faces are paler and darker. Clothes are old and faded. Language degenerates into abuse, and the air carries the smell of spices and leather and glue and sawdust.

Still they continue, and the streets grow narrower until they become mere lanes with names that jar on the ear. Rough blocks of stone take the place of macadam and there is no pavement. Eons of time separate the dilapidated dwellings from modern times; the windows are narrow slits with iron bars. There is less movement, stalls are few and far between. Features are coarse, faces are darker and beards begin to sprout. There is less clothing. No shirts with the trousers, no underpants with the gallabiya. Language breaks down to a jargon of grunts, and kitchen smells ride on the air. Still they continue and the winding lanes lead to alleys paved with dirt, covered with filth and water and slime. There are no stalls; goods are displayed on push carts or a showcase nailed to the wall. The houses have shed their coating of paint and the iron bars on the windows. Children and flies swarm in abundance. Features are coarse and swollen as though bitten by wasps. Clothes are threadbare, some are unclothed; language is loud and shrill, and the smell of slime and decay falls like a pall on the dismal scene.

As they keep on toward their destination the winding lanes and alleys lead to a place without substance where everything melts into everything else. The raised ground, compounded of years of accumulated dirt, welds with the dilapidated buildings groaning with age. The slimy ground is the same color as the dusty walls. The smell of the earth mingles with the smell of humanity, and the low broken murmurs mix with the barking of dogs and the creaking of old gates, and the dead slow movement of inanimate creatures. The low grimy dwellings are a continuation of the graveyard, stretching forward as far as the eye can see. And the obsequious Farghali leads the way, a grave expression on his face, befitting the grave situation. People greet him and he answers curtly. They treat him with deference, him, the mean janitor, while back in al-Gabalaya Street nobody knows the all-powerful judge.

They walk on through the crumbling buildings propped, like the people, against one another for support. The old lean on the young, the children lead the blind, and the walls support the sick. All are strung together like the beads of a rosary. One spirit inhabiting many bodies. Time does not exist. The child suckling at its mother's breast is the same one who crawls on the garbage heaps, and the same one girt with talismans against the evil eye. He is the child who died and the child who escaped death. He is the apprentice at the workshop, the one who fools around imitating actors and calling abuse. He is the youth in overalls drawing on the stub of a cigarette. The one with a job or out of work. He is that one near the wall, crazed with opium and Seconal and unemployment. He is the old man who prays all day calling benedictions on the children, lamenting the past as he paints himself a glowing picture of the world to come.

And the betrothed bride. She is the children's mother with the colored head-cloth or the black veil. She is the beating mother and the beaten wife. She is that one rummaging for food to feed the hungry brood.

Farghali's voice comes dimly to Abdallah. He is pointing at the only upright building in the lane saying proudly it is his house, insisting they go in, not forgetting to curse Shohrat who is the cause of his disgrace. Abdallah asks where the blind alley is and whether Shohrat's house is still far. Farghali replies that they have almost reached it. They walk on, followed by inquisitive looks. And behind every suspicious look the word 'stranger' forms, implying danger and distrust.

The women at their doorsteps are weaving conversation out of their idleness. They lean their heads together as they watch the strange procession. The whisper travels from doorstep to doorstep. 'Police,' some say in a hoarse whisper. 'Health authorities,' hope the optimistic. Then they recognized Farghali, and their whispers die down.

And children. Scores upon scores gather in front and behind and on either side, their eyes bleary with ophthalmia and trachoma, and misery looks out of their haggard faces. Swarms of flies come in their wake. One child shouts as he hurls a stone at Farghali who reproves him mildly. Soon it is a game. The children gather round Farghali who chases after them and they scamper away with the flies behind them. Soon they come back and resume their game as the flies resume their buzzing.

Farghali is not sure which is Shohrat's house. He asks one of the women sitting at their doors who points to a house not far off. The name is carried from mouth to mouth, collecting conjecture as it travels. The women leave their places to join the procession of children. Their black veils and the dirt ground and the shouting of the children and the low mumble of adults are all one. The earth boils under the hot sunshine and the stench from its bowels escapes to the sky.

Farghali and Sharaf, surrounded by the curious crowd, wait at the door while Abdallah goes up alone. The house is dark. The interior is like the mouth of a toothless hag. Matches won't light and they drop to the slimy floor. Shohrat is on the second floor, at least that's what they said. The first floor is pitch black and the stink is foul; an army of rats seems to have gnawed at the decaying walls streaked with traces of brine and leakage. Dank, moldy, as if just emerging from a flood. A woman washing at the door of a room in the entrance, one bare white leg exposed, stares at him with suspicion. Her hands stiffen; she can neither let go of the washing nor cover her bare leg. The stairs are worn and shaky, its wooden steps rotten and missing in places. His shoe creaks, and he is panicky with the danger of falling. For the hundredth time the light from the match is blown out by a dank breeze blowing from an invisible source. A cool dank breeze that chills his marrow, while outside the sun burns hot. The second floor can hardly be called a floor. A bare framework like the ribs of a skeleton forms the roof. Old tottering sloping walls, and a door on the landing. It is made of old rough unpolished wood, grayish blue, smudged with the remains of dried-up dough, the excreta of birds and animals, and the bloody imprint of a human palm, flanked by the drawing of a face like a witch's, chalked by some child.

He stretches a hesitant hand to knock on the door.

'I want a word with you,' he says to the face that appears in the doorway.

She pales beneath the look he pours on her like a searchlight. Apprehension and fear look out of her eyes. It's Shohrat. She greets him in a broken voice and opens the door wider to let him in. She is wearing a man's old gallabiya slit down the front. Her paleness has traveled to her feet making her toenails white. He is embarrassed. This trembling woman stole his watch. He was out for her blood when he started on her trail, but now he wavers. He stands debating whether to go on or to turn back. Having come this far, he must go on.

'I want a word with you,' he says as he had planned. But his tone is not as he had planned. She lets him in, pale and apprehensive. She tries to hide her embarrassment behind a wan smile. He plans his retreat as he enters. Anything might happen. She might scream for help; he might be assaulted and robbed or killed. Three children emerge from somewhere. A girl, ten years old, tall, dark, skinny, with beady eyes and an expressionless face. Her hair is black and shiny, exuding an odor of petrol, one plait undone and a wooden comb planted in the crown of her head. Two other children, a boy and a girl, or possibly two girls or two boys. They cling to their mother's skirt. Out of the dark, penetrating the smell of petrol, four pairs of eyes are fixed on him with mistrust. He swallows.

'I want a word with you,' he repeats mechanically. Shohrat comes to abruptly as though in response to a stimulant.

She sends the children away and shuts the door, but they linger behind it, their eyes shining through the cracks like glow-worms. His head is spinning. The room is close and narrow. A faint light filters through a window high in the wall. A decrepit four-poster, rusted all over, with a grubby mattress. A coarse moth-eaten sack full of something is propped against the wall. A rabbit is sitting on it. At the other end is another grubby mattress, and empty tin cans and chips of wood and a miscellany of junk lie scattered about. There is a picture of the Imam Ali on the wall. He is shown smiting an infidel with his sword, but the infidel is still sitting upright in his saddle, his feet firmly in the stirrups, in spite of the gash in his head. Something stirs on the mattress: a man, tall and dark and bald as the water cooler standing beside him. He is stretched out with a scowl on his face, his belt unbuckled, with filthy underwear showing through his open trousers.

'I want a word with you,' for the third time.

'Yes?' Faintly with a tremor.

'Where is the watch?'

She stiffens and beats her breast with indignation. She denies with the fluttering of her eyelids and the increasing paleness of her face. He repeats his question. She repeats her denial. Intuition assures him she is the thief and he returns more vehemently to the attack. She tries to reply and the words die on her lips. He shouts and she cowers, holding on desperately to her pride. The screams of the children rise above theirs. The eldest tries to take them away as she hears what is being said to her mother. Scenting danger they refuse to go and leave her alone.

His anger grows and he threatens her with the police. He is at the door. She appears not to believe him so he goes to the door. It creaks open. Then he takes her to the window and they both lean out. 'Alright, Officer,' he calls and Sharaf replies with a wink. Abdallah's face remains frozen and he pulls Shohrat back inside. 'Hand it over or you get a year in jail.' She stumbles on her way. 'Think of your children.' She stops dead in her tracks at the word 'children' so he batters her again with more stress on 'the children.'

There are no tears in her eyes. The sleeping man turns and groans as he dreams. Shohrat calls out to him but he sleeps on in despair. Abdallah's anger grows and he repeats his threat while something inside him whispers: this mother is fighting for the entity of her family.

And his anger rises, giving his face a fearful mask, and he makes a final threat, and her eyes look into his. There is not a grain of pity in them, nor is there a grain of cruelty in his heart. He does not know why he threatens, why he persists, why he has no mercy, nor why he is not more ruthless. 'You can search,' she says, and he knows she is guilty. He kicks things over with his foot. The sack is full of dry corn cobs. Under the bed there is an old wooden doll and old rags and the smell of mildew. A pile of worn shoes in a blanket of dust beside an iron tube. The cupboard is one meter wide, painted brown under a thick coat of grime. Inside, a dead roach and a boiled potato, two onions and a sealed packet of salt. Looking below, his eyes shine as he starts identifying some of his belongings. Decorated candy boxes, a wooden box with inlay, red pencils, lead pencils, the top of a fountain pen, part of an old lighter. 'For the children, to play with,' Shohrat explains. Also an old mended sock. A deep sense of shame makes his heart sink and the blood rise to his head. 'Hand it over,' he hisses for the last time.

The husband stirs as he shoos away the flies with a sleepy hand, and the voices of the children at the door grow louder. Shohrat opens her mouth and then shuts it again. Noises come from her throat and her hair is disheveled. She trembles inside the floating gallabiya, one hand frozen on the other, and a distraught look in her eye. There are moments when he comes to his senses and he realizes he is putting on an act while this woman is standing bare in her misery. The powerful traits of her face which once had brought him low have withered with her suffering. There is no joy in victory. He is torn by many factions.

The tears come. She has found her voice. 'Those things, I found them, I swear. I was going to return them.' The simpleton! How could she cave in so soon. And he had thought he was in for a long struggle.

She moves to the open cupboard and fumbles inside and comes up with a broken glass. She pokes two trembling fingers inside and pulls out his watch. She hands it over without looking up. Buckets of iced water are pouring on him. The storm quietens down and his heart feels like lead and the horrible putrid room becomes unbearable. The watch is shining brightly in his outstretched palm, and the sight of it fills him with a childish joy. He turns it over in his hand, shakes it, puts it to his ear. It is still running, pointing at the exact time. Four twenty-five. He must go.

At the top of the stairs as he starts to move, he suddenly slows down, gripped by a feeling that he has done wrong. He calls Shohrat who reappears, her little brood clinging to her dress. The eldest girl watches her mother, her face expressionless, her hands holding on to her undone plait. Abdallah hesitates then he asks Shohrat why she did it.

'My pay is too little. You refused to lend me . . . .'

He asks her again.

'The blouse, I had to pay the seamstress.'

He presses her.

'I am ashamed to appear in a *melaya*.'

She doesn't weep though tears are falling from her eyes like rain from a cloudless sky. Her answers are vague. He wants to know why she didn't pawn the bed or sell it instead of stealing. Because it isn't their bed, and more tears stream down.

'Then whose bed is it?'

'Umm Hanem's.'

'And who's Umm Hanem?' She is the woman with whom they share the room.

A gruff voice from inside is asking with a big yawn what the matter is. She turns to answer as he steps aside to go downstairs in a hurry. Once in the open he takes a big gulp of fresh air and dashes forward unheeding of the crowd before the door. They follow him with their eyes. Large probing eyes that want to know what the gentleman has done to one of their own. Farghali presses him with an ugly smile. 'Well?' he asks, but Abdallah pays no heed and Farghali won't give up. He persists, relentlessly, like the splutter from his mouth. The curiosity of the crowd closes in on Abdallah like a ring of barbed wire. They want to know. He pulls out the watch and straps it on his wrist and he hears their murmurs grow to a rumble. The news is starting to travel. The women huddle together whispering, and they send their voices to the sky asking God to protect them from evil. The men growl whilst the children prattle and reports of the incident fly from casement to casement. Shohrat is being torn to pieces and her mangled remains are tossed from mouth to mouth, while she stands pale, silent, frightened, resigned, and helpless.

When he reaches his car it is like reaching a lifebuoy. Sharaf is not there. He's washed his hands of the whole affair, explains Farghali, he said he could stand it no longer. Abdallah is not astonished, he expected that from Sharaf. Farghali's profuse apologies alternating with threats and menaces as though he counted himself responsible for the whole universe, irritate him. He gets into his car and presses the starter the same way he presses on his bad conscience.

Once more the wide orderly streets come into view. Once more the people are clean-shaven and well dressed and their features are fine. He leaves the push-carts behind and joins the fleet of taxi-cabs and buses and private cars. The nightmare is over. The air is lighter, the world looks brighter, everything smiles as he looks at the familiar surroundings of Qasr al-Nil Square. Here a light breeze begins to blow, bringing people back to life after the lethargic heat of the day. The mighty river flows eternally under the crowded bridge. The tall buildings on the horizon look like pigeon houses. The city is breathtakingly beautiful.

When he reaches his flat he goes straight to the terrace and throws himself in an armchair and tries once again to sort out the events of the day.

8

During the interval nothing had changed. There was the same old study with the same old terrace overlooking the Nile, watching the shift of scenes. The glaring light of day was slowly fading as if an invisible hand were turning off the sun-disk. The city paled as the light faded. The rays of the sinking sun dazzled the eye as they broke on the window panes. The sky was tinged with red and, below, the city took on the evening hue of steel before it settled in nocturnal blackness. It was almost totally engulfed by the night except for the myriad lights speckled on the surface.

The terrace was alone to observe the scene. Judge Abdallah was far away, brooding, motionless, scanning the face of the sky. His thoughts were hovering round a spot, lost in the shadows, somewhere beyond the minaret of al-Azhar. From time to time the metallic sheen of his watch would flash before his sight, and a scathing sensation would gush like a hemorrhage, urging him to fling it away into the river.

But he never did. Nor did he sit up all night on the terrace. In the morning he was on his way to work as usual, accompanied by his customary headache. The watch was still on his wrist reminding him of that nightmare excursion. He would hold it up for all his friends to see before he started to tell them the story. He had to drop many details. When he came to the blind alley, the scathing sensation returned and he would gloss over some of the descriptions and move hurriedly to the next part.

He never allowed Farghali to speak to him of Shohrat. Nevertheless, he was not against picking up whatever news Farghali communicated. How she had turned bad, and got a reputation and styled herself Amira.

One day driving down al-Malika Street he slowed down as he happened to catch a glimpse of her standing at a bus-stop. She was obviously not waiting for the bus. Her lips were painted with real lipstick, and she was wearing the same skirt in which she used to come to work, but what particularly caught his eye was the new blouse that matched the skirt.

Translated by Wadida Wassef

Did You Have to Turn on the Light, Li-Li?

———∿∿∿———

I t was a joke at the start. Perhaps it was a joke in the end too. Actually
it was not a joke in the real sense, but an incident, rather, which happened to involve those fabricators of jokes who were past masters of
the art. It was not the fact that all those people who normally go to bed at
dawn should rise at that hour in order to pray, which was the joke, or the
fact that for the first time in the annals of the quarter of al-Batiniyya—that
den of opium, Seconal, and hashish—the people answered the call to prayer
which came from the minaret at the break of day.

Nor was there anything odd in their praying with their heads foggy
with dope. Forgetting that they have already recited the *Fatihah* they
recite it another time, but they forget the words and then they remember them in the middle of a prayer so they start all over again. The joke,
actually, came just as they were about to end the prayer. The incident is
still one of the cherished tales they are fond of recounting. People
around there were drug addicts for the most part, reared in banter and
humor, for whom jokes and anecdotes were a staple diet. No sooner
would an incident occur than they would seize upon it, adding frills and
embellishments until they made of it a fantastic epic to rival the best of
their local lore.

Oddly enough, the first prostration had gone in perfect order, so had the
second, and only the third prostration, the salutation, and the uttering of the

words 'There is no god but God and Muhammad is the Prophet of God' remained to terminate the prayer.

'God is the greatest!' called the Imam as he kneeled for the third prostration. They all kneeled after him, albeit a little awkwardly, their joints stiff from disuse as most of them had not performed their prayers for longer than they cared to admit. Ten long rows piously repeated 'God be praised' three times, and waited for the final response from the Imam to conclude the prayer. When that failed to come on time some began to suspect their count was wrong. So again, slowly, they repeated it, but still the response failed to come. A few resigned themselves to waiting, only too glad to rest, their dizzy heads still laden with dope, but most began to wonder what had happened as it was becoming clear the situation was rather odd. Still, they were hopeful that the Shaykh would presently pronounce the words 'God is greatest' and all would be well. But the longer they waited the more their suspicion was confirmed that they were facing a crisis. All sorts of possibilities began to storm through their bowed heads, which none of them dared to raise.* Had the Shaykh been suddenly taken ill? Or had he passed out, or simply died? Or could it be some devil had induced him to take a whiff of hash, and he was suffering the consequences now? Yet in spite of these conjectures they still expected the response to come and restore peace to their minds which by now had gone on a wild rampage in the realms of fantasy.

Exactly how long they waited no one was certain. According to some accounts it could have been two minutes or it could have been two hours, that is, if one were to disregard exaggerations which affirmed that the pause had lasted until echoes of the noon call to prayer began to reach them from al-Azhar. There are also those who insist they are still kneeling up to this moment.

But what was certain even to the most befuddled was that an unusual length of time had passed and that all was not well with the Shaykh. He had certainly not pronounced the *takbeer* for which they were all waiting and

---

* According to religious law any wandering of the eyes, of the mind, or any coughing or irregular motion will annul the prayer and the worshiper must begin again.

which would have put an end to their kneeling posture, and the snoring wheezing out of all those drooling jaws.

At this point each one of them found himself faced with a problem he had never encountered before. What exactly should he do now, and what do the laws of religion say with regard to a situation like this? If one of them were to move and raise his head, would that annul his prayer, and possibly that of the entire congregation? And would he alone take the blame? Being freshly-returned prodigals made them once again recall visions of a God who promised reward and punishment, wielding paradise and the bottomless pit of hell. To the newly repentant new transgression was more than they would want on their consciences.

But time was starting to weigh, and wicked thoughts began to assail them. Like scoffing for instance, not only at their predicament but at the thought of what might arise if the Shaykh had got it into his head to take a snooze or, even worse, he had simply dropped dead. They would probably have to remain in that posture till the following day, or possibly till doomsday before someone discovered them, as the mosque was not a place people around there were fond of frequenting, for merely to walk past it stirred the conscience. But they were afraid to dwell too long on their devilish thoughts or on the ridiculous situation they were in, since they were irreverent by nature, and they dared not succumb to impiety for fear of adding to their sins. Even the most optimistic were forced to admit that they were in a real predicament when the light of dawn began to break, and the wan light of the electric lamp slowly faded. It was pitch black when they had started to pray and now with daylight appearing no doubt remained that the prostration was uncommonly long. The sporadic sounds of coughing, growing increasingly more frequent, were the only signs of impatience with a situation which did not promise to end soon. It was impossible to know what had happened without raising their heads, and if they raised their heads they annulled the prayer. None was willing to take the lead and bring upon himself the opprobrium of such a deed. All were waiting for someone else to start. The blame would then be on him. There was a vast difference between the guilt of one who leads and one who merely follows. The prolonged prostration was becoming an undisputable fact and it lasted until it defeated all doubts and misgivings and any inclination to laugh at the matter.

And since there is no joke so far, and since the real laughs haven't started yet, let us leave them as they are, prostrate, each of them fearing to be the first to trespass.

For that's exactly how I left them. I, Shaykh Abd al-Al, Imam of the Mosque of al-Shabokshi, in the quarter of al-Batiniyya.

Did you have to turn on the light, Li-Li?

Yes, it is I. Glory to him who makes the night follow the day. Sleep is in my voice for I wake with the cries of the dawn. I am the climber of the dark spiral staircase of the minaret. I fear for my chest and for my voice from the morning dew. The cold invades my eyes and I shut them from habit. I know that my call to prayer falls on deaf ears. The Godly are few in this quarter, and the truly Godly prefer the mosque of al-Azhar, not far from here. It serves nothing to strain my voice for it is drowned by the amplifiers from the forest of minarets surrounding mine. My call is for myself, for I am content to know my voice has reached God; that He knows I call for the ordained prayers as He has ordered. I am content to know He forgives the people of these parts whether they sleep or they wake. For in sleep they shut their eyes on their wrongdoings and when they wake it is only to do wrong again. Perhaps it is providence that got me appointed to this mosque, endowed long ago by a Turk who had whipped and looted his way to fortune. By building a mosque and making his grave lie near the *Kiblah* he hoped to buy redemption. He believed that the people's prayers, generation after generation, would bring him nearer to paradise. Even paradise you want to reach on the backs of others, you Turk!

I am the new graduate from al-Azhar. I loved God from childhood, and of my own will linked my existence to His faith. I smile at those who imagine I entered the famous school in order to become a chanter of the Qur'an because God endowed me with a pleasing voice. That is not the reason why I chose to enter al-Azhar, nor why I started to learn the Qur'an when I was a boy. The reason goes beyond that. A call from God. . . . It had to do with my place in a universe where none but He deserves to live.

Did you have to turn on the light, Li-Li?

How dazzling was the light in the midst of total darkness. One lone lamp in one lone room on the roof which seemed to flood the whole of al-Batiniyya where it crouched like a deserted camp. The houses, old and crumbling, bulged with living beings. My flock, my burden, or more precisely my defeat. My defeat at attempting to awaken God in the hearts of those who wanted to forget His existence.

I struggled, and at the end of a week there was a spark that kindled hope. I struggled more. They cast aside their false promises and their voices began to rise. I pressed on. They came, threatening, their eyes sparking fire. Listen. We don't want a wet blanket around here. If you want to stay here, mind your own business or you'll get what you're looking for. Nevertheless, instinctively I knew they were good folk, that in their hearts they accepted God and that they sought Him. But in their lives there is no place for a total God. He must accept them as they are, they will worship Him in their own way or not at all. According to their brand of religion prayer was two prostrations every Friday, and although they fasted by day during Ramadan, from sunset to sunrise they fed on weed. No transgression there. Show me the text where it is prohibited. As for alms, the rich gave freely. Sometimes in kind, as the faith commands. The pilgrimage to Mecca was the crowning glory for big-time traffickers which allowed them at least to swear by the Prophet's grave when they made a deal. Five people only have I barely won over, the rest had no faith in me. I realized the fault was mine. Before I could lead them I had to know them; I had to live their lives to change their ways. I had to be of them so that they be of me. Theirs was another language. They had other values, and other concepts, and special keys that opened the door to their pale. I went out to them, I sat in their cafés, I visited their homes. I never frowned on their doings. My heart was with them as I watched and listened, and slowly came near.

Did this have to be, Li-Li?

It was ordained, whether it was she or another. I did not know that purity to that extent was seductive, nor did it occur to me that in spite of my devotion to God I was only a youth of twenty-five. I am chaste. Happy. Even in this quarter where the ancient residents, like the new, had taken refuge from the world. Then as now they were fond of meditating, except that now they dwell on levity while those of old dwelled on the sublime which led to the fountainhead: to God.

I did not comprehend except when the signs became frequent, and unmistakable in spite of the purity of my intentions. One day I happened to recite to them. They liked my voice and they called me again. I knew then that I had touched their hearts. The doors that until now were shut in my face began to open. They wanted nothing of me but my voice and my recitation. They rejected the preacher, and the mentor, and the Imam; only my voice could draw them where I wanted them to be. God in the abstract is hard to conceive, so let the beginning be through His word.

The listeners who gathered round me were all men. I did not know that they screened a larger audience of women. The moment I began a recitation the rumor spread like wildfire and in a flash they flocked down and came to listen, sighing with every cadence. Trouble began. Every time I went to the mosque I found a woman waiting for me. Always with a question or the pretext of one. But I never allowed my eyes to travel from the ground. Still, I was making headway. I had succeeded in getting them to pray and I was happy to see they were urging the men to do the same.

One day I was asked a question that rocked me to my bones. It was a young woman. Those feet upon which my gaze was fixed could only belong to a young woman. Faltering a little at first and then becoming bolder, she told me that for months her husband had deserted her bed; she tried everything to bring him back but nothing worked. His addiction was the cause. There was no hope of a cure and she feared the evil path. What was she to do?

Soon the questions became confessions. Master, I obeyed the devil and gave in to the delivery boy whom my husband sent with the vegetables. What shall I do? What shall I do, Master, for I saw you in a dream? What must I do, Master, when my brother comes stoned in the early hours and will not let up until I yield? Every night I yield. I want to repent. Will God accept repentance from the likes of me? I want to repent at your hands, Master.

There was no hint of repentance nor a shadow of restraint in the way she clung to my hand.

Satan.

These people had long and frequently given themselves up to him. For long years they had strayed in the paths of ruin and they knew no other. Satan. Around me and everywhere. In the woman's low whisper. In the look aimed at my back burning like a red-hot iron straight from the flames of hell. To face the devil without flinching I learned to master the bold stare and by that I lost the timidity which made of me the object of their lust. And with a withering look, I was able to stay their gallant approaches.

Did you have to turn on the light, Li-Li?

'My name is Li-Li, haven't you heard of me?'

A bold stare deflected my gaze where I looked. Naturally, I had heard of her. She accounted for half the rumors and gossip and all the contentions that kept the quarter humming. Part-English, part-Egyptian, she was the wonder of all time with her glossy red hair and honey-colored Egyptian eyes. Li-Li was the fruit of a week-old marriage between her mother Badia and a British soldier called Johnny. The morning after he spent the night with Badia, unlike our shifty lads, instead of giving her the slip, the dolt asked her to marry him. A week after they were married he was called back to duty and she never saw him again. He got killed in the war. To that short-lived union Badia owed a monthly allowance she had never dreamed of, which for twenty-five years she cashed in regularly at the British Embassy. For the first time money ran freely through her hands, which tempted her to run a small business financing local small-time pushers.

It was there that Laila, as her mother called her, grew up. Li-Li was the name her English grandparents gave her when they came from England after the war to see their grandchild. They tried by every means to get custody of the infant but Badia clung stubbornly to her child.

She gave her an education in spite of the sundry characters going in and out of her flat where she chose to sit at the door. Sometimes she sat in the doorway down in the street, generously exposed and totally indifferent to what people would say in a neighborhood where she counted as a rich woman, and where she ordered the men to run her errands. She carried on openly with one or another without a qualm. But Li-Li, she would get an education. She'd see her right through to the end. She'd make a lady of Li-Li.

Educated or not the European is an enticing creature, much more so when the heady wine of Egyptian blood runs through her veins. Although she received an education Li-Li did not learn. She was ambitious. Even as a child she was aware that she was a cut above others. Even when she served cheap drinks in seedy cabarets where she joined foreign troupes, or when she haunted the offices of second-rate impresarios. She never doubted that one day she'd be a great lady, that she'd know fame and glory and that the world would be at her feet.

'God be with you and light your way to the true path.'

'You light me the path and gain your reward from heaven.'

'The light is in you. It must come from your heart.'

Did you have to turn on the light, Li-Li? Did you have to?

'I want you to teach me to pray.'

'I have a book. You can have it.'

'I want you to teach me, privately.'

'God forbid that I should sin. Go, and may He forgive you.'

One day the allowance stopped coming; the money dried up; the mistress was ageing and ill health set in. Li-Li's pitiful earnings were all that remained.

Many times I tried to avoid her but she stood in my way wherever I went, her eyes like electric sparks flashing from pole to pole, now Saxon now Egyptian, her devastating beauty beyond anyone's reach. They tried force, money, crawling on their knees, but Li-Li gave herself only to foreigners. That was the secret she revealed to no one. In the end, as with all stubborn cases, they gave up and took her as she was. They bowed to the fact that she belonged to no one, and since she belonged to no one she belonged to them all, for all to guard and protect; forbidden and desired.

Light.

A window of shining light.

I am blinded.

The light is near. Only across the narrow street. The minaret is on a level with the window. I gazed inside. One look swept me up like a whirlwind from the pit of somnolence to the peak of awareness. An awareness full of terror, as I realized I was facing something wondrous and overwhelming.

There is a high wooden bed in the room, what else besides I do not know. A woman is reclining on the bed, one leg slightly bent, her milk-white form half clad in a flimsy garment that barely covers her breast. It is the first time in my life that so much of a woman's flesh is revealed to my sight. I came round to myself half-way down the stairs gasping for breath as I fled. My terror turned to a sweeping fury.

I am caught in a snare.

I who came here to conquer the devil. My ambition dwindled until I am content merely to ward him off, to shun his abode, and beware of his many disguises. I find myself at the break of this day caught in a snare. I, who sought to defeat him in others, I run for fear he defeats me in myself. But my plea, you demon, is that you tracked me down when I did not know you existed.

How often was your wickedness engraved on our hearts until you came to be the image of evil. Not once have you been coupled with beauty, although that is where you love to lurk. In the shape of a woman, in the folds of luxury, or in the sweetness of a smile. That's where you hide your bait.

I went back upstairs.

What I saw I erased from my thoughts. The light from the window, the room, the street, the house, the whole area I blotted out of my mind. Let it be a war, a blazing raging war.

Oh, God! My cry sounded strange to my ears for that was not the sound of my voice. After the benedictions my call went up from my depths to the vault of heaven, sharp and shrill and endless. A powerful call that bore with it the frailty of mortals and all their limitations, as it reached out to the Omnipotent and Everlasting. But now it rose in a feeble gasp, shackled by my impotence, never to reach the heavens but to crash down from the minaret and perish on the ground.

My heart grows faint. I am afraid. Not of the devil but of myself. How often have I caught myself, too ardently lending an ear to those meretricious and lustful women. I cannot help the searching look in my eyes, nor can I ease the pangs of deprivation or the torments of my flesh.

Oh, God!

I was pure as the crystal fountain when I followed Your ways. Solitary, as though I were the only creature of Your hand. To gain acceptance I know I must go through the ordeal. So let it be a hard one.

I shall not flee.

I shall look and take my fill of her. The agony is past bearing. By allowing the lesser sin I shall triumph over the greater one.

It is she, Li-Li. The devil incarnate. Temptation in the flesh, tossing in her sleep, her body spilled on the bed, an incandescent glowing mass of flesh. There. There is her breast and there her belly. Her hair slides gently down to cover them. She turns and it slides back.

Oh, God! I cry for help. Not the cry of earth to the immensity above but my own desperate call as I sink. I continue to gaze for I cannot tear my eyes away. How evil is man. How evil I was to think I could conquer the devil alone. Alone I am nothing. My strength derives from God and what there is of Him in me.

Satan has me in his grip. My eyes he has riveted to Li-Li's white form, and with all his might he seeks to wrench from me my very soul. How little I knew the extent of my weakness.

Oh, God, who answers every prayer. All powerful God who knows my impotence. You who gives will to the slave, who knows my suffering, have mercy on me. Though I bear up I am defeated. I am horrified to discover at the crucial moment the frailty of what I believed to be my strength. Face to face with the devil, I know this is my battle for survival.

Oh God, will You leave me to fall? Will You have me err? Will You forsake me for Satan to rule and dominate. Help me my God, for I am in the abyss. Come to my aid for You are my only hope.

Why did you turn, Li-Li? Why did you let your flimsy covering fall away from your body, so dazzling white? So white that it shines with a light of its own. Stark naked, heaving and dashing, twisting and turning, your soft limbs languidly scattered at your sides. . . . What blazing hell is this that dwells in you which neither the rising dawn nor all the cold in the world can cool?

All in the glaring light.

Did you have to turn on that light, Li-Li?

It was not his loud voice that roused the people from their sleep for none of them could remember ever being roused from his torpid slumbers by a call to prayer. In truth it was an intimation of something marvelous and beautiful which called them from their beds. The voice was filtering through to their rooms like a heady perfume seeping into their sleepy nostrils; warm and tender like a melody in a dream. But they know they are not dreaming; they know they are thrilling to the stark reality of that voice.

Oh, God!

How often that call is uttered. In prayer and supplication; in sorrow and in gladness. How often did it come with the last breath of life and the first beats of existence. Uttered by the child, and the man, and the sinful, and the repentant. By the hopeful and the desperate wavering between hope and desolation.

All woke to that one call. Like a magnet it drew them out of their beds and into the streets with a feeling in their hearts they had not known before. A joyful feeling that they were close to God. A merciful God whom they had nearly reached.

They met in the mosque, the water from their ablutions hardly dry on their faces. Having never met before at such an hour or such a place they looked at one another like strangers meeting for the first time, their ears picking up the soothing strains of the call to prayer; food for their souls for when they shall hunger.

Presently, and in great confusion, they began to flock outside heading for the minaret to seek Shaykh Abd al-Al. They needed to know whether the voice was truly his, whether it was truly of this earth or whether it flowed from heaven. So great was their rapture they did not realize that the Shaykh had come down without sending out the full call to prayer. Pale and sallow he descended from the minaret and with a sign of his hand

stopped the rushing crowd. Immediately he went to the *Kiblah* and prepared to pray.

Yes, I prepared to pray for now I was worthy to pray.

Because I have triumphed I am worthy to pray. The first sign of victory
was when I was able to recover my erring sight. When my voice awakened Li-Li from her sleep and she sat up, the satin curves of her body
undulating languidly on the bed. Rapturously she turned her gaze on me.
Desperately I fought, my whole being torn with anguish, just as she was
torn with anguish—the anguish of joy and pure exhilaration. Then she
got up and stood leaning out of the window. That instant I looked away
and I returned to my senses—a ruin, the very dregs of a life.

I looked up to the sky in my gratitude. I was no longer myself. My
stock of faith I lost in the raging battle. In triumph and with a bleeding
heart I went down. Prayer is the balm. I turned my face to the *Kiblah* and
prepared to pray.

They were still prostrate when the sun shone down on the nave. Some had
gone to sleep, others were snoring, and the rest were lost in private meditation. They were all still waiting for the words 'God is greatest' when a
sudden raucous laugh burst upon them. It was Me'eza the Dope who was
in the habit of seeking refuge in the mosque whenever his wife turned him
out of the house. He nearly split his sides laughing before his words came;
sheer drivel, but at least they came.

'Look at the dopes,' he said, 'praying without a leader.'

In triumph and with a bleeding heart, I went down. Prayer is the balm. I
turned my face to the *Kiblah* and prepared to pray. I opened my eyes and
Li-Li's naked form appeared before me, throbbing, voluptuous, her silken
hair falling in ripples down her sides. Forgive me oh God, for I have concealed from You the truth. The devil has won the day.

While all were kneeling together, like a stray flock come home, I stole
through the window by the *Kiblah* and in a flash I was knocking at the
door on the second floor of the house opposite. Wrapped in a bed-sheet

Li-Li opened the door.

'I have come to teach you to pray,' I said with terror in my smile as I started to unbutton my cloak. The bed-sheet slipped from her shoulder. Sharply she pulled it back.

'Sorry, I bought the English record that teaches prayer. I found I understand it better,' she said as she turned her back and switched off the light.

Did you have to turn on the light, Li-Li?

Translated by Wadida Wassef

Death from Old Age

———✺———

I t was on just such a morning that Amm Muhammad died. What annoyed me was that people took his death as a matter of course, no reason for anyone to grieve or mourn or even to sigh in sorrow.

That day I had started work as usual signing birth certificates which made regular citizens, recognized by the state, out of new-born infants. As a matter of fact my job reminded me of Sayyedna Radwan, guardian of the hereafter. For just as no one could leave or enter that abode without his sanction, no one could enter or depart from this world without mine.

I used to start the day warranting certificates with a long queue of mothers standing in front of me waiting to have their infants' vaccinations checked. Forty days ago these infants were only a name on a slip of paper, and now they already had a few weeks of life behind them and incipient problems. I rather enjoyed my work in spite of the many troubles I was bound to encounter. It was refreshing every morning to inspect the tiny mites so full of the vigor of new life. Their mothers were all young and newly married and happy to be mothers. They'd probably started to collect since early morning in their best clothes, their eyebrows freshly penciled and their eyes carefully lined with kohl. It was no use trying to keep their line straight for they kept on falling out to go and look at some other woman to see what she was wearing and take a peep at her infant to compare it with their own. There was no malice intended, of course, but they all saw to it that their babies were properly decked with wolves' teeth and amulets, and the first thing they did when they got home was to read the charms against the evil eye.

After the women it was the schoolchildren's turn to line up. Their noisy clatter filled the room. The same children who not so long ago had been carried in here in their mothers' arms. Now they were back again on their own two feet to get certificates from the office to admit them to school. Then there were the young workers; boys and girls who came for a statement that they were above twelve years of age, which the law on the employment of juveniles required before they were allowed to embark on their lifelong struggle for their daily bread. That lot was never noisy. They just stood, dazed and bewildered, with the awed look of those about to probe a dark interior.

By the time I was through with them I could tell from the racket outside that the next batch was collecting. Male voices in an uproar of oaths with angry references to justice and humanity and the government and the waste of time. Nothing would calm that lot. Not even the repeated assurances of the orderly who vainly tried to keep their line straight, his fist tightly clasped on the measly tips he was collecting from them. He shook his head many times and assured them they would all take their turn. Yes, they will be granted leave. Yes, they will pass the medical examination. Dr. Khaled is a kind man. Yes, he is in a good mood today. Just a little patience friends, and you'll get your ages estimated. You'll all be getting what you came for. Everything in good time. Just a little patience. Then they started trailing in, a long queue of people obviously unused to discipline. All you saw was the restless faces of men caught up in a mad race to grab the loaf out of the other fellow's mouth. Coarse boorish faces bruised and toughened by the daily encounter with life in the raw.

By ten o'clock I was through with the world of infants and youngsters and adults and I prepared to enter the sphere of the dead. They, too, have their problems. Death is by no means the end of a man. As a matter of fact in dying a man gives a lot more trouble than he ever did while he lived. If the penalty for smuggling someone into the world without a birth certificate is a fine of one pound, the penalty for smuggling him out without a license is a term of imprisonment. And while the state never bothered much about an individual during his lifetime, it suddenly gives him the greatest attention the moment he expires. Just as the law cares nothing for how he lived but will move heaven and earth to know how he died.

Suspicion in some cases is a crime, goes the saying. But the legislator takes the opposite view: that it is a virtue in most cases. Accordingly, anyone who dies is assumed to have been murdered until it is proved otherwise. It was my job to get 'otherwise' proved. My job was to certify the death, to examine the body, and to sniff for evidence of foul play. And after having made an approximate guess as to the cause of death, put it down on the death certificate. Only then did the deceased have a right to get buried and start off for the next world.

At ten o'clock then, my dealings with the world of the dead began. The first people I had to see from that sphere were the undertakers' assistants when they came in and crowded round my desk. Amm Muhammad used to be one of them. I never noticed him at the beginning for they all looked alike. And although assistants are usually associated with the young, those were a curious lot, the youngest of them well over sixty-five. There was something unwholesome in their senility, unlike the common run of pensioned or retired officials many of whom retained a youthful appearance in spite of their gray hair and wrinkles and rounded backs. These men were somehow disfigured by old age. Their bodies were shrunk to a feeble tottering frame, and their faces were shriveled and dry as a raisin. The tall appeared taller, and the thin appeared thinner, while the short could hardly be seen. Invariably there was a white stubble sprouting on their thin haggard faces, and their eyes were bleary from more than one disease. Their work-clothes may have differed in color and quality but they were all equally old and worn, and reached no lower than the knee. Their headgear, too, was the same for all. A long narrow rag of some sort, wound round a frayed, shapeless head-cover of some sort, or simply round their naked pates.

They were quite something to look at, what with their great age and the way they were rigged out, in addition to their many infirmities. They looked like creatures from a distant planet where everything is moth-eaten and decrepit.

Their work began from the moment a man gave up the ghost. Just like the angels who conveyed the soul to heaven, these undertakers' assistants took care of the departed until they got him safely underground. Some people imagine that the undertaker's job is easy, but in reality it is much more difficult than simply conveying the soul to heaven. Some may also be under the impression that it is an unpleasant job, which is another mistaken notion. It is a job like any other. If people work only to make a living then any job is unpleasant, which means that work must have rules and regulations. Here the rule was for the boss to sit in the shop and receive the death notices. It was he who dealt with the clients and cashed in advance payments, and only in rare cases did he personally undertake to wash the deceased.

After he clinched a deal, his assistants took over. They'd run to the house of the deceased in order to get him dressed. Then run for the doctor at the Health Department office. Then back to the shop or to the herbalist's. It was they who had to heat the water and carry the body on their lean arms to the wash-basin and wrap it in the shroud before they placed it in the coffin. Sometimes too they were made to help carry the coffin to the mosque or to the graveyard. The coffin usually had long rough handles of unpolished wood that settled viciously on the lean old neck, sometimes making it bleed. Very often it was heavy, and the distance always long. Summertime was hell. But the biggest torture were the obese.

So at ten o'clock it was their turn to come in, crowding before me, each of them stretching a skinny arm with a death notice. Each trying to get me to start off with him first, to see his client and give him the burial license which would allow him to get on with his work before it got late.

There was something in those boys at once pathetic and grotesque. I couldn't resist a quip sometimes.

'And when shall we be writing out one for you too?' I used to say to the first of them to reach my desk.

The poor devil could only laugh. They were always anxious to please me, and they generally went along with anything I said. That's why I was astonished one day when one of them did not respond when I made the same quip to him. I stared at the man. He looked just like the others. The only difference I noticed was that a slight shadow covered both his eyes like a winter cloud.

'What's wrong with you?' I asked, seeing that something was obviously wrong.

'I wish I'd died in her place,' he moaned sadly.

'In whose place?'

'Didn't you hear? My daughter. She died.'

'When?'

'Yesterday. The primus stove blew up in her face. She died in the hospital.'

I didn't believe him, for his blank expression hardly altered as he announced this news. I had to ask his Mo'allem, who was not his boss alone but that of three others as well, all equally ancient. This one did not conform to the traditional image of mo'allems, who were usually corpulent hulks with fearsome mustaches. He was only in his thirties, tanned and clean-shaven with a severe expression on his face though at heart he loved to frolic. The business had come to him upon his father's death but not before he had sown his wild oats and knocked about for a while. Looking at him anyone could see he was sharp and clear-witted and knew what he was about. Although he was young he wore the traditional dress of well-to-do Mo'allem: a bright red tarboosh and a woolen cloak over his silk caftan, the rich embroidery round the neckline showing through the opening in the cloak. He wore elegant black shoes and in his hand he held the inevitable amber beads.

He confirmed what the man said. It was true that his daughter had died in hospital and that by her death he was left alone in the world. I felt sorry for him as he stood so forlorn, leaning toward the ground as if an invisible force were pulling him down, precipitating the moment when he would be laid there for good. He just stood, motionless and dry-eyed.

'Ah well, Amm Muhammad,' I said, 'don't upset yourself. This is the way of the world.'

As I said that, I realized I was not even sure of the man's name, I was only guessing it was Muhammad. Actually I called them all Muhammad and out of deference to me they all answered to that, as if it didn't matter to them any more whether they had a name of their own.

'Yes,' he mumbled, 'I wish I'd died in her place.'

It is not uncommon to hear such expressions in circumstances of over-whelming grief and one takes them for what they are, a mere burst of emotion. But in the case of Amm Muhammad the way he spoke left no doubt he meant what he was saying.

From then on I began to take an interest in the man, as well as in all the other Amm Muhammads. I found out the reason why they were all so old, almost as if to do their job it was an essential requirement to be elderly. Most of them, I discovered, were retired school janitors, office boys, or police constables. They took odd jobs during the first few years of their retirement until their strength was gone and they were quite worn out. After that the only way for them to make a living was as undertakers' assistants. That is if they were lucky enough to find a vacancy. The job did not require much physical strength, and the wages were so poor that none would accept them—none but an old man on the brink of death from weakness and star-vation. And yet, in spite of their years when the most they could do was lie in their beds and wait for death to come, their duties were most strenuous.

I'd gone with Muhammad on hundreds of calls, and every time we went through the same act. He was always in a hurry to get the burial license from me in order to get on with his work in time to be able to attend to other business. There was the boss to consider, and like all apprentices he was anxious to please him. So he was always trying to dissuade me from going all the way to the house of the deceased as the journey back and forth took too long. He wanted me to sign without leaving my office. But orders were orders and mine were to examine the body before giving a license. He used to get excited and swear to me that the death was natural, that there was not the slightest suspicion of foul play, that he himself had undressed the body and examined it. He had pulled the hair and stared into the eyes and felt the bones. My comfort was all he was interested in, he assured me every time. I'd shake my head stubbornly and he'd shake his in despair as he started to run in front of me. 'As you wish then,' he would say. 'Have it your way.'

After a while he would stop.

'I swear by God, my Bey, it's an old man this time. A simple case of death from old age.'

'Death from old age—in full possession of faculties,' was the term used in the case of an old person's death when no other cause of death is apparent. The phrase 'in full possession of faculties' is thrown in for legal purposes where a legacy is involved and litigations amongst heirs are likely to arise. It was a common expression widely used by health inspectors, civil servants and undertakers, and it was only natural for Amm Muhammad to adopt it too.

Seeing that it was no use persuading me to stay back he would trot on in front of me to show me the way. We went to crowded areas; crowded with people and houses and flies and everything imaginable. There were more people than houses, and more houses than space, and about a million flies to each individual. Everything was piled up in heaps as if the work of someone in a hurry. And Amm Muhammad trotted along on his skinny bow-legs, with sweat streaking his face, tinier in stature than a wizened monkey. It was a struggle for him to catch up with me and a struggle to run ahead of me, and a struggle to clear a path for me to proceed. Acting as self-appointed policeman he starts to direct the traffic, signaling carts to halt, and ordering vegetable hawkers to stop yelling and waving their arms about, and to make way for the 'Bey.' He gets out of breath but he manages to keep up some sort of dialogue with me to keep me entertained. He curses the crowds and those who disobey his orders. There's no good left in the world any more. In the old days death came in plenty, and business was good. I ask, panting like him, whether we still have far to go. Oh no, only a few steps, just round the corner. So I proceed and after hundreds of steps we have still not reached the house or the body. We keep winding in and out of lanes and alleys and the people who see us go by turn their faces away with a visible shudder, wondering whom we are after. Amm Muhammad keeps trotting on, in front and behind and on both sides of me, trying his best to ward off the disaster of my losing patience and deciding to put off the business to the next day.

Finally we reach our destination. Amm Muhammad picks up the hem of his gallabiya and holds it between his teeth as he rushes on double-quick to make way for me. No sooner do I step into the house than I am greeted with terrifying screams followed by a chorus of wails.

'The doctor has come for you, my love!' they cry, as if the doctor were Azrael himself. But Amm Muhammad pays no attention.

'Hey, out of the way, you,' he shouts. 'This way, my Bey. Get out of the way, I said. God damn those women, where the hell do they all come from! This way, my Bey.'

The black bundles crowding the room begin to move but not before they have peered into my face to take a close look at the doctor. At last there is no one in the dead man's room but the nearest relative, Amm Muhammad and myself.

'There, my Bey,' says Amm Muhammad, rushing toward the body, hardly waiting to recover his breath. He rips the cover away to reveal the dead man.

'See? I told you, just dandy. Not a scratch.' He goes on as if in self-defense, wanting to prove he was right when he said the death was natural.

'Here's the chest. Look. And the belly. And here's the mouth, clean as a whistle. And the hair.' He pulls at the hair to show me there is no evidence of poison. He becomes irritable as it is nearly midday, and he wants to have finished by then.

'And the legs, here.' He pulls up the leg. 'I told you, my Bey, it is only old age. Look at the back.'

He tries to haul the body over but it proves beyond him even though he calls God's saints to his aid.

'Lay off, damn you,' his boss would scold gruffly as he takes over. But Muhammad insists on helping if only by supporting a leg, or straightening a finger.

When the examination was over and we have left the room, Amm Muhammad would still not take his eyes off me, like a schoolboy awaiting the results of an examination. He breathed with relief only when I signed the certificate and he held it thankfully in his hand like a gift from heaven. Then he would bite on his gums and his pupils would dilate, and his smile would say, 'I told you so.' And he would scurry down ahead of me, back to my office.

One day I saw a tear in Amm Muhammad's eye. A tiny liquid speck, as if it were the last drop in his sockets. It came after he'd received a quick slap on his face from the boss. He had made a mistake. I had gone to examine a body and it was still not undressed when I got there. Before I had time to reprove the boss for it, the latter had come down with a slap on Amm Muhammad's face as if to show me it was not his mistake and that he had seen to it that justice was done. It made me furious but Amm Muhammad never moved. He just stood with his hands on his cheek, a guilty expression on his face, like a reproved child.

One day I went to my office and found it packed with Amm Muhammads, all standing glum and silent as usual, decrepitude having sapped them of even the energy to talk. I was not a little astonished when I found them crowding my office, for I was not used to having so many at a time. As soon as he saw me their boss came forward with a broad grin on his face wishing me every kind of good morning, fragrant with jasmine and roses and honey dew, which he accompanied by a great roar of laughter. Then, as if he suddenly remembered something, his expression changed. He stood with his fists resting on his belly and an expression of profound grief on his face.

'Didn't you hear?'

'Hear what?'

'The man, he died.'

'What man?' I spoke carelessly as the boss was in the habit of talking to me of people and things I had never heard of as if I knew all about them.

'One of my boys.'

'You mean Muhammad?'

'That's right, God give you a long life.' Then immediately his professional look came back and he was brisk and businesslike. 'If you please doctor, for the sake of the Prophet, kindly let us have the death certificate without delay. You know, it's summer, and him an old man and all that.'

I couldn't help a smile. Only yesterday Muhammad was trotting all over me on our way to a call, and today he was dead and his boss was as eager to rush him through his own burial as he himself used to be for his clients.

'Well, my Bey, what do you say?'

'So he went and did it,' I murmured, addressing no one in particular.

'That's right, and if God hadn't sent us a new boy, heaven knows how we were going to manage today.'

'A new boy?'

'That's right. There he is. Come, Guindi.'

Guindi came. Another shriveled old man no less decrepit than the others. He hadn't got into his official clothes yet for he was still wearing a crumpled, shapeless tarboosh.

'If you will be pleased to sign, my Bey,' the Mo'allem was saying.

'No, I've got to see him first.'

'Well, it's not as if he's a stranger to you. I just don't want to put you to any trouble, that's all. I wouldn't be deceiving you; after all, he was an old man, and you knew him. You can sign right here, "old age," that's all there is to it.'

Here all his boys joined in to back him, eager to do their departed colleague a last good turn. But I insisted on what I said, if only to have one last look at Muhammad. After all, we were pals.

Presently, we left my office and set out for Amm Muhammad's house. It was a grim procession, with me in the front and the Mo'allem at my side holding his gallabiya up by the hem with one hand while he gesticulated with the other, telling me all about Amm Muhammad's funeral and how he was giving it to him free although times were bad, and one never knew. Behind us came the rest of the Mo'allem's crew. People stopped to stare as we went by, wondering who the eminent person could be whose death formalities required the whole lot of us.

The house where Amm Muhammad lived was out of the way, at the foot of a hill. It consisted of a large courtyard with an enormous heap of garbage in the center, surrounded by rooms, most of them dilapidated but not unoccupied in spite of that. Our arrival did not stir the slightest motion. Not a wail, not a cry, not a sob went up. Everything seemed to be going on much as usual, as if death had never called there. Only a few dogs began to bark when they saw us coming but they stopped and scampered away when the Mo'allem shouted at them.

The room was dark and only the open door let in some light. Amm Muhammad was lying near the wall covered by old German newspapers; nobody could explain how they found their way there.

'Alright,' shouted the Mo'allem to the new boy.

The 'boy' bent down and removed the newspapers with trembling hands. Amm Muhammad lay stretched out with his face to the wall like a punished child. He was wearing his work clothes, his body was shrunken, and his feet, so often seen scurrying as he went on his rounds, were now lying still in a thick cast of dried mud and dirt.

'There,' the Mo'allem was saying, 'nothing wrong at all. Turn him over; let the Bey see him properly.'

The old 'boy' tried to haul him over but the effort proved beyond him. I could imagine then old Amm Muhammad rising from the dead and reproving him in his own gruff way.

'Lay off, damn you. Here, my Bey, I'll turn myself over. No need for you to trouble. Here I am, absolutely nothing wrong. Here are my legs.' And he stretched out his legs, two long desiccated twigs. He took off his clothes and stood naked in the middle of the room, a skeleton in a covering of skin with not an ounce of flesh between. Amm Muhammad turned himself round. 'I told you, my Bey, I'm an old man. Here's my arm.'

He tried to stretch his arm but it seems the rheumatism which had long troubled him when he was alive had left him with stiff joints so he gave up and went on to show his head, a little shrunken ball, the cheeks sucked into the mouth, and one jaw clamped on the other.

'And here's my hair,' he said, pulling at the little that was left, 'and my feet,' he added sticking out his two colorless feet that looked as if they had been dead for decades.

The effort of thus displaying himself must have tired him for he lay down again turning his face to the wall.

'You could have spared yourself the trouble. I told you, it's only "old age,"' and he sighed as he settled down.

I came round to myself at the sound of the Mo'allem's voice.

'Well?' he was saying.

'You may go ahead.'

Immediately a great bustle started as the Mo'allem removed his cloak and stood like a captain on deck briskly giving out orders.

After a while Amm Muhammad was settled in his coffin and the coffin was settled on the bearers' backs, all of them his pals. They started on their way, the coffin swaying as they carried it out of the house where not a sound or a single wail went up to bid farewell to Amm Muhammad.

After the Mo'allem had checked that everything was all over and that he had done his duty in giving his 'boy' a decent funeral, I was surprised to see him suddenly go back and squat on the ground near the wall, hiding his head between his knee. I saw him give vent to a long muffled sob, and in a low sad lament he called Amm Muhammad's name over and over.

When his sobs subsided, remembering formalities, he lifted a tear-stained face to me.

'You did sign the license, Doctor, didn't you?'

I nodded.

'Wasn't it . . . .'

'Yes, "old age".'

He wiped the tears from his eyes.

'And "in full possession of faculties" . . . .'

'That's right. "In full possession of faculties,"' I replied.

Translated by Wadida Wassef

The Shame

—⟋∿⟍—

I believe they still refer to love as The Shame over there. They probably still hesitate to talk about it openly, making only covert allusions, even though you can see it in the hazy look in their eyes, and when the girls blush and shyly look down.

Like any other, the farm was not a big one. The few houses were built with their backs to the outside, the doors opening onto an inner courtyard where they celebrated their weddings and hung their calves when a sick one was slaughtered to be sold by the *oke** or in lots. Events were few and could be foretold in advance. Day began before sunrise and ended after sunset. The favorite place was in the doorway where a north breeze blew and where it was pleasant to doze at noon and play a game of *siga.***

Nothing much happened, and whatever did happen was predictable. You could be sure for instance that the scrawny little girl playing hopscotch would marry in a few years. Her complexion would clear and her angular body would take on softer curves, and she'd end up with one of those boys in tattered gallabiyas next to their skin, diving off the bridge like chained monkeys to swim in the canal.

---

* One oke is equivalent to approximately 1 kilogram.
** A game of draughts where pebbles are used for pieces and the ground serves as a board.

Sometimes things did happen that were neither expected nor predictable. Like the day screams were heard coming from the field. They
ripped the vast emptiness of the countryside, warning of some fearsome
event. And although at first the people did not know where the sound was
coming from they found themselves running to help, or at least to find out
what had happened. But that day there was no need for help. The men
returning to the farm tried to avoid answering when the women asked what
had happened. For they could not bring themselves to say that Fatma had
been caught in the maize field with Gharib. For both were no strangers to
the farm. Fatma was Farag's sister, and Gharib was Abdoun's son and the
matter had been plain to all.

It was a small farm where everybody knew everybody else, and private
affairs did not remain private. People even knew when someone had money
hoarded away, exactly how much, where it was kept, and how it could be
stolen if one had a mind to. Except that no one ever stole from another. If
at all, they stole from the farm crops; petty thefts like a lapful of cotton or
some corn-cobs. Or sometimes they would dip into the drainage canal of a
rice field when the watchman wasn't looking, and take all the fish without
sharing it with the bailiff as the understanding went.

Everyone knew Fatma and all there was to know about her. Not that she
had a reputation or anything like that. It was just that she was pretty; or to
be more accurate the prettiest girl on the farm. But that was not the point,
for if a fair skin was the yardstick by which beauty is measured in the countryside, Fatma was dark. The point was that no one could explain what it
was about that girl that made her so different from the others. Her cheeks
were hale and ruddy giving the impression that she had honey for breakfast
and chicken and pigeon for lunch, when her daily fare was plain curd cheese
and pickled peppers, onions, and scorched fry. Her eyes were black and
beady and incessantly alive with a piercing look which made it hard to hold
them for long. To say that her hair was soft and black, and that her floating
black gown did not conceal her provoking curves would not do her justice.
It was not her looks that made her what she was, but her intense femininity.
A gushing, throbbing, devastating force which it was hard to trace to any
definite source. The way she smiled, the way she turned her head to look

behind her, the way she asked someone to help her with her water jar; her every movement was a provocation. There was witchery in the way she tied her only cabbage-green headcloth at a slant to reveal her smooth black hair. There was witchery in the dimples in her cheeks when she smiled, and in the trail of her rippling laughter; in the very sound of her languid, fluid voice which she knew how to modulate and distil into drops of the purest female seduction, every single drop of which could quench the lust of a dozen males.

Fatma aroused men, almost as if she was made for that. She even aroused the dormant virility in little boys. When they saw her coming, they felt a sudden urge to uncover themselves. And they often did, raising their gallabiyas well up above their knees, and no amount of shouting or scolding would make them let up, for they themselves could not explain this urge to expose themselves in her presence.

That's why she was a worry to Farag, her brother, who was a poor lonesome fellah who owned nothing but his cow. The bailiff would not let him have more than three feddans to cultivate. His attempts every year to increase his share by half a feddan invariably ended in failure. Nevertheless he was a strapping hulk of a man. In one meal he could devour three whole loaves of bread, if he had them, and down the entire contents of the water cooler in one gulp. The calf of his leg had the proportions of a thigh. But his life was a torment on account of his sister. She lived with him and his wife who had a flat nose and a pale face and was a good sort on the whole, except when she drew Farag's attention to his sister's breasts, insisting that Fatma wobbled them on purpose when she walked. Also to the kohl with which she lavishly bespattered her eyes, and the chewing gum she was always asking people going to market to bring her. Farag had no need to be reminded of all this. He could see for himself, and it made his blood boil. Yet he had no real reason to reprove Fatma. She was no different from the other girls. They all dressed alike, they all smeared their eyes with kohl, and they all chewed gum. She was never caught in dubious situations, and her conduct was above reproach. Even when his wife accused her of coloring her cheeks with the wrapping paper of tobacco cartons, he had unwound his turban and wetted one corner with his spittle and rubbed her cheeks with it until he nearly drew blood, but nothing had come out. All he could do that day was glower at her, contenting himself with giving her a sharp scolding, while Fatma could think of no reason why she deserved to be treated that way. Warned and threatened by Farag, she well understood the meaning of The Shame. She was not guilty of it, nor did it even cross her mind to contemplate it. Indeed she would rather have died.

Because she knew that people loved and spoiled her, she behaved like anyone used to receiving affection. She was natural, and her reactions came from her heart. She knew her looks were what attracted people to her so she took care of them, never appearing unwashed or uncombed. When she worked on the fields she protected her hands from getting scratched by slipping on the socks she borrowed from Umm* George. She was even careful not to offend when she spoke by using bad language or coarse expressions. Everyone loved her; everyone was her friend, and she loved them all in return. That was why she could not understand why her brother was so harsh with her, or the reason for the poisonous looks he kept darting at her.

Nor did Farag himself. All he knew was that he had to answer for his sister and for her screaming femininity. Every lustful look directed at her dug into his flesh. He could not wait to marry her off, preferably in another town, and rid himself of the responsibility. But in this respect Fatma was not doing so well; suitors were few, or none to speak of. For who was the fool who would want to be saddled with that heap of seduction? And once married what was he going to do with her? People in those parts did not marry in order to enjoy beauty and then put up walls to protect it, because in the first place they did not live for enjoyment. They were happy enough to survive. When they married it was for the sake of an extra pair of hands, and eventually a progeny to swell the labor force. For this reason Fatma remained without suitors.

Not that the farm lacked men or young boys, and Fatma like other girls worked as hard as any of them, going to the fields at dawn and returning with the call for prayer at sunset. But unlike the other girls she stirred trouble

---

* A respectful form of address to married women in rural society, the name being derived from the name of the person's son. This Coptic woman has a son called George, therefore she is addressed as Umm George: mother of George.

wherever she went. That's why Farag lived in constant fear which he concealed behind a boisterous front. Much of the jolly atmosphere of the farm
came from him when he fooled around with the men and made a mockery
of their false airs of decorum. He challenged the boys to swimming races,
and toppled baskets off the women's heads, and even the most demure did
not escape his pranks. At weddings he wore his white gallabiya and his raw
silk turban and cropped his hair short; he shaved his beard smooth and
danced for the groom. He never failed to shower the bride with the traditional gift of money, not forgetting the bailiff and the cattle overseer, and
anyone else standing around. All from the money he made on the side stealing cotton from the storehouse, or filching a bale on its way to the truck.

He spent lavishly and filled the farm with his exuberance, and he was
popular everywhere. So that though his sister's irresistible appeal caused
even the stones to stir, and though the men, torn with their passion, smol-
dered with desire for her, Farag was a friend to them all. In deference to him
they looked away when they met Fatma, and when one of them allowed a
sigh to escape, someone was always there to call him to order.

And so Fatma remained like a luscious fruit, ripe yet forbidden. None
came near her, or allowed anyone else to come near her, while their hearts
continued to pine. Old and young lusted for her. But Farag was always
there. His wild laughter reminded them of his presence and warned them of
The Shame, and they would return to their senses and rush to perform their
afternoon prayers, or go round to the corner shop for a glass of tea.

And today she was caught in the maize field.

Not for the first time. She was always being caught with someone. Now
in the maize field, now behind the stables, now under the thresher. Always
by imagination. Rumors which invariably turned out to be false. For there
was bound to be rumor wherever she went, just as sighs were bound to rise
in her wake.

There was no malice in the people. They were decent kindly folk who
wished for others what they wished for themselves. You could see their
goodness even in their geese as they collected near the threshing floor, and
cackled down to the canal to splash about and teach their young to swim.
At sunset they returned, hundreds of them cackling back to their pens which

they found by instinct. And when a foolish one strayed into a neighbor's pen by mistake, your neighbor would be at your door with the stray creature even before you realized it was missing.

Everyone on the farm was under Fatma's spell. She was loved by all. If she went to a wedding it was she who outshone the bride. This strange magnetism was the reason why they feared for her. They feared she might slip, for they could not believe a woman so desirable could long resist The Shame. Their conviction of this even led them to pick the man with whom she was likely to commit The Shame, and that was Gharib.

Gharib was the son of Abdoun. In spite of his age no one called Abdoun 'uncle.' He was an irritable old man addicted to chewing tobacco and drinking sugarless coffee. He quarreled on the slightest provocation. Even the bailiff took care to keep out of his way. He was never known to have had a decent word for anyone. His talent for swearing was revealed at its best when a calamity befell the farm. Then he would take his position by the canal, like a bird of ill omen, and holding his gallabiya up by the hem, he would curse and swear, at the same time spewing out his tobacco chew and spluttering abuse on the peasants as if they alone were responsible for the misfortune. But nobody seemed to mind him for they knew there was no harm in him.

As for Gharib, he was mistrusted by all. He was rude and impudent, and he grew a forelock which he was fond of showing off, smooth and shining beneath his white woolen skull-cap. What's more, he had an eye for women and thought nothing of setting out to seduce them—which was why people were wary of him—without much caring whose wife it happened to be.

In spite of his father's ungainly appearance, Gharib was a good-looking boy, and although weather-beaten, his complexion was not too dark. He spoke little but his speech was engaging, perhaps because he sounded so carefree, speaking with the raucous rasp of an adolescent. Somehow he escaped the doltish look common to peasant boys, his clothes were always clean, and he was quick and sharp-witted which was probably what made him so smug. He worked tirelessly, and sang lays, and he owned his own equipment for making tea which he was always pressing on his friends. When night fell, he could not bear the narrow confines of his house, and he would go outside to seek the comfort of the hay near the barn. There he would sit, proudly feeling his thighs and his chest, and brag to his friends about his amorous exploits—a field where he was highly proficient and they were hopelessly inept.

His flirting was flagrant and undisguised. He would eye the women boldly from the legs up, with a glint of irony in his look, or it could have been a repressed chuckle. He couldn't help it if his look unsettled them. A woman knew when he looked at her that way that he divined her thoughts, and if her thoughts were dwelling on The Shame, which more often than not was the case, she would realize he was stripping her with his eyes and she would get so confused trying to cover herself up that her defenses would weaken and she could not help but succumb. As the number of his victims grew, so did his vanity, and the glint in his eye became bolder still.

There was something in the boy that set him apart from other men. Perhaps it was his intense virility. It was enough for a woman to catch sight of the back of his neck or the cord of his underpants for her limbs to melt. He didn't worry much about his methods. All means were fair which led him to a woman. At weddings he used to force himself into their midst making them freeze where they stood. At the mill he was only too pleased to carry their basket or turn the wheel of their hoppers. Even the sick he did not spare. And except for his fear of the bailiff's rifle he might even have sneaked in to Umm George by night. When people complained to Abdoun, he flared up at them, his face contorted into an angry scowl. 'There he is,' he would say, 'do what you like with him. I wash my hands.'

But there was nothing much anyone could do. For though Gharib was short he had the strength of a bullock. He was quite capable of lifting the heavy iron waterwheel with one hand while he broke a man's neck with the other, the same ironical glint never leaving his eye.

Of all the men he was the most virile, and of all the women Fatma was the most seductive, and it was only natural that they should be coupled by gossip. And yet they were poles apart. Fatma avoided him because of his reputation, while secretly he was intimidated by her. Although he could deftly handle the bailiff's servant girl, or Shafia, the widow with the many children, when it came to Fatma it was a different matter. For Fatma was a creature apart.

Sometimes he liked to brag to the boys, sleeping on the hay with him, that she was in love with him, and that she sent him messages. But he was the first one to despise himself for his vain boasts. He worked in the fields like a stallion, everywhere sweeping the women off their feet with his irresistible appeal. But with Fatma he was quite powerless. For her part she feared him, so that if he happened to greet her, his heart pounding as he did so, her reply would come curt and timid. She feared him because she feared The Shame while he feared her because he feared to fail, and all the time their names continued to be linked and Farag continued to hide his misgivings behind his show of goodwill, while playing up to Gharib who was the source of his greatest fears. It all went on covertly. On the face of it they were all happy kinsfolk living in brotherhood, and the farm was small and Abdoun's house was only three houses away to the right of Farag's, and there were practically no incidents of geese going astray.

Meanwhile they all lived on the brink of expectation. Things were bound to come to a head, like waking up in the middle of the night at the sound of a gun-shot or a cry coming from the fields to announce she had been caught there with Gharib.

It wasn't long before it happened.

It took no one by surprise. They took the incident for granted as something they had expected sooner or later. Even the children—in their private world where they fabricate their own gossip and hold their own notions about grown-ups—even they realized that Fatma at last had committed the forbidden thing their parents had long warned them against. Fatma had committed The Shame.

So when they saw Farag leaving the field for the first time without his turban, his head uncovered, his waistcoat unbuttoned, with mud clinging to his trousers, and when they saw his ashen face and trembling mustache and his bloodshot eyes, they huddled close to the stable wall as, instinctively, they felt the enormity of what had befallen Farag. They followed him stealthily through the gateway of the farm until he reached his house. They saw him bawl at his young son who was drumming on an old rusted can. They heard him ask his wife in a low hoarse whisper to bring him his water-pipe, and stood watching him as he inhaled deeply, puffing out the smoke in dense clouds like those which came from damp logs burning in the oven.

When a few men began to go in, they were emboldened to creep in after them. But they were careful to stand near the door watching what was going on with diffidence. Not that anything fearful was going on. Farag, pale and silent, was puffing away quietly, regularly renewing the supply of tobacco, while the men sat round him, embarrassed and self-conscious. When one of them stirred uneasily, feeling compelled to say something to soften the blow, Farag would look at him and quietly offer him a puff from the water-pipe to keep him silent. The thing he had dreaded for a long time had happened at last, and nothing he or anyone else could say was going to make it change.

He remembered how he used to watch his sister's body moving beneath her torn floating black gown, or see her flesh through the holes; how whenever he watched her laugh or speak, or even eat, the blood would race to his head and he would look at her with eyes like hot pokers, or burst into wild laughter by which he hoped to conceal his lurking fear of the impending disaster. Often he had asked himself what he would do if—God forbid—the thing should happen. His hair would stand on end at the thought and he would look at Fatma again and wish he could wipe her off the face of the earth. And now that it had happened it was his duty to act like a man and a brother. It was his duty to kill her and kill Gharib—kill the sister whom he had carried in his arms as a child across the canals, and whom his dying mother had left to his care. It was his duty to kill Gharib, the worthless dog he had sheltered and fed, always half expecting to be betrayed.

Only blood was going to redeem what had happened. But before he made himself guilty of their blood, their own guilt must be proved. He was about to bring ruin on himself and his wife and his children, and it must not be for nothing. Let him smoke then and wait before he took up his knife. The decision was cold, and merciless, and irrevocable. For Farag was a farm man, and farm people were accused by village folk of being lax in matters of morality. He was going to show them that farm people have a moral code as lofty as their own and that they do not tolerate The Shame.

An enormous black mass with myriad arms and heads was seen coming in the distance, moving in a cloud of dust. It was the women marching resolutely in their ragged black gowns, driving Fatma before them, white as a sheet, the color gone from her cheeks. There was no trace of beauty now in her face, and her head was covered with her shawl like a woman in mourning as she stared about her, her face a deathlike mask.

They made a lot of noise as they came nearer, arguing in shrill tones. Some said she should be taken to the farm-steward's house while others insisted her place was in her brother's house and that it was more proper for her to be taken there. After a good deal of squabbling she was conducted to the steward's house which stood in a corner of the farm, while the children stopped at the door and waited.

As for Gharib, they said he was last seen heading for the fields. He had run away, perhaps never to return, they said.

Suddenly all was confusion, thoughts were blurred and vision was impaired and no clear course of action seemed open. The men kept silent while the women heaped curses on Gharib, asking God to blight him with a deadly plague. Yet even the women's loud jabbering failed to lift the gloom that was slowly settling on the farm making even the dogs cower quietly in their corners.

Over at the steward's house the ring was closing in on Fatma. She was being badgered with questions, but even before she answered no one was prepared to believe her. She told them she had been taking Farag's breakfast to him in the fields that day, that she was just crossing the canal when Gharib suddenly appeared out of nowhere and tried to grab her by the hand and pull her to him. She fought him and cried out for help. Here she interrupted her rambling account. But the women urged her on. People came to her rescue, she went on, but Gharib had vanished into thin air. They did not believe her. There was more to this. No there wasn't, Fatma insisted. That wasn't true, and they shook their heads and each presented her own interpretation of Gharib's grabbing of Fatma's hand with all the color her imagination could bring to it. They were seized by a mad fever to know exactly what had happened, which grew increasingly wild and more persistent as Fatma refused to say any more. Even the men sitting round Farag, far from Fatma and her circle, seemed to have caught the same fever although they appeared more restrained.

'Wait and see, folks,' someone would say in kindness, 'perhaps nothing happened.'

No one could ignore any longer what they had tried to suppress, now that it had happened. No one was astonished for it was not difficult to imagine the result when a man found himself alone with Fatma, much less when that man was Gharib. Who was going to believe that she had resisted? If she had indeed been alone with him, all was lost. The important thing now was to find out if all was really lost. Even Farag, as he guessed at the people's secret thoughts, wanted to know the truth not for its own sake but in order to make sure that Fatma was no longer his sister and that he was free to deal with her as he saw fit.

Strangely enough, women are bolder than men when it comes to such matters. They were quick to whisper it first amongst themselves, and then to Farag's wife—who had left the house to go weeping and wailing over Fatma—and then to Fatma's aunt. When they told Fatma herself, her face darkened, her nostrils quivered with anger, and a few tears fell from her eyes, fewer than the drops of juice squeezed out of a green lemon. She screamed at them that she was not going to let them do anything of the kind. She swore on the Qur'an that she hadn't been touched. 'You're afraid of the examination, so something must have happened,' they all said. All of a sudden she flushed crimson, unable to utter a sound. She who had once believed it herself, and who had been told by others that she did not know what it was to be shy.

Had such a thing happened in a village the people would have done everything to cover up for one of their own. But on a farm where nothing stays hidden, what was the use? Everyone, old and young, was on tenterhooks to know if the inevitable had happened to Fatma as they had predicted.

The horror of what she was about to face made her grow faint. They splashed water on her face and put an onion to her nose to make her come round. Her head reeled at the thought that she was being accused of the most infamous of crimes, that she was entirely at the mercy of these people, defenseless against their savage prying, within sight and hearing of her own brother and her relatives and all those who used to love her and whom she used to love. She looked up at the circle of women and pleaded for mercy. They only stared with mournful eyes from which all doubt had gone. 'Very well,' she said with a stony face, 'I am ready.'

By then Farag's head was in a daze from too much drawing on his water-pipe on an empty stomach. His head was lowered, resting on his hand. Were he not a man he could have been taken for a grief-stricken widow bemoaning a dead husband.

There was no one on the farm more expert on such matters than Sabha, the *mashtah*,* who was not a professional like the others. She owned an old manual sewing machine and took in sewing for men and women alike. She looked younger than her years, with a clear complexion and a good-natured motherly air about her. But when she spoke she betrayed herself for what she was: a tough, matter-of-fact woman who had knocked about a good deal, with much experience of both men and women, and who did not inspire much confidence.

When Fatma announced she was ready they should have called in Sabha, but they hesitated. They were keen on having the truth, and although Sabha was experienced in such matters and they were certain that she would know immediately what there was to know, they did not trust her, for she was held in disrepute. True she was the only dressmaker on the farm and she sewed for everybody, but to be seen in her house, even though only to try on a gallabiya, was compromising. It was well known that Sabha did not mind herself and her house being used as a screen for the clandestine meetings of men and women who had a perfectly good reason for being there. No one of course had actually seen anything. It might have been true, just as it might have been a groundless rumor, but what was certain was that Sabha was a shady character. She might find out the truth and withhold it, or she might say the opposite of what she knew. 'There's only Umm George,' said Farag's wife.

---

* A washer or tire-woman whose profession is to help women with their toilet, particularly the decking-out of brides on their wedding day.

The women agreed immediately. Umm George was the only 'lady' on the farm, and the only one who was educated and could read and write. What was more she came from the town, where people knew all about everything.

The children pushed and shoved as they crowded round the long procession leaving the steward's house on its way to the bailiff's. Eager yet dejected, the crowd stumbled on down the narrow lanes littered with dirt and piles of rice straw. It was still daylight although the sun was going down. Fatma, in their midst, walked blindly on, her face ashen, her heart sunk to her feet, feeling with every step that she was trampling on it. Trampling on her innocence, and the sweet memories of her childhood, and the days of her girlhood when she sang at wedding feasts, dreaming of her own wedding day, and the music, and the ritual night when her hands would be dyed with henna—the night when all would stand waiting for her to come out like a queen. And now they were waiting for her too. Hundreds of eyes riveted on her everywhere she looked, ravenous and brutal, raping her without shame as she staggered on, bleeding in her heart, barefooted, humiliated, driven without mercy.

Her friend Hikmat tried to pull her veil down to cover her face but she pushed it back. What was the use of covering her face when all of her was bare?

Sadly, inexorably, the mass of women moved on, heads and arms squirming, a trail of children and hungry dogs behind, all enveloped in a veil of dust. The geese along their path were scared away, and overhead the birds and doves flew to their nests and the women trudged on, grim and resolute, till at last they reached the bailiff's house.

At that moment Dorgham the watchman was having another of his fits, bawling as usual, while nobody paid attention, for people by now were used to his outbursts. He was the only man on the farm who came from Upper Egypt, and he had been watchman to that threshing floor since the day he arrived. He was now well over seventy and still at the same job. He had a huge black head and thick black features constantly knitted into an angry scowl. His hair was kinky and now quite gray, and his long white whiskers made him look like a mastiff. Sweat was constantly pouring from his face so that it glistened as though it were smeared with grease, and he spoke in fierce grunts which nobody understood. The sight of anyone coming near the threshing floor was enough to send him into a rage. After living thirty years on the farm he still did not know anyone by name, nor did he care to, and so long as people stayed away from his threshing floor he left them alone.

Now he was barking at Gharib whom he had discovered hiding under a pile of maize. They boy had just come out of hiding, sneaking back to the farm in order to watch the result of his atrocious act. His already dusky face had browned to a dull tan. He wore his skull-cap low on his forehead, no longer displaying his cherished forelock. It was a much subdued Gharib huddling there beneath the maize, glum and repentant, as his own depravity revealed itself to him in all its starkness. As the procession approached and Fatma appeared he sank deeper in his hiding place and looked away.

It was his dread of Fatma and the fact that she was unattainable that had kindled his desire. And the more desperately he wanted her the more distant she had seemed. He had not intended any harm. All he wanted was a little recognition, a sign that she was aware he existed, if only a careless look over her shoulder. But that never came, and he retaliated by an even more fevered pursuit of other women, never for a moment giving up his passionate longing for one look or one word from Fatma.

That wasn't the first time he had hidden, watching for her as she carried her brother's breakfast to the field, swaying in her black gown, the sweet breath of her body blowing over the trees, and the meadows, and the stream, filling the earth with her fragrance. Many times before he had stood watching for her, unobserved, afraid to be discovered, but that day for the first time he did not care if he was. He wanted her to see him. For the first time he longed to commit that Shame which had kept him sleepless and tormented, tossing on the straw. And yet he would have been content only to speak to that girl who was neither his sister nor his mother and listen to her timid reply.

No sooner had he appeared before her, emerging from the field, than she stood rooted where she was as though she had seen him stark naked. As though it were The Shame itself looming before her. That very Shame of which Farag's bloodshot eyes, branding her like fire, had given her warning. The basket fell off her head. She screamed in panic. Everyone came rushing at the sound. In one second the whole world was tumbling about her ears as Gharib took to his heels and vanished in the fields.

Contrary to what they expected, Umm George crossed herself and expressed her genuine sorrow over the whole affair, promising to do her best to help to find out the truth. She swore by the living Christ that she would get her husband to lock up Gharib in the police station, and get the police officer to tie him to the tail of a horse and hang him on a telephone pole. Umm George was well known for her piety. She was well-bred and dignified. Nobody knew her real name. She used to force her husband to take her to church in town every Sunday morning in spite of his grumbling. He was used to spending Saturday evenings drinking *arak* in the neighboring village where Panayoti, the grocer, also served liquor to those who wanted it.

Umm George was fair and short with graying hair and three dots tattooed on her chin. She knew all about Fatma, and she was rather fond of the girl. Often she used to send for her to come and help her with the biscuits Abu George* couldn't do without for breakfast. Or sometimes just to keep her company, or to fill her in on the latest gossip as she was forbidden to mix with the women of the farm. Had it not been for the difference in age she might have been her best friend.

It was with the deepest humiliation that Fatma stepped into the bailiff's house. She was going there now not because she was wanted, but in order for Umm George to arbitrate on her honor; the woman who only a few days before had kissed her mouth saying that had they been of the same religion she would have taken her for wife to her brother who was a cashier in the province of Beheira.

She stood petrified on the threshold but the women dragged her in and her veil slipped off her head. Umm George went round to see that George

---

* Father of George.

was out of the house and that he doors and panes and shutters were properly barred. Fatma fought with all the strength of instinctive shyness, but
they had fallen on her, forcing her down on the bed while one woman tied
up her hands and two others got hold of her legs. Many hands stretched
toward her: veined, ugly, dry hands. Eyes bulged, intent in their search for
honor, seeking to guard it. Burning, piercing, boring through her, even when
they no longer knew what they were looking for. Umm George was all in a
quiver as though she were the one about to go through the ordeal. She kept
rebuking the women, in vain, at the same time reassuring Fatma, also in
vain, while the struggle went on amidst muffled cries that gradually died to
a chill whisper. A stillness heavy with expectation hung over the room and
spread slowly outside, to the house, and onto the farm, and over the whole
universe. It hung gloomily over the heads of the people sitting with Farag
and those hanging around near the irrigation pump or out in the fields, following in their imaginations what was going on at the bailiff's house.

The whole farm was lulled to a hush except Dorgham. Only one man
was there to give him an ear and that was Abdoun, Gharib's father. Lifting
his gallabiya by the hem he had rushed to the threshing floor in search of
any living soul before whom he could vent his fury and curse Fatma and his
son and the entire farm—even if only Dorgham.

Suddenly a loud trilling-cry coming from the room where Fatma was
imprisoned, tore the silence. It was followed by other, alternating with cries
of, 'All is well! Thank God, all is well! Honor is safe.'

Only then did Farag look up. 'Bring her to me,' were the first words
he uttered.

A few moments later, no sooner had Dorgham's vociferating died down
that a tremendous racket was heard starting near the shaft which fed the old
waterwheel. It was deep enough to hold three men standing on one
another's shoulders, and there just at the edge was old Abdoun catching his
son by the scruff of the neck, and with all his tottering strength trying to
throw him in. From all around men had gathered round him in an effort to
quell his fury and save Gharib from his clutches. Every time he failed to
budge Gharib his vituperations redoubled and his curses poured like burning lava. Anyone watching this performance could have no doubt of

Abdoun's genuine intention of drowning his son. But there was something, perhaps an imperceptible inflection in his voice, or in his choice of insults, which suggested that Abdoun was at heart not ashamed of his son. If anything, that he was secretly proud to have sired a seducer no woman could resist, and that his son was accused of rape.

Meanwhile at Farag's house a regular massacre was about to take place. Farag was beating Fatma with the coffee grinder, and Fatma was howling with pain. Farag's wife was screaming in terror lest he should kill his sister and get himself into trouble. The neighbors' wives were screaming too, while everyone else from inside and outside the house rushed to hold him back, in vain. Farag was like a maddened beast heeding nothing but his wild intent to murder his sister. And yet there was something wanting in the measured force of his blows and the look in his eye strangely void of emotion. It was just that although Fatma's innocence was proved, and his honor was untouched, he felt bound to perform some spectacular act by which to reply to the people's gossip and the many speculations that had crossed their minds.

Of course Abdoun never drowned his son, and Farag never murdered his sister. The sun went down as always, and as always people brought their cattle home from the fields, having loaded the donkeys with their fodder. Smoke began to rise through the cracks and over the roof-tops of the mud houses, and cooking smells drifted in the air with the glow of sunset. The men went to evening prayers, and the women finished going up and down to feed the animals and lock the chickens in their coops for the night. By the time the call to the night prayer echoed above the rooftops, all was quiet on the farm again. Everything concerning the incident had been hashed and rehashed until there was nothing more to add. Heads began to nod, lamps flickered and died. Sleep crept in with the growing darkness and tired bodies stretched on their mats and lay still.

After everyone had gone to sleep and Fatma was alone, weary and broken, she began to cry. Her tears flowed in spite of herself, streaming down onto the mud oven where Farag had forced her to sleep without mat or cover. Her body shook with her sobs, so did the chicken coop by her side, and the oven, and the house, and the entire farm, until she nearly woke the people from their sleep. She gave herself up to her pain and wept far into the night, racked by her suffering.

During the days that followed, well-meaning friends tried to persuade Farag to accept Gharib when he proposed to marry Fatma, but he wouldn't hear of it and they had to give up. As for Gharib, he never talked about Fatma any more. As a matter of fact he stopped talking about women altogether. He cut his forelock and he took to observing the prayers regularly, but that did not prevent him from hanging around the farm, and loitering by the open window of Farag's house.

Fatma, on the other hand, was locked up in the house, forbidden by Farag to step outside or even to go to work although he was in dire need of her earnings. It made no difference, for she had renounced the world, and was quite content with her seclusion. The bloom was gone from her cheeks, and her eyes had lost their luster. She had grown to look like a sluggish beast: cowering, inert, unsmiling. There was submission in her voice, and her tone had lost the sparkle where her intense femininity rang with every inflection.

Nevertheless none of all this lasted very long. Fatma did not remain a prisoner forever, and Gharib's zeal for prayer fizzled out, and Farag went back to his boisterous clowning. For after many and many a market day, everything that happened was stowed away in the storehouses of memory. Peacemakers had seen to it that Abdoun was reconciled with his son, and all was well between them. Gharib even grew his forelock again and once more he was entertaining his friends with tales of his amorous exploits. Not without a shade of bitterness. For Fatma was up and about again, ravishing as ever, wearing her headcloth at a slant, holding her gown by the hem, her willowy grace driving the men out of their senses. She greeted everyone on her way. Everyone except Gharib; not deliberately, but simply because she did not see him, as if he had never existed.

Fatma had returned to her old way of looking and talking and smiling and bewitching the men just as before. But people wondered sometimes. She had acquired something new, something they did not know her to have before. Or perhaps one should say she had lost something: that thing that gave her purity. The quality that gave sincerity to her smile and made her anger real. She had lost her innocence. Now she was a creature of guile and deceit and concealment.

That was not all. If Farag happened to catch her leaving Sabha's house, and he dragged her home, and locked the door and grabbing her by the hair asked her what she was doing there, she could stare him in the face and answer boldly, 'I was having a fitting. Get out of my way.' And she would shake herself free of his grip and stand in a corner of the room rearranging her hair, with her lovely eyes looking straight at him, defiant, unflinching, and unabashed.

Translated by Wadida Wassef

His Mother

———⟋⟋⟋———

He found it on a winter's night. The third tree before the subway. One of the weeping willow trees on the bridge over the Nile at the end of Qasr al-Aini Street.

It wasn't the first time he'd run away. He'd tried old railway carriages left to rust on disused track, and had to put up with being woken by the watchmen on their rounds and given a good hiding, until he fled from the railway and tried sleeping under lorries in Darrasa, in crannies in the wall at Fumm al-Khalig, in crannies and rubbish dumps, cattle sheds at the slaughterhouse, lots of other places, but people always chased him off as if he were a dog that was rabid or mangy.

Since his mother's husband had driven him out of the house he'd been on the run. He used to love his mother and she loved him. He'd never seen his father and then one day that man came and it was as if the strength and energy left her and all at once she seemed weak. The man would come in drunk or stoned out of his head, and empty his crazed outpourings into the depths of his mother who lay there squirming about. The sound of her panting and moaning reached him and he felt different toward her. She was different, this new husband of hers had reduced her to a formless stream of dissolving female flesh, and her heart was gradually turning away from her son.

That's what he felt then and he went on feeling it, that every day his mother was growing further away from him and nearer to this man, remolding herself or caving in like melting butter to accommodate herself to him and his violent outbursts, until one day he woke up to the fact that his mother was gone from him, taken by the man as surely as death had taken his father. When the new marriage bore fruit and his mother's stomach swelled up with a child, he realized that the final thread that had been keeping him attached to this room where they all lived had been severed, and then the man told him to leave school and get himself apprenticed to a joiner. He appealed to his mother to help him, but he wasn't surprised when she yelled at him to shut up and not wake the baby. And what's wrong with being a joiner? At least it'll teach you a trade, you little bastard. Bastard am I? So that's what she thinks of her marriage to my father now. With tears in his eyes, he gave in. But the joiner was hard, and the boy would often daydream and let his mind stray from the job, then the joiner used to take his hammer to him, or sometimes lay into him, cursing and swearing, with one of the wooden clogs off his feet. So he ran away from there too.

He tagged along with other boys who roamed the streets begging and scavenging for scraps and cigarette ends. He worked as an errand boy and if any of the places he worked for gave him a night's lodging they made him pay for it with his flesh, and the self-respect of the child-man who'd been forced to grow up quickly. He paid with his most precious possession, and ran away again.

But then he found he had to escape from all the others who were running like him. There was the one-eyed man who tried to teach him to pick pockets, and the blind beggar who wanted to be led around and who was always nudging him from behind with his prick. Then a woman who scared him when she grabbed him one night and tried to cuddle him. Running in the daytime wasn't a problem. He could always find something edible on rubbish heaps. No, he wasn't like a stray dog or cat. He knew how to rummage around and choose the right things, and always used to come upon something fresh or at least it wasn't rotten, then he rinsed it clean in the river, even if it was just a scrap of bread, and put it in the sun to dry and get hot ready for when the other ingredients for the feast turned up. The problem was finding somewhere to go at night, and on a winter's night he found it.

A weeping willow's trunk seems to be made up of its roots and that's why they call it locally the tree of tenderness: its roots protrude above ground, twining together, and dry out intertwined and create a trunk which grows stout and huge with the passing years so that it can bear the weight of the giant tree. And because the trunk is really the roots growing up close to one another, it isn't a solid round mass. There are gaps large and small in it, either open at both ends or closed from one side, making a little shelter with a roof and a single entrance.

One night he was making his way along miserably. He didn't cry any more because when a person feels miserable nearly all the time he doesn't cry. Crying is a form of hoping for a solution, or asking for hope, or a request to the Almighty to show us a way out, grant us some respite, however brief. One result of continual suffering is that you can't even feel the pain any more.

It had begun to rain. Then with a bountiful hand the sky began to pour down water in torrents, emptying the streets, leaving them cheerless and creating in the spirit still abroad in them a strong sense of fear and desolation and a violent desire to weep.

He sheltered under the tree from the torrential downpour which had drenched him to the marrow of his bones, and in the little bit of light which got through from the brilliant glare of the street light he saw the opening and went closer. He examined it and marveled when he found that it had a depth to it like a cave. A cave with bumps and furrows on the inside of it, making it look like an old woman's mouth filled with the stumpy remains of her crooked teeth.

It was as if he'd gone into a magic place, a cave of delights, for it was happiness just to have the sensation that the stair-rods and watery bombs had stopped beating down on his head and penetrating his thin garments. A tremendous feeling of joy engulfed him; he was like a tramp who'd been presented from on high with a fairy-tale castle. This feeling persisted, effacing from his mind all the humiliations of a life spent running away, assaulted and hounded out and always on the move. He was only aroused from his reverie when it occurred to him that there might be snakes and rats and other biting, stinging things sharing his hideout with him.

To frighten him more the lightning started up. And by the light of its intermittent flashes and the unwavering glow filtering through from the street lamp, he began to inspect the floor of this vegetable cave inch by inch, then its walls, and found nothing except part of a dog's skeleton that must have been there for ages. When he'd flung it away and cleaned up the ground with an old bit of rag, and squatted down to rest at last, he felt that he was the happiest person on the face of the earth, happier than a king or a rich man or Firmawi himself who owned all the greengrocers' businesses in the area.

He was so happy he wanted to resist the drowsiness that started to creep through his body and would draw him, it the succumbed, down into a sleep unlike any other he'd ever had. Here he wasn't on anybody's property, he wasn't near a warehouse or a shop so they'd pick him up on sus. The police couldn't see him, nobody could, human or devil, and he tried to keep awake to savor something that he'd been without all the time he was homeless—a tender mother in whose embrace were warmth and security and protection from all the evils of mankind.

He struggled to fight off sleep, aided by the severe cold, and every time he noticed the thunder and lightning and the relentless downpour outside the cave and him protected from it all by the old tree's embrace, he felt like a drowning man who'd been rescued and dragged up on the shore. In his strong fortress, surrounded by wild beasts howling and licking their lips, he could stick out his tongue at them in the sure knowledge that their claws couldn't reach him and they were roaring only in impotent rage, and where he was it was safe as houses lined with velvet, downy velvet of the tree's substance which had begun to incline toward him sending out currents of warmth from an unknown source.

He woke up and it was morning. The rain had stopped, but the noise of the street and the rattle of the trams sounded as if they'd been going for hours. For a long time he lay, staring through the opening at the passersby and the traffic. Half asleep, he ruminated on his past life, stopping when he reached the point in his thoughts where he had found this new place to live because between the night that had just passed and the whole of his previous life was a sharp and irreversible divide.

With a hand made weak by sleep on the end of a slack and indolent arm he began to feel the inside wall of the hollow as if he was turning over the contents of a treasure chest between his fingers. He realized that he was hungry with a sort of keen, pleasant hunger that he'd never felt before. But first he had to wash his face. The Nile was close at hand. What luxury, his castle even had running water laid on, and an abundance of places to piss and shit in.

It seemed that once his housing problem was solved, all sorts of means of earning his bread offered themselves to him. He'd only taken a few steps along the street when a woman who'd just got off the bus asked him to carry her suitcase. Although it was heavy it felt as light as a feather to him and she gave him twenty pence for the short distance he carried it. He breakfasted for the first time on brown beans and bean rissoles and onions, and drank tea and smoked a whole cigarette. He roamed the city streets and by the end of the day he had enough on him to buy his dinner and go to the cinema and still have ten pence over to begin the next day with.

As he went home after sitting through two films he felt that he was going back to a place already dearer to him than any other he'd lived in. Only one thing bothered him, when he thought about it, which was that he'd find that another occupant had taken up residence in his absence. But it was still standing vacant, waiting for him, and if he hadn't been scared that he might be going off his head, he would have rushed up and embraced its walls and sung Abd al-Halim's song out loud to passersby. She's my heart's joy and my desire, she's all my life to me. His greatest happiness was that he had something that belonged to him, a place of his own, and it was like coming upon a family where the father hadn't died and the mother didn't have a husband who hurt him and mangled his self-respect. The wanderer of the sea of life had found a place to rest.

But the night was cold and he lay there with his eyelids tightly shut, finding it hard to sleep. What did it matter even if he spent the whole night awake? In the morning the place would still be all his and no one would wake him if he did fall asleep. He was in his own home.

It grew so cold that he began to shiver. He would set aside some time the next day to look for a rag or an old sack to cover himself, as the cold had become unbearable. However much he huddled up and pressed against the inside wall of the tree, so soft compared to the rough outside wall, he felt no warmth at all.

Near dawn he felt that there was some warmth beginning to surround him very gradually and he wondered if he was feverish. Maybe the cold had made him ill and he was going to start coughing and sneezing? If he caught something now it would finish him off for sure. He put a hand on his forehead and compared the heat of his hand to the heat of his body. No, no fever, but there was a palpable warmth coming from somewhere, and it was only when out of habit he stretched out to stroke the inside wall of the tree that he realized the heat was coming from there. He was scared and almost started to shake again out of fear of this strange anonymous warmth.

He must have been beginning to invent things, for a thought had flashed through his childish mind that the tree was warming him up like any mother might do when her child cuddles up to her feeling cold. Even if it was an absurd notion it pleased him and he relaxed so that his teeth stopped chattering and his limbs stopped trembling and he drew his knees up to his chin and slept.

As he depended on the tree completely, and it had become his refuge from the wicked world outside so that he even began to go back there for a siesta when spring came and brought the hot weather with it, he was surprised when be found signs that the tree too felt lost and bereft of close relations. The hollow seemed to be changing and taking on a different shape and then he saw it, a new branch thrusting its way out from the opening. He patted it and watered it assiduously until in a few weeks it grew bigger and nearly filled the entrance, making a door and almost hiding it, so that only he could tell where it was.

Without him realizing what was happening, and of course without the tree realizing, there came to be more between them that dependence, or affection, or coolness in summer and warmth in winter. He loved it more than he'd loved his mother. It was everything in the world to him, home and shelter and loving embracer.

He didn't know how much time went by, a year or ten years, because time had stopped for him the moment he discovered the weeping willow.

Life pulsated through the tree now and the sap ran in every dried up twig, and although he had managed to get a job as an errand boy in a big shop and earned a regular wage he couldn't tear himself away from the tree's embrace. But gradually he began to feel that the hollow was getting too small for him, as without noticing he'd got bigger and his arms and legs had grown longer until the day came when he could no longer squeeze himself inside.

That's the way it goes, and one day he'd had to collect together the things that he'd stowed away in the tree's nooks and crevices and say farewell to the hollow and go to share the attic room with his friend and colleague at work. He spent many long nights not knowing how to sleep on a bed, he who was accustomed to being curled up comfortably in the tree's living embrace. But time passed and he grew accustomed to sleeping in a bed. He became a man and delighted in working hard all day and sitting up with his friends late into the night, so that he forgot all about the tree and couldn't even remember the street where it had stood, because he moved away and went to live and work in Shubra.

One day his boss sent him on an errand to Fumm al-Khalig and suddenly he found himself jumping off the bus at the end of Qasr al-Aini Street and hurrying toward it. He stood horrified, looking at it. Its green leaves had withered and its branches were dry and the door covering the entrance had collapsed. It was as if it had died and he felt a lump forming in his throat and then the tears came and he wept. His mother.

Translated by Catherine Cobham

An Egyptian Mona Lisa

—⟋ℳ⟍—

This isn't my first attempt; it may even be the third or fourth. Every time I think of writing it down, I get the feeling the language I'm using is much too crude, too stilted and hollow to put what I want to say into words. The language we use to speak and write was, I feel, created to depict imposing phenomena and great sensations, things like rocks, for instance; and even if we reduce the scale a little, I still sense it's meant to depict things like sand and pebbles—whereas what I want to portray is something soft, musical, delicate, and subtle, like those many particles that seem to cling to the sunlight when it pours into a dark room. No! It's not even like the sound of a violin or the plaintive warbling of a flute, but, rather, a melody you can only hear when the world's cacophony dies down and all creation is silent. Your entire being is purged then of all those anxieties and ephemeral, earthbound feelings that always manage to distract you. You're infused, totally, with the proper sense of the words 'mercy,' 'love,' 'affection,' and 'man,' all of them timeless concepts in whose fulfillment the abiding hope of humanity lies. There's plenty of strain involved in preparing yourself for this sensation and a lot of contemplation and silence too. But when it's been done at last, you'll find a gentle, soft melody seeping in to your inner self, not just through the ears but through your very being, as an actual part of it. This is done, quite simply, by transforming your very self into the melody, till the two merge in one profound, transparent unity.

How can I find words to describe it, when all our words are fashioned with particular concepts in mind, things that are totally clear, evoking no doubts or stirrings of the spirit? How can I find words to describe a tenth of the excitement, or just one hundredth of that shuddering sensation, or the incredible palpitations, so muted they can hardly be heard at all?

How can I find colors to describe the complexion of Hanuna, the Christian girl? It wasn't white or flaxen, it was neither European nor Oriental, neither Upper Egyptian nor from the northernmost part of Lower Egypt. It had a blue tinge to it; not the kind of blue you associate with life-less things but, rather, the blue of dawn breaking or of a calm sea when the waves are transformed into gentle cries turning back to their home on the humble, prostrate shore, calling you on to plunge into the sea and follow its blue expanse forever.

How can I begin the story, when I've no clear-cut beginning in mind? It's just a series of relationships between people—a common birthplace, the days of infancy, then childhood, a faded black blanket, a room with no one in it but us, holy bread, then a New Testament with lots of pages in an Arabic with a special flavor to it.

I was an adolescent then, at that stage of life when you feel there's a world there, something that's real; that there's morning and sun and moon, and people too. Far, far away there are lands on this side of the salt sea and across and beyond it. Then there were the pumps, incredibly large, black, and oily, with their perpetual slow, solemn noise. Vast quantities of water were drawn into the sluices by some secret magic then emerged, roaring angrily, in a headlong torrent. Cows and sparrows there were too and pious saints of God, holy scriptures and verses that had to be memorized, all about a strange, incredibly beautiful heaven and a hellish fire that made your whole body shudder, retribution, torture, this world and the world to come. Then there was Shaykh Mustafa's can; now that was something very urgent and immediate. His turban used to tilt forward more than it should, and he had long legs, coming to a point at a pair of knees that looked like the heads of matches. He'd cross his legs, letting his faded, gaping shoes dangle, and when he shook his turbaned head at you and said, 'Listen to me, boy!' that was something very real, something we couldn't see or feel, something quite apart from things like the Night of Power,* or death, or the steady affection I felt toward my father. There was something about the shaykh's will. It kept out of sight, reluctant, apparently, to show itself. Perhaps it was worried at the effect it might have on us; for, if we'd encountered it, we might all have died of sheer fright. It really was something quite unusual, different even from demons, who do finally, after all, have something amusing about them. This, though, never remotely provoked laughter: it was severe, grave, protective, and compassionate, all at the same time.

'I want to be like you,' I told Hanuna, even though I didn't really mean it.

She must have been a year or two older than I was. She was certainly taller, though not as strong; but in any case, she was always more intelligent and had more common sense. It's at this point, in fact, that I can't put things into words. Her soul had a feeling that radiated like a glow from nowhere, which reached you through some indirect path. It enveloped her words, her walk, the way she'd raise and lower her head and chew the small piece of consecrated bread with her front teeth—a rite of such bizarre innocence and purity and elegance that it made you believe. She didn't seem like an earthly creature at all, more like someone from a further stage of humanity, forging a link between the angels and themselves.

I can't remember what it was she said to me; to tell the truth, I can't even remember if she replied at all, or what it was she had to say about the Gospel, holy bread, and the Kyrie Eleison (which, she told me, means 'Lord, have mercy'). Some months earlier I'd heard the priest who came from the city recite it at Africa's wedding. All I can remember is that her replies made me aware there were other people in the world beside Muslims. Up till that time I'd imagined the whole world was Muslim. This other, new religion was filled with things that woke your imagination and stimulated curiosity; and all the more so when I learned from Hanuna that the Christians had a church in the local capital, with a large picture of the Messiah in it, as well as candles and electric chandeliers. Everyone, she said, sang there; in fact, their whole worship involved singing.

---

* The Night of Power (Lailat al-Qadr) is the twenty-seventh night of Ramadan, the month of fasting. Muslims spend a long part of this very holy night in prayer and supplication and they ask God to grant their specific wishes.

I couldn't understand any longer just why I felt such a bond with Hanuna, as my thoughts followed her on her way to sleep. Could it have been because I wanted to learn more about this religion of hers, or was it surrender to that irresistible, unending radiance that drew people and things toward her, transforming everything she did into some sparkling event, delightful, and subtle, and exciting?

One thing I do know though. I won't say I began to feel a firm bond tying me to her; rather I slowly became aware that I never left her, as though I were her shadow. It was only when I wasn't with her that the feeling came; when I was, I never realized what I was doing. I was enmeshed, totally, in one long, continuous meeting with her. My only concern was to look at her and follow what she said and did, like a person baffled by some unbeliev-able, constantly recurring miracle, who can't distance himself from his feelings, remaining in a state of baffled intoxication that he can't leave and that won't leave him for a single second.

As far as I can tell, that's just where the problems of this world start. We simply won't tolerate what happens in the world, the spontaneous interplay of events along with those impulses of energy and growth that come into being, then develop, disperse, and flourish. With our foolish wills and the laws drafted by our narrow-minded ancestors, we're forever interfering with everything. We take it for granted someone has evil or, sometimes, good intentions, and so we poke our noses into things, striving all the time to make injunctions, to suppress and disrupt, and so pervert the rules of life itself.

What possible harm could there have been, I wonder, in letting a rela-tionship like ours continue? It was like a small, gentle flower amidst the impenetrable forests of people's temperaments and characters and those complex, intermeshed social relationships of which we knew nothing. What did it matter that I was the pump engineer's son, while Hanuna's father was a local big shot? Or that I was a boy and she was a girl? Or that people gos-siped a lot (even though there weren't many living in our settlement)? They all had homes the Irrigation Ministry had put up for them near the enormous pump building. There it was, a settlement with its own little society, together with the pumps, in some faraway place in the northern part of the Delta; a small representative set of people (though it seemed to me then like a quarter of the world), Muslims and Christians together. But for all that, there were a thousand problems, a thousand thorns to prick and hurt relations between these few human beings in this spot at the ends of the earth.

It all started when my mother complained to my father. He'd lost one of his legs; either it had been amputated or else mashed up in the pump propeller, I don't know which—the whole subject was mostly avoided, since it seemed to bring back such painful memories. Ever since it had happened, though, my father had been dominated by my mother. Since he only had one leg, my mother grew three, along with ten hands and a hundred tongues. And so, one day, my dear father stopped me on my way to Shaykh Mustafa's school and told me plainly I had to come straight home afterward.

He didn't want, in his kindness, to hurt my feelings by mentioning Hanuna's name or the things we'd been doing together, preferring to leave me to work the rest out for myself. I had no inclination to argue either. To tell the truth, I'd decided instantly to disobey the injunction and carry on meeting Hanuna without telling him. How could I just stop doing something when my own will had no control over it anyway? It was simply the way I was. It seemed as natural as being hungry or being thirsty and drinking; I just did it, without any recourse to thought, or weighing up the different possibilities, or making decisions. When we're young, we tend to be more honest with ourselves, and what we want is more heartfelt than life itself. Finally we were young children in a world that didn't submit to life or its laws, to a life regulated, legislated and governed by grown-ups. They always had to interfere, and, when they did, it forced us to stop and deceive them, to tell lies and hate them as much as we hated to be punished.

I've no idea what happened to Hanuna.

Our usual meeting place was by the millrace, the deep center into which all the water pours from the major canals and from where the pump apertures raise it up to a higher level, to that of the Mediterranean. Then it can be pumped out again and fed along the irrigation canals. The Delta water level, in the northern part especially, is below sea level, which is why it has to be pumped higher. But I didn't find her there. I waited for a long time, gazing at the water as it rushed through the millrace, spinning round in huge circles that became gradually smaller and shallower. Then they started spinning even faster, till they made a funnel-shaped hole. A man could be swallowed up in that, people said, and never come out alive.

She didn't come. Finally I went and stood a little way from her house. By this time, I was beginning to realize just how mean-spirited grown-ups could be: they'd done their dirty work, and that one long, sweet day was over forever.

I spotted her in the window. It was late afternoon, and the sun had changed from the fearful, hot ball of noontime fire to a gentle yellow lamp lighting up the window and the room beyond. And there, in the middle of this vivid yellow floor, stood Hanuna. The sun's rays gave her face a strange-colored glow, which shone out through the gloomy iron bars, a glow that transformed her face into another sun, smothered, faded, and hidden. Still I stood there, waiting for some picture, a glint in her eye even, to show she'd seen me or wanted me to be there. But she stayed silent and motionless—the very picture, indeed, of the Virgin Mary herself, like that picture hanging in her room, but hanging, now, there in the window. I had to see her. I knew her mother, who, though reputed to be so hotheaded, had always been very good to me, seeming, almost instinctively, sympathetic to my friendship with her daughter. Often I'd sneak an orange or some sweets into my pocket, and she'd regularly ask me to give my mother her regards—which I never did, knowing well enough how the two women felt about one another.

The door was open. Should I knock? I went in.

Hanuna's mother was just that moment coming out of the kitchen, her face, along with her clothes and the strands of her white hair, covered with soot from the stove. She smiled momentarily, as if realizing why I'd come. Then her expression froze. It was as though she'd suddenly remembered the problem and the threat. She stumbled and stuttered, but couldn't get a single word out. Then she turned back toward the kitchen, as if she hadn't seen or heard a thing.

What was I to do now? I took her gesture to mean approval and shot into the room like an arrow, to find Hanuna standing there smiling, waiting, with her head still bowed. Although I couldn't see it for myself, her expression was, I'm sure, one of delightful, innocent cunning, of the kind lovers often have. Then, to my astonishment, she acted in a way I'd never seen her act before: she put out her hand for me to shake. I put my own hand out with all the energy I could muster and shook hers so firmly it seemed to hurt her. We'd met often enough and walked and done things together, but this was the first time we'd shaken lands. Her hand was small, whereas mine, for all the two years' difference in our ages, was larger. But it wasn't just that. Hers was a slender hand with refined, delicate fingers at the end, so that you felt as though you were clutching a collection of pencils. They weren't pencils, though, but fingers on a hand, alive and warm, as though all her particular vibrations were focused within them. It wasn't just a hand but a pounding heart, the same heart I'd heard beating before. When I brushed past her breast with my face, something awestruck, something feverish swept through me.

'You look like the Virgin Mary!' I told her.

She raised her eyebrows in alarm and disapproval. Then she smiled again, as though I'd simply said something clumsy. Yet she asked me, even so, how she looked like the Virgin Mary.

'When I saw you through the window, Hanuna,' I replied, 'you looked like the Virgin without the Messiah.'

How I loved calling her by her name—as though just pronouncing it brought enjoyment and left an enjoyable taste in my mouth. 'You're Hanuna,' I went on. 'I'm the Messiah and you're the Virgin. Let me be your Messiah, and you'll be my Virgin.'

She almost struck me. In fact she did slap my hand, but very gently, to scold me for saying such a thing. But by now the idea had seized hold of my mind. It wasn't just a whim of the moment; it must have been growing inside me that day we were alone together, as usual, in their home. I'd gazed at the picture of the Virgin Mary caressing her child, Jesus the Messiah, its colors old and faded. From Mary's head rays shone out in all directions, while Jesus was a beautiful baby, smiling happily like a son who knows he's in his mother's arms, that she'll cherish him and love him. Mary was smiling too. There was just a trace of a smile in her face and on her lips, as though she knew someone was painting her portrait and she wanted it to include the smile of a mother really happy with her son.

As I turned to talk to Hanuna, I suddenly felt I wanted to be a baby once more, so that I could cuddle into her embrace, and she could be as happy over me as the Virgin Mary was with her Messiah. But when I asked her that day to be my Virgin, with me as her Messiah, I wasn't really thinking of becoming a little baby again, embraced by its mother. Behind it, rather, was desire that had long been burning fiercely inside me. I wanted to hug Hanuna, to take her in my arms and embrace her. I wouldn't do it violently or brusquely, for I was aware how slender, delicate, and fragile she was. No! I'd embrace her gently, with loving affection. I wanted to enclose her completely in my arms and chest, to make her smaller and then put her some way into my own heart. That, it seemed to me, was the only way of stilling my constant wish to be close to her and bound to her forever.

I wanted to get really close to her, so much closer than we'd ever been with girls when we'd played at being married in the old storehouses.

Hanuna gazed at me for a long time. It was the first time I'd seen her gaze at me in such a strange way. I'd often wondered what she thought of me, how she felt toward me. I didn't feel the way she treated me showed any sign of a particular 'special' relationship—rather that she saw me as a boy of fourteen, just another boy to those eyes of hers that had seen sixteen springs come to full bloom. There was something there, bound together by companionship, by familiarity and mutual agreement, but nothing more than that.

Suddenly, now, I sensed a certain gleam in her gaze, possessing that quality I'd so often yearned for, the quality of emotion. I felt it was a look being directed at me, Muhammad, and that she was using it to say a lot of things the eye would be ashamed to put into words. The look she was giving me was the only way of expressing it. In fact, the eye was just incapable of putting such things into words—or so it seemed to me—and *her* eyes above all. Faced with such a glance, all I could do was move closer to her. We'd often been close together as we walked and had even linked arms, but this was the first time we'd ever moved this close. For all the dreams and desires swirling inside me, I'd never imagined that what was happening now would ever happen: that Hanuna would suddenly clasp me to her bosom with a rapid, trembling gesture and plant a furtive kiss on my forehead. Naturally I blushed crimson; then I raised my head, bringing us face to face. We were both panting. Then came the second, incredible surprise. I found her leaning toward me—I was a little shorter than she was—then, before I knew what was happening, she'd kissed me on the lips. Like the first kiss, it was soon over, but we were both quivering with excitement. I felt her trembling lips, pursed together, as she imprinted them on mine. The kiss was swift as lightning, but it sent electricity through me, and there was the flavor of mint too. Every pore in my body opened up to it, and my heart sprang to life, like a bird awakening in early springtime. The whole thing left me dazed and excited; I'd never felt anything quite like it before. I was as though the kiss itself made me aware, all of a sudden, that Hanuna was a girl, with that quality distinguishing the female sex. She had the attribute that makes women wear particular colors and that kind of clothing, put on all kinds of perfume and jingle around in bangles, rings, and necklaces. It was the same thing that made her breasts swell out and gave her a skin as soft as silk, made her voice like a tuneful melody. How different that sound was from a man's voice, coarse as his body, prickly as his chin, and dark as his face and the hair on his chest.

So Hanuna was female! The reason this so surprised me was that I'd never conceived such an idea before or even dreamed of it. For me Hanuna was like the Virgin Mary, like a goddess: the great promoter of those happy feelings with which creation abounds. Good God—may He be praised and forgive me my sins—she was female! As I still embraced her in my arms, it flashed into my mind, for the merest fraction of a second, that this was the eternal virginity of creation I held in my hands. That was the feeling I had, and it wouldn't go away in fell into the chamber of my mind and refused to leave. There it stayed like the profoundest of aspirations, a prisoner of veneration for convention, reason, and tradition, a wish that the smaller self would fuse into the larger, that you could love God to the stage of utter oblivion, that the eternal bond between you and the great cosmic secret would be forged at last.

Even if I'd managed to picture Hanuna as a female human being, to bring her down from heaven to earth as a body with flesh and bones, still I could never have linked such a picture with myself. I couldn't conceive of anything between Hanuna and myself that might lead me to treat her like other girls. Like someone possessed, I strove desperately to return the saint to her place. Again the feeling came that she was the one great thing above all else, that the beauty, grace and superior quality she bestowed on the world set her above the level of mankind, raising her to the heavens. I made a mighty effort to recapture that feeling, hoping it might restrain this young man now quivering in response to the call of womanhood. Hanuna herself, with equal suddenness, had been born out of the same call.

But I was trying for the impossible. All the saints in the world can't prise apart man and woman, those two great forces in life, when they've once come together. There's always a third factor involved too, the fiendish law that can't be defied. And so I returned her kiss, shaking all over my body, every bit as excited as she was. To do it, I had to summon up all my virgin manhood. I didn't care any more whether she belonged on earth or in heaven, whether she was a saint or just an ordinary girl. She loved me and I loved her, and she had started it all. What I had to do now was seize the chance with joy, to bathe naked in that strange, surprising sea that had suddenly opened up between her lips. How her heart pounded as she lay there on the sofa, with my ear close to her bosom, a pounding that almost made the heavens and earth shake! It made me tremble. In her face I sometimes saw the earth in all its beauty, sometimes the heavens in all their sanctity. Now, for a moment, she looked refined, now earthy, she blushed and then turned pale, seemed depressed then wore a virgin smile, stirred up like the sea in all its awesome splendor as it urges and seethes. There she was, speaking yet saying nothing, while her body swayed from side to side, speaking without uttering a word. She was a virgin, and so was I. Neither of us knew it; or we may have wanted to know, while knowing all the time. Suddenly the blinkers were taken away, those blinkers that shield our eyes, preventing us seeing our true selves, as we are in our very depths. The fever we felt wasn't the kind to make you swoon into unconsciousness; it was an obsessive quest for achievement, for pleasure and discovery—and so part of the cosmic secret itself. At last it was revealed! It was the same feeling you have on the Night of Power, as you stand there waiting for that moment when the gates of heaven open before you and heaven's secrets are revealed. You have the same feeling when a woman divests herself, before your eyes, of the greatest secret she has, for you and you alone.

Each time I tried to think of her as a girl, a female I felt on the threshold of some enormity that would make earth and heavens shake or as though I were about to commit some heinous crime, the worst possible crime a human being could commit. I remember how, each time I felt this way, overwhelmed by a sense of deprivation, I held her, squeezed her tight, and bit her. There she was, alive and warm and female. I groveled in her, in my own feeling of deprivation, in her saintliness, in the greatest crime a human being can commit, in the fact that she was a human being, and in the time I spent worshipping her. I'd worshipped her before, and now here I was holding her, in a fashion inconceivable in the wildest fantasies.

What can I say? Should I say the saintliness that wrapped her round, giving a certain air to her voice and even the movements of her hand, simply sprang from the female in her, womanly rays, sacred and gleaming, rays of her whole kind and femininity, focused and magnified in Hanuna's light, all femininity and female? Many years have passed now, and I've known plenty of women. But she was the female that day, and ever since, to this very day, I've never had the same sense of being the man, that man.

It was as if the water in the millrace had slowed to utter calm and the pit it made had been leveled out, with everything becoming quiet and still again; as though the sea bursting out from between her lips, across the whole world, had a surface like glass once more.

She looked shy, yet as though she regretted nothing. I felt shy too. We'd hardly finished trying to put ourselves to rights when something flashed by the door, and I knew at once what it was. It came from the glasses of Mi'wad Effendi, her father! He was a tall, refined man, with eyes that always looked tired and always, whatever the time of day, had in each corner a piece of white-colored mucus or some residue from iritis, I'm not sure which.

I felt shy. But I was like a believer too, who, for the first time in his life of faith, achieves absolute, unquestionable communion with his Creator. The wonder's complete then, and faith becomes a mission for him, a certainty prepared to sacrifice life itself for the cause, in all simplicity. And so, when Hanuna scuttled from the room like a frightened cat, and my heart started pounding as it does when young boys are caught, I stilled the pounding with all the zeal of a visionary filled with faith, who, by so doing, can restore the link with what he'd been doing some moments before. For me that meant Hanuna and everything connected with her. This believer, I told myself, would carry on his relations with her, come what may. The world might be turned upside down; Mi'wad Effendi might strike me or quarrel with my father; Hanuna's mother might give mine a piece of her mind, or maybe my own mother would throttle me; my father might drag his old gun from the cupboard and shoot the whole Mi'wad family or else just me. Well, let it all happen! The worshiper prays to his God, the beams of the sun lead back to the sun itself, the night will always have its stars. My relation with Hanuna was still more inevitable than these. It had endured and always would, till the day I died or we both died together. It might even last beyond death itself.

These amazing feelings were all well and good. But, as Mi'wad Effendi stood there, tall and sedate, my expression somehow changed. It seemed to be borne off. All the blood in my body seeped from my veins, as though pouring out and drenching the floor of the room. I stood there, motionless, my eyes dry. My head was bowed low, and I awaited my punishment. Yet I knew, too, that everything had finished before he arrived, that he could have no idea of what had actually happened. But there I was, still waiting for him to punish me. If only he had! If only he'd struck me or cursed me, or even told my father so he could punish me. But all he did, after a long silence, was say:

'I thought you were a gallant boy, Muhammad.'

That's a word to stick in your mind for life, never to be erased. It rings in your ears constantly, rising up suddenly, from the darkness of the past, forming itself on your lips as you repeat it, while a shuddering shame envelops you just as it did when you heard it for the first time. Whenever you remember it, you recall it completely, with the same tone and manner in which it was said. I don't know if months or years have passed since it happened—the days passed bleak and full of tedium, stretching aimlessly and without end. Again and again I'd go to the house, hoping for a glimpse of her, knowing, though, that fate had struck, that her parents had given her the strictest orders not to see me, that I should perish on her account. Sometimes, very rarely, I'd catch sight of her from a distance and gaze my fill at her with a faraway look, like a man looking up at the stars, with the holy passion prompting me every so often to move nearer, to venture into her sight. I'd call to her, now whispering, now aloud, beckon to her with a trembling hand that sometimes felt cut off from me, at other times as though it could leap in the air along with my whole body, to come between her eyes and the horizon. Not once did she seem to recognize my existence, as she stood fixed in the heart of the square yellow window with its iron bars. Surely, I felt, surely she must know I was there; yet she was not aware of my presence or else refused to recognize it. She must have promised her parents, and Hanuna's promise was sacred like Hanuna herself, never to be betrayed. I'd melt with passion as I remembered her, as I shall remember her always till eternity itself, every move she made, every word she uttered, every look that spoke on her features. I'd melt with longing and passion, ready to die from the memories. Did my love have to seek final fulfillment? Wasn't it enough just to be near her? Wasn't that easier than the void this final break brought with it? I felt like the hero in one of those Arabian Nights stories, who was left in a palace with seven gates and ordered not to open the final one. He lived happily in the palace but couldn't resist the last, alluring temptation of that seventh door. And so he opened it and saw what no eye had seen and no mind conceived—then found himself outside the palace in the very magic spot where he'd entered, along with six men clothed in black who sat there constantly weeping and wailing. Those were the ones who'd followed that same course before—and now I'd become the seventh. Did I really have to open the seventh door, seek out the greatest happiness? Now I was sorry and wept; the world had become bleak, the days never ending like a gray, withered old crone, the nights without midnight or dawn or morning, life itself without time. Then autumn came. Rumors spread that I refused to believe; the day was fixed and the night came. There was celebration all over the colony, but its heart was in the great central square. Lights pierced the darkness with their sparkle; there were countless candles, sending the smell of their wax far and wide. Her cousin had come in from the countryside to marry her, and now they were celebrating the wedding. The clergyman who visited from time to time had arrived from the state church, and everyone was singing and repeating after him, 'Kyrie Eleison, Lord have mercy, God have mercy.' Hanuna came, in her snow-white clothes and jasmine necklace and veil, her face made up too heavily. Her gaze, though, wasn't painted; it was distracted, terrified, and lost. As the many hands pushed her forward, she moved like one hypnotized and playing a part. The smile on her face was pale and fearful, and by her side was a young man she might never have seen before that evening, a big man in a black coat, with a thick black mustache, his hair gleaming from the brilliantine he'd used. The bridegroom strutted proudly, like someone who'd just clinched a favorable deal, savoring the moment, booming with laughter, for no apparent reason sometimes, from the very depths of his chest. And beside him walked Hanuna, meek as a dove beneath the touching, thrusting hands, her smile pale, her eyes wandering and searching for something among the stars, as though she were the Virgin who'd lost her Christ. The Virgin was submissive, patient, solitary, searching the heavens for some escape. Who knows? Perhaps she was looking for me as I crouched on the roof, watching with suffering and longing, as everyone repeated, 'Kyrie Eleison, Kyrie Eleison.'

Translated by Roger Allen and Christopher Tingley

The Chair Carrier

——ɰɰ——

You can believe it or not, but excuse me for saying that your opinion is of no concern at all to me. It's enough for me that I saw him, met him, talked to him and observed the chair with my own eyes. Thus I considered that I had been witness to a miracle. But even more miraculous—indeed more disastrous—was that neither the man, the chair, nor the incident caused a single passerby in Opera Square, in Gumhouriyya Street, or in Cairo—or maybe in the whole wide world—to come to a stop at that moment.

It was a vast chair. Looking at it you'd think it had come from some other world, or that it had been constructed for some festival, such a colossal chair, as though it were an institution all on its own, its seat immense and softly covered with leopard skin and silken cushions. Once you'd seen it your great dream was to sit in it, be it just the once, just for a moment. A moving chair, it moved forward with stately gait as though it were in some religious procession. You'd think it was moving of its own accord. In awe and amazement you almost prostrated yourself before it in worship and offered up sacrifices to it.

Eventually, however, I made out, between the four massive legs that ended in glistening gilded hooves, a fifth leg. It was skinny and looked strange amidst all that bulk and splendor; it was, though, no leg but a thin, gaunt human being upon whose body the sweat had formed runnels and

177

rivulets and had caused woods and groves of hair to sprout. Believe me, by all that's holy, I'm neither lying nor exaggerating, simply relating, be it ever so inadequately, what I saw. How was it that such a thin, frail man was carrying a chair like this one, a chair that weighed at least a ton, and maybe several? That was the proposition that was presented to one's mind—it was like some conjuring trick. But you had only to look longer and more closely to find that there was no deception, that the man really was carrying the chair all on his own and moving along with it.

What was even more extraordinary and more weird, something that was truly alarming, was that none of the passers-by in Opera Square, in Gumhouriyya Street or maybe in the whole of Cairo, was at all astonished or treated the matter as if it was anything untoward, but rather as something quite normal and unremarkable, as if the chair were as light as a butterfly and was being carried around by a young lad. I looked at the people and at the chair and at the man, thinking that I would spot the raising of an eyebrow, or lips sucked back in alarm, or hear a cry of amazement, but there was absolutely no reaction.

I began to feel that the whole thing was too ghastly to contemplate any longer. At this very moment the man with his burden was no more than a step or two away from me and I was able to see his good-natured face, despite its many wrinkles. Even so it was impossible to determine his age. I then saw something more about him: he was naked except for a stout waistband from which hung, in front and behind, a covering made of sailcloth. Yet you would surely have to come to a stop, conscious that your mind had, like an empty room, begun to set off echoes telling you that, dressed as he was, he was a stranger not only to Cairo but to our whole era. You had the sensation of having seen his like in books about history or archaeology. And so I was surprised by the smile he gave, the kind of meek smile a beggar gives, and by a voice that mouthed words:

'May God have mercy on your parents, my son. You wouldn't have seen Uncle Ptah Ra?'

Was he speaking hieroglyphics pronounced as Arabic, or Arabic pronounced as hieroglyphics? Could the man be an ancient Egyptian? I rounded on him:

'Listen here—don't start telling me you're an ancient Egyptian?'

'And are there ancient and modern? I'm simply an Egyptian.'

'And what's this chair?'

'It's what I'm carrying. Why do you think I'm going around looking for Uncle Ptah Ra? It's so that he may order me to put it down just as he ordered me to carry it. I'm done in.'

'You've been carrying it for long?'

'For a very long time, you can't imagine.'

'A year?'

'What do you mean by a year, my son? Tell anyone who asks—a year and then a few thousand.'

'Thousand what?'

'Years.'

'From the time of the Pyramids, for example?'

'From before that. From the time of the Nile.'

'What do you mean: from the time of the Nile?'

'From the time when the Nile wasn't called the Nile, and they moved the capital from the mountain to the river bank, Uncle Ptah brought me along and said "Porter, take it up". I took it up and ever since I've been wandering all over the place looking for him to tell me to put it down, but from that day to this I've not found him.'

All ability or inclination to feel astonishment had completely ended for me. Anyone capable of carrying a chair of such dimensions and weight for a single moment could equally have been carrying it for thousands of years. There was no occasion for surprise or protest; all that was required was a question:

'And suppose you don't find Uncle Ptah Ra, are you going to go on carrying it around?'

'What else shall I do? I'm carrying it and it's been deposited in trust with me. I was ordered to carry it, so how can I put it down without being ordered to?'

Perhaps it was anger that made me say: 'Put it down. Aren't you fed up, man? Aren't you tired? Throw it away, break it up, burn it. Chairs are made to carry people, not for people to carry them.'

'I can't. Do you think I'm carrying it for fun? I'm carrying it because that's the way I earn my living.'

'So what? Seeing that it's wearing you out and breaking your back, you should throw it down—you should have done so ages ago.'

'That's how you look at things because you're safely out of it; you're not carrying it, so you don't care. I'm carrying it and it's been deposited in trust with me, so I'm responsible for it.'

'Until when, for God's sake?'

'Till the order comes from Ptah Ra.'

'He couldn't be more dead.'

'Then from his successor, his deputy, from one of his descendants, from anyone with a token of authorization from him.'

'All right then, I'm ordering you right now to put it down.'

'Your order will be obeyed—and thank you for your kindness—but are you related to him?'

'Unfortunately not.'

'Do you have a token of authorization from him?'

'No, I don't.'

'Then allow me to be on my way.'

He had begun to move off, but I shouted out to him to stop, for I had noticed something that looked like an announcement or sign fixed to the front of the chair. In actual fact it was a piece of gazelle-hide with ancient writing on it, looking as though it was from the earliest copies of the Revealed Books. It was with difficulty that I read:

O chair carrier,
You have carried enough
And the time has come for you to be carried in a chair.
This great chair,
The like of which has not been made,
Is for you alone.
Carry it
And take it to your home.
Put it in the place of honor

And seat yourself upon it your whole life long.

And when you die

It shall belong to your sons.

'This, Mr. Chair Carrier, is the order of Ptah Ra, an order that is precise and was issued at the same moment in which he ordered you to carry the chair. It is sealed with his signature and cartouche.'

All this I told him with great joy, a joy that exploded as from someone who had been almost stifled. Ever since I had seen the chair and known the story I had felt as though it were I who was carrying it and had done so for thousands of years; it was as though it were my back that was being broken, and as though the joy that now came to me were my own joy at being released at long last.

The man listened to me with head lowered, without a tremor of emotion: just waited with head lowered for me to finish, and no sooner had I done so than he raised his head. I had been expecting a joy similar to my own, even an expression of delight, but I found no reaction.

'The order's written right there above your head—written ages ago.'

'But I don't know how to read.'

'But I've just read it out to you.'

'I'll believe it only if there's a token of authorization. Have you such a token?'

When I made no reply he muttered angrily as he turned away:

'All I get from you people is obstruction. Man, it's a heavy load and the day's scarcely long enough for making just the one round.'

I stood watching him. The chair had started to move at its slow, steady pace, making one think that it moved by itself. Once again the man had become its thin fifth leg, capable on its own of setting it in motion.

I stood watching him as he moved away, panting and groaning and with the sweat pouring off him.

I stood there at a loss, asking myself whether I shouldn't catch him up and kill him and thus give vent to my exasperation. Should I rush forward and topple the chair forcibly from his shoulders and make him take a rest? Or should I content myself with the sensation of enraged irritation I had for him? Or should I calm down and feel sorry for him?

Or should I blame myself for not knowing what the token of authorization was?

Translated by Denys Johnson-Davies

Rings of Burnished Brass
A story in four squares

―――∽∞∽―――

The first square

Her back had become a mass of squares, searing, red-hot, little ones inside big ones, full of pain. She should be gentle and think clearly, be tender. But she had never wanted it to be like this, didn't want it now; she must cry out and push him away with all harshness.

'What are you doing? Stop it. Stop it.'

An unexpected development, and she assumed he would react wildly and terrorize her into submission. But, lying half on his side with his leg bent up and his hand hovering, uncertain what to do next, he was silent. His eyes were wide open in astonishment, and his features were those of a child who has done wrong in spite of himself, and wants to be good.

'What's the matter?'

He was scared to come near her, or touch her. She didn't answer. What could she say? How could she make him understand things which she herself, even though she felt them, didn't know how to shape within the limits of comprehensible words. Was this the time to retreat, to make the final renunciation? But how could she, when what she had envisaged as the most abhorrent, the most preposterous turn of events had already come to pass?

Consumed with rage and despair, she felt a hand, like a cat sneaking up to take what it knew it shouldn't have. She pushed it aside with a strength and lack of pity that she hadn't intended, uncharacteristic of her and unfamiliar.

There was silence, so dense that the harsh rattle of the street, the light-hearted cries of playing children, the hum of life outside, was swallowed up. Would Sayyida Zaynab* punish her? She shuddered. Was she losing her mind? Should she scream, or run out, as if there was something to escape from, and tell everybody? Or simply kill herself?

Her mind gave way to distraught meanderings, and before she could think of anything else she glanced sideways at him, imperceptibly, barely moving her eyes in their sockets, and then stopped abruptly: without a sound, without any gathering of pressure, or any concentration of energy on his part or even a shift of position, tears made their way slowly from between his closed eyelids and left their tracks gleaming on his cheeks. And so once again, she was caught up in a rush of feeling like a whirlwind, that made her forget everything and go to him impatiently, embrace him with arms that froze with longing, rain down anxious kisses upon him, summon all her energy to keep him from being hurt, bathing his cheeks and his eyelids with her tongue and, in her excess of desire, delighting in the taste of his tears.

She was finished. Suppose it was his fault, then so be it. She would sooner die than see him weep again, and it was her fate, or her bad luck, all determined in advance—the crowd at the door of Sayyida Zaynab, the push from behind when her foot was poised in mid-air. She had been quite certain that nothing could stop her from falling and her only hope had been that she would not crack her head on the big square tiles. But the arrangement was perfect. As she went down, bound for certain disaster, a hand came out to save her. It seemed not to belong to anyone, as if it were a hand from the skies, but it prevented her falling any further. Then as she lost her balance in the process of recovery an arm went round her, sturdy and capable, and for a split second it made her feel, perhaps for the first time since before her husband had died, quite safe.

So she hadn't fallen, and no bones were broken. But Sayyida, Mother of Hashim, Mother of the Helpless, I did you wrong. Forgive me. Her bag.

---

* Granddaughter of the Prophet. Patron saint of women and the infirm with a mosque containing her shrine in Cairo. Sayyida: 'lady.'

There was the other hand holding it out. And only they did she begin to realize that the arm was still around her. She expressed her thanks, backing away in the confusion of extricating herself from a predetermined fate. What did he say? She didn't know. In the end she had looked into his face, and the shock of it: he was hardly old enough to shave, and all the time she had assumed that she was dealing with a man.

'Why are you crying? Have I done something? Is it me that's upset you?'

'You pushed me away.'

'And that's what upset you!'

'You did it violently, as if you hated me. And you do, you despise me. You want someone rich, and respected. And I'm poor, and the poor don't have feelings as far as people like you are concerned.'

And in spite of himself, of perhaps because he chose to, he burst into tears. She took him in her arms. He didn't understand, it was ridiculous to expect him to. She possessed no faculties which made her capable of expressing to him the feeling that nothing mattered except that she had found him, and at that moment he was dearer to her than the whole world.

'What shall I do to make you believe me?'

'Don't push me away.'

'But I'm old enough to be your mother.'

'She died ten years ago. I haven't got a mother, you know that.'

He tried to speak but the tears choked him. He wanted to tell her how he felt like the abandoned castle in the story when life began to stir in it again. It had happened when he first put his arm round her and she felt not flabby and fat but ladylike and delicate and so soft that you could feel it even through the black silky layers of her clothes. He could have accepted her thanks and gone but he stood there, hesitating, wishing for a moment that she would need him again.

The next step was not arranged by fate. It was true that she had twisted her foot, but she would have been quite able to bear the slight pain and proceed alone. Why then, when she tried to walk, did she exaggerate her suffering and the extent of her injury? Was it because she had noticed that he wavered and that, strange as it may have seemed, he appeared to want her to want him?

With neither a word of objection nor a sign of acceptance from her he walked along beside her supporting her under her arm with a gentleness and tenderness that she had long since forgotten, like that of sons before they become men and transfer their affections to their wives and lovers.

Their stately progress might have been expected to end at the first bus or tram stop or the sighting of a taxi but they continued walking. She didn't request it and he didn't inquire. No conversation passed between them except when from time to time she asked him, 'Am I tiring you?' and he denied it each time with mounting scorn.

'What shall I do to convince you that you're very dear to me?'

'Don't push me off.'

'But I could be your mother. It's not right.'

She was always taking refuge in that, but the way she said 'your mother' was as if she didn't want him to believe in it. With her death his own mother had deprived him of herself and of all female company. Now she, this 'lady,' was giving it back to him all at once and he felt as if he were dreaming, and discovering his hunger and loss for the first time. When he'd supported her, the pressure of her comfortable affectionate body had almost driven him wild, and he had visions of her adopting him as the son she'd always wanted and leaning on him every day with this comfortable familiarity. But then his arm had appeared to begin to take on a life of its own, far removed from any of his thoughts about her. The body which it encircled seemed to melt, luxuriously, and in spite of himself his arm, with its torn overalls hanging off it, participated, and transmitted to him through all her clothes—expensive but much too warm for the time of year—that feeling of softness. The only maternal characteristic left in her then was the trembling softness common to serene well-covered, well-satisfied women who remain feminine well into their sixties, although she didn't look even fifty. In his mind he compared her favorably with the wife of their neighbor the taxi-driver, who after seven years of married life looked as if all the things that had identified her as a woman had withered away.

'Are you tired?'

'A little.'

'It'll be better like this.'

And he supported her with his whole arm so that it encircled her. Now they had come into the area where he lived and she began to learn about him: that he was eighteen, that he worked with his father mending calor gas stoves, was an only child, and that his mother had died during an operation. She had also begun to understand why Sayyida Zaynab was angry with her.

This was not the first time she had gone to her, under protest, and the way there had been long. She had become a grandmother for the fourth time, and mother of a brilliant young company director, a university lecturer with a doctorate, tipped to become a government minister, a used car dealer, the richest of them all, and a daughter who was married and worked abroad.

Her contentment was justified, and need know no bounds. She had done her duty with consummate success, although her late husband had died along the way. People acclaimed her as an exemplary mother, and her children came to visit her at every religious festival and on every special occasion. You're looking well. You will come, won't you? What have you been doing with yourself? But they were only words.

Three men and a woman who didn't need her any more. They talked indulgently to her and teased her gently, and began to make fun of the old things in the flat that had accumulated over the years. Things that they had accorded love, even veneration, while they were growing up. Certainly there were still many ties that bound them so that she was anxious when she learnt that one of them was ill, and they in turn expressed concern for her blood pressure and her diabetes, but it was altogether different from the days when they were her children and she was really their mother. Theirs was the concern we feel for an old toy, when we hold it close and try to burrow into it, hoping to find just one jot of the comfort that it used to offer us; and she was as happy as them if she could give them what they wanted, solace perhaps in the face of that larger society where they now lived their lives, even though a gulf of many years separated them from those early days—except at Friday dinner-times.

From the early morning, she slaved with her old servant to make for each of them what he or she liked best. And in a tumult of noise and gaiety they began to arrive. There was the son whom she would still remind you used to be so pale and skinny when he was a child, grown into a husband; a husband of some long standing with sons and daughters who called her 'Tante,' and 'Granny,' and 'Grandma.' Her boy had become a whole separate family, and had secrets of his own, and whispered and made signs to his wife or to another brother. Only she was excluded from the game, and stood apart.

The food was brought, and they ate. And although deep inside her she had long ago realized that it would have been better for all of them if her cooking had remained a sweet memory, growing more pleasurable with the passing of time, the present reality, staring her in the face, was that they had quite lost their taste for it, and swallowed it with difficulty. For their wives had given them other food, such things as it would never have occurred to the mother to think of preparing, and the meal and their exaggerated approving comments had become a worn-out ritual that she could hardly stomach, as indeed had the whole business of their Friday visits to her.

Her children came to watch their own children hugging the old grandmother, and then amused themselves by making them practice saying her name; and perhaps the occasion aroused a faint childhood memory here and there. It was a charade, and when the players tired of it they would retire, each one in a corner with his wife, or in a group discussing something of no relevance to her. Then from time to time, perhaps at the jolt of a slow-reacting conscience, one of them would lean across toward her with a word, a compliment, or a perfunctory kiss, and it would dawn on her that, although she was in her own home, making them welcome, giving them food, she was an encumbrance that they would feel compelled to cast off before long. And sure enough the chain of discoveries would begin.

One would look at his watch and draw his breath in sharply: 'I forgot. I've got a lecture.'

And the distress of the minutes or hours which she spent with the rest of them, discomfited by her awareness that each one of them must be searching for an original idea, a respectable excuse, that he might use in order to get away himself. Even the children tired of listening to her telling stories and asked to have the television on, and in desperation she would go to the kitchen sometimes, to take refuge with the servants, only to find them immersed in gossip about their ladies and gentlemen and the neighbors, and the latest weddings and divorces amount singers and film stars. In the end after all the dreadful noise and uproar she was alone again in the vast high-ceilinged flat. Even the old servant had taken the afternoon off.

It was nobody's fault. Life was like that, and her children only needed her as a decorative appendage, mother embalmed in the 'family' flat. When her husband had died she hadn't thought for a moment of remarrying or changing her style of life for they were there, her children, not allowing her out of their sight for a moment, so great was their need for her. And she in turn would not let herself be apart from them for long, for she wanted them always to be able to take from the waters of the verdant spring that flowed within her; her greatest happiness was to give herself to them, although it was only natural that the day would come when they no longer needed her. But what was she supposed to do when the mother in her lived on, potent and unsubdued, for she had married and had had children while still young?

'For heaven's sake, why not visit the Sayyida?'

Like a miracle from on high the suggestion came to deliver them from their difficulty, these sons who would enjoin despair and old age on their mother. They wanted her dumb, incapable, passive, dead above the earth's surface in readiness for the time when she should be transported to its depths, as if to erase from their minds the living articulate reality. She wasn't an old woman yet, even if she wasn't as young as she had been when their father died, and old age was something she would resist with all her might, in the near future at least. They wished it on her in part to justify to themselves her being alone, for a life of solitude is taboo for a young girl or a woman in her prime, but acceptable for an old woman. And so the suggestion that she should visit the Sayyida seemed like an answer to prayer.

Have mercy on us, Sayyida.

On Fridays, after the family lunch when she had had the enjoyment of seeing them ranged side by side around the lavish board, the men with their children, the daughter with her husband, and had dandled the grandchildren in turn on her lap, she was to go to the Sayyida and spend the rest of the day at her devotions.

And next year, God willing, you'll go on the pilgrimage to Mecca, and we'll rely on you to pray for us dearest mother, and don't forget to pray that

Muna will be successful and Hamada will get his degree, and that the chairman of the board will resign and leave the way clear for me.

'What do you think about it, mother?'

And they all turned to the youngest brother who had begun to look as if he had found the buried treasure: the Sayyida every Friday, and if you get bored, you can always go to Saint al-Husayn on Mondays, and Saint Hanafy on Thursdays if you like. We're ready to help.

O yes, they were always ready to translate warmth of feeling, courteous attentions and filial duty into their cash equivalents, perhaps because they had begun to have money, while they no longer needed sympathy and demonstrations of affection.

Her fall was obviously devised by the Sayyida to show her anger, for she had never gone to her on her own initiative: she had been pushed by others, not into pious devotion, but toward a fate which she was powerless to stave off.

'We've walked a long way. I'm rather late. Shall we look for a taxi?'

'Are you fed up?'

She stared curiously at him. On his childish features the first vestiges of manhood were visible, giving him that particular beauty common to his age, a radiance which shines out irrespective of individual attributes. He had shaved his mustache, although you could almost count the roots of the shaven hairs one by one. His beard crept hesitantly down the sides of his face only to burst forth triumphantly like a fountain right in the middle of his chin, around and within a dimple. The look in his eyes was not insolent like a man's might have been, nor was the scope of his vision yet subject to the strictures of his will and his defining and limiting awareness. Yet he did not have the impudence of a child, rather the look of somebody who has begun to recognize the existence of other people, and as he looked at them, they were able to look back at him unobstructed. Her eyes had never met with such an entreaty before as, perhaps against his will, he seemed to beg her not to go. There was a world of difference between that and the doctor of philosophy or the company director saying to her, as they closed the door behind her at the end of one of her visits:

'Please . . . please, Mummy, stay and have supper with us.'

'Do you want to go? Won't you rest for a bit. To give the pain a chance to ease off.'

She gazed again at the insistent appeal in his eyes, and couldn't withstand it. It embarrassed her, for he didn't confirm his insistence with words, but left her to make the decision, and bring all her desire to stay into operation to crush her resistance to the idea. And so she asked: 'I really am tired, but where can I rest? I'll have to go.'

But with native cunning, he proposed an alternative. His father was in the shop. Their home was only a few steps away. It had a small sitting-room and one other room. Did she think it would be suitable?

Was he so naive that he didn't realize that anywhere would be suitable since she had received his urgent summons, and that it was what she most wanted to do, to make him happy, as far as it was in her power to do so, and that a wild spirit was surging through her making her capable of anything. She had ignored it always before, and tried to kill it, and her children had ignored it, and everyone around her had preached their values and received wisdom at her in an attempt to stifle it till it died of hunger and neglect and deprivation. But now that it had raised its head so violently it seemed to whirl her along on a magic carpet to a land of youth, vibrant, rumbling and pulsating with the movement of life, in its depths and its heights and on the surface of it: a land of sheer terror.

The look was not all need: at the heart of it there was desire silently burning, like a noiseless howl. But even if there was hell itself there, she, with her will, undertook to extract what she wanted from his look and compel it to give up the rest. He was a child, nothing more than a child, although he was taller than her, and was looking down at her, as if trying to steal a glance at himself through her eyes and see the things that weren't childish in him, the things that a woman might secretly want to take from him.

It was a risk and so she had to feel confident that her view of things would prevail—that she would give him a mother, even if only for a few hours, and that, perhaps unwittingly and very briefly, he would be a son to her; and that in any case she could no longer run away from what was to come.

It was strange, since his arm was still round her supporting her, and in Hanafy Street there were many eyes with little else to do but stare in search of a moment's excitement, strange, that they did not look with disapproval. Even the neighbors assumed she was a rich aunt dutifully seeking out her poor relations. So used were they to accepting all that they were subjected to that they wouldn't even have had any doubts when, as they got near to the top of the stairs leading to the flat, the hand supporting her moved down a little, feeling her back, and growing bolder.

She didn't want any time to be lost in feeling uncomfortable with him, so she made him understand, gently, that she had come with him not to rest, but because he had aroused maternal feelings in her. And it was only natural that she should tell a lie at this point and explain that this was because he reminded her of her own son whom she had lost when he was about the same age. He was motherless, and she was a mother whose children no longer aroused her maternal feelings or had any need of them. So she would be his mother for a little while but if any misunderstanding arose she would leave without further ado.

Of course he showed horror, and reassured her, and accepted her conditions, sure that she meant what she said, and deciding to himself that he would comply and enjoy her mothering him at first and then perhaps if he was lucky get the woman afterward.

'You mean I'm like your son now?'

'And I'm your mother.'

'It's nice idea . . . right, what are we going to do then?'

'What mothers do.'

She took off her outdoor clothes and, as water swilled over the floor that hadn't been cleaned for years, bent down with zeal, in spite of the pain, to polish and clean, while he went in and out noisily singing, happy. She sent him out with a basket and money and he came back with meat and vegetables, and soon the smell of cooking rose up. As the old gas stove slowly cooked the food in the clean orderly room, she went to the bathroom and washed everything she could lay her hands on, including his overalls, so that he sat there in some old clothes she had found for him, a little boy still.

With the washing nearly done, and the smell of food that was ready to eat, and his singing, grown more lusty now, and interspersed with little involuntary chuckles, she felt a happiness such as she had never known before, perhaps not even on her honeymoon. She hadn't married a sweetheart but—as people used to do in those days—an eligible man introduced to the family by a relation; and had it not been for the long cohabiting, the child-bearing, and her sweet disposition, she would have hated him, or who knows, perhaps she would have loved him, at least felt passionate sometimes, unsettled and changeable, instead of that everlasting sameness never soaring upwards and never sinking to the depths.

He had not known happiness like it even when his own mother was alive: for all her long suffocating kisses, she had never spoken to him without swearing at him, and when she took him in her arms his tender feelings were wounded by the thorniness of her rough affection. She had tried to temper it, be more motherly and gentle, but her insensitivity, her coarseness, had always reasserted itself. Now he could hardly remember her, or how he felt about her. All that had gone before was subsumed in his present happiness as, impetuously rushing here and there, laughing, teasing, he was alive as never before. Just as she had expected, her mothering had made him a child again, and this had restored touches of brightness to her that had long since faded, as if she'd just given birth for the first time.

Childishly he lifted the lid of the pot tasting scalding pieces of partly cooked meat, and she reproved him, then told him, in no uncertain terms, that everything in the flat was clean except him, and he was to have a bath, before the meal too. How he relished the situation as he tried to put off the torture till after lunch and she insisted in that deceptively soft way, which you realize belatedly is more intransigent than any abuse.

'Are you going to bathe me then? You're my mother aren't you?'

He knew that he would be refused—he wasn't a baby, but perhaps he did it to find out just how far she would go, to what extent she had become the mother, and at what point she would recoil for shame. She pushed him in the direction of the bathroom, but he did not sense great disapproval. She was absorbed in the game, and what lay behind it was shrouded in obscurity.

'Scrub my back for me. Nobody's done that for me since my mother died.'

Even had she been gifted with extraordinary powers of insight, nothing would have made her understand why she accepted. She shouted at him to sit cross-legged with his back to the door; the loofah was eaten away and she couldn't help her hand coming into contact with his back. The muscles were firmer and harder than she had expected, and this made the heap of living flesh inclining toward her somehow unknown and fraught with danger.

She asked him if he'd scrubbed behind his ears with the loofah, only to discover, after a string of such questions, that he hadn't yet learnt how to bathe himself. Not only had he been deprived of a mother when he was young, but also of love, of a heart full of tenderness for him, of someone to insist that he ate, that he was clean and wholesome: he had been orphaned a thousand times over.

When she had finished and he was squirming to avoid the water pouring over him she had a sudden shock. His genitalia were visible to her for a moment and all at once there could be no more deceiving herself. For hours she had had an image of herself with a beloved son whom she'd come upon by chance, but this slender youth with the manliness that was in him was never he. He was a stranger born of quite another woman, and he had a father whom she had never seen, and a long life before seeing her of which she had only a shred of knowledge.

It was a momentary revelation but he realized, and understood, and was as confused as she was. All was changed when the spontaneous currents of motherly and filial feeling had been severed by a passing glance, and they had to take up their roles deliberately, with embarrassment, and the dreadful participation of the will. The bath ended suddenly, faded out by tacit consent, as if it was the cause of the tragedy.

Strange, after that confused medley of feelings, that, like a random spark, a small feeling of happiness came to her, as it might have come to any mother discovering one day that her son was no longer a child. The question that hung unresolved, as evening gathered in his father's shop, was one that she had not liked to articulate, but the answer came unsolicited: the father would be in a café with friends, smoking till after midnight, straining at a spluttering narghile, spluttering in turn and then relapsing into longer bouts of coughing. Similarly unsolicited came her reply that all that awaited her were the great high walls of the empty flat, and the prayer mat.

'I'm cold. The dirt must have been keeping me warm.'

She laughed at the joke but his teeth began to chatter in earnest. He rushed to fling himself down on the rug, for the high sofa was his father's bed, and pulled the blanket over him, and sneezed several times. If there had been a stove or wood, she would have lit it, but as she searched anxiously for something to protect him from the cold and allay her fears for him, she found nothing there except herself. Making him turn his back toward her, she took him in her arms, thrusting forward her legs and stomach to encompass him, holding him tight until gradually he stopped trembling.

A great feeling of tranquility crept over him, while she was intoxicated, her work done, like a mother who has given suck. But she recognized that her emotion was not because she had warmed him and he had grown still and passive, momentarily savoring a mother's embrace: for him it was a stage on the way to other quite different feelings—not of physical desire, but of something stronger, of tenderness and affection—and she might have been expected to respond to the change, to the strangeness in him, and not to the familiar and accessible. But from utter terror she stifled all such feelings within her.

The second square

Call it love or something else, she did not doubt the depth of her feelings: no one on the face of the earth was dearer to her, even her own children. He meanwhile had found a refuge unlike anything he had known; his drug-addicted father, the women who lusted after him and pressed against him on the narrow stairs, all the miseries in his life, faded into oblivion, and in his rebirth all his dreams were incorporated and past and future deprivations made good.

Call it love, or heaven—and the supreme happiness to him just then might well have been to abandon himself to the dreams which began to dislodge him from reality and bear him gently to sleep; just as her dozing could have been a sign of satisfaction after years of gnawing hunger.

But far away from them and their minds' visions of delight, their bodies were in contact, without an intermediary, leaving their minds to drift where they would while they formed irreversible links.

Bodies don't imagine and dream; they only know how to express themselves by clinging together and holding each other in love or hate, while dreams have imagined confrontations in an intangible world. The physical attraction began against the wills of both of them.

He curled up and grew smaller, in imperceptible movements, as if, left to himself, he would have buried his way into her like a fetus. She, with the decisive behavior of one who has made up her mind to be in opposition, sought to reunite him with his strangely curled-up physical existence, and with his life—his father, the room, his clothes hanging up to dry. She began with his hand—which she had saved, with foresight, from an untoward action—squeezing it in her own fingers, but then took all of him to her as if to put him back where he belonged. The feeling of love which has no physical element at the outset, formed in the imagination, is changed vehemently by close proximity, although the imagination, the idea of the love, and the sensibilities, still participate in the physical attraction which flares up. And even if he had been an angel and she a saint, or if the punishment for it was burning alive, or death at the stake, if the whole world had joined forces to stop them, the outcome would have been the same. The strength of such attraction is part of the mystery and power of life, and suggests that there is a stronger commitment in the scheme of things to uniting what is separate, then to mere propagation and survival.

When mutual affection creates attraction, and then the two beings touch, nothing can come between them. She called upon the saints and the holy men of God, and the Sayyida; upon her past self-control, her father's fond smile, her late mother with ten pilgrimages to her name; and she uttered verses of the Qu'ran, and all the imprecations she knew to drive out devils. And he sought help in the teachings of his Sufi sect and with his shaykh and in the other commands and prohibitions heaped up in his memory. But the hunger of flesh for flesh, the thirst of mouth for mouth, and the urge of legs to twine themselves around legs always triumphs.

Their two bodies lying close were heirs to laws of life more complicated and awesome than all the struggles of humanity to escape from them. What lay between them still was the torment of suppressed emotions that exploded triumphantly from time to time, and forbidden areas, which became accessible by degrees. She clung grimly to her last line of defense as a mother whose children were successful, educated, and in desperation she invoked them as a protection in the existing situation and a guard against what was to come—a safeguard at least from the sensations that were gradually paralyzing her will. Her intention was to stop the gaping void in her consciousness of herself as a mother, restrain her power to give from reaching its limit, at which point, God forbid, it would take only a simple impulse to turn it into a desire to take, a particularized desire for him as he lay small, egg-like, waiting.

All this time his longing for her as a mother was reaching unbearable proportions, so that he wanted her for himself exclusively, to a degree that would mean she was barred from all other human relationships. The superficial characteristics of motherliness were not enough for him and he searched straining to reach, and capture for himself, the center and essence of the motherliness in her: the mother can always accommodate herself to any number of children, but only one man gets the woman and she is his alone.

Their reactions to each other, bold sometimes, embarrassed and inhibited at others, took place in the presence of a long history of rules and prohibitions, eclipsed from time to time by other laws of life which asserted themselves more strongly. He would begin to behave like a lover and she would scold him like a mother, or she would hold him hoping to quieten him down and her motherly embrace would catch fire; and the four, the son and the woman, and the mother and the young man, would show no mercy to each other, nor to specters from their present lives or others made sacrosanct by the passing of time. In the flame of the rising heat things burnt which are considered incombustible, and prohibitions melted away. The past and the future disintegrated, leaving only the woman taking refuge in the mother in her, and the son distraught, seeking the female hidden inside this mother.

But after all, and however much the affair may seem to have become of purely sensual concern directed by automatic responses, the human body possesses a strange and magical member, the mind, without whose participation and concurrence it would not move an inch independently.

She made a desperate effort: she had summoned her children before her like an army of storm-troopers and from their ranks leapt her grandchildren condemning their grandmother's behavior, while their fathers looked at her through the scornful eyes of their wives. She thought of her husband and the years of struggle after his death, and her dogged refusal to marry again; past history massed to ward off one decisive moment in the present. As if in answer to her fervent prayers the miracle happened and the mother and celibate widow resumed control, the horror of what she was doing struck her forcibly and she let him go.

Perhaps it was because he had little past to be aware of, or else it was a characteristic of the difference in their ages, but he could not bring himself back to the present or hide the desire which had begun to blind him. He had reached the point where it was too late for him to stop or go back. Just as it was inconceivable that the situation should have arisen, so it was now inconceivable that it should be reversed.

The third square

The squares, whose surface was eaten away and whose edges protruded unevenly, were the big white stone tiles of the floor in the flat. The worn cheap rug was not enough to camouflage their rough edges, and they and the high sofa and the three-legged metal table and the window full of washing spread out to dry were their witnesses. They were witnesses not to the fact that a woman in her fifties had gone home with a boy of eighteen— walking although she'd twisted her ankle—nor to the fluctuations of rejection and desire; more accurately perhaps to a battle being waged inside each one of them. The nature of the battle was obscure and ill-defined because clouds of varying degrees of embarrassment swirled about it and enveloped the surrounding area: there was to start with the simple embarrassment of the mother and son recognizing each other as man and woman, and suddenly the lover in him came to the fore and he embraced her neck and covered it with kisses. They were frenzied boyish kisses, and she whispered firmly:

'You mustn't do that. I'm old enough to be your mother. My children are older than you. I'm a grandmother, don't you believe me?'

As speech had ceased to have any effect she used her hand, pushing him away gently as a mother would to a son who was annoying her. And the annoying son advanced upon her insistently once more, so she showed him the gray hairs, to make him believe, only to discover, with him, that this inflamed him more. Whenever she portrayed herself in the image of his mother or tried to evoke filial responses in him, this had an effect the reverse of what she had intended, on a youth who now appeared to be aroused by the very fact that she was a mother, his mother. Worse still, every time she convinced herself that his behavior so far fell within the definition of what could be properly expected of a son, she felt impulses rearing up inside herself which frightened her because they made her unfamiliar to herself. The characteristics of this woman were not in keeping with the one who had been a dutiful daughter whom her parents had brought up, educated and married off so that she could beget children who bore children in their turn. She was more feminine than anything she had imagined in her life about herself as a woman, and she was imprisoned, and rumbling menacingly, threatening an explosion whose repercussions would extend God alone knew how far. These impulses, this unfamiliar woman in her, were like a powerful extension of her motherhood, reaching out, and she had an unconquerable wish to engulf him and possess him, to make him once again a part of her, because, with her children there looking on, this boy, this stranger, still seemed to her closer and more son-like than any of them.

And he wavered between shyness of her and desire for her, shy even of his masculinity, but shyer still of her femininity. It was as if he wanted to distill the motherly qualities in her until he found the woman, or to take the motherly feelings in her which were exclusively for him, and manipulate them until they became those of a lover. But be she mother or lover, it no longer satisfied him to clasp her to him or lie still in her embrace. He moved to her impetuously to join with her, to be absorbed into her and extinguished, like a planet returning to its mother star after a long weary circling.

For all that passed, there was something inside her which hadn't stopped since the shrine. It reminded her continually of its presence and shouted at the top of its voice: 'No . . . no . . . no.' It had grown fainter sometimes, perhaps, but all the while it was really gathering momentum, until she started up, pushing him away with all the fierce strength she possessed. As if a sharp object had hit him on the head, he woke from his reverie, the rejected orphan, sensing the unreality of what had charmed him.

It was only then that tears began to gather in his eyes in spite of himself and run down his face, and he looked straight in front of him, grief-stricken, without hope: his mother was lost to him and he was like a child standing alone, watching other children with their mothers and fathers dancing up and down for joy.

This was the expression bathed in tears that she had noticed when she glanced sideways at him, and that had stopped her in her tracks. Come what may, she could never let him feel bereaved a second time; it was the glance of a mother to a son at a crucial moment which threatened to call her motherhood into question. And these were the impetuous huggings and kissings that washed away his tears and caressed his broken features.

'Why were you pushing me a way then?'

'I won't do it again.'

'It wasn't an answer, but a decision. And she acknowledged that she might go straight to hell for it.

'Come here. Come to me.'

She didn't take him in her arms nor did he take her. The distance between them that had remained so great all along was swallowed up, and time evaporated.

The lightning flash as the two poles made contact rocked the square-tiled floor and rattled the windows, and would have brought the whole house down if it had gone on for longer.

The fourth square

When she went back to her big flat, she found it small, and in the mirror the expression reflected there was one she hadn't seen for thirty years.

When the next Friday came, her children were all surprised at the old woman that they had intended her to be, bursting with life, more mobile and energetic than them, and exuding joy like a girl again.

'Didn't I tell you—the Sayyida's done wonders already!'

It was quite unprecedented when she was the first to make her excuses, and her pretext was ready-made: the Sayyida couldn't wait.

There were many catastrophes in the universe, many disruptions in the ordering of human affairs, but the regularity of her appointments with the

Sayyida was never broken. After she had filled their stomachs with food and nourished them with a strange tenderness, like a spurt of oil from an abandoned well, and cared for them, and smothered them with maternal feelings, which had become almost too much for them to take, she made her excuses and went to visit the Sayyida.

And every time, with terror, she caught sight of the saint's shrine in the distance and muttered 'Forgive me.'

It was as if time had ceased to exist for her and had no effect on her life, since she had met him. The day when it moved on again was one that she had always taken into her calculations, and foreseen coming, but still when it came she was surprised. She stood where she was, confused, not wanting to believe that the hand wasn't there this time and wouldn't lead her to the room of squares in Hanafy.

When the hours went by and he didn't appear, she began making her way hesitantly to the shop, which was not far from the mosque and the Sayyida's shrine. But she came to a halt before she reached it. He was there, the owner of the shop since his father died, but he was not alone. In front of the shop was a girl, about eighteen, perhaps less—and she did not cease to wonder at the perfection with which she had wound her robe about her. He was haggling with her about the repair of a calor gas stove in words that were full of intimacy and hinted at an understanding of another sort, and the girl was laughing and he was smiling.

She looked at him with new eyes, as if she hadn't seen him properly since the first time, the first time . . . .

He was quite different, unshaven, and his beard had begun to grow profusely, black and thick. His laughter was manly, less sweet, and his voice was harsher, with a decisive no. He no longer looked at the world with welcoming eyes and marveled at it, but looked only to mark out his own path in it. He had grown up, that was clear, joined the ranks of men, where mothers are a burden.

She felt no need to give vent to her misery, and she could stop the world spinning round her, for she wasn't annoyed or sad or surprised, nor even resentful toward the girl, or him. She realized in a vague way, with no ill-feeling, that she too no longer had anything to give him, no more motherliness, no more feelings of any sort; the lush green volcano had run dry.

In the mirror of her handbag she examined her gray hairs, quite visible despite the dye, and the lines around her eyes and on her neck. And she moved away, in the direction of the mosque.

Secretly she asked forgiveness, and it was as if it were granted, for in her humility and submission a desire came to her, and she went toward the saint's shrine.

She stood there for a long time, not knowing what to say or do. Then she had an inspiration, or obeyed an instinct, and approached the brass wall surrounding the shrine. Alongside the other men and women there she grasped one of the burnished brass rings worn down with much use. She gripped it tightly, clinging to it as if the ground at her feet was opening to swallow her up.

No one needed her now, and she needed no one. This was real loneliness as she had never imagined it could be. Like the first signs of winter, noiselessly, it had come. There was no escaping from it: it was as decisive as the change which made her son into someone else's father, or her as she had been into her as she was now, returning to be a daughter, to a mother that didn't exist.

Perhaps that was why they called her Mother of the Helpless, for a human being is no longer a human being, if not father or mother, son or daughter. When a man's manhood, and his fatherhood, is at an end, he becomes a son again, and the same is true for a woman—a rule with no exceptions. But just for the moment she was utterly alone, like Sayyida Zaynab herself who was surrounded by men and women clinging to the rings on the outside of her shrine, each one of them alone like her, driven on by the hope that they could become sons and daughters again—their best hope the saint, the mother of those who have nothing.

And the saint was alone in her grave while the crowd jostled around it, desperate to the point of tears to catch hold of one of the rings and extricate themselves from their loneliness, feeling that in her they had found a mother, even if she were mother of them all. She was alone in her grave. And around her the men and women clung alone.

God have mercy on the saint as well as all of them.

Translated by Catherine Cobham

The Shaykh Shaykha

———〜〜〜———

V ast and numerous are God's countries, and each village has its fill of everything, the old and the young, boys and girls, people, families, Muslims and Copts—a vast realm regulated by some laws and made sleepless by others. However, there are exceptions, as in our village which was distinguished from God's other countries by the presence in it of this living creature that cannot be classified as one of its inhabitants or people or even, for that matter, as one of its animals. It could not be considered the missing link either—this nameless, self-existent being whom they sometimes called Shaykh Muhammad and sometimes Shaykha Fatima, but only at times, and for the sake of expediency because he had in fact no name, no father or mother, no one who could tell where he came from, or whose study frame he had inherited. As to his having human features, he had features all right: he had two eyes, two ears and a nose, and he walked on two feet, but the problem was that these features of his took completely inhuman shapes. His neck, for example, leaned horizontally on one of his shoulders like a plant that has been trampled down at an early age and has grown crawling alongside the ground. He always kept one eye half-opened and the other one tightly closed, and he never once narrowed the one or widened the other. His arms dangled from his shoulders in a way that made one feel they were not connected to the rest of his body, like the sleeves of a washed garment as it hangs to dry.

His short, heavy, kinky, brushlike hair brought home a problem that called for attention since there were no tokens of femininity in it, and that it was also devoid of any tokens of masculinity. His body was heavy, of average height, and solid and large like a wall, but his face bore no signs of a beard or a mustache. His voice might have settled the dilemma of his sex, thus admitting him in either the world of women or that of men had it not been for the fact that he did not speak, and never even moved unless he was injured or in pain. A shrill hiss would then break out of him that could not be identified as a female or a male hiss, or even as a human hiss at all.

He rarely walked, and when he did, he toddled along as if fettered. Standing was his favorite occupation. He could go on standing next to you, or in front of your shop, or in your courtyard for hours and hours, like a sinless culprit, and it never even occurred to him that he could move. No one knew how he ate or wherefrom. Whenever he was offered food he refused it. Some people hold that he fed on grass from the fields, that his favorite dish was clover and that he drank, like the cattle, from the irrigation canal. All this was idle talk, however—mere idle talk for no one ever dared claim to have been an eye-witness.

Had such a creature ever existed anywhere else, people would have considered it a phenomenon worthy of study and research. They would at least have published his picture in the newspapers and he would have been interviewed. However, our fellow villagers did not in the least consider him an abnormal creature—he was a different kind of creature, and that was all. So long as he lived amongst them, harming no one, bringing no evil upon anyone, no one objected to his life: it was a sacrosanct sin for anyone to protest, or for someone to stare at him or ridicule his standing posture or his twisted neck, for all that was God's will, and if the Maker wills something, there's no escaping his will; no worshiper may question His order, even when it seems to go wrong. How often is the order disrupted so that the world seems chaotic; how many are the possessed, the half-witted, the disfigured and the insane? At all events, they all do and must live, bound together by the solemn, slow procession as it marches to its endless end. All there was to it was that the villagers treated the Shaykh Shaykha with a special kind of awe unadulterated by that blending of veneration and scorn with which they looked upon the holy and the possessed alike. It was also devoid of that blending of pity and disgust with which they looked upon the crippled and the sick. It could have been the awe normally inspired by the sight of something alien and eccentric which, through its very abnormality, unveils the essence of the wonderful Order that encompasses the world and the people, an awe inspired by the order itself rather than by its violation. Whenever he came upon a group of people, they would avoid looking at him determined as they were not to make him feel they had noticed his presence. One or two might steal a quick, probing glance at him, but they would immediately avert their eyes, and their mouths would carry on their conversation regardless of the fact that he was standing nearby, rooted in his place like the trunk of a tree that has suddenly sprouted from the earth. But when his long stations attracted the children's attention so that they crowded around him, irreverent and fearless, to watch him, the adults drove them away. One of them inevitably set out to chase them even into the crevices and alleys of the village. And woe to them if one of them ever thought of teasing him or pricking him with a cotton twig to make him emit that mysterious, shrill hiss of his!

The Shaykh Shaykha thus spent long years in our village, and people absolved him of all the duties of men, animals and plants, but he nevertheless kept all their rights. He cold stand rooted to the ground like a plant or hiss like an animal if he wished, or move around freely like a human being, and no one would rebuke him or stand in his way. He could walk into any house and keep crouching in any of its corners for as long as he wished and his presence would never disturb the household. They never even felt his presence as though, at his arrival, he became part of the premises, the moment or the air. The women undressed in his presence and so did the men and, in his presence, families discussed their most intimate affairs. A man would sleep with his wife or another woman, plots would be contrived and complaints filed in front of him, and a person would whisper to the other when wishing to reassure him that he may speak up freely: 'Speak up, man, speak up . . . . Don't be afraid . . . . There's no-one here but you and I and the Shaykh Shaykha . . . . Speak up!'

Nevertheless, a rumor would break out every few years and would then die down, feebly melting away and vanishing on people's tongues as soon as it reached them. They once said that something peculiar was going on between him and lame Na'sa. In fact, she was often seen searching the night for him with her eyes. Sometimes, she even inquired about him, and she was often seen coming out of the vacant lot near the mosque where he spent most of his nights. According to one rumor they were certainly having an affair. Owing to another, he was her son and had been born in that state because she had got pregnant while whoring with his bad-blooded father, a man from the city where Na'sa went to sell cheese, milk and faggots of firewood at dawn. However, people did think it over a thousand times before believing any of these rumors since Na'sa could hardly have been considered a woman at all. She had a robust frame like men, she was harsh in dispute and tough when she joined in brawls: she beat up the men one by one and walked out uninjured without ever even tearing her clothes. Her husband died when she was young and she rolled up her sleeves and went into many feminine jobs, but she was more like a man in disposition, and this probably prevented her from ever remarrying and made her settle down in the end for a job that called for her strong muscles and big bones: she carried firewood, hay, meal, and whatever men could not or would not carry. Her only equipment was a round pad made out of rags that she had stitched into the shape of a doughnut, and when she placed it on her head she could carry a camel's load. She would walk untiringly, steadily carrying her burden, haughtily stumping the ground, while she twisted her legs foppishly to make her anklets—that she never parted with and that were perhaps the only sign of her femininity—tinkle. Such were, one by one, the distinguishing traits of that woman who could grind at the heaviest burdens and at the hardest tasks. Her only shortcoming was that, unless she carried a load, she could not walk properly: she wobbled along like a grasshopper as her steps wavered between a feminine swing and a masculine steadiness, and hence they nicknamed her 'the lame.' The men gave her that name out of envy, and the women in disparagement, and they all did it unjustly. Could anyone as rough as she was ever have had an affair with the Shaykh Shaykha and could anyone possibly imagine that she could ever have been a boy's mother, even if her son happened to be that very same creature?

Nevertheless, they insisted. They said that she hid him after his birth in the vacant lot where he took refuge after he grew up. They said that she breastfed him in secret, nursed him away from the reach of inquisitive eyes, and finally let him go as a full-grown boy with teeth.

One year there was more prattle than usual about the lewdness of women and their debauchery. Some even went as far as claiming that certain sex-starved females living on the outskirts of the village went to the Shaykh Shaykha, certain as they were of his absolute silence.

A story went around once that the Shaykh Shaykha was not, like the rest of humanity, the son of a man, but that he was rather the son of an ape. They said that a village woman, weary of her sterility, had resorted to a gipsy who prescribed her a 'woolen cloth' that she used and that, much to her bad luck, the cloth was imbibed with an ape's sperm which made her conceive and deliver the Shaykh Shaykha. They said that she was so appalled by him when he was born that she handed him over to a gipsy whose silence she bought and whom she paid to nurse him. The gipsy took the newborn baby along in her wanderings around God's countries, brought him back when he grew up and left him just outside the village.

Another strange story spread the following year, certifying to the contrary, stating that the Shaykh Shaykha was no other than the son of 'Abdu al-Bitar who sheared the donkeys and pared their hooves before nailing their new iron shoes on them and who—but only the tale-tellers can warrant this claim—had a predilection for their females in general, and for Shaykh al-Bilidi's, the *ma'zun**'s, she-ass in particular. They said that Shaykh al-Bilidi got rid of the newborn so that no one would suspect him or his son who was reputedly addicted to the same vice.

Idle talk, tales, rumors, unfounded and faint and infrequent but recurring. People thus reaffirmed their determination to solve this living riddle. There had to be an explanation, a reason to his presence among them. There must indeed be a reason for everything; even the irrational must have a rational motivation. However, there were only rumors and anecdotes that

---

* Official authorized to perform civil marriages.

did not explain or clarify anything, some of which were told for the sole purpose of entertainment.

The Shaykh Shaykha might very well have stayed on in the village as the perfect embodiment of a present-absent-mounted-walking-inexistent-living being had not one of the 'Ubayda boys run toward the mosque, panting, collapsing, seating himself, trembling, almost fainting, amidst the crowd that usually squats all night near the mill's alley:

'What is it boy! What's happened?'

Stuttering and rattling like all the 'Ubaydas, he said:

'It seems the Shaykh Shaykha can hear and speak like a windbag!'

'How's that boy? It's impossible! Utterly unbelievable! How did you find that out?!'

The boy swore on his father's grave that he was walking near the vacant lot when he heard two people talking in muffled voices that they gradually raised, so he went closer and found the Shaykh Shaykha talking to lame Na'sa, using words as correct as anyone's. He could not believe himself so he went even closer, but Na'sa charged and he ran away and came, panting and trembling, to tell the story.

Naturally, no one in the assembled crowd believed him, and neither did all those who heard the news later. They all agreed that the boy was raving. Surely he must have been so scared of the vacant lot that he had imagined it all. The two speakers could also very probably have been djinns. Indeed, this was far more probable than the Shaykh Shaykha being able to speak, to utter or to understand words at all. Could he possibly have deceived everyone for so many years? And besides, why should he have deceived them, what could he have gained from doing so, why should he have tortured himself, standing for hours, sleeping like an animal, living like a worm?

However, despite the convincing arguments and the people's adamant refusal to believe one word out of what the boy said, despite themselves and, unintentionally, whenever they saw the Shaykh Shaykha nailed to the ground near one of their gatherings, their looks became inquisitive and suspicious due to the sheer possibility—although it was an irrational possibility—that the boy could have been telling the truth. What if the

Shaykh Shaykha had had the capacity to see and hear and understand everything that had been said and done in front of him all his life?

Whenever that question arose in their heads, they shook them in horror
and refusal. What a great catastrophe, in fact the calamity of calamities, if
it were true! All those years during which he had been treated like a haunt-
ing creature that cannot see or hear or understand, he had actually been able
to witness the circumstances and secrets of every inhabitant of the village,
which no other human eye had ever witnessed. Every human being in the
village lives like a boat: part of him rises on the surface of the water for
every eye to see, and the rest remains underwater, invisible. Even if sharp-
sighted people can fathom what comes close to the surface, it is quite
impossible to perceive the deeply submerged parts that no hand, eye or ear
can reach out for. They cannot be reached unless their owner lifts them out
since he alone knows about them. If man is a being who has secrets, and
if it is in his human nature to conceal certain things and to hide them deep
within himself, it is also part of his everlasting nature to hide them against
his own will so that he is compelled to yield from time to time, to come
out with them, to expose and analyze them, maybe years later, but he must
come out with them, maybe just for himself, in writing, or to the person
closest to him or most remote, provided they seem capable of keeping a
secret. The Shaykh Shaykha sometimes played this part for some people,
and he sometimes saw what nobody else had ever seen or heard what
nobody else had ever heard for the simple reason that he was nobody. He
was like a tame animal, like a pet cat or dog, for instance. The horrors that
cats and dogs witness in households! If pet cats and dogs could talk no
one would be able to live. For a man to live as an individual, he must wrap
himself in garments and clothes to shield his body and its secrets, and to
live as an individual within a community, he must hedge parts of himself
behind walls and call these parts secrets: they contain his being, his keys
and his innermost longings which distinguish him from others and safeguard his integrity. The family, with all its members, must surround itself
with a thick-walled house so it can also have an existence, an identity and
an independence of its own. Even the village should surround itself with
an imaginary wall and boundaries, and a nationality as well as words like

'my village' and 'my fellow-villagers' to preserve itself from destruction and dissolution.

If the news were true, therefore, it would be a great catastrophe, even if there were the slightest doubt as to its veracity. This might not yet mean the destruction of the inner walls that protect and separate them all, but it would at least mean a chink in every wall: a chink, through which whatever is inside can seep out so that a day of havoc, certainly more frightful and horrid than the day of judgment, would begin.

From then on, they began to cast on the Shaykh Shaykha looks filled with fear and dismay that hovered around him, blinded by the fever of suspicion, while the Shaykh Shaykha remained as he was: his neck bent and his blue garment tattered and stained. If he stood, he kept on standing, and if he sat he did not move, one eye half-open and the other one as tightly closed as ever. His features were as they had always seen them—hard, frozen, still; they had obviously always been still. Even now that suspicion drove them to surround him, to accost him, to talk to him and to question him, he never moved, and no one ever caught the least flicker of emotion on the surface of this compact block of flesh, bones and fat.

It was a while before the storms stirred by the news began to abate and give way to acceptance and contentment. Fear had seized everyone of them at the thought that a chink may have well been started in one's wall through which a conscious eye had peeped, discovering whatever there was inside. This fear now abated, giving way to serenity while the suspicion that went along with it gradually froze into conviction.

All this would have ended like any ordinary gossip had it not been for another incident that was not reported by a coward or a boy but by full-grown men who saw it with their own eyes and heard it with their own ears and who were ready to repeat it under oath. On a market day, in al-Sa'dawi's shed under the bridge where passersby have coffee, tea or *ma'assal** the

---

* A mild-tasting tobacco prepared with molasses, glycerine, fragrant oil, and essences.

conversation turned around the 'Ubayda boy's story. The Shaykh Shaykha was standing motionless in the sun on the bridge, heavily drenched with perspiration. Lame Na'sa at some point became the unavoidable subject of conversation and several men defamed and slandered her, carelessly boasting as they told real events and facts, to the point where the sense of competition drove one of them to swear that she had tried to seduce him. At that point, they all suddenly heard a scream or, more precisely, something like a scream because what they heard was not a real scream nor was it a cry for help or a howl. It was more like an explosion, a roar or a camel's snort, followed by a long moan. Then, which is even more important, a word was spoken, and some heard 'God forbid!' while others heard 'God damn you!,' and each of them swore that he had said the truth. At all events, one thing was certain: they had all heard human speech issuing from the vicinity, and when they turned round they saw the Shaykh Shaykha leaving his place in the sun and moving faster than he had ever done, instantly disappearing into the nearest maize field to reappear no more.

However, despite everything that had happened and despite the general consensus and agreement of those present, if you questioned each one of them individually a day or two later, pressing him, putting him on his oath, he would answer: 'Actually I can't swear to it . . . . God alone knows . . . but if it were not him who could it have been? The bridge?'

How many oaths were given and how many threats made! The village was in a turmoil of controversy; many of them insisted that they had been duped as they had never been before by the Shaykh Shaykha who has shammed the deaf and dumb act for years to pry into their circumstances and secrets and to rob their hoards.

Many others would sooner believe the bridge could speak rather than the Shaykh Shaykha. However, all the disputes and disagreements only went from mouth to mouth while a sharp fear massed up inside all of them and, whenever anyone recollected whatever he had said and done in the presence of the Shaykh Shaykha and realized that he had said and done an awful lot, his fear would turn to terror and frenzy. He would then turn the village upside down to find him, if only to catch sight of him, since perhaps seeing him, just seeing him, might restore one's peace of mind and all that talk might turn out to be lies, only lies, a dreadful harrowing nightmare flooding the village and its people.

Furthermore, the Shaykh Shaykha was not to be found anywhere despite the great number of people who looked for him. This only made things worse, for where had he been and to whom was he now repeating his stories?

At all events, his disappearance did not last long. A few days later, they saw him returning from town, and the strangest thing was that Na'sa led him by the hand. As soon as the news spread, the whole village was there: young and old, especially the women who seemed terrified, trembling with anger and fear, making up a big black spot in the tight human circle that crowded around Na'sa and the Shaykh Shaykha. The eyes of the whole village were riveted on the two of them avidly and resentfully. Yet nothing about the Shaykh Shaykha had changed: same blue sack, same short hair— the only thing was that his twisted neck had started to straighten up. Furthermore, the laughs that broke out of him whenever someone asked him a question or addressed him were rather dismaying. They were strange laughs that were more like words than like laughter.

As for Na'sa, she kept silent for a while and then, as if suddenly unable to control herself, she broke out asking them why they were thus assembled, insulting them, cursing their fathers, from the youngest to the oldest: 'Bastards! Lice! What do you want?! What business is it of yours if he is or is not my son and if he is or is not dumb?! He was ill and I assisted him: is that a crime? And even if he had not been ill, if he had been in good health, if he had been able to hear and see, what could he possibly have heard or seen? We're all in the same boat; whoever slanders will be slandered and whoever hides his fault from his neighbor will find that his neighbor hides a similar fault from him! What could he possibly have seen or heard?! Get out of my way or I swear if I ever lay my hands on one of you I won't let go until I've choked the life out of him!'

The people listened to Na'sa in stupor and amazement, not knowing how to answer her; as they witnessed this sudden outburst of fervor that stripped her of all shame and restraint. She was even willing to confess, for example, that the Shaykh Shaykha was her son and was even ready, if need be, to reveal his father's name. Their ears were deafened by the lava that poured out of her mouth, and they had no solution and no answer to what she said.

But sooner or later they had to disperse. The next day came, and the day after, and the Shaykh Shaykha started going out on his own again, roaming around the village, standing in his customary way near the gatherings as they sat or stood in a corner. The conversation would stop for a while at his arrival, but if it were resumed, if someone began to talk and happened to look toward the Shaykh Shaykha as he talked, the Shaykh Shaykha would startle him with his newly acquired laugh, and the laugh would engender all sorts of doubts in the man's head, and he would then stutter and feel compelled to keep silent since, who knows, while he now sat lecturing on matter like robberies and thieves, the Shaykh Shaykha could be making fun of him for that measure of wheat that he had seen him steal in the barn on the day of storage. Or maybe he laughed because he knew about the bloodstain on the hem of his gallabiya for he stood in the same place that day and, finally maybe he made fun of him, because only yesterday he had sung a completely different tune in another gathering where the Shaykh Shaykha had also been.

The next day came, and the day after, and people began to realized that their worst fear had come true. They realized that the Shaykh Shaykha's laughter was the very peephole that had been cleft in every wall, that the contents of their hidden, secret storerooms were now menaced, that they now stood naked in front of the Shaykh Shaykha, stripped of everything that shielded them and protected their personality, their dignity and their integrity, and that they could not live in the same village with him, with a human being who knew everything about them and who confronted them with his strange, horrid laugh wherever they went.

It had become unavoidable, then, that people should wake up in terror one morning due to the echoing screams of a howling, broken heart: 'My son . . . . My darling . . . .'

Feet rushed in fear toward the voice which surged out of the vacant lot. It belonged to Na'sa, and they were really taken aback by the hail of stones and rocks that she hurled at them. She bitterly sobbed and cursed, saying that he had been deaf and dumb all his life and that she wouldn't let them get away with it . . . The Shaykh Shaykha lay down in a pool of blood at her feet. His head had been smashed with a stone.

Translated by Ragia Fahmi and Saneya Shaarawi Lanfranchi

It's Not Fair

———ϖ———

We had a friend called Abd al-Magid, whose very name was synonymous with hashish. One of the few real connoisseurs of the stuff, his experience of it was both vast and various. While we always found him permanently high, we could also be sure that his pocket invariably housed yet further reserves.

Many were the days when Abd al-Magid became for us an endless topic of conversation. He was a man whose every word was a joke, his every retort a play on words, and at the mere mention of his name each of us was able to recount tens of stories about his experiences with Abd al-Magid or his antics.

Abd al-Magid worked as a doctor at a large hospital. While most people believe that doctors are necessarily short, stoutly-built, pot-bellied, and thick-necked and that they wear spectacles and a benign air, Abd al-Magid was quite the opposite, being tall, lean, and of a pallid complexion.

But I don't want to digress about Abd al-Magid (which would be only too easy), for his life story was like that of life itself: having found a beginning to it, one never succeeded in discovering an end.

The point of our story is that he was once on night duty and had to stay awake in readiness for the various accidents the city would be hatching. He was not one to let such an occasion pass without making the very minutest preparations for it. He had therefore smoked until his eyes, though not white, were not yet red but had become a sort of betwixt and between of delicate pink. And so, seated in the casualty ward, he waited for the shouting hordes of the ill and ailing to flock in.

Right in the vanguard of these hordes a problem presented itself. A police officer entered accompanied by two constables in charge of a short, bowed man with sunken cheeks. Placing numerous papers on the doctor's desk, the officer briefly put him in the picture. He informed him that they had raided a hashish den and that everyone had made his escape except for this one man whom they'd managed to arrest. On searching him they had come across a piece of hashish which he had somehow managed to swallow. They had therefore brought him along so that the piece might be retrieved by the judicious use of a stomach pump.

The problem intrigued our friend Abd al-Magid: it was one that possessed a certain charm and the solution to it differed from anything else that had come his way so far. He gazed at the handcuffed man standing in front of him and inquired of him in a tone that mingled authority with guile, 'Come along—did you swallow it or throw it away?'

The man answered in a tone of utter meekness, prodigious humility, and extreme childlike innocence. 'Me, sir? Swallowed what? . . . Honestly, I don't even know what the stuff looks like! By the Prophet, I've been wronged! It's not fair!'

Abd al-Magid looked at him: the man had gone up in his estimation. He smiled as though to say, 'That's the way, my lad! May God protect you!'

In addition to this silent encouragement, Abd al-Magid insisted that the handcuffs be removed. After a short argument, the officer—red-faced, yellow-mustached, and blue-eyed—agreed.

While it is the doctor himself who should undertake the business of the stomach pump, it can in no sense be termed an operation and can easily be carried out by any nurse. The doctor therefore ordered the male nurse Abd al-Salam to prepare the solution, and the prisoner—still accompanied by the two policemen—departed to another room, leaving the doctor and the officer alone in the office.

As it was impossible to remain silent forever, the conversation broke ground on the subject of the girl pictured in the magazine held by the doctor, branched off when the two of them discovering that they had been contemporaries at the same secondary school, that they were both crazy about the songs of Umm Kulthoum, that the officer lived in Abbasiya, where Abd al-Magid had a group of friends, and that neither of them had yet taken his holiday because their respective bosses were always giving pressure of work as an excuse for their not being spared. Before the series of discoveries had come to an end the officer said, 'My dear fellow, it's really enough to drive you mad! There we were, just settling down to a great session on the roof of a house of someone we know in Heliopolis—a friend of ours had just got back from Palestine absolutely loaded with the stuff. The party was all set, with Umm Kulthoum singing "The Moonlit Nights Have Come," and we were just warming up and feeling on top of the world when along comes a detective with a search warrant. What could I do? I had to break away from the party and go off with him. What a bloody life it is! Honestly, isn't it enough to drive you mad?!'

The doctor agreed with him that it was truly maddening, while he gazed at the officer's beautiful eyes, whose blue pupils were foundering in a pool that, though not white, was not yet red but was a sort of betwixt and between of delicate pink. Before he could agree with him further and recount a similar experience that had happened to him one night when he was high, Abd al-Salam the nurse entered with a cry of joy, as though he had discovered America.

'Here's the piece, sir. The man brought it up. It's a good two piasters' weight.'

'Two piasters' weight?' interposed one of the policemen. 'I'll cut off my right arm if it's not a good quarter of an ounce and then some.'

'And it's a lovely piece, too—real quality stuff,' said the other policeman, with a knowing nod of his head.

The doctor and the officer hurried out of the office and stood either side of the short man, who was lying on a table and emptying his stomach of all its contents, both good and bad. The doctor called out to Abd al-Salam to put the piece of hashish, together with everything else brought up by the stomach pump, into a sealed envelope as a court exhibit.

The officer's pink eyes sparkled with joy at having proved the crime and having the evidence safely under seal. The man was led away, placed once again in handcuffs. As he walked off between his escorts, he could be heard muttering in a weak, agitated voice, 'It's not fair. By God, it's not fair.'

House of Flesh

———⟋⟋⟋———

he ring is beside the lamp. Silence reigns and ears are blinded. In the silence the finger slides along and slips on the ring. In silence, too, the lamp is put out. Darkness is all around. In the darkness eyes too are blinded.

The widow and her three daughters. The house is a room. The beginning is silence.

The widow is tall, fair-skinned, slender, thirty-five years of age. Her daughters too are tall and full of life. They never take off their flowing clothes which, whether they be in or out of mourning, are black. The youngest is sixteen, the eldest twenty. They are ugly, having inherited their father's dark-skinned body, full of bulges and curves wrongly disposed; from their mother they have taken hardly anything but her height.

Despite its small size, the room is large enough for them during the daytime; despite the poverty of it, it is neat and tidy, homely with the touches given to it by four females. At night their bodies are scattered about like large heaps of warm, living flesh, some on the bed, some around it, their breathing rising up warm and restless, sometimes deeply drawn.

Silence has reigned ever since the man died. Two years ago the man died after a long illness. Mourning ended but the habits of the mourners stayed on, and of these silence was the most marked, a silence long and interminable, for it was in truth the silence of waiting. The girls grew up and for long they waited expectantly, but the bridegrooms did not come. What madman will knock at the door of the poor and the ugly, particularly if they happen to be orphans? But hope, of course, is present, for—as the proverb says—even a rotten bean finds some blind person to weigh it out, and every girl can find her better half. Be there poverty, there is always someone who is poorer; be there ugliness, there is always someone uglier. Hopes come true, sometimes come true, with patience.

A silence broken only by the sound of reciting from the Qur'an; the sound rises up, with dull, unimpassioned monotony. It is being given by a Qur'anic reciter and the reciter is blind. It is for the soul of the deceased and the appointed time for it never changes: Friday afternoons he comes, raps at the door with his stick, gives himself over to the hand stretched out to him, and squats down on the mat. When he finishes he feels around for his sandals, gives a greeting which no one troubles to answer, and takes himself off. By habit he recites, by habit he takes himself off, and so no one is aware of him.

The silence is permanent. Even the breaking of it by the Friday afternoon recital has become like silence broken by silence. It is permanent like the waiting, like hope, a hope that is meager yet permanent, which is at least hope. However little a thing may be, there is always something less, and they are not on the look-out for anything more; never do they do so.

Silence goes on till something happens. Friday afternoon comes and the reciter does not come, for to every agreement however long it may last there is an end—and the agreement has come to an end.

Only now the widow and her daughters realize what has occurred: it was not merely that his was the only voice that broke the silence but that he was the only man, be it only once a week, who knocked at the door. Other things too they realized: while it was true that he was poor like them, his clothes were always clean, his sandals always polished, his turban always wound with a precision of which people with sound eyesight were incapable, while his voice was strong, deep and resonant.

The suggestion is broached: Why not renew the agreement, right away? Why not send for him this very moment? If he's busy, so what—

waiting's nothing new? Toward sunset he comes and recites, and it is as if he recites for the first time. The suggestion evolves: Why doesn't one of us marry a man who fills the house for us with his voice? He is a bachelor, has never married, has sprouted a sparse mustache and is still young. One word leads to another—after all he too is no doubt looking for some nice girl to marry.

The girls make suggestions and the mother looks into their faces so as to determine to whose lot he shall fall, but the faces turn away, suggesting, merely suggesting, saying things without being explicit. Shall we fast and break that fast with a blind man? They are still dreaming of bridegrooms— and normally bridegrooms are men endowed with sight. Poor things, they do not yet know the world of men; it is impossible for them to understand that eyes do not make a man.

'You marry him, Mother. You marry him.'

'I? Shame on you! And what will people say?'

'Let them say what they like. Whatever they say is better than a house in which there is not the sound of men's voices.'

'Marry before you do? Impossible.'

'Is it not better that you marry before us so that men's feet may know the way to our house and that we may marry after you. Marry him. Marry him, Mother.'

She married him. Their number increased by one and their income increased slightly—and a bigger problem came into being.

It is true that the first night passed with the two of them in their bed, but they did not dare, even accidentally, to draw close to one another. The three girls were asleep but from each one of them was focused a pair of searchlights, aimed unerringly across the space between them: searchlights made up of eyes, of ears, of senses. The girls are grown up; they know; they are aware of things, and by their wakeful presence it is as if the room has been changed into broad daylight. During the day, however, there is no reason for them to stay there, and one after the other they sneak out and do not return till around sunset. They return shy and hesitant, moving a step forward, a step back, until, coming closer, they are amazed, thrown into confusion, are made to hasten their steps by the laughter and guffaws of a man interspersed by the giggling of a woman. It must be their mother who is laughing, also laughing is the man whom previously they had always heard behaving so correctly, so properly. Still laughing, she met them with open arms, her head bared, her hair wet and combed out, and still laughing. Her face, which they had instinctively perceived as nothing but a dead lantern where spiders, like wrinkles, had made their nest, had suddenly filled with light; there it was in front of them as bright as an electric bulb. Her eyes were sparkling; they had come forth and shown themselves, bright with tears of laughter; eyes that had previously sought shelter deep down in their sockets.

The silence vanished, completely disappeared. During dinner, before dinner, and after dinner, there are plenty of jokes and stories, also singing, for he has a beautiful voice when he sings and imitates Umm Kulthoum and Abd al-Wahhab; his voice is loud and booming, raucous with happiness.

You have done well, Mother. Tomorrow the laughter will attract men, for men are bait for men.

Yes, daughters. Tomorrow men will come, bridegrooms will make their appearance. Yet the fact is that what most occupied her was not men or bridegrooms but that young man—albeit he was blind, for how often are we blind to people just because they are blind—that strong young man full of robust health and life who had made up for her the years of sickness and failure and premature old age.

The silence vanished as though never to return and the clamor of life pervaded the place. The husband was hers, her legitimate right in accordance with the law of God and His Prophet. What, then, was there to be ashamed about when everything he does is lawful? No longer does she even worry about hiding her secrets or being discreet, and even as night comes and they are all together and bodies and souls are set loose, even as the girls are scattered far apart about the room, knowing and understanding, as though nailed to where they are sleeping, all sounds and breathing aquiver, controlling movements and coughs, suddenly deep sighs issue forth and are themselves stifled by more sighs.

She spent her day doing the washing at the houses of the rich, he his day reciting the Qur'an at the houses of the poor. At first he did not make it a practice to return to the house at midday, but when the nights grew longer and his hours of sleep less, he began to return at midday to rest his body for a while from the toil of the night that had passed and to prepare himself for the night to come. Once, after they had had their fill of the night, he suddenly asked her what had been the matter with her at midday: why was she talking unrestrainedly now and had maintained such complete silence then, why was she now wearing the ring that was so dear to him, it being the only thing by way of bridal money and gifts the marriage had cost him, while she had not been wearing it then?

She could have risen up in horror and screamed, could have gone mad. He could be killed for this, for what he is saying has only one meaning—and what a strange and repulsive meaning.

A choking lump in the throat stifled all this, stifled her very breathing. She kept silent. With ears that had turned into nostrils, tactile sense and eyes, she began listening, her sole concern being to discover the culprit. For some reason she is sure it is the middle one: in her eyes there is a boldness that even bullets cannot kill. She listens. The breathing of the three girls rises up, deep and warm as if fevered; it groans with yearning, hesitates, is broken, as sinful dreams interrupt it. The disturbed breathing changes to a hissing sound, a hissing like the scorching heat that is spat out by thirsty earth. The lump in the throat sinks down deeper, becomes stuck. What she hears is the breathing of the famished. However much she sharpens her senses she is unable to distinguish between one warm, muffled heap of living flesh and another. All are famished; all scream and groan, and the moaning breathes not with breathing but perhaps with shouts for help, perhaps with entreaties, perhaps with something that is even more.

She immersed herself in her second legitimate pursuit and forgot her first, her daughters. Patience became bitter-tasting, even the mirage of bridegrooms no longer made its appearance. Like someone awakened in terror to some mysterious call, she is suddenly stung into attention: the girls are famished. It is true that food is sinful, but hunger is even more so. There is nothing more sinful than hunger. She knows it. Hunger had known her, had dried up her soul, had sucked at her bones; she knows it, and however sated she is, it is impossible for her to forget its taste.

They are famished, and it was she who used to take the piece of food out of her own mouth in order to feed them; she, the mother, whose sole concern it was to feed them even if she herself went hungry. Has she forgotten?

Despite his pressing her to speak, the feeling of choking turned into silence. The mother kept silent and from that moment silence was ever with her.

At breakfast, exactly as she had expected, the middle one was silent—and continued in her silence.

Dinner-time came with the young man happy and blind and enjoying himself, still joking and singing and laughing, and with no one sharing his laughter but the youngest and the eldest.

Patience is protracted, its bitter taste turns to sickness—and still no one shows up.

One day, the eldest one looks at her mother's ring on her finger, expresses her delight in it. The mother's heart beats fast—and beats yet faster as she asks her if she might wear it for a day, just for one single day. In silence she draws it off her finger; in silence the eldest puts it on her own same finger.

At the next dinner-time the eldest one is silent, refuses to utter.

The blind youth is noisy, he sings and he laughs, and only the youngest one joins in with him.

But the youngest one, through patience, through worry, through lack of luck, grows older and begins asking about when her turn will come in the ring game. In silence she achieves her turn.

The ring lies beside the lamp. Silence descends and ears are blinded. In silence the finger whose turn it is stealthily slips on the ring. The lamp is put out: darkness is all-embracing and in the darkness eyes are blinded.

No one remains who is noisy, who tells jokes, who sings, except for the blind young man.

Behind his noisy boisterousness there lurks a desire that almost makes him rebel against the silence and break it to pieces. He too wants to know, wants to know for certain. At first he used to tell himself that it was the nature of women to refuse to stay the same, sometimes radiantly fresh as drops of dew, at other times spent and stale as water in a puddle; sometimes as soft as the touch of rose petals, at other times rough as cactus plants.

True, the ring was always there, but it was as if the finger wearing it were a different finger. He all but knows, while they all know for certain, so why does the silence not speak, why does it not utter?

One dinner-time the question sneaks in upon him unawares: What if the silence should utter? What if it should talk?

The mere posing of the question halted the morsel of food in his throat.

From that moment onwards he sought refuge in silence and refused to relinquish it.

In fact it was he who became frightened that sometime by ill chance the silence might be scratched; maybe a word might slip out and the whole edifice of silence come tumbling down—and woe to him should the edifice of silence tumble down!

The strange, different silence in which they all sought refuge.

Intentional silence this time, of which neither poverty nor ugliness nor patient waiting nor despair is the cause.

It is, though, the deepest form of silence, for it is silence agreed upon by the strongest form of agreement—that which is concluded without any agreement.

The widow and her three daughters.

And the house is a room.

And the new silence.

And the Qur'an reciter who brought that silence with him, and who with silence set about assuring for himself that she who shared his bed was always his wife, all proper and legitimate, the wearer of his ring. Sometimes she grows younger or older, she is soft-skinned or rough, slender or fat—it is solely her concern, the concern of those with sight, it is their responsibility alone in that they possess the boon of knowing things for certain; it is they who are capable of distinguishing while the most he can do is to doubt, a doubt which cannot become certainty without the boon of sight and so long as he is deprived of it just so long will he remain deprived of certainty, for he is blind and no moral responsibility attaches to a blind man?

Or does it?

Translated by Denys Johnson-Davies

Farahat's Republic

———✍———

No sooner had I made my way inside with the guard than I experienced an immediate feeling of depression. Though not the first time I had entered the police station, it was the first time I'd seen it at night. I felt, as I stepped across the threshold, that I was making my way into some underground trench utterly unconnected with the present or, indeed, the immediate past. The walls were covered half-way up with a blackness that resembled paint, while the other half was enveloped in a general gloom; white patches scattered here and there merely served to emphasize the ugliness of the rest. The floor was so slimy you couldn't tell if it was made of asphalt or just plain mud. The all-pervading smell, whose quintessence defied definition, gave one a sensation of nausea. From lamps of great antiquity on which the flies had settled and laid their eggs, lamps the greater part of whose light had been condemned to life imprisonment within themselves, a pale light emanated; the little that did succeed in escaping acted more as a protecting veil for the darkness than it dispelled, and when it did fall upon objects and people merely brought out their mournful and ugly aspects.

On being enveloped by all this, having become an inseparable part of it, with people around me wearing expressions of great gravity and going around as though under hypnosis, with the boxes of fruit and hand-carts, the café chairs confiscated by the Municipality police and stacked up in one corner, their owners strewn around the walls and corners, collapsed in exhaustion on the ground, heads lolling forward on to their laps, and the policemen in their black uniforms looking like *afreet*s of the dead of night; while enveloped by all this I felt that I too must surely have committed some forgotten crime and I wished I might escape from the place as soon as possible. However, as I was to be detained at the police station for the night and sent up before the Parquet the following morning, I was unable to leave. They were at a loss where to put me, the detainment room being full, while the other room in which political prisoners were generally kept was a teeming mass of women under surveillance and ladies of easy virtue, so that in the end they could do no better for me than leave me, together with my guard, in the duty officer's room.

Despite its size the room was too small for the persons it contained. Of these the duty officer himself was the most striking. He was sitting at his desk like a commandant of police, on his right the muzzles of more than fifty stacked rifles, behind him a wooden board fixed to the wall and weighed down with every sort and kind of chain and fetter, shields, axes and helmets, while on his left stood the usual old iron chest. Seated thus, it seemed to me that there were no limits to his power and the awe he must inspire, that he would be capable of quite simply taking a bite out of my arm or gouging out my eye with a finger. I was certain, however, that he was no concern of mine nor I of his.

I found myself abandoning everything within me, everything with which I was preoccupied, and joining that army of eyes directed at him by the people crowded before him and separated from him only by a low wooden railing.

At first it seemed to me that he wasn't a living creature but merely a body fashioned from the black paint that had been used on the walls, his head one of the helmets hanging up behind him, his eyes rifle muzzles, his tongue most certainly a whip. But when I had calmed down a bit and got used to the place, I observed how he wore his cap at a most dignified yet fearsome angle, how his officer-type overcoat was buttoned right the way up—contrary to the usual practice—and how the skin of his face was drawn back so tautly, with such severity, that all the wrinkles in it disappeared and it became as smooth as the stretched skin of a drum. There was an intenseness about his gaze that made one feel that he not so much looked at people as pecked and stung them; his voice, required to perform feats of which it was incapable, snarled and roared, staccato as bullet shots, with unintelligible words.

Observing all this, he struck me as being like one of those prisoner-of-war Italian generals we used to see. Then it happened that a Sergeant or Master-Sergeant—I don't remember which—came and stood before him.

'Farahat,' he called out.

I was amazed how he addressed him with such informality. My amazement, however, disappeared when he again said:

'Farahat . . . Mister Farahat.'

The duty officer made no reply till the man had addressed him by 'Sergeant-Major . . . sir!'

I had drawn close and was leaning, as were several others, on the wooden railing. I was thus able to hear his accent which contained faint traces of the countryside of Upper Egypt; his high-pitched voice betrayed the wide open spaces in which he had grown up, betrayed too the bellowing and barking required by his job: it had added to it the sort of grating rattle that befalls the local café wireless from having its volume turned up too high too often. The image of the general went completely from my mind as his features took on an aura of awesome authority. I saw him then purely as Upper Egyptian: a nose as big as that of Ramses, a high angular brow like that of Mycerinus, and the imprint of his advancing years that indicated a crowded history in the service of the police, for he had inevitably spent whole decades in it to reach the rank of Sergeant-Major, having joined the force as a simple private. I saw his ageing body as it really was, straight in parts, twisted in others, forced into its uniform, heavy boots and leather belt, which had themselves imposed a shape upon his body in the same way as the iron gives shape and dimension to a tarboosh. It was quite apparent he enjoyed being duty officer and wanted people to treat him like a real honest-to-God officer, which no doubt he had been dreaming of becoming for three-quarters of his lifetime dreaming of the day when his shoulder would carry its one pip. It was clear, though, that his shoulder would be carrying nothing of the sort, for though he would sometimes undertake the role of duty officer, the time for his being pensioned off was imminent and for him the dawn star was more attainable than that of a second lieutenant. . . . And when my eyes moved away from him and I looked round the room I could see the empty desks vacated by their owners, the filing cabinet, the old fan placed above the safe, which looked as if it had not been used for at least ten years and over which the grime had made spidery tracings, and the electric lamp with its shade of sheet iron dangling down from the ceiling alongside Farahat's head bent over the papers before him. While the people crowding round the wooden barrier were a thoroughly mixed bunch, they were at one in their anxious, sadly angry looks and set, depressed expressions. Most of them, having been charged, were returning, joined together by a long chain, from being investigated at the Parquet.

After a while I realized that they attached no importance to their armed guard, the chain or to Sergeant-Major Farahat himself; his barkings were countered by bellows or sometimes with a riposte no less telling than his own. Then one of them exploded in rage because his identity and record cards had not yet arrived from the Identity Investigation Department and he was having to stay under detention till they did. He rained down curses on all and sundry, bewailing the unfairness of the world and his own accursed bad luck and poverty; if it had not been from some last vestige of respect for authority he would have heaped down curses on the duty officer too for good measure. I noticed that the officer in Farahat was undergoing extreme embarrassment as he listened to them ranting and raging while being unable—as real officers, in his view, should—to still the clamor because of their numbers, savagery, and defiance. When he had finished with them and they had gone off, a policeman at the head of the line and another bringing up the rear, the chain clinking and clanking and the prisoners still swearing and cursing, Farahat heaved the heavy sigh of someone at his wit's end.

When I again directed my attention to Farahat I found he was looking extremely old, so old you would have thought he was some item that had been lighted upon in a surprise police raid and, after being confiscated, had been sealed with a red tarboosh and uniform and had remained on in the government stores as an exhibit, deteriorating and growing more and more ragged, though without the seals themselves suffering any wear. His eye traveled over those present and he said:

'Ugh, I swear to God hard labor's easier than this lot.'

His eyes came to rest on me. They contained a clear invitation. I, who had been sitting for hours in silence listening, responded to it and found myself saying:

'Oh, is there so much work then?'

Like someone who has waited a long time for release he exploded: 'I should say there is, sir. This isn't a job, it's a circus, a madhouse. People have gone crazy. What are they up to? It's no skin off their noses! It all comes down on our heads. By the Prophet, I'd prefer to work in irons for a hundred years than sit around here for an hour. And what really drives you mad is that it's all so much nonsense . . . it's all lies . . . all false allegations, I swear to you. There's the fellow who's gone off and done himself an injury, and the one who's lost his hammer, and the chap who says he was fast asleep and his cap did a bunk. Why go any further? Hasn't she been standing there since early morning? What's up with you, girl? I'm not Sergeant-Major Farahat if she doesn't say they beat her up and stole her jewelery. . . . What's up, girl? What's the matter?'

The 'girl' was one of those standing in front of him. She was wearing a black dress which the magician of poverty had changed to a drab grayish color; round her head she had wound a faded handkerchief which hid but little of her short coffee-colored, kinky hair, the ends of which were twisted and ragged. Her face was a dark brown and the *kohl* on her eyes had been smeared by tears. 'Umm Sakeena,' she said meekly, 'and the girl Ayyousha, her niece Nabawiyya and the boy—'

'What of them? What of them?'

'They attacked me and hit me in the stomach,' and she began sobbing.

In a flash she was in full flood. Her voice choked with tears, she added, 'And Umm Sakeena . . . . She bit me . . . here . . . in the shoulder . . . and gave me a poke in the stomach. The girl Ayyousha pinched my ear-rings.'

The Sergeant-Major's voice was thick and guttural from the guffaws of laughter he gave vent to. 'See what I mean, sir?' he said. 'D'you see? Didn't I tell you? I swear to you it's all a pack of lies, an absolute fraud. I ask you, can you imagine her owning so much as a brass button? What ear-rings are these, my girl, they've taken? The crown jewels?'

'Gold ear-rings, Bey, and two bangles—'

The Sergeant-Major turned to me and said in a tone that reminded me of the comedian Naguib al-Rihani: 'Who d'you honestly think is the victim in this story?'

'Who?'

'Me! It's me, sir. Such barefaced lying is worse than robbery with violence. And the hell of it is that the report about it has to be in two copies and what's more it's I who'll be writing out the two copies.'

He faced round to the woman, piercing her with a searching look which contained a hint of fleeting laughter. He took hold of the pen and opened the large report ledger as though opening Mitwalli Gate. 'So . . . may the good God put an end to your life and mine that I may be spared all this.'

When he had finished writing the preamble to the report he asked her: 'What's your name, girl?'

He didn't wait for her to answer or concern himself with her reply when it came; facing round to me he continued with what he had to say, though I felt that he was talking more to himself than to me: 'By the Prophet, it's I who is the victim. And not only in this case, in a thousand cases, a billion. Perhaps you don't believe it. Then come and have a look at the day-book. We started off today with a rape on the highway and then following on that there's number 592, a pickpocketing of a wallet which was said to contain 147 pound, 83 piasters and a couple of postage stamps. I swear by God, all that it had in it were the two postage stamps and being on oath as it were, two and a half piasters as well. The next case is the theft of some copper. They say in the statement that the copper weighed 50 pounds and they accuse the maidservant, a mere chit of a girl who'd hardly herself be weighing more than ten pounds . . . and so on and so forth. From early morning I've had writer's cramp. And it's all just chickenfeed, rubbishy talk and lies. My dear chap, forget it.'

He turned to the woman.

'Why don't you say something, girl?' he asked. 'What's your name?'

Before she had answered he gave a laugh, like someone who has remembered a joke, and said: 'Or what about the body they found in the rubbish dump which didn't have an owner—or rather whose owner wasn't known? They found he'd given up the ghost just like that, without anyone saying so much as a harsh word to him. Tell me, though, why should he choose this particular rubbish dump to go and die on? D'you mean to say he had so little choice he couldn't have walked to Shobra for instance? God have mercy on his soul, he's dead when all's said and done, but why should it be I who suffers? Anyway, the long and short of it is that we're all destined for affliction and grief just as our ancestors were. . . .' He turned his head toward her.

'What's your name, woman?'

'Khadiga . . . .'

'Khadiga what? Speak up.'

'Khadiga Muhammad . . . .'

'Get a move on, woman . . . Muhammad what?'

But before she could give a reply he laid aside his pen and, resting his elbows on the page, placed his head between his hands. From under the brim of the cap, with the lamp in front of him swaying like a pendulum so that the shadow of his head moved along the wall behind him, backwards and forwards like a large monkey, he said:

'By the Prophet, I'm the victim, I swear it. It's not for nothing I've got old before my time! Thirty years' service, I tell you, and every day it's been just like this. I've been through it all, from Manzala to Uneiba, from Arish to Mersa Matrouh. I've seen men murder for a stick of sugar-cane, burn down a barn for a corncob. . . . People have gone crazy. It's not for nothing one goes gray.'

He stopped speaking suddenly and swooped down upon a hand that was gravitating toward the desk and gave it a violent, petulant thump.

'I've told you a hundred times to find yourself another blotter. Is this the only piece in the whole of the station? I take my refuge in God, are we at a gipsies' fair?'

Having said which he waited till the owner of the hand had disappeared discomfited, then turned on me his serious face with its tightly drawn features.

'One bursts a blood vessel and these sons of bitches don't give a damn and just fool around.'

As he talked he motioned with his eyes toward the telephone room where some policemen had gathered round a flaccidly corpulent colleague; some were holding his hands behind his back and the others were attempting to pull his trousers down, while the man panted and struggled with such strength as his obesity allowed.

Out of the corner of my eye I noticed that Sergeant-Major Farahat was smiling and chuckling; then, oblivious to everything else, he craned his neck forward so as to follow the battle. He looked really sorry when it ended with the victory and escape of the man with the large stomach. At this he raised his voice and spoke in his wholly Upper Egyptian accent:

'Ah, you set of old women—you couldn't even manage to deal with that flabby fellow.'

He had scarcely finished speaking when a side door opened and the Assistant Superintendent appeared in the courtyard. The station suddenly became deaf and dumb, everything was frozen over by the air of sternness that descended.

'You say your name is Khadiga Muhammad what?' the Sergeant-Major asked the woman gravely.

I left him to his questioning for I had become engrossed in the night patrol which had begun to collect in the courtyard. When duly gathered together it was a truly remarkable sight: two ranks of complete darkness with only a glimmer of yellow brass buttons and above the darkness a conflagration of bright-red tarbooshes. In front of each rank was another rank of hands stretched out dejectedly supporting rifles. Murmurings could be heard in the darkness and bursts of laughter that died with the speed of shooting stars. Occasionally an elbow would move out sideways from the outstretched hands and nudge its neighbor.

The Assistant Superintendent inspected them with his nose pointing skywards like a turkey cock and his eyes on the button that didn't shine, the boot which was not as black at it should be. To and fro he went, then entered his room. It appeared that he had just dined for when he came out again he was still chewing and there was a sheen on his lips. Once again he made his inspection, drying his hands which he had just washed. Boots and the butts of rifles crashed down on the ground several times. To some punishment was meted out, others were merely reprimanded. Then:

'Slope arms! Shoulder arms! Patrol, quick march.' And off went the night patrol, wheezing and reeling. Bringing up the rear was a corpulent policeman who was trying in vain to keep his ill-proportioned body in step.

On the departure of the patrol, the station courtyard became as empty as a coach on the night train approaching the terminus. Returning to Sergeant-Major Farahat, I found that he was still questioning the woman.

'And where did they attack you?'

'Inside the cinema.'

'And what made you go to the cinema, girl?'

'Mahmoud.'

'Mahmoud who?'

'Mahmoud!'

His Upper Egyptian origin was again in evidence as, with knotted brow and without writing in the report, he asked:

'And what, my girl, would this Mahmoud be?'

'My cousin.'

'Ah, what a cock-eyed country it is, you sons of bitches,' he said, putting down his pen. He extracted from his pocket an old metal box of the sort in which expensive cigarettes are sold. I saw that it contained two plain cigarettes and a cork-tipped one, also a packet of matches. He lit one of the plain ones and murmured one or two cryptic remarks about fathers and grandfathers. He dispelled any ambiguity when he said, speaking to himself: 'Cinema . . . huh . . . Cinema, they say, do they! What the hell would you be going to the cinema for? The likes of you don't go to the cinema!' Breaking off his conversation with himself, he leaned back, crossed his legs and asked the woman:

'And why should you be going to a cinema with a boy like that?' His eyes searched round in my direction, perhaps wanting me to bear witness to her answer. I therefore said to him:

'What, isn't the report done yet?'

'Not yet . . . . Will it ever be finished? I'll be right along, I know I've kept you waiting. Just a minute and I'll be free for you.'

It was clear he thought I was somebody with a complaint or an informer—most likely the latter. Perhaps, though, he found me well cast for the role of a listener to whom he could unburden himself on one of his long nights on duty and had thus decided to postpone my departure. Smiling, he wrote down something, then said:

'After all, you're being entertained. Honestly, isn't it better than the cinema?'

With a sigh he asked the woman:

'Huh, and why did your former husband plot against you? What's this rubbish about having gone off to the cinema? Come on, speak up, girl, why did your former husband plot against you?'

'The point is I had an order against him for maintenance.'

He jotted down a word or two and gave me a look of distaste.

'Stories! The cinema! What are these stories they make up? They might as well boil them up and make soup of them.'

'Why, don't you like it?'

'Like it? How can I like it? A film must be really interesting—not all this clowning and dancing around that gets one nowhere.'

He took up the pen and rested the nib on the ledger. Instead of writing, however, he said listlessly:

'Once when I got fed up with stories I made a film.'

His lack of enthusiasm caused me not to listen all that carefully to him. His words, however, had an odd ring about them and I asked:

'You did what?'

'I made a film—a story.'

'How did you make it? You took part in it or what?'

'No, I made up a film specially for the cinema.'

I was about to dismiss the whole matter and laugh, thinking that he had no doubt been the witness of some incident or crime with which his life teemed and that he rather naïvely wanted to make it into a film.

'What sort of film would this be?' I asked, checking my laughter. Quite simply, without hemming and hawing or sitting upright or putting down the pen, or even paying attention to the woman and other people at the barrier, he said:

'There was an Indian came to Cairo, a very rich man, one of those who have as much money as we have poverty. The man came and put up in one of those terribly posh hotels, let's say Mena House or "Shabat,"' and there was some poor wretch like ourselves . . . .'

Suddenly all my senses were wide awake. I leaned heavily over the barrier so as not to miss a word.

A woman came forward demanding help, half-screaming. She was fair-skinned and good-looking and her eyebrows were penciled with exquisite care.

'What's up with you, woman?' Sergeant-Major Farahat growled at her. 'What's wrong—end of the world come or something?'

'Help! Help, the lad's beaten his mother to death.'

'What lad, woman?'

'Our neighbor's son.'

'And what's it got to do with us?'

'What . . . ? Aren't you—may the Prophet protect you—the police?'

'Is it right for the police to come between the lad and his mother?'

'Eh! . . . And when the chap kills her brother?'

'That would be a different kettle of fish. In that case we'd be off and arrest him.'

The woman gave up in despair and retired into a far corner with the policeman who was guarding me. She began recounting the story to him in whispers, largely with the aid of her eyebrows. Then she left the station, with the policeman lost in amazement and delight at the whisperings of those eyebrows. Sergeant-Major Farahat again turned his attention to me.

'What a load of calamity it all is!' he said. 'Some lad I must say! Enough of that . . . . This poor fellow was out of work, meaning, as the saying goes, that he was an employee of the Sun Company—packing sun into bottles all day and hawking them round at night. Ha ha! That's how it was. Yes, indeed! As I was saying, this Indian was once leaving the hotel when he dropped a diamond which today would be worth at the very least seventy or eighty thousand pounds. The Egyptian fellow, seeing it, picked it up and handed it to the rich Indian . . . .'

'What diamond are you talking about, you old humbug?'

We turned round together to find that the person who had spoken was a tall sergeant carrying a file, who presently asked Farahat:

'What've you done about the deceased whose name's not known?'

'What d'you want me to do?' Farahat fired back. 'Walk round the streets saying "Anyone lost a body?"'

'I went to the hospital and saw him.'

'Happy to make your acquaintance.'

'Look here, old chap, his eyes are honey-colored, his hair's gray and on his right temple—'

'What are you telling me all this for? Did I send you to ask his hand in marriage? You'd be better off getting on with your work. Honey-colored indeed, you lanky oaf.'

Then he turned to me: 'When the Indian man came to give the Egyptian some money he swore by everything holy he wouldn't take a single millieme. In vain did he try to persuade him but there was nothing doing. He therefore went up enormously in the Indian's estimation, who was really won over to him. Well, the days came and went and the rich fellow went off to his country at a loss how to reward the Egyptian. He then decided that the best way was to buy him a lottery ticket. . . . Do you know how much the first prize was? But let's wait till we have a drink of tea.'

He went on clapping his hands till the boy from the canteen arrived. He asked for tea and had a lengthy argument as to the orders he had consumed that day, the boy saying three and he insisting that it was only two. But even when the tea had been brought the dispute remained unresolved.

We heard the Assistant Superintendent's door being opened. When he came out and stood stretching himself in the courtyard, Farahat resumed his questioning of the woman.

'Huh, what's it all about?'

'When I got the order against him, he came along wanting me to give it up. When I didn't agree he sent his mother, his sister and his cous—'

'Whoa . . . . That's enough up to here. They attacked you in the cinema?'

'Yes, and they went on hitting me till I almost had a miscarriage . . . .'

'What?'

'You see, I'm six months pregnant.'

Sergeant-Major Farahat, overcome by curiosity, laid aside the report. 'Good God! Who are you pregnant by, girl?'

'From him, Bey—from my divorced husband.'

'When?'

'Before he divorced me.'

'And why did your husband divorce you when you were pregnant?'

'Because he had sworn to.'

'Sworn to? And when did he divorce you?'

'The first day of Ramadan last. I broke his mother's water-jug when I got up to prepare the *sahour** and he made a triple oath that if he didn't break my arm in return, he'd divorce me.'

'And he broke your arm?'

'No, he divorced me.'

'By the Prophet, I felt in my very heart this would be it. . . . So, his mother's jug is the cause. So, because his mother's jug gets broken last Ramadan I get myself steamed up for the whole of today—the victim of one piaster's worth of jug. Listen, my girl, have you any other statements to make? Anything else you'd like to say?'

'Yes, Bey, it was Ayyousha who pinched the ear-rings from me, while her mother . . . .'

'Ugh! Anything more to say, apart from what you've already said?'

'But I haven't said anything yet.'

I was unable to refrain from laughing and Farahat's anger also turned into a loud guffaw. He finished off the report, gave a sigh and a yawn, and then shook his head.

The woman went out bearing a note sending her for a medical report. To my amazement all the people who were standing around went out with her.

'Huh, how much was the first prize?'

'You still remember? It was for a million pounds. After all, it too cost a lot of money!

---

* The pre-dawn meal during Ramadan.

'He bought a hundred tickets so as to make sure of winning, and when the draw came along one of them won the first prize—a million pounds free of tax. It never occurred to the man to be greedy and keep it for himself without anyone being any the wiser. Not a bit of it. What did he do? Off he went and bought an enormously big cargo-boat which he loaded up with the very best quality Indian silk, a bit of ivory, a few ostrich feathers, a bit of fine woolen cloth and cashmere and classy furniture. Then he sent the ship complete with all its crew to Alexandria. After that, he sent the contract of sale and the bill of lading fully paid up to our friend in Egypt. That's to say he had nothing to do but take receipt of it.

'Then, lo and behold, the ship arrived at Alexandria—something absolutely out of this world. And who does it belong to, chaps? Why, so-and-so. Well, to cut a long story short, the fellow sold the goods on the ship and used the money to buy another ship. So he kept one ship going off overseas fully laden while the second was returning home also fully laden. Now, if a tiny parcel so big costs one so much to send by rail, you can see what a ship like this would make from a trip . . . .'

At that moment a short, thin man came rushing in, wearing a gallabiya all covered in oil and stains, his head bare and his feet in wooden clogs that made a most excruciating sound. He darted in like an arrow, an expression of immense pain on his face.

'Effendi . . . Effendi . . . .'

His entry irritated Sergeant-Major Farahat. As though someone had aimed a punch at the tip of his nose, he turned on the man and thundered at him:

'What's up with you?'

'There's nothing up with me, Effendi. It's that bastard of a boy who threw a brick which broke the pane of glass of the shop window, a pane of glass that you can't get these days, genuine Belgian pre-war crystal. Three meters by three it was. May God bring about your ruin as you've brought about mine, you bastard.'

'What shop's this?'

'The Friendship and Fraternity Grocery in the main street.'

'I know it—the one on the corner opposite the garage?'

'That's it, may God prosper you. May the Lord never bring down upon you . . . .'

'And which window was broken—the one on the street or the other one on the lane?'

'The big one, Effendi, the one on the lane.'

'Then it's not ours,' said Sergeant-Major Farahat, dissociating himself from the matter and preparing to continue with his story. 'It's Boulak's.'

'How's that, Bey, when the house is in your district?'

'The side that overlooks the lane is under Boulak.'

'Please, Effendi—'

'I've told you it's nothing to do with us. Go to Boulak station.'

'Ple—'

'Scram! A *khamsin* wind take you!'

The man darted out like an arrow, clip-clopping in his clogs. Farahat waited till the hammering of the clogs had died away, then endeavored to recreate the atmosphere which had been disturbed by the grocer. He leaned far back, tilting his chair; then he took off his cap and held it in his hand, twirling it round or fanning himself with it.

'The man was extremely fed up with all the European ships, but in the space of a year God was good to him and he expanded a lot. Bit by bit he began buying up all the ships of Alexandria so that there wasn't a single one, English, Italian or what you will—all were flying the green flag.'

I noticed that Sergeant-Major Farahat's features had relaxed; they had shed all that sternness and distaste and had taken on an expression that had about it the contentment of old age; his eyes wandered about in the sky of the room like two dreamy butterflies; his voice was free from all discordance and flowed with a sweet, casual elation, so that the words issued from his mouth as though sweetened with honey. You could not help loving them, loving their tremulous resonance as they stole forth unhurriedly into the lugubrious silence that reigned over the police station, giving it the air of a funeral marquee at the end of the night when nothing can be heard but the hissing of the pressure-lamps and the murmurings of people paying their last respects.

'The man came to have countless ships, the smallest of which would have been ten or fifteen times as large as this station. But was he satisfied with this? Not at all. The money didn't go to his head, so with the income from the ships he went off and bought an enormously large textile factory in which he employed about half a million workers. After one month the profits from the textile factory paid for a glass factory. The glass paid for flour mills—and rice-hulling works, then some cotton ginneries, a bit of sugar—a bit of gas—a bit of paper—a bit of machinery—a bit of steel— Anyhow, the day came when he owned all the factories in Egypt.

'But this untidy state of affairs didn't please him at all. So he gathered up all the factories and put them down in one place measuring a thousand feddans. No, what's a thousand? A thousand wouldn't be enough. More like ten thousand, of which five thousand were for the factories and the other five for the workers to live in. Not any sort of houses mind you. Oh no. Real homes they were with gardens and balconies and everything laid on— chicken coops, rabbit hutches, the lot. And That's not all! He didn't make any profit at all from workers' sweat. The man who did work worth five piasters got five piasters, the one who did work for ten got ten. Forgive my saying so, but a worker will put his heart and soul into his job when he's properly paid. We're a people who've had an inheritance of hard work handed down to us from father to son ever since the time of the Pharaohs. Instead of making a meter of cloth the worker would make two; instead of just one shoe he'd make a pair. That's how it was—give and take, give me my right and take yours. Also the worker himself was completely changed, with tip-top clean clothes, his overalls nicely ironed to go to work in, then returning in the afternoon to change into his best suit, 'Nisr' tarboosh and patent leather shoes. And what cafés there were! What gardens! What casinos! What splendor! And the people all looking nice and gay and happy. There was no unpleasantness, no hard times, laughing the whole day long and having fun. At night they'd go to the cinema. These cinemas are terribly important. In every street there was a cinema and by order everyone whoever he might be had to go. And as for the films, they were absolutely tip-top. As for police, there weren't any—just a constable who instead of having to be out for eight hours on patrol would have a kiosk all made out of glass, right in the middle of the street, and a small office, and anyone who wanted anything would come to him. . . .

'Hang on, 'cos the vermin, begging your pardon, have arrived. Let's see what today's catch is like.'

I had in fact heard a slight noise coming from the direction of the door but had been too absorbed by what Farahat was saying to pay any attention. I turned toward the doorway and found it crammed with four or five plainclothes men, tall and broad, and all wearing felt skullcaps, every one of whom held a fistful of unkempt children in each hand and old beggars whom they dragged behind them, the gallabiya of one child tied to that of the next. The plain-clothes men looked like enormous giants and alongside them the children were tiny and dwarfish, like frightened chicks. They crossed the courtyard and the procession arrived at the wooden barrier; they were accompanied by the din they were making, which Sergeant-Major Farahat put a stop to with:

'Enough! Shut up, the lot of you! Line them up in front of me. Stop that yattering, God strike you blind!'

The remainder of the plainclothesmen went off and the line fell in quietly.

Sergeant-Major Farahat again leaned back in his chair, still in a state of euphoria.

'And then?' I asked.

'Well, along came machinery from Germany right away and engineers and workmen got busy and off they went cultivating the whole of the desert. Just imagine all this sand once it was cultivated. An express train traveling for seven days wouldn't reach the end of it! And the great thing was that there was none of that nonsense called ploughs and waterwheels and such rubbish. Everything was done by machinery—irrigation by machinery, threshing by machinery, fertilizing by machinery. There were even machines for gathering up the cotton and cutting the clover. And the peasant who did the work didn't know any more about such things as gallabiyas, skull-caps, yellow slippers and all that tomfoolery. Not on your life! It was all suits—khaki pants to the knees, clean white hats and shoes with double soles that never wore out. Off the peasants went to work in crocodile line, working up to noon only and coming back in line too. It was the same with the women, except that they were in one field and the men in another. And the houses were all of stone. Gas lamps were absolutely out—everything was electric and the cost of consumption was borne by the landlord. Every row of houses had its own canteen in which they all ate and then they'd all go home for a siesta and later they'd file off to school so as to learn to read and write and get to know their rights and duties. But, sir, not to make too long a story of it, the man, having so much money, lost all interest in it—it had become as common as dirt to him. The fellow who owns that sort of money can't help but get bored with it—like someone who eats apples every day. So one day he announced over the radio—oh yes, I forgot to tell you he'd made a radio station and linked it up with every single house; well, he announced into the microphone that he was giving it all up.'

Now Sergeant-Major Farahat was looking at me as though thinking about some other problem.

'Hey, you, what d'you think you're doing standing there?' he suddenly addressed himself to the constable. 'Haven't you got any work to do?'

'The fact of the matter is,' said the constable disjointedly, 'he was handed over to me.'

'Handed over? Why?'

'To guard him.'

Sergeant-Major Farahat turned and looked at me in a way he had not done before. He went on staring at me; no doubt he found that I did not lend myself to the role of a murderer, a thief, or a kidnapper. I don't know what he meant when he said, slowly and with a great deal of uncertainty:

'Oh, this gentleman. Are you one of them?'

'Of whom?' I said, smiling, 'Anyway, what did the man announce over the radio?'

He continued to gaze at me and then said absent-mindedly:

'Forget it—it's all just so many words. You don't really believe it, do you?'

The skin of his face tightened till it again became as taut as a drum; he pulled down his cap to its accustomed place over his forehead, and swooped down upon the old beggar who stood at the top of the queue, withering him with his gaze and then burst out in his customary bellowing:

'Say something, you animal! What's your name?'

Translated by Denys Johnson-Davies

The Greatest Sin of All

———ɷ———

D on't let the title scare you. The story itself is enough to make you die laughing. But Muhammad Husayn never laughed as he told it, nor did he see anything in it to raise even a smile. Quite the contrary. His voice would shake so much that he almost started crying. Sometimes, if there were any knowledgeable or enlightened people among his audience, he used to ask them imploringly whether what he had done and was still doing was a dreadful sin; could he be sent to hell for it?

The fact was that Muhammad used to be rather surprised when his audience burst into uncontrollable fits of laughter and found it hard to compose themselves. Muhammad was one of those peasants whom the village women would nickname *gid'an* meaning 'smart lads,' not because he had any particularly remarkable qualities, but more likely because he was young, single, and carefree.

Nevertheless, a "smart lad" he was. He did not wear a gallabiya made of the expensive fabric called *sakarota*. He was not known to be a café habitué and had never gone to the provincial capital. He was just one of the many peasants who had been credited with the greening of our country for the past seven thousand years or more. For, no matter how hard he worked in the fields, he never tired of it; no matter how much he ate, he was always hungry. Never in his whole life had he worn a gallabiya. He was always running around in his underwear, pantaloons, and undershirt. Over the undershirt he used to wear a waistcoat, the color of which had not only faded but the shiny outer material was torn all over the place with only the lining barely visible. The undershirt was threadbare and full of holes, and the pantaloons had some ineffectual patches badly sewn on by his mother whose eyesight was fading; in fact, she used to lose patience just trying to thread a needle.

In any case, Muhammad was a young man, eighteen years old, although he looked thirty-eight. He had experienced all the follies of youth, and had even had some flirtatious encounters with women. He used to sing to the girls working in the fields, and was also known to exchange words and glances if he happened to be working with them or if they were at the mill together.

However, his sexual experiences had begun with animals, from goats to cows to water buffalo, and ended up with the local women of ill repute who used to succumb to a mere look with such ease.

In any case, he had never even dreamed of what would happen to him. One hot, godforsaken summer day, he had spent the entire morning running after the donkey of the Qanadila, the rich farmers for whom he worked as a manure carrier for their fields which were some way away. He had actually completed thirty loads, which meant in effect that he had run about sixty kilometers. He had covered half of them running behind the donkey, while he had ridden the animal for the other half and its protruding vertebrae had almost broken his back in two. Running or even being lynched was a much better idea than riding the animal.

On this particular day, he felt thirsty, so thirsty that he started dreaming of water. Such was his thirst that he blocked out of his mind even the possibility of asking for a drink of water from the Qanadila house; they kept their water in large water jugs, and it was always hot and brackish. Shaykh* Sadiq's house was the only place to get a real drink of water, or rather from the clean water jug of Umm Gadd al-Mawla. Her cold, filtered water with the clean cloth over it to keep the dust and flies away, that would revive his spirits.

---

* *Shaykh* (masculine), *shaykha* (feminine): a title of respect often used to refer to a religious person, whether or not he or she fulfills a religious function or office.

So, as Muhammad was goading the lazy donkey into action, he made up his mind to hurry up to the house of Umm Gadd al-Mawla. He peeped in through the door. His eyes took a while to get used to the semidarkness which pervaded the inside of the house. Just then, he felt himself nailed to the ground out of a feeling of shyness, deference, and respect. There was Umm Gadd praying, or, to be specific, kneeling. He saw the breadth of her body in such a way that he could not help but stand there with a bashful reverence and awe. The prayers did not last long. Soon she ended her ritual by addressing her greetings to the angels, turning to left and right. On one turn to the left, she turned even farther to see who was standing there.

He apologized for interrupting her and asked whether he could take a sip of water. Umm Gadd nodded in agreement without saying a word (she was in the process of finishing her prayers) and gestured to the water jar. Muhammad went over to it at once, tilted it sideways, filled the small cup and had a drink. He drank two cupfuls which quenched his thirst and felt himself panting with instant satisfaction. He was grateful to Umm Gadd or Shaykha Sabiha as they used to call her, not because she was a *shaykh*'s wife or even because she used to pray and keep on praying, not greeting anyone without covering her hands so as not to negate her ritual ablutions;* not for those reasons, but because she preferred to wrap her head in a white veil, something which none of the other women did. Yes, he felt a debt of gratitude to Shaykha Sabiha and was anxious to repay her somehow. So, on his way to the door, he asked her if he could do anything useful for her. She thanked him for making the offer.

He made a move toward the exit so as to catch up with his donkey which had left him and gone its own way, but, before he could get there, he heard the word, 'But . . . ,' and turned round to find a slight smile on Umm Gadd's face which revealed her short, decayed teeth. She asked him hesitantly if he would mind lifting the reserve water jug and pouring its contents into the larger jar so as to raise the level which was very low. That was all she wanted. In one rapid movement, Muhammad lifted the heavy jug and, without even

* The *wudu'* or ritual washing is required of Muslims before they pray; any interruption during the entire process requires that the person praying start from the beginning again.

leaning it on the rim of the jar, poured in the water which gurgled and gushed in spurts.

Muhammad did not notice Shaykha Sabiha at that moment; she was eying him for the first time since he had entered the house. In fact, she was not looking at him as a whole; her gaze was fixed on his two black legs etched out of hardship and matted with thick hair. She was not looking at his legs exactly, but rather at the muscles in his calves which swelled as he stood on tiptoe trying to maintain his balance while pouring the water. Something in his calves had suddenly hardened of its own free will like a piece of steel, something which could only be found in a man's body. This was nothing new to Umm Gadd al-Mawla; her husband, Shaykh Sadiq, had something similar. However, by comparison his legs were thin and puny like bamboo sticks. They would stiffen too if he happened to be on tiptoe or to be walking, but in his case, the stiffening produced a small, flattened lump which was hardly noticeable through his skin.

This was not the first time that Umm Gadd had made a comparison between her husband and another man she had seen or met casually. She had been making these mental comparisons for several years, or, to be precise, for four years, ever since the craze had come over her husband. It had made him go to excessive lengths in his devotions—prayers before noon, extra prayers during Ramadan, the fasting month, staying up all night during *mawlid*s,* performing dervish rituals, making himself the imam of the local ritual group, and joining the Dimirdash order.** He became all spiritual and started speaking to her about the holy masters, saints, al-Ghazaali*** and the great devotees; he even made her wear a white veil and carry prayer beads. Actually, Umm Gadd was not surprised at this change that had come over her husband. Shaykh Sadiq had been thin and sickly all his life; low-voiced and pale, he ate little and was prone to bouts of heartburn and colitis. He never missed the five prayers

---

* Celebration of the birth date of one of the famous figures in Islamic history, and usually the occasion for festivities and religious observances of various kinds.
** One of the orders of dervishes or Sufis, the mystics and, in many ways, the purveyors of popular religion in Islam.
*** Al-Ghazaali (d. 1111): the greatest of the Islamic theologians.

a day and would never hurt a flea. Even in his youth, when young people were quite happy to wear skullcaps, he was the only one to wear a turban. He was a peasant, an expert on agricultural matters. He loved the land as well as tilling the soil. He used to be worried sick about animals and was never happier than when they delivered little ones, perhaps even happier than when a son of his own was born. The few square yards that he planted were always green. But this new spirituality had only come over him during the last four years, almost as though it were timed to coincide with the puberty of their son, Ismail.

However, this spirituality seemed a pretext for him to vent his wrath on her for not praying. If she did pray, he would still nag her until she fasted for the prescribed six days and gave her no peace until she agreed to wear the white veil. At first, she tolerated all the changes this illusion brought about with some reluctance. He neglected his land, never found anyone to look after it or keep it irrigated, he ignored her, the house, and everything else. Instead, he devoted himself totally to his prayers and devotion sessions which began at dinnertime and went on till after the dawn prayers. Then he used to come home, go to bed, and sleep until just before noon. Because of that, they lost their turn at the local waterwheel and could not get their allocated amount of irrigation water. The wheat in their fields thus had no water, the ears stayed empty and parched, and, as a result, they only got a couple of bushels yield per acre.

At first, she accepted the situation with indignation, and that developed into a patient tolerance which was followed by a sense of resigned desperation. Eventually a feeling akin to contentment took over. But the very crisis, the heated discussions which they would have, and the nagging, all these things pushed her into asking him to put aside his prayer beads, pick up an ax, and till the soil. She used to compare her husband to the other men in the village, both in his presence and behind his back. But this was the first time that she had ever drawn a comparison between a part of his body, the calf of his leg, and that of another man!

Muhammad, of course, was totally unaware of what was going on in her mind; even if he had been, he would not have understood. Umm Gadd stood up suddenly and came over. She stood beside the water jar, stretched out her hand, and tried to take the jug away from him. 'That's quite enough, my dear lad,' she said, 'quite enough. You must be tired out by now.'

He pulled the jug toward himself and held on to it stubbornly. 'God be praised,' he said, 'impossible. How can you say I'm tired?'

'By the Prophet Muhammad,' she replied, 'you shouldn't do any more. God preserve your youth! Listen to me!'

'By Him who created the Prophet,' Muhammad said, 'impossible!'

They kept pulling at the jug this way and that till his elbow brushed her white veil and pushed it aside a little. His arm touched her arm, his undershirt her dress, and in particular, the calf of his leg brushed against hers. Suddenly, Muhammad's heart started pounding as if someone had caught him unawares and thrown him into the canal. At that moment, he came to realize that Shaykha Umm Gadd al-Mawla was a woman, standing there beside him. She was neither young nor beautiful, and did not tie her kerchief in a provocative manner. Her complexion resembled her husband's: somewhat pale. Her eyes were small, her voice soft and husky as though it were emerging from an opening in her back. She had the same odor as the color of her veil, emaciated grayish white. Even so, he could sense the woman in her.

How was it that he came to feel all this in spite of her veil and the obligatory prayers which she had just completed? How could it happen in spite of her snub-nosed son around whom certain special flies seemed to congregate (although, looking at him, you would have found it difficult to believe that he had been born of a woman)? How was it that he came to be aware of the woman in Umm Gadd? Who was responsible for it? He could not tell. When he saw the veil sliding off the top of her head and saw her head, hair, and face without a veil, he felt that it was all over. Instead of holding on to the handle of the jug, he put his arms around her neck, with no premeditation or cunning but instinctively, just like that, and then grasped the water jug too so that she was firmly within his grasp. She tried to free herself. 'Be careful,' she exclaimed. 'Now you've negated my ritual ablutions!'

But he paid no attention and merely tightened his grasp so as to force her into total silence. At that moment, all he wanted both for her and himself was total silence, simply to remain together in each other's embrace.

'No, no, please, I beg you!' she protested. 'Shaykh Sadiq will be back shortly.'

'Where is he?' he asked with a hoarse voice which seemed to echo from an internal call uttered for all eternity.

'He must be performing his noon prayers,' she replied. 'He'll be coming home soon.'

'When can we . . . ?' he asked.

'After dinner,' she replied.

At that, Muhammad's knees began to shake as thought they had been stricken by some earthquake which also overtook his voice. 'But won't he be here then?' he asked with his upper lip trembling.

'No,' she replied. 'Tonight he has to go to another of those *mawlid*s.'

Muhammad went almost mad for joy and hugged her so hard that he almost broke her ribs. He lifted her off the ground and spun both her and the jar around out of sheer happiness, the greatest, the most wonderful happiness he had ever experienced in his life.

It was on the rooftop, one like that of Shaykh Sadiq's house and most other houses in the village, a rooftop full of pitfalls and booby traps, rice chaff, corn husks, old rusty agricultural tools, and lizards, on that self-same rooftop that they had their rendezvous. Umm Gadd was very scared and thought a thousand times about calling the whole thing off. She kept cursing herself for what she was doing, but, in spite of it all, she still left the ladder lying against the wall. It was missing a few rungs, and the pieces of wood were tied together crudely with rope. She left it there and waited for Muhammad to climb up. A thousand inner voices kept urging her to get up and leave, but iron chains kept her riveted to the ground. An overwhelming force like time and fate made her ears deaf and her eyes blind to everything. She put the ladder in place, snuggled into her veil, and massaged her face with a few drops of rose water which she borrowed from a neighbor. All this she did as though she were hypnotized, driven to an inevitable fate.

The odd thing about it is that Muhammad never even used the ladder to climb up to the rooftop; it was not that high. He made it in a single leap like some demon. Once there, he could not see very clearly. In fact, his eyesight was no better at night than by day; he could only see things clearly if he rubbed his eyes, and, if he did so they turned red, and, if that happened, he saw things double. Now he really did see two things. The grain silo actually was the grain silo, but the other thing he saw was Umm Gadd. She had seen how confused he looked, but stayed where she was, not daring to utter a single sound. Instead of starting his search, Muhammad also crouched down beside the silo on the other side. If he had listened to his own intuition, he would have hidden inside, for he was really dead scared himself. He was afraid that Shaykh Sadiq might return home suddenly. The thought of God's wrath had him worried too, not to mention the way the neighbors would gossip if they ever found out. And yet, in spite of his apprehensions, his heartbeats were throbs of pure joy, an all-encompassing joy. When he could not explain this sensation to himself, he settled on the notion that it must be that thing called *love* which people kept talking about so much. For this was the first time in his life that he actually had an assignation with a woman in her own home and that she had agreed to meet him. This time, it was not out of hunger either or the need for the price of a few ears of corn to broil. This time it really was for himself, for his sake, 'for the beauty of his dark eyes,' to coin a phrase. In fact, the blackness of his eyes was white because of the cataracts which marred their vision! But, even if he had been totally blind and Umm Gadd completely paralyzed, they would still have met that night. His whole being was vibrating in anticipation. He was drawn to her by some mysterious force, and neither darkness, silos, nor firewood were going to stand in their way.

So their meeting took place, he in his undershirt and pantaloons, with his rough-skinned face puckered and blotched, she with her small, wan body which looked inexplicably pale and her distorted smile which dangled to one side. But Muhammad did not notice such things for he was completely immersed in other thoughts. His mind was paralyzed with fear that Shaykh Sadiq might come back and also with the fear of God and the neighbors. His body meanwhile was preoccupied with hers. They both stood there trembling, while the world around them was steeped in a darkness which carried with it no glimmer of hope.

From far away, as though from the very heavens and stars above, came the resounding voice of Shaykh Sadiq. He was beginning the *dhikr** in the dervish circle. As he chanted disjointed, indistinct phrases, the bodies of the dervishes kept swaying. Their voices became louder and hoarser, and seemed to be coming from souls which were heaving with fear and hope, rebellion and need, which were filled with power of will and a sense of the inconceivable, with an intense capacity for patience and a long drawn-out feeling of aggravation.

At almost the same time, the ceiling of the house (which was thatched with dried branches) began to shake and throb to the very same rhythm, exactly like heartbeats or feverish gasps. It continued, meaninglessly and aimlessly, until the branches themselves began to squeak and the chaff and corn husks whispered to each other as though to exchange meaningful messages. Rumors began to spread, and sinful murmurings were everywhere.

The voices of Shaykh Sadiq and Muhammad were singing the same tune and keeping in tempo with each other, and the swaying of the entranced bodies below matched the swaying of the bodies on the roof. The trembling voices of the dervishes in the *dhikr* were exactly like those of the couple coming together on the roof. The same motion seemed to embrace the entire universe. The beat went on relentlessly. The lizards stood absolutely still, a strange thing which they do sometimes as though in reaction to the tremendous cosmic movement going on all around them. There they stand, watching and witnessing if required. They came back to life again only when the voices of the dervishes started to become confused, and some of them began to speak in strange tongues—in Syriac—rising and then fading away. The movement on the ceiling stopped too, and all the whisperings and rumors died away in their cradles on top of the firewood on the roof.

This was the first but by no means the last time that Muhammad found his way to Shaykh Sadiq's house, and particularly to the roof. It was impossible for him to stop. Whenever he heard Shaykh Sadiq calling the faithful

---

* A Sufi ritual involving the repetition of the name of God and other formulaic utterances to induce a state of trance. This is frequently accompanied by the swaying of the body and, in the case of the Mawlawis, by spinning the body around in a circle.

to prayer, organizing a *mawlid* or putting an evening of *dhikr* together, he used to drop whatever it was he had in hand and head at once for Shaykh Sadiq's house. With a single leap he would be on the roof. There he always found—that was the strangest part of all—Shaykha Sabiha wearing her white veil, as though she too had a regular rendezvous with her own husband's voice.

In those particular days, Shaykh Sadiq was extremely happy. His wife had completely stopped arguing with him about costs and reminding him of the land that had to be tilled. She was content to give such advice to her son, Gadd, who had gotten into the habit of picking up the ax from its usual place and strolling over to the fields. Moreover, Shaykh Sadiq began to notice that his wife was becoming a truly pious woman, a Shaykha as people used to call her. There was now a genuine sincerity to her prayers and she used to beg God's forgiveness from the bottom of her heart for all her sins, past and present. He no longer had to remind her to give alms and perform extra religious obligations. As a result, he now abandoned all his previous restraints and removed the final obstacle which prevented him from devoting himself completely to prayer and meditation. He got a thousand-bead rosary to replace the one hundred-bead one he had been using so far. Every night, he used to recite a special litany from the Chapter of Yasin in the Qur'an. Now, there was bound to be a *dhikr* every night somewhere.

The more Shaykh Sadiq immersed himself in this new spirit of devotion, the more rash Muhammad became. He would go to the rooftop of the Shaykh's house twice in the same evening, and sometimes during the day as well. Things reached such a point that, whenever Muhammad heard the voice of Shaykh Sadiq calling people to prayer or entreating the Lord during a *mawlid*, he would feel this incredible sensation surging through his body. A hot flush would come over him which almost made him blind.

But habit, like time itself, has the characteristic of blunting things. With habit, Muhammad became much less enthusiastic about dropping whatever he happened to be doing every time he heard the Shaykh's voice as he prayed in confidence or asked for God's aid. These fits of indifference now became more and more frequent, and they may have been responsible for loosening his tongue. He was now more prepared to open up to his friends and let them in on his secret, perhaps the only personal secret he had. Later, he told his acquaintances too, and eventually he was quite willing to tell it to any audience. That happened when the story succumbed to the usual fate of any well-kept secret and became the talk of the village. It did no harm to any of the people involved, but was just a story which became casual gossip. The only difference was that, at the end of every narration, Muhammad's voice would crack and he would become emotional to the point of tears. 'Will I really be damned forever to eternal fire,' he used to ask, 'as punishment for what I've done?'

When we were children, we often discussed the story. Whenever we came to the point which was of utmost importance to us as youngsters, the question of heaven and hell and who would be doomed to what, we used to assure each other and come to a raucous and unanimous consensus that the two who would be irretrievably doomed to the fires of hell would be Muhammad and Umm Gadd. It may well have been this very odd unanimity which made me ponder more and more on that question. I was forced to smile at a frivolous, ironic voice inside me which used to pop up suddenly in front of my eyes like a clown. With a binding oath it assured me that Shaykh Sadiq would inevitably be the one to enter hell, and through its largest gate at that.

Translated by Mona Mikhail

from
City of Love and Ashes

---∞∞---

1

The tram terminal in Shubra al-Balad is more than just the beginning of a tramline. It is a pivot of constant interplay between Cairo and its suburbs, between the city and the many factories scattered around it. You see village folk here coming to the capital, awestruck by the city, breathless at the drone of the great bustle and the new world. You see sullen workers in the bustle too, resentful of the city but unable to escape it.

And—on this particular January day—you see Hamza standing as usual waiting for the tram to leave the long tail of cars crammed at the beginning of the line and make its way to Ataba Square. As he waits he breathes in deeply, with pleasure, for the terminal was also a pivot of constant interplay between the constricting life he lived in the morning among the white coats, vats of dye, and test tubes and the free and open life that began once he stepped onto the station platform.

He stood and narrowed his eyes slightly behind his glasses to be able to see the scene more clearly. He observed the people as he fidgeted nervously. The faces that attracted his attention were serious and harsh; he imagined their luster was the spark of hidden desires being set free, the outbreak of revolt, and when their voices reached him he always took them as the rustle of demonstrations or the roar of strikes. In spite of the cold, and the gray clouds that hid the sun, there was a smell in the air, a peculiar smell that made the body tremble, like the smell from the barrel of a rifle just fired.

A tram pulled away from the line of cars to start its long journey. Hamza practically sprang onto it to claim a place among the many people standing. By the time the conductor had finished issuing the tickets the passengers had quite relaxed, and any barriers of reserve and alienation among them had lifted. Hamza pricked up his ears to listen to their conversations. Not the usual altercations, apologies, jokes—just the English . . . . The English . . . . Battalions, commandos, Kafr Abduh, tanks . . . . Erskine and the Egyptian troops . . . . Four English soldiers killed . . . . The waterworks blown up . . . . Their day will come, the bastards . . . . By God, we'll turn them out of Egypt dancing and singing all the way . . . . If we had weapons . . . . We need weapons . . . . Where can we get them? . . . Where? There are ways . . . . If only they'd come out and fight us man to man!

Three halts from the beginning of the line, halfway between Shubra al-Balad and Cairo, Hamza got down. There were no buildings here, just broad stretches of cultivated land, telephone poles, huts made from tin sheets, and mounds of piled garbage.

He walked for a time across deserted land until he came to the leveled patch with the tent erected on it. A firing post had been set up at one end of the patch of land; at the other end there were wooden barricades, and in front of them a ditch. A sign on the tent read 'The General Committee for Armed Struggle' in small letters, and beneath it in larger letters "Shubra Training Camp." He found the sign hanging crooked, so he straightened it. He saluted, and his salute was returned by a large, dark young man wearing long yellow trousers and a long-sleeved, turtleneck jersey. The young man had seen him coming, and had left his seat at the firing post and come to meet him. Hamza greeted him and they went inside the tent out of the bitter cold. Hamza sat on a box with handles on the sides, while the young man sat next to him on the ground. Hamza rubbed his hands together to warm them and blew into them fruitlessly. His teeth chattered as he spoke. 'It's cold.'

'Very.'

'A cup of tea'd go down nicely, Hasan!'

'You want some tea?'

'Go down nicely, Abu Ali.' Hamza called Hasan by his familiar nick-name.

'Tea. We'll make you some tea.'

The young man went off to a two-legged gas burner, a tin can, a large earthenware pitcher full of water, and a jar of sugar, and pulled a half-ounce packet of tea from his trouser pocket. While he was lighting the burner, Hamza asked him, 'Nobody been?'

'Not a soul.'

'Somebody was supposed to come at two o'clock, and it's two-fifteen now. Didn't he show up?'

'No, he didn't.'

'Strange.'

'Nothing strange but the Devil!'

Then the young man looked at him, smiled, and added, 'I don't believe it.'"

'What don't you believe, Hasan?'

'That we're going to make a training camp.'

'Why?'

'It just doesn't look like it.'

'Tomorrow it will, know what I mean?'

The burner flared up and filled the tent with flame and smoke that almost caught the roof. The young man cursed it and all its kind. After the storm had settled, he asked Hamza, 'You like it strong?'

'No. Not too strong.'

'But Mr. Hamza, those few miserable weapons we have aren't worth an onion.'

'Don't worry. You have the pistol? Give me it.'

'Why?'

'Just give it to me.'

The young man got up and went to another box. He opened the padlock and pulled out a pistol with a shining barrel. Hamza took it and examined it. He closed one eye and looked down the barrel with the other, muttering, 'It's full of dirt. Give me some kerosene and a rag. It's Italian. The English took it from the Italians. And we took it from the English.'

He stood up from the box he was sitting on, lifted its lid, and rummaged inside until he found a screwdriver. Then he closed the box, sat down again, and began loosening the screws of the pistol.

They heard movement outside. The young man raised a flap of the tent to look out. 'Odd!' he exclaimed, still looking out. 'What are these people doing here?'

'Who is it, Hasan?' asked Hamza, absorbed in shifting a stubborn screw.

The young man came back in. 'A well-dressed man and a woman.'

'Where?'

'Next to the tent.' Then the young man raised his voice through the tent opening: 'What do you want, sir?'

A rather nasal voice replied. 'Where's Hamza?'

Hamza, still busy, said, 'That must be Saad. Come on, Saad, come in.'

Saad entered, nervous, wan, and short. He wore a leather jacket and dark glasses. 'What's going on?' he blustered. 'An hour I've been looking for you! Put up a sign, man! Raise a flag over the tent when you're in it! Good morning!'

'Good morning,' said Hamza. 'Sit down, Saad.'

'I won't sit down. I have somebody with me. It's work. You think I never do any work. It's an unending struggle! Come in, Miss Fawziya. Please come in. Come on in, don't be afraid. There's only people here!'

A young woman stooped to enter through the small door of the tent. She stood by the door confused and hesitant, staring at Hamza and the pistol, which was now in black pieces in his hands, and at the other young man standing in the middle of the tent in his high-necked, blue woolen jersey, like a genie just emerged from the lamp.

Hamza looked up at her. She was of medium height like him, but thinner, and had a small, white face, dark red lips, and thick hair. She was wearing a light brown coat, but still she shivered from the cold and her pallid face trembled. Despite her shaking, there was a particularly warm and lively light in her eyes.

Hamza stood up quickly, made room for her on the box, and stretched out his hand to greet her, and when he found it was covered in kerosene and rust he offered her his wrist to shake instead. Her fingers around his arm were as cold as ice, but her grip was unexpectedly firm.

While all this was going on, Saad in his stuttering manner said, 'This is Mr. Hamza, who's responsible for the training camp.'

'Glad to meet you,' she said, with no trace of timidity.

'And this,' continued Saad, 'is Miss Fawziya, secretary of the Women Teachers' National Resistance Committee.'

Hamza's expression changed immediately, and he greeted her again, this time with the hand he had just cleaned.

'They have a marvelous campaign,' added Saad. 'As you know, we were rounding up donations, and I went to collect from their school in Munira, where I was introduced to her. And I found it was more than a matter of donations, so I decided she ought to meet the committee right away. I thought I'd better bring her to you, right? Congratulate me, then!'

Hamza looked at him without knowing whether to commend or reproach him; certainly Saad should have told him about this before bringing her to him. Before he could decide what to do, the tea was ready and the large young man poured it into three cheap, blue, thick-bottomed glasses, then poured the rest into a tin jug that had been covering the mouth of the pitcher. As he stretched out his hand to Fawziya with the glass, he said in his harsh voice, 'Here. You're shivering like an eel.'

Fawziya ignored this, took the glass from him, and clenched it in both hands. Saad, despite all attempts to dissuade him, insisted on drinking from the tin jug.

The tent was filled with slurping sounds as they drank the tea, and its steam rose from their mouths and from the glasses alike. They were suffused with a sudden intoxication of warmth on this freezing cold day.

All the time, Hamza stole surreptitious glances at Fawziya. This was almost the first time that work had brought him into contact with a young woman. In the depth of his soul he had no faith in women or in what they might be capable of achieving, even though he was always saying there was no difference between men and women and that women had the same rights as men. In any case, how could a young woman shiver from the cold with a coat like that? And as thin as she was, how could she plunge into the kind of battle they were embarking on and stand with him shoulder to shoulder?

'Very good, what you've done,' Saad was saying, 'Very good indeed. When did you put up the wooden barricades out there?'

'Yesterday.'

'Very good. Excellent. And when will the training start?'

'Tomorrow.'

'Amazing! That's great! Wonderful! Tomorrow really?'

'Yes.'

'Marvelous. You deserve to be congratulated. It calls for a celebration. And, God willing, you'll have a hundred men to start with. You must have at least a hundred.'

'We're starting with ten.'

'That's not enough! Too few. Not enough at all. How come?'

'It's enough. Why were you late? Weren't you supposed to be here at two?'

'No. No, no. Two-thirty. I swear on my honor it was two-thirty. No, no, no—when it comes to appointments I'm meticulous. Very meticulous. If it's two-thirty, it's two-thirty. I swear on my honor it was two-thirty. I'm meticulous with regard to appointments especially.'

'Your appointment was two o'clock. And drop all this stuff about honor, know what I mean? Let's go.' And Hamza stood up.

They all went out, the tea filling them with the confidence to face the cold. The world outside was amazingly still and silent, and the empty plot was desolate. The sky was heavily overcast, and it looked like rain. And far away over there was Cairo, an ash-gray dust hanging over it. Its houses appeared crammed together, nothing standing out but a few apartment blocks and the minarets that looked from a distance like the chimneys of a huge, disused factory. The ground they were standing on was soft and gave slightly under their feet. A light, yellow wind blew up in a fury, animating the straw that littered the ground, some strands flying up, the rest shuffling around.

Fawziya asked, 'Is this the camp?'

'Yes,' answered Hamza, looking at her and contemplating her small nose, whose pointed tip had reddened in the cold.

'And are there many volunteers?'

'Not many, but every day there are more. Tomorrow this will all be full of parades and drills.'

'And who'll be doing the training?'

'Volunteer officers.'

'From where?'

'The army.'

'How's that? With a permit?'

'There's no such thing as permits.'

'So the government turns a blind eye?'

'Is there a government?'

'Goodness! Of course! Who rules the country?'

'We do! We rule. The people.'

Fawziya stared at him for a while as if in disbelief.

In the meantime, Saad had left them and gone to jump from the top of the wooden barricades to look at the ditch. Then he lay on his stomach at the firing post, holding an imaginary rifle.

'Saad's very odd,' said Fawziya, 'Look what he's doing!'

'Yes. He's keen.' He was silent for a time, then he said, 'But tell me, Miss Fathiya, did you give Saad any donations?'

'Fawziya. My name's Fawziya'

Hamza's ears reddened with a deep blush, and he stammered his apology.

'But I came specially to forge a direct link with your committee,' Fawziya went on, 'because the main aim of our committee is to serve the armed struggle.'

'Very good.' Hamza spoke carefully and cautiously, still scolding himself.

'We'd collected a bit of money to buy first aid supplies for the Fedayeen, but it looks like you need the money more.'

'It's true we always need money.'

'So can I meet you tomorrow to give it to you?'

'Certainly.'

'Where?'

'Let's see . . .' And Hamza pulled a small diary from his pocket and turned the pages. He lifted his head, and his glasses shone in a ray from the sun that had managed to beat the clouds and squeeze between them. 'Can you come here?'

Fawziya thought for a moment. 'Four o'clock?'

'That's just fine.'

Then Hamza raised his voice and called to Saad. He took him aside, where they whispered together for a while. Then they shook hands. Fawziya too shook Hamza's hand, and he noticed that she did so with a firmness unusual for a woman of her type, as if she were an old friend.

The last he saw of her was a smile and the loose belt of her coat flapping behind her in the wind.

Hamza went back to sit in the tent, to the pistol and the rag and the kerosene. Every now and then he shook his head and said, 'Strange!'

'What's strange?' the large young man asked.

'Nothing,' said Hamza, lost in thought.

2

At four o'clock the next day the camp was animated by the presence of ten young men in training fatigues. The ground shook under their feet as they marched up and down in file. Every now and then their trainer screeched his orders. Hamza and the young man were down in the ditch, each with an adz, digging deeper wherever it was not deep enough.

As he shoveled away the soft earth, Hamza raised this head and saw her. Only then did he remember it was time for their appointment. He experienced a certain pleasure as he watched her vague form approaching at a distance. He waited until she came nearer then climbed out of the ditch and made toward her, so weighed down by shoes caked in dried mud that he had no alternative but to take them off.

Fawziya shook his hand in her usual vigorous, enthusiastic manner. She suppressed a laugh at his rolled-up trousers, his shirt decorated with countless medals of mud, and his socks from which his toes protruded in defiance of both elegance and the cold.

He took her away from the camp: he found that the small parade of young men became confused and distracted and winked secretly when they saw her. Before he had a chance to say anything, she opened her purse, took out a bundle of money, and handed it to him. 'Twenty-seven pounds fifty,' she said. Then she added with a smile, 'First installment.'

Hamza was genuinely delighted: twenty-seven pounds was two Lee Enfield rifles and several rounds. 'Well done,' he said, reshuffling the bills.

He invited her to sit beside him on the ground, which she did without hesitation. She began to tell him about her committee, and about herself when he asked her. A teacher in Munira School, she had read widely and understood much, but done nothing. But when the Battle of the Canal began she felt impelled to discuss the situation with her teaching colleagues, and the discussion led to the formation of the committee. Hamza nodded his head, encouraging her to go on, and it was almost as though with each word he looked at her anew and tried to convince himself that women were indeed capable of action.

Before she left, he flipped through his diary. 'Next Wednesday, from seven o'clock on, I'll be in Heliopolis all the time. We could meet there to arrange how to keep in touch.'

She thought for a while and said, "I have six lessons on Wednesday . . . but I'll be there anyway."

'Nine o'clock by the Baron's Palace—okay?'

'Okay.'

'And if anything happens and we can't meet, you know what to do?'

'What?'

'Make it the same place and time the following week, know what I mean?'

This time it was Hamza who grasped her hand vigorously, almost taking it with him, and she left.

Hamza found his mind wandering after her, thinking about her—about her small but determinedly agile size, as though there were a secret generator feeding her with an inexhaustible energy; about the rapid expressions that chased each other across her face and her quick responses to his own expressions: he laughed and her expression leaned toward laughter; he frowned and he could read sadness clearly in her face. Every time he looked at her he was amazed at the feeling that had overtaken him—the feeling that he possessed a strength no one else possessed and that he could perform miracles. And he thought about her delicate, elegant features, in every pore of which were grace and hope. She seemed indeed like a young child, needing only a pinafore to become a schoolgirl.

Hamza might never have broken free of his reverie, but he soundly scolded himself and dived back into the ditch to go on trimming its sides.

3

The next evening, Hamza was sitting in a café in al-Qarin, in Sharqiya District. The café was in the center of the village on a square that appeared by accident among the houses and was never meant to be a square.

At that time, al-Qarin lived on the news of battles, stories of valor, the preparations of the English—and was mobilizing a strike against them. Hamza had just concluded an arms deal: three machine guns, five pistols, and a box of ammunition. They would be delivered in Cairo early on Sunday morning.

Evening in a village like this was a new experience for Hamza. A few wan mantle-lamps and some kerosene lanterns, with or without glass. People walking up and down, coming from the darkness of one street to disappear into the darkness of another. Slow, lifeless movement. Cattle roaming about, cattle being led home. Impossible to believe that over the years the people of this village alone had killed hundreds of British soldiers, and that because of their hostile actions against the British Empire questions had been raised in the House of Commons.

The clock struck eight-thirty, and Hamza listened to the news, which all the villagers gathered to hear. As it was read, an intense silence spread, like the silence at Friday prayers when the imam is giving his sermon. But strangely the radio made no mention of the previous day's slaughter at Ismailia. The news was quite ordinary. It occurred to the café owner to listen to what the English had to say, on the news of the BBC Arabic service, so he came over to the radio and stood there searching among the stations. Hamza was more interested in the man himself and his gaunt, meager, miserable face at the radio twisted in intense concentration as he followed the tuning needle; more interested too in the people who had not yet dispersed, whose mouths were still analyzing the news, passing it on, prognosticating, threatening. But he suddenly paid attention as all his senses awoke to the voice in London announcing that martial law had been declared in Egypt. Hamza hurriedly left his seat and stood by the radio, his ear practically glued to the speaker. 'Fires annihilating Cairo . . . . Foreigners slaughtered in the streets . . . . Plundering, looting, and murder in broad daylight . . . . Explosions all over the capital, blood running in its streets . . . . Prime Minister Nahhas calls for martial law . . . . Martial law declared . . . . Sections of the army called out . . . . Situation of grave danger . . . .'

Hamza wasted no time in hiring a cab to take him immediately to Tall al-Kabir, where he waved at every passing vehicle until one stopped to pick him up.

Voices assaulted him, passing on vague, dark, unconnected rumors in a vortex. But when he arrived at Cairo Station and saw the thickening columns of smoke livid in the sky, the many blazing buildings appearing dark red in the black of night, the tongues of flame rising from them like the tongues of devils, the incandescent fires, the charred timbers, shops with doors ripped out and contents smashed, all parts of the Cairo he loved hemorrhaging ruins and rubble as its trembling buildings pondered their destiny, soldiers in battle dress and helmets, police car patrols, the resignation of the cabinet, martial law descending blacker than the smoke in the sky and more terrible than the flames consuming the land: when he saw and heard all this, he felt the air filled with the shades of a dark and sinful hand, and the smell of conspiracy mingled with the smell of the gunpowder of an aborted detonation. The signs pointed to a black future.

There was an old vendetta between Hamza and martial law, with a long and bloody history that went back to 1948. He realized it was imperative to find another place to hide out: under the new state of affairs the room where he now lived was not safe at all.

He was obliged to take a taxi, the only form of transport available. Inside, it was mercilessly stifling. Every now and then the question floated to the surface of his consciousness: would Bedeir rescue him this time too?

The car stopped in a street in Dokki. He climbed out, rang the bell of apartment 9, and went on ringing it. It was around midnight, and the apartment was steeped in darkness. Finally the door opened and Bedeir peered out, with his large head and his great towering body, shivering in the cold.

When Hamza briefly apprised him of the situation, Bedeir refused to believe it. They sat by the radio as the announcer intoned over and again:

'Gentlemen! We await an important bulletin.'

The bulletin came at twelve-thirty. At one, the new cabinet was announced. Hamza asked Bedeir if he could stay with him for a few days. Bedeir agreed, though it seemed to Hamza grudgingly.

Translated by R. Neil Hewison

Modern Arabic Literature
from the American University in Cairo Press

Ibrahim Abdel Meguid *Birds of Amber* • *Distant Train*
No One Sleeps in Alexandria • *The Other Place*
Yahya Taher Abdullah *The Collar and the Bracelet*
The Mountain of Green Tea
Leila Abouzeid *The Last Chapter*
Hamdi Abu Golayyel *Thieves in Retirement*
Yusuf Abu Rayya *Wedding Night*
Ahmed Alaidy *Being Abbas el Abd*
Idris Ali *Dongola* • *Poor*
Radwa Ashour *Granada*
Ibrahim Aslan *The Heron* • *Nile Sparrows*
Alaa Al Aswany *Chicago* • *Friendly Fire* • *The Yacoubian Building*
Fadhil al-Azzawi *Cell Block Five* • *The Last of the Angels*
Liana Badr *The Eye of the Mirror*
Hala El Badry *A Certain Woman* • *Muntaha*
Salwa Bakr *The Golden Chariot* • *The Man from Bashmour*
The Wiles of Men
Halim Barakat *The Crane*
Hoda Barakat *Disciples of Passion* • *The Tiller of Waters*
Mourid Barghouti *I Saw Ramallah*
Mohamed Berrada *Like a Summer Never to Be Repeated*
Mohamed El-Bisatie *Clamor of the Lake*
Houses Behind the Trees • *Hunger*
A Last Glass of Tea • *Over the Bridge*
Mahmoud Darwish *The Butterfly's Burden*
Tarek Eltayeb *Cities without Palms*
Mansoura Ez Eldin *Maryam's Maze*
Ibrahim Farghali *The Smiles of the Saints*
Hamdy el-Gazzar *Black Magic*
Tawfiq al-Hakim *The Essential Tawfiq al-Hakim*
Abdelilah Hamdouchi *The Final Bet*
Fathy Ghanem *The Man Who Lost His Shadow*
Randa Ghazy *Dreaming of Palestine*
Gamal al-Ghitani *Pyramid Texts* • *The Zafarani Files* • *Zayni Barakat*
Yahya Hakki *The Lamp of Umm Hashim*
Bensalem Himmich *The Polymath* • *The Theocrat*
Taha Hussein *The Days* • *A Man of Letters* • *The Sufferers*
Sonallah Ibrahim *Cairo: From Edge to Edge* • *The Committee* • *Zaat*
Yusuf Idris *City of Love and Ashes* • *The Essential Yusuf Idris*
Denys Johnson-Davies *The AUC Press Book of Modern Arabic Literature*
In a Fertile Desert: Modern Writing from the United Arab Emirates
Under the Naked Sky: Short Stories from the Arab World

Said al-Kafrawi *The Hill of Gypsies*
Sahar Khalifeh *The End of Spring*
The Image, the Icon, and the Covenant • *The Inheritance*
Edwar al-Kharrat *Rama and the Dragon* • *Stones of Bobello*
Betool Khedairi *Absent*
Mohammed Khudayyir *Basrayatha*
Ibrahim al-Koni *Anubis* • *Gold Dust* • *The Seven Veils of Seth*
Naguib Mahfouz *Adrift on the Nile* • *Akhenaten: Dweller in Truth*
Arabian Nights and Days • *Autumn Quail* • *The Beggar*
The Beginning and the End • *Cairo Modern*
The Cairo Trilogy: Palace Walk, Palace of Desire, Sugar Street
Children of the Alley • *The Day the Leader Was Killed*
The Dreams • *Dreams of Departure* • *Echoes of an Autobiography*
The Harafish • *The Journey of Ibn Fattouma* • *Karnak Café*
Khan al-Khalili • *Khufu's Wisdom* • *Life's Wisdom* • *Midaq Alley*
The Mirage • *Miramar* • *Mirrors* • *Morning and Evening Talk*
Naguib Mahfouz at Sidi Gaber • *Respected Sir* • *Rhadopis of Nubia*
The Search • *The Seventh Heaven* • *Thebes at War*
The Thief and the Dogs • *The Time and the Place*
Voices from the Other World • *Wedding Song*
Mohamed Makhzangi *Memories of a Meltdown*
Alia Mamdouh *The Loved Ones* • *Naphtalene*
Selim Matar *The Woman of the Flask*
Ibrahim al-Mazini *Ten Again*
Yousef Al-Mohaimeed *Wolves of the Crescent Moon*
Ahlam Mosteghanemi *Chaos of the Senses* • *Memory in the Flesh*
Mohamed Mustagab *Tales from Dayrut*
Buthaina Al Nasiri *Final Night*
Ibrahim Nasrallah *Inside the Night*
Haggag Hassan Oddoul *Nights of Musk*
Mohamed Mansi Qandil *Moon over Samarqand*
Abd al-Hakim Qasim *Rites of Assent*
Somaya Ramadan *Leaves of Narcissus*
Lenin El-Ramly *In Plain Arabic*
Ghada Samman *The Night of the First Billion*
Rafik Schami *Damascus Nights* • *The Dark Side of Love*
Khairy Shalaby *The Lodging House*
Miral al-Tahawy *Blue Aubergine* • *Gazelle Tracks* • *The Tent*
Bahaa Taher *As Doha Said* • *Love in Exile*
Fuad al-Takarli *The Long Way Back*
Zakaria Tamer *The Hedgehog*
M.M. Tawfik *Murder in the Tower of Happiness*
Mahmoud Al-Wardani *Heads Ripe for Plucking*
Latifa al-Zayyat *The Open Door*